Time to Stop Ru

John Fitzgerald

Time to Stop Running

I dedicate this book to the gentle hares of Ireland and all who strive to protect them from man's inhumanity.

1

What's happening?

Where am I?

Why is the world so…different?

He blinked and looked again.

It can't be gone. But it is. Why is this happening?

Sadness threatened to overwhelm him. *Please make it come back.*

The more he questioned his predicament the more his heart ached for something…some place…that he'd somehow lost or left behind.

But where am I now?

Glimmers of understanding pierced his consciousness. His world had faded, receded from him. All gone: those lovely meadows…the dancing rainbows of light…the landscape bedecked with happy flowers and rolling hills.

Gone too was the all-encompassing love of enlightened… *resplendent* beings.

Now, he felt loved too, but in a different way. The hare he snuggled to for affection and security exuded compassion and a mother's love.

Yes, that's it.

It came back to him, but from where he didn't know. This hare was his *mother*. She had enabled him to cross from that world of perfect peace and joy he had known… to this one.

Vague fragments of memory eluded him. The more he tried to grasp at those images inside his head the hazier they became. A jumble of thoughts and instincts vied for his attention, teasing and taunting him as if to test his understanding of where he now found himself.

Sorrow and confusion enfolded him as he looked around to survey his habitat. There was grass…and clay. Beyond these, high leaves and chubby yellow flowers protruded. But the grass and the leaves and the flowers didn't shimmer and glow as they ought to…as they did in that *other* place.

He was lying with the larger hare in a little hollow in the grass.

Mother. The thought came to him again, as if planted in his mind from elsewhere.

He cast his eyes skyward. That molten orb wasn't in his world…the one he'd called home just a few hundred heartbeats ago.

Another memory sputtered within: An ethereal meadow where a soft green sward quivered gently and he sat facing…spheres of burnished gold, changing to blobs of light and then, gradually, to solid forms.

They were hares….five of them…beings so advanced in wisdom that their radiance almost blinded him. From a world more exalted than his, he knew. They were transmitting knowledge to him…instructions too…for his new life.

The world he was about to enter, they informed him, was high on the list of the nastiest in the whole universe. Challenges unheard and undreamt of in the benevolent state of existence he would shortly forsake, awaited him.

All hares had to experience this World of Hard Knocks. It enabled them to grow and evolve spiritually and become better hares. Pain they must endure, terrors and privations; but they'd also learn lessons of survival, sharing, and self-sacrifice.

A frightening array of enemies they'd face, the most lethal and treacherous of these being…the Humaniks.

But there was an upside to it all. Their earth lives would be short, and once their lessons had been learned, death would release them from their school of suffering and again they'd enjoy the peace of Hare Heaven….all the more so for having known the trials and challenges of the Earth World.

"Tipsy". An abrupt sound startled him…brought him back to the present: His new reality.

How different it was here.

"Tipsy." Again, that sound prompting him.

"What's that?" he muttered.

The soothing voice of the large hare…his mother…repeated the word, adding: "You are a darling leveret. I've had a dream about you" she crooned as she licked his head, inside which snippets of information and recollections were settling themselves into place.

He was beginning to make sense of his new environment. Without thinking he answered her: "So that's my new name."

She drew back, her eyes denoting bewilderment. "What? You're talking already. Oh, Harold, come here…see this!"

A grumpy looking hare shuffled into the grassy hollow in the earth. He looked quizzically at Tipsy. His mother was all aglow with pride. "Go ahead, Tipsy…say something!"

"I was just reacting to Mum telling me my name is Tipsy. You see, in the world I was in before coming here I had a different name, but…for some reason I can't remember it now…"

The grumpy hare's mouth opened wide and he exchanged startled glances with Mum. "Ostara must favour you, son" he said gravely, "normally a leveret doesn't speak for at least a few weeks. And what's this about another world?"

Tipsy pondered for a moment. "It's fading now, with every heartbeat it's moving further away in my head, dissolving and disappearing. But I know I was…elsewhere…before I…before I arrived here. And I know that all hares were in that other world prior to reaching this one…and that we all return to it after death."

"Well now, hold on there, son…The priest hare tells us there's a place somewhere up in the sky where hares go when they die. But no hare knows what that faraway place is like."

"I don't understand. Dad, I was there, as surely as I am here now. So I just know."

Dad grunted and sniffled. "I hope you're right son. We live in hope. Anyway, I'm off to the beach for a jump and a run…and maybe a running jump if I'm in the mood. You'll be running soon, Tipsy; maybe sooner than most leverets judging by your progress at the talking. See you both later!"

Tipsy was exhausted. It must be all the thinking he'd done. He mentioned this and Mum said it wasn't natural for a new born leveret to think so much.

He yawned. As he drifted into sleep he tried to visualize that glorious Other World, but only the faintest dots of remembrance lingered, and those were fading fast.

Somehow, he felt, he must adjust to his new situation and accept the challenge of whatever it was he had to endure in this… what was it that the advanced being had called it? *The World of Hard Knocks.*

***

2

Tipsy felt better now. The pangs of longing had grown less painful, and only the tiniest fragments of memory remained of that perfect world he'd left behind. He still knew he'd prefer to be back there. But with each passing moment his acceptance of his new situation deepened.

Mum and Dad had encouraged him to leave the nest in the grass, his home, and explore the wider world. He'd already ventured out over short distances when his parents were away. He'd be sure to return before they'd got back, partly out of fear of the unknown…what he might encounter on his travels, but also to avoid worrying those loving, protective hares who'd facilitated his entrance into this unfamiliar world.

Mum had told him about it: The Island, it was called. It was an expanse of terrain upon which hares lived, but also other creatures. It was called an island because on all sides this territory was surrounded by water, a great ocean that was itself populated by creatures that lived underneath the surface, unlike hares that lived on solid land.

The island wasn't the entire world. Beyond its shores were vast lands that hares on the island knew about only from stories passed down from their ancestors.

There was a belief, based on tradition, that hares fared badly in those alien lands, though Mum stressed that such beliefs might just be scary stories invented by mischievous hares to frighten the rest of them, "as if we weren't timid enough!"

The hares on the island all got along reasonably well, Mum assured Tipsy, apart from occasional disagreements and…then there was the matter of male hares competing for the attention of female hares, but that was something he'd learn about when he grew to maturity.

"About those other creatures on the island", Dad had interjected, casting a worried look at Mum, "You want to be careful of them, son. Most of them are harmless. Don't bother us hares. But then, well, there's the falcon." Dad rolled his eyes around in his head, his whiskers wobbled, and a short but tense silence followed.

Tipsy looked to Mum, then back at Dad, who continued, in a sombre tone: "The falcon is our greatest enemy. He flies above us, watching and waiting for any sign of a leveret, or even an old hare like me, and, if we're off our guard, he swoops and…that's the end of us. Unless of course we see him diving. Then our speed may save us. So be vigilant, son, and be alert for danger from the skies…"

Mum coughed lightly, as if to interrupt Dad. She smiled and said: "The greatest enemy of all, though thankfully he does not dwell among us here on the island…is the Humanik…"

Tipsy shuddered at the mention of this creature. Again, a vague recollection of that Other World flashed inside his head…The resplendent ones advising him. Yes…they too had cautioned about that strange, hostile, and powerful creature that all but ruled the world he was to be born into.

But why? If Humaniks didn't live on the island, why worry about them?

Mum seemed to read his thoughts, or maybe she just guessed what he was thinking. "Humaniks *did* live here once, but no hare alive today remembers them. Their homes can be seen, what's left of them. Some Humaniks have come here visiting, but only to capture fish from the sea. We think they probably ate the fish, like the gulls do."

Watching his parents depart, Tipsy decided he'd take in more of the island today, see what kind of place it was that he'd been sent to…because he had the persistent feeling that it wasn't by accident that he arrived here.

He had a mission, some kind of purpose, but that too had faded from his mind, though he knew, somehow, that he'd rediscover what it was. Perhaps an exploration of the island might offer a hint?

Scrambling out of his hollow in the grass, Tipsy set off in search of knowledge and understanding. He grumbled to himself as he went*: why can't I just remember why I'm here instead of having to learn it all over again and snatch at fading memories?*

***

3

Tipsy stood on the crest of a hill gaping at the lake. Mum had told him about this vast expanse of water. She described it by pointing to a little puddle near the nest. "Now, imagine those few drops growing wider and deeper by the heartbeat...tiny ripples become larger ones..."

Funny how it didn't look like water... at least from where he sat: It was so calm, apart from miniscule quivers of movement...and it wasn't the colour of the puddle Mum had compared it to. That was translucent. He could partly see the flattened grass, clay, and pebbles through it.

But this was...a pale blue, with what he might have mistaken for wobbling stretches of sky, complete with puffy white clouds, on its surface... had he not been aware that the sky was above him...way up there...not spread across this vastness of water. Though he wondered *why* it resembled the sky to such a degree. He'd ask Mum about that.

He settled in front of a large jagged rock close to the lake. *But not too close. Mustn't fall in.* Mum had cautioned that he must learn to swim before plunging into the water. He began nibbling at the lichen that grew like whiskers out of the rock, reminding him of his own fuzz that he'd washed and cleaned earlier.

Food was everywhere on the island, Mum had told him: in the fields, between stones, and along the cliffs. There was the luscious heather, though that wasn't abundant in the cold windy wet time when the sun, despite its fiery splendour, didn't give as much warmth.

Mum had explained that Ostara reduced the heat of the sun a bit at certain times to let hares gain vital experience of discomfort...otherwise life would be too easy and hares, she said, would just laze about all day in the balmy warmth, failing to learn the lessons of life for which they were born into the world in the first place.

One of those lessons was to cope with climatic harshness, to achieve warmth by vigorous exercise, making up for the weaker sun by creating heat within their own bodies. Another lesson, she emphasised, was that of survival by running and hiding. Other creatures used strength and the instilling of fear to overcome enemies. For the hare, violence was not an option.

The beach was another place to get food. Tipsy hadn't seen that part of the island yet, but Mum had assured him the food to be found there was most nourishing. Hares differed on the subject of its appeal to the palate: Some craved it, while others tried it once but couldn't bear the sight of it, let alone the taste, afterwards. Tipsy couldn't wait to discover how his own taste buds reacted. First he must locate the beach.

He accelerated his pace. He marvelled at how he could use his legs to cover long distances. Especially his hind legs. They had more power in them than his front ones. Another lesson learned. With each passing sunrise and sunset he felt his strength growing. He found himself sitting atop a steep hill. Instinctively he knew the descent would be easier than his slower climb to the top. Had he done all this in that other world? He couldn't recall. But he was learning, or was it relearning…fast.

He sauntered down the gentle grassy slope, sliding effortlessly but slowing when he saw what looked like a different surface at its base. Alighting on it he felt a hardness he hadn't encountered yet. This wasn't grass or clay. And it was cold to his feet. He moved tentatively along it. Rock, like the fragments he'd encountered near home. Mum had told him he'd find a lot of this hard substance on the island.

Though mostly flat and even, this rocky surface had nasty little protrusions in it. These prodded his feet and contact with them made him wince. He had just cursed his luck in pressing his left hind leg against a sharp object when something flew past him, emitting a low whistle followed by a shriek.

A bird. He'd seem similar ones from his nest, fluttering overhead, and also pecking with their funny noses in the ground near home. Mum said they were foraging for food. This one was all black, apart from his orange nose. No, *a beak,* that's what Mum called it.

The smaller birds were no threat to a hare, she'd explained. As he moved on he quickly adapted to the rougher ground beneath him. There was a knack in avoiding the prods and discomforts. Just took getting used to, he guessed.

A pleasant aroma came to him. He'd been looking straight ahead and hadn't noticed until now the tasty mosses that grew in crevices from the rock he trod upon. He paused to sniff at a clump of juicy growth; wondering if it was safe to eat. Mum had urged caution as some alluring foliage or plant life could sicken or even kill hares. How was he to know if this was safe?

He just felt it was okay, and that instinct alone prompted him to try it out. He nibbled at the tiniest morsel he could scoop into his mouth, and swallowed it. He lay still, contemplating his decision to risk illness or death. Not feeling bad so it must be safe. He helped himself to several mouthfuls of the moss, smacking his lips with satisfaction.

He ran further, reaching the end of the hard surface and…he drew back in horror: Before him was a drop and he'd almost fallen from a great height. Something else Mum had warned him about: Mind the cliff, she'd advised, her eyes full of dread. He edged forward, carefully this time, and surveyed the vast panorama that stretched below and ahead of him.

The cliff, for this must be it he assumed, extended sharply all the way down from where he stood to an expanse of ground that was neither grass nor rock, but some form of dusty surface. The wind was tossing little cloudlets of it back and forth.

Didn't clouds belong to the sky? Maybe there were earthly ones too. Then it struck him: That must be the beach down there. It matched Mum's description, now that he thought about it.

Beyond that unfamiliar territory so far below was a vast tumbling mass of water. It extended to the far horizon and rolled towards the dusty earth of the beach. Seemingly in turmoil, it crashed in upon itself in giant splashes, spewing upwards in frothy plumes and spluttering forth as if driven by some hidden unstoppable force.

There was a visible rhythm to its movement and a pattern to its thunderous roar at the edge of the stretch of ground that Tipsy gazed down upon nervously.

So far, since his birth, apart from his glimpse of the lake, he had only seen and tasted small puddles of water. It quenched his thirst and Mum said all hares need to drink it to stay healthy and survive. But this…this must be the great ocean of which Mum had also spoken: So much water, enough to keep hares drinking for eternity.

He must find a way down from the cliff to get a closer look. For now, he was content to close his eyes and inhale that lovely air. It smelled and tasted nicer than the air he breathed back at the grassy nest. His eyes fluttered open again at the sound of loud squeaking.

He beheld a throng of birds hovering overhead, circling above him, and what a racket they made. Their cacophonous crying was out of tune with the more soothing sound of the ocean, but that wasn't what troubled Tipsy.

Some of those greyish white creatures had broken away from the rest and were...no doubt about it...flying right down towards him.

Instinctively Tipsy turned and ran; heading straight for a yellowish weedy patch that he hoped would offer cover. The screeching of those hostile birds grew louder, and almost burst his eardrums as he leapt into the large clump of high growing shrubbery.

His heart beat loudly, its hammering almost as loud as the shrill screech of the birds as they flapped and soared somewhere close by. Light breezes brushed against his panting body through spaces in the foliage, presumably fanned by those awful creatures.

Then the menacing racket subsided and silence returned. Tipsy listened attentively. He heard only the nearby chirping of small birds, and the musical heave of the ocean. Either the large birds had lost sight of him or were unable to pursue him into this flowery cocoon. Tipsy didn't care which.

He ventured from his hiding place, thanking Ostara as Mum had taught him to do whenever he felt grateful for deliverance from danger.

Ostara was the creator of the entire universe, Mum had told him, and both his parents spoke her divine name with great reverence. Looking up he saw the large birds were flying back over the ocean. They must have forgotten him.

Tipsy had enough exploring done for this day. He retraced his steps back to the nest. Boy, had he something tell Mum and Dad this evening!

***

4

Tipsy approached the cliff edge again, but this time he wouldn't be caught unawares. He knew about the drop, and he wouldn't be doing anything as silly as falling to his death.

Mum had complimented him on learning quite a few lessons on his last foray across the island. He had faced a possible threat from those birds. Gulls they were called, Mum had informed him, and Dad had laughed heartily at how he'd outwitted them by taking to his heels and finding a refuge. "Quick thinking Son," he'd crooned, "your date with the hereafter hadn't come yet."

Mum shook her head and repeated her warning about predators. Gulls tended to give themselves away so that gave you a chance to escape. The falcon was a bigger menace.

Mum had then usefully told Tipsy how he could reach that dusty piece of ground, the *beach*, at the bottom of the cliff without having to fall off the edge to his doom.

Tipsy proceeded along the route she'd described, taking in many new vistas. He savoured the fluffy texture of multi-coloured vegetation that he couldn't resist shuffling through instead of just running around to avoid.

The flowers: red, yellow, blue, and purple, were soft and fluffy and their perfume went straight to his head when he sniffed. They were edible too, he suspected, like most of the growth on the island, but he'd already scoffed lashings of moss and other easy pickings.

After every twenty steps he cast a cautionary eye skyward. No falcon… and no gulls. He skipped over rocks scattered in a field that was itself bordered by heaps of bigger rocks and clusters of small stones. He climbed one of the rocky barriers, dislodging pebbles and a few larger stones as he clambered into the next field.

The roar of the ocean became audible, as a distant hum at first but then, as he quickened his pace, he heard again that awesome roar and the surging cascade of motion.

Emerging abruptly onto a rocky surface that sprouted mosses and thick slivers of plant life he gasped and couldn't move. The ocean: stretching beyond the beach to the far horizon.

He felt dwarfed by its vastness. He thought of what Mum had told him about it. The water lapped the shore continuously, and always looked as if it might cover the entire breach, but it never did. It kept a respectful distance; thanks to Ostara having ordained that a limit was imposed on its progress towards the strand.

Tipsy ran along the delicate smooth sand, creating dust clouds as he kicked it up in the air behind him. It was so soft...and warm too. He sneezed. Grains got into his nostrils. He kept running until he was close to where the water was striking the beach. He sat and marvelled at how Ostara had restricted its movement. It surged towards him, bubbled and frothed and splashed...but then, it retreated, only to return shortly afterwards to repeat this watery ritual.

Tipsy felt thirsty, and ventured to drink from this endless supply of water. It had no sooner passed his lips when his stomach heaved. He spat it out onto the sand. It had a bitter taste that wasn't to his liking. Not like the water that fell from the sky. Somehow, he knew there had to be a catch. All that water. *Too easy.*

He ran along the fringe of the waterline, breathing in that lovely, invigorating air. That felt good, whatever about the water.

A far off screeching made him pause. He scanned the sky, squinting to avoid being dazzled by the glistening molten orb whose heat and light sustained this world. He saw gulls flying, but they were out over the ocean, so hopefully wouldn't be bothering him.

Another sound distracted him. Glancing to his left, he saw two other hares, one a leveret like himself, and the second an adult hare. The large hare looked ancient. His fur had strayed from reddish brown to a greyish hue, and was speckled with white. His eyelids drooped and his whiskers hung down as if something deep in the earth pulled at them.

His ears too were sagging, as though weary of the world. But he had a strange commanding presence, a curious dignity.

He shouted a greeting to Tipsy, as if to make himself heard above the roar of the sea. Though Tipsy didn't understand the word he used, he acknowledged him out of courtesy.

The leveret said nothing, just stood gazing at his own feet. Tipsy remembered what Dad had said about most leverets not learning to speak until at least thirty sunsets had passed.

Walking over to the pair, Tipsy introduced himself. The adult hare said: "pleased to meet you, I'm Father Buck."

Tipsy was confused. "But you can't be my father. Dad is back home right now..."

The hare laughed. "No, I'm called that because I'm a priest. I look after the spiritual needs of all the hares on this island. The Wise One, the supreme spiritual leader who outranks me cannot leave his residence so I keep an eye on things for him. I must say I'm impressed. You can speak and you're quite young."

Tipsy felt bashful. "So I've been told."

"Is there anything you wish to know, while you're here? About life or its true meaning...that sort of thing?"

Tipsy reflected. "Well, yes. I was telling Mum and Dad about the world I lived in before I came here to this one. Seems it's not so common to remember Hare Heaven, as I believe it's called."

Father Buck looked perplexed, and a hostile frown distorted his countenance. He began licking his whiskers awkwardly, and remarked: "No hare remembers Heaven. You mustn't lie...to your parents or anyone else."

Tipsy was highly offended. "But I'm not lying, Father Buck...though my memories of that other place have almost gone now..."

"Listen here to me: that's blasphemy. When we die, Ostara will take us onto eternal rest, but we must not seek proof of this sacred truth..."

"Why not?"

"Because...because, why then there would be no place for faith, and faith is everything..."

"But, Father Buck... isn't it better to have proof... the truth right in front of our snouts, than to have to believe and take someone's word for it?"

The hare priest raised a paw and motioned Tipsy to stop talking. "No more nonsense. Where do your parents live? I'll be having a word with them about your attitude!"

"But, I don't understand..."

The old hare sighed, and his angry visage mellowed somewhat. "Look, religion is all about faith. If we had proof there'd be no room for faith. Without faith there would no challenge, no test of our devotion to Ostara. It would knock the good out of religion. It would be like...like being able to appear anywhere you want to without having to run. Sure, it would be useful; in many ways, but then you wouldn't have the joy of running, would you? And all that you get to see and hear and touch along the way. Faith is what makes life worth living. Ostara wouldn't have it any other way."

Tipsy thought of a dozen other questions, but restrained himself. "Thank you, Father Buck. That is most enlightening."

The priest beamed, seemingly glad of the compliment. "Say hello to Jockser," he hummed, "this is his first view of the ocean."

The leveret gaped shyly at Tipsy and nodded.

"Jockser believes he has a vocation to be a priest. Though he can't speak yet, his parents spotted his devotion...recognised the signs. Little fellow's always gazing at the moon. Praising Ostara is for him more important than playing, or even eating. He's to begin training when he's a little older. There's been a decline in hare vocations to the priesthood in recent times. I'm the only priest left, since

Father Scut died, and I wonder sometimes if anyone listens to me. Worrying it is, the way hares are disregarding their faith and acting as if only this world mattered. I'm told some hares haven't prayed for ages. They'll pray, though, when it suits them…at the end!"

With a flourish Father Buck turned his back on Tipsy, and quickstepped towards a grassy hill, kicking sand all around him, with Jockser scampering in tow.

I admire his faith in faith, Tipsy thought, still unconvinced by the notion of believing without proof, especially when you knew something was real and didn't need to say you just "believed"...or, more worryingly, when you had strong reasons for doubting and were expected to have faith. *Must ask Mum and Dad about that.*

***

5

"Hey, care to join us for a run?" Tipsy was barely out of the nest, setting off to explore the island a little more, when he heard, and then saw, the other leveret who'd called to him.

He was older and bigger than Tipsy, and sitting atop one of those stone walls that Mum said Humaniks had built long ago when they lived here.

"A run…I suppose…where to?"

Before the leveret answered, another three hares, older than leverets, leaped up onto the wall and sat alongside the leveret who had spoken. One shouted: "Let's have a race…across the island…to the lake?"

The leveret shrugged; "why not?"

Tipsy agreed. The five of them clustered together, and then lined up in readiness. Tipsy had slept well and felt energetic, so he hoped he'd have the stamina for this test.

A hare with part of his left ear missing shouted "go" and they all bounded forward. At first none of them attempted to outrun the others, and Tipsy respected this apparent lack of concern for getting ahead. Two hares were chatting as they ran, staying alongside each other to facilitate the conversation.

Tipsy reckoned this must be the norm so he slowed deliberately to stay with the youngest of the hares, who introduced himself breathlessly as Mossy. "We run casually for a while," he explained in a slightly macho tone, "then we get serious…no hurry. It's only a game."

"You like running?" Tipsy asked Mossy.

"Yeah, next to eating it's my favourite routine!" He went silent, before adding: "So long as nothing's chasing me…"

Saying this, Mossy glanced upward ruefully. "Don't think he's around today…"

A reference to the falcon, Tipsy presumed.

The others had dropped back behind Tipsy and Mossy. They seemed in no rush. They all ran at a leisurely pace over rocky terrain that was also slimy and slippery. The rain must have fallen on it as Tipsy found himself slipping and sliding. One hare shouted an oath as he landed on his back, his four legs flailing the air. He uprighted himself quickly and resumed his run, to the amusement of the others.

Grateful to be away from the rough ground, they savoured the soothing brush of primroses and dandelions against their bodies and the lush gorse that almost swallowed them up as they ran, pushed, or leapt their way through it, the perfumes of the assorted foliage a pleasant distraction as they progressed.

A succession of those Humanik stone walls faced them. They climbed each one easily, careful of the loose stones that tumbled under them as their feet made contact with these odd structures. One hare shrieked with annoyance as pebbles dislodged by the leveret in front of him struck him in the face.

On they went, the sun warming them and a light soothing breeze counteracting its life giving heat in a pleasant balancing act. Then, abruptly, the oldest hare stopped and held up a commanding paw. They were sitting on a high hilltop. Tipsy could see a huge expanse of land that included the lake. From his present vantage point, it resembled a light blue patch in the middle of the landscape.

"Okay, guys" the hare announced: "All of you ready? Last one to the lake is a dumbo…go!"

Tipsy had allowed his mind to wander at the sight of the lake and the spectacular view from the hilltop. The others were scampering down the hillside before he took a first step. He had to make up lost ground. With fierce resolve, he leapt as if to clear a high wall. His hind legs absorbed the impact as he alighted on the grassy surface of the hill. He then broke into a ferocious run.

The world around him became a blur. Time dissolved into itself. The wind half carried him and his feet were surging through air currents. Instinctively, he halted at the edge of the vast body of water, little clods of uprooted earth flicking past him.

The lake. But surely…? How could he be here that quickly?

He looked around him. Over there, across five fields separated by walls…just arriving at the bottom of the hill in the distance, were the others…running strenuously. Tipsy waited patiently, nibbling on a sprig of wild thyme and trying out some lichens he hadn't tasted before.

When the others arrived at the lakeside, they regarded him with a mixture of wonder and exasperation. Mossy, out of breath, shook his head and said: "That was astonishing. No hare can run that fast!"

The older hare was silent, suspicion distorting his features. Finally he blurted: "You didn't know a shortcut by any chance?"

Another hare answered the question for Tipsy. "There's no shortcut…just a straight run from the top of the hill, through those fields, to the lake. I salute your athleticism, Tipsy. I didn't think such speed was possible. If I were superstitious I'd say it was a miracle. But I'm not…"

Tipsy blushed. "I just ran…Sorry if it looked like showing off, lads. Anyway, forget about running. These herbs are delicious, and you really must try the moss."

Tipsy and the others relaxed and enjoyed a nap by the lakeside after gorging themselves on the luscious vegetation. Tipsy found the lake, which lapped gently at its edges, a calming influence.

There was something alluring about its still, unruffled waters, so different to the surging power of the ocean…though he liked the beach too, apart from the racket the gulls made. Closing his eyes, he reflected on his success in outrunning the others… so easily.

What did it mean?

***

6

Tipsy was landing one surprise after another at the feet of his parents.

His memories, shrunk to mere pinpoints now, of a previous life in a wondrous world beyond description, had held them entranced. As had his breathless account of how he'd outrun dozens of hares, young and old, in races across fields, up hills and along the sun-kissed beach.

He relished the prospect of telling them about today's developments. They'd been impressed by his faster than normal acquisition of the power of speech, so he was sure they'd be bowled over by what had happened that afternoon.

He rested on his way back to the nest to reflect on his enhanced communication skills. Frolicking on a hillside amid clumps of gorse and glorious weeds earlier that day, he'd been distracted by wasps buzzing overhead. *Don't let them sting you!* Another hare had warned good-humouredly.

Tipsy's head turned to the humming tiny creatures that flew lower than birds, eyeing them suspiciously and wondering if they'd bother him. One wasp broke ranks with the rest and headed straight for him. Bracing himself for impact, and possible evasive action, Tipsy was startled to hear a voice say, "I won't sting you…I'm just curious. What are you?

"I'm a hare," Tipsy replied.

Two other hares ran to his side. "Hey, Tipsy who're you talking to?" they asked.

Before he could answer the wasp spoke again. "You can talk to me…Astonishing. Don't be afraid. I'm flying off, hare…see you!"

"Bye then…" Tipsy said, and, turning to his mates he murmured that something very odd had happened. When he told them exactly what, they burst out laughing.

"Impossible" one guffawed.

"Not even funny" the other said grumpily.

Tipsy shrugged, regretting he'd told them, and wondering if perhaps he'd imagined the wasp conversing with him.

His doubts vanished when, shortly after, away from the other hares, he was passing by a bush brimming with purple berries. He paused to eat a few. He recognized them as ones that were edible and non poisonous to hares. No sooner had he plucked a mouthful of the juicy fruit when he heard another voice, not squawky like the wasp's… but not like a hare's either.

It had a pleasantly soft whistling ring to it. He saw the little creature gazing up at him. It had something in its beak. It gulped, swallowing whatever it was. "That was tasty. I wish I could squash as many berries into my beak in one go the way you do".

"Maybe you don't need to… you being a bird and so much smaller than I am!" Tipsy responded casually.

The bird's beak opened wide, and its tiny eyes seemed poised to burst with alarm. "You can speak my language…I must be dreaming!"

"I don't think so…A wasp spoke to me earlier."

The bird stepped back, flapping its wings. "Excuse me, I have to fly" he lisped, and disappeared into the folds of a happy sunbeam. The rays dazzled Tipsy as he watched the bird flutter away.

Heading home, a multitude of voices and cadences vied for Tipsy's attention. He had to block them out. From the grass and clay he trod upon, insects commented in spasmodic mutterings on his presence, a spider weaving a web between two stones in a broken wall blurted: "What are looking at? Ever seen a Harry longlegs at work before?"

A butterfly paused in mid flight, its stunning yellow and red wings flapping elegantly: "Enjoying the sunshine, hare?" it queried.

Tipsy's reply: "Yes, and you?" sent the gentle creature spiraling away in shock and confusion.

A wriggling earth worm wrapping itself lazily around the stalk of a dandelion said "Good afternoon, not a bad day" and Tipsy heard the musings of low flying birds of different sizes and plumages. Further up in the sky gulls wheeled and dived, over the ocean. Their raucous chattering resolved itself into distant cries of "when am I going to get supper", "out of way, I saw that fish first", and "I've being flying all day and I need a rest guys!"

Tipsy's head rang with a cacophony of words and voices, diverse, dissimilar… but all somehow intelligible to him. What should he do? He'd be shunned and scorned by the other hares if he persisted in claiming he could commune with other species. But he really could. He hoped Mum and Dad would have answers, but this time he had the uneasy feeling they might not.

***

7

Tipsy inhaled the invigorating sea air. What a lovely sight from the cliff-top: the mighty ocean lapping the strand. He'd go to the beach later for a meal of seaweed. That's if he was still hungry after sampling other fare that came his way. No point in planning for meals. There was such a wide choice on the island. He closed his eyes to relax, but as the daylight dimmed his whole body shuddered. An ear splitting racket drowned out the rhythmic crashing of the waves below.

Gulls overhead. What else? Circling and squawking in angry hordes. Tipsy wasn't unduly worried. They made so much noise but that was an advantage. You had plenty of notice of their presence long before they might take a notion to attack. And sanctuary was near if they did target him. He'd thwarted them last time. Not that you could ignore them. Careless or unsuspecting leverets had succumbed to their sharp claws and nasty beaks, Mum had warned him.

Tipsy watched them wheeling about and listened to their shrill cries, some of which resolved into words. Snatches of exchanges reached him, all trivial nonsense to do with their search for food, fish that eluded them, and complaints about other gulls getting more food than themselves.

A pleasant breeze from the ocean fanned Tipsy's fur. He ventured to the cliff edge, careful not to get too close. The sun to his left was too bright to look at, but he squinted to admire its fiery circle of warmth. He imagined his body absorbing the heat and felt energized by it.

Gulls flew across the radiant disc. Besmirching stains. *Time to go home*…Mum would expect him about now. No point in worrying her. He had taken a few steps away from the cliff edge when something prompted him to stop. What was it?

The gulls!

Their strident babble had suddenly abated, and they flew erratically, chaos replacing their focused gliding and gyrating of just moments ago. Some soared higher; some flew in disorganized haste out over the ocean, while others dispersed further inland at a ferocious rate.

Something had distracted them and their nervous mutterings had changed quickly to outright panic. Their fleeting silence gave way to even louder shrieks, rising to an ear shattering crescendo that made Tipsy grind his teeth.

Then he saw the cause of their alarm. A huge bluish grey bird with a white breast and enormous wings was hurtling down on them, seemingly from out of the sun, whose golden white beams the creature blocked and distorted as it flew through the radiance at terrific speed. The gulls scattered in all directions, a crazed fear seemingly driving them, their cries a chorus of discord that Tipsy thought for a moment would break the sky the way a hare's paw could shatter a small sheet of ice.

Then the bird hovered, suspended as if about to rest or stand on thin air. But it didn't. Tipsy watched goggle-eyed as the creature's mighty flapping wings closed tight around its body and it started falling.

Had it died? Why was it…? It kept falling, like a stone dropping from a great height. But no…it wasn't dead.

Tipsy was riveted to the drama high above him. A heartbeat before colliding with a gull the great bird's legs shot out, striking the frantic and grossly outmatched flier with stupendous force. The stricken gull fluttered for a few seconds and went still. It began to drop…plummeting haphazardly and directionless. It must be stunned or injured…but the large bird, its wings now flapping again, pursued it downwards and fastened its beak on the rapidly descending gull, which emitted a low squeal.

The triumphant bird flew gracefully across the sky, the struggling gull dangling from its beak. The predator's awesome wings reminded Tipsy of oversized tree branches swaying in a storm. No other bird flew close to it as it made off with its petrified captive, presumably on its way home. Tipsy reckoned they'd all be afraid of such a powerful adversary.

Though he didn't like the gulls, he felt sorry for that one up there. He visualized it being eaten, its captor ripping it apart back in the nest…feathers and guts littering its terrifying abode. *Thank Ostara, we hares don't eat other creatures.*

Before the great winged marauder had disappeared from sight Tipsy realized he'd caught his first glimpse of the dreaded falcon.

***

8

Dad looked bemused, maybe a little worried, Tipsy thought. Mum just sat there, shaking her head, saying nothing.

They'd both just listened to Tipsy's account of how he'd discovered his ability to communicate with other creatures and understand their languages. Before that he'd recounted that scary episode involving his first sighting of the dreaded falcon. Seeing the powerful creature was intriguing enough, but watching it attack and capture the gull was spine-chilling, and Tipsy conveyed the terror of it to his parents.

That got their attention. Both had gasped with horror, despite already knowing what the bird was capable of. But then Tipsy broached his newly discovered gift.

He feared he'd gone too far. They'd shown their displeasure when he'd told them about his encounter with Father Buck and his disagreement with the priest hare on the subject of faith and what lies beyond the veil of death. Hares generally left spiritual matters to the priest. It wasn't wise, Dad said, to contradict their pastor. One might, he advised, need Father Buck's services at the hour of death, even if he tended not to be anywhere near when the big moment arrived for most hares, and the priest wasn't as fast on his feet as he used to be.

Dad broke the silence, dropping a sheaf of assorted flowers and herbs he'd been nibbling on. "Are you absolutely sure, son that this isn't just your imagination? That you didn't get a knock on the head? I've heard of hares that saw and heard all sorts of strange things…after a little mishap."

"No Dad, I seem to know the language of every living creature, at least all the ones I've come across on the island…"

Mum coughed lightly and cast a benevolent gaze on Tipsy. "I didn't mention this…to either of you" she announced.

Dad glowered. "What haven't I heard?" he said grumpily.

"I had a dream last night…I didn't pay much attention to it, but now …A ghostly white hare that shone brighter than the sun appeared to me. He told me that you, Tipsy, were special. In what way he didn't say…but he repeated: Your son has a special purpose that will, in time, be made known to him."

Dad rolled his eyes around. "Oh, now I've heard it all…have you both gone crazy?"

He left the nest muttering to himself, leaving Mum sitting there in a daze. She was tearful. "I don't know what it's about Tipsy, but it's clear to me…you are no ordinary hare! Ostara must have blessed you in a way yet to be revealed. That dream…it was more vivid than any I've ever had…"

She seemed lost for words. She looked at her son with a new found reverence and compassion. Tipsy kissed his mother. Exhaustion overcame him as he settled in the flattened grass beside her, struggling to process the astounding events of the day.

***

9

Tipsy inhaled the crisp salt sea air as he floated and splashed in the water.

He loved it. Mum was right. Swimming was something he wouldn't have to learn. It would come to him. Many hares went from birth to death, she'd told him, without ever crossing water.

But the hares on the island were privileged to be surrounded by a great ocean. It was theirs to explore…but he mustn't swim too far.

He was keeping count of the heartbeats. Well, more or less. This was his third time in the ocean, and he found each plunge more enjoyable and relaxing. His hind legs paddled furiously but far from feeling tired his body pulsed with renewed energy.

He dived under a surging wave. *Can't breathe down here. What's to see?*

Vast numbers of sea creatures, darting about in large groups as if directed by one mind. *How lovely to share this strange underwater world with the fish.*

Before his first swim the only fish he'd seen were dead ones washed up on shore: An unpleasant and unsettling sight. Even sadder was to see a fish wriggling furiously on the beach.

Odd…he couldn't breathe underwater and had to surface shortly after submerging. But the fish had the opposite problem. They seemed to breathe underwater and struggle when out of it.

Sometimes a fish would be washed in by the tide and find itself stranded. Some of these fish he saw being taken by birds that circled above the island, watching for their chance to swoop.

Hares didn't eat other creatures, thankfully, so Tipsy couldn't figure why birds would want to kill the fish.

He marvelled at the endless varieties of colour exhibited by the sea creatures. The rainbow in the sky paled in comparison to the multifarious hues that sparkled and shone and tantalised beneath the waves. *Time to turn back*.

He resurfaced. Though the water was cold his body was pleasantly warm. *Peculiar.*

But he wasn't complaining. His panoramic vision took in the broad sweep of the ocean as the splashing around him almost drowned out the hissing and whistling of the strong sea breezes. Another sound distracted him: A sharp screechy noise...somewhere overhead. His eyes glanced heavenward. *Oh no, please…not that.*

A huge gull was diving towards him, its angry eyes like two dark pebbles over its ugly beak, its wings flapping and its whole frame outlined grotesquely against a blotchy sky. It seemed to be falling and diving at the same time…in Tipsy's general direction.

Tipsy instinctively dived too, right down into the depths. *Can't stay down here too long.*

He gasped and spluttered, water surging into his mouth and filling his lungs. Fish stared blankly at him, flailing their shiny bodies, as if to say: *Hey, this is not your domain. What are doing here?*

The gull's greedy head appeared close to his own, but was turned the wrong way, its eyes directed elsewhere. It made no sound underwater. Suddenly, mutely, it grabbed a curious fish and disappeared from view.

Unable to hold his breath any longer Tipsy surfaced. As he gasped for air he caught a glimpse of the gull flapping upwards, the squirming fish clenched firmly in its beak.

Swimming ashore, Tipsy felt as sorry for the fish as he'd felt for the shrieking gull taken by the falcon.

***

10

Waxy Bumbleton Crossbar stood atop the Peak of Jackdaw Mountain, leaning against the gigantic stone cross that devout folk faced morning and evening when called to prayer.

It wasn't really a mountain, just a hill, but a high enough one that overlooked most of Broc Peninsula.

He sweated and panted and puffed, holding his belly that waddled in flaps of fat out over his trousers belt. His doctor had advised a strict and, Waxy thought, far too intensive exercise regime to lose some of that potentially life-threatening flab he'd accumulated.

Years of easy living had taken their inevitable toll. Having inherited a fortune from his father…and a thousand acres of grazing land that he leased to farmers, he hadn't to work a day in his life unless he wanted to: Hence his cursed descent into obesity.

Wiping the sweat from his brow with a hankie, he admired the view of all those patches of green sward, the stunning patchwork of hedgerows, the winding roads and laneways, and the cluster of small towns and villages. His own domain…the bungalow with its splendid view of Jackdaw Mountain, was just a speck on the dagger-shaped stretch of land that jutted out into the Atlantic.

Most mornings he stood looking through his bedroom window at Jackdaw. Now here he was, reversing the process. He wondered if someone was at this moment observing him, maybe through binoculars. He sat down on the moss-encrusted stone chair at the foot of the cross. The County Council had installed the seat for locals and tourists who regularly ascended the hill, some as sightseers, others to pray or gain God's blessing for the climbing effort.

Waxy shielded his eyes from a cool but still dazzling sun. He was glad he'd made it to the peak. The walk and the climb might prolong his life by a few months, if the doctor wasn't having him on. Relaxing and enjoying the panoramic sweep of the Peninsula, he tried to see himself as others probably saw him.

Friends and neighbours envied him, he knew, believing he hadn't a care in the world owing to his wealth. But they were wrong. His passion in life was also a source of worry and involved almost as much work as any of those factory hands, office clerks, builders, doctors, or farmers had to face into: The converted ex-farmyard at the back of his bungalow had served him well as a greyhound training venue. Not for testing speed and stamina. No. Tracks could look after that.

What Waxy offered the trainers of the Peninsula and beyond was the prized opportunity to test their dogs in the most effective way possible. It wasn't everyone's cup of tea. He knew that only too well. But since when could you ever hope to please everyone?

There were people out there who cared more about animals than people. Crazy. They'd throw a fit if they dropped in at the wrong time and witnessed training. The sight of a few cats, rabbits or birds being utilized for blooding would upset their weak stomachs and liberal sensibilities.

Idiots! It wasn't strictly legal, but that wasn't a problem for him, because the trainers were keenly aware of this so they weren't going to incriminate themselves with loose talk.

Waxy smiled at the thought. The law was a funny creature. What was legal today could be a criminal offence tomorrow. What one country banned another might promote as a tourist attraction. Yet, in one's own mind no offence was committed if one's conscience was clear. It was just a question of not being careless.

With hare coursing it was different. While blooding was illegal, thanks to misguided politicians of another era who couldn't appreciate its value to the greyhound industry, there was no law in Ireland against his beloved field sport of hare coursing. It was more than a pastime to him. It was an expression of everything he was and aspired to be: a proud upholder of tradition and Irish cultural values.

The Bumbleton-Crossbars had been dedicated hare coursers since his great grandfather, Timmy the Scut Crossbar, founded Ballycrossways Coursing Club back in the 1850s. It was one of eight clubs initiated in the same year on the Peninsula. Now it was the sole survivor, the other seven having disbanded for a variety of reasons: Shortage of hares was a major headache for clubs in recent years, but there were also those accursed antis.

Waxy rose from the stone seat, anger seizing control of him. He'd promised himself he wouldn't let his mind be troubled by those…*morons*…on his morning walk. Now, here he was, again ruminating on that persistent distraction , a threat that grew alarming at times, then faded, then resurfaced…like some foul disease that one tried to banish with every form of treatment available but that kept rearing its ugly head, again and again.

He remembered a time in his childhood when the threat simply didn't exist. In his father's day there wasn't as much as a whisper against hare coursing. Not anywhere in Ireland. But then, about half way through the 1960s, squeaky liberals began to poke their noses into the lives and pastimes of decent sportspeople, with their nonsense about the "rights" of hares.

He remembered how his father had exploded with laughter when he heard about that opening caper from the antis. It was an apt response. Weeks passed, months. Then, a handful of hippies from Dublin gathered outside a major coursing event in the Midlands: A scruffy, bedraggled gang, clinging to home-made placards with slogans denouncing his sport. A picture of them appeared in the *Irish Times*…as if their pathetic stunt deserved any publicity.

That was then. Now protests were commonplace, and they'd even got their political friends to call for a ban on coursing. *Well, they'll find that our political friends are more powerful than theirs.*

He clenched his fists. Turning to descend Jackdaw Mountain and return home, he swore he'd die before he'd allow those enemies of hare coursing get the better of him. He was club secretary, returned to that position year after year unopposed. But he was much more than that. He was the driving force without which coursing on the Peninsula might have succumbed to the ravages of modernism and those daft notions about animals having "rights".

If you take on Waxy Bumbleton-Crossbar you'll be sorry. The "rights" if hares! What about our own ancient rights, our traditions stretching back to the days of the warrior Finn Mc Cool who hunted hares blindfolded and ate them raw?

He spat on the dirt track as he heaved and panted and kicked up clay, glad of this opportunity to lose a few pounds. He must weigh himself back at the house and see if this five mile grueling hike was worth it.

***

11

Tired of chewing tree bark, though it was tasty and nourishing, and helped to sharpen his teeth, Tipsy decided to explore the island a little more. There was so much to see, and Mum had told him that many heartbeats would pass before he'd encounter all there was to perceive and experience.

He ran, leaped and skidded over patches of damp gorse, the splashes of bright yellow succulence tempting him with their flavorsome aroma. Nicer than bark any day he'd discovered, but Mum had drummed into him that tree food was better for his health and growth.

He raced along the edge of a steep cliff, venturing a little too near the edge sporadically out of a reckless, daring sense of adventure.

Careful not to fall off, Mum had warned. That would mean death, which would be tragic and also brainless because such a premature end was easily avoidable. The hare faced so many enemies, if not on this happy island, but falling off a cliff would be stupid as well as sad since no predator would be responsible.

He approached the tangle of weird structures he'd already passed some time previously…two or three sunsets ago. Mum had explained that these were the remnants of old Humanik homes. Apparently they abandoned them at some point.

Thank Ostara those Humaniks left the island! They were no friends of hares. Everyone knew that. It was one of the first lessons he'd learned shortly after he drew breath…*when was it?* In that other season…when the sun burned warmer than now and flowers gave off those lovely perfumes…and everything looked brighter on the island, not like now, with all those yellow and red leaves from the trees heaped in clusters; this season of shorter days and longer nights.

The beams from that heavenly orb had shone a little too brightly as he'd sat in his grassy home and listened to those words of advice and wisdom.

Tipsy spotted something, a flicker of movement between two broken stones in a Humanik former home. *Careful not to court danger.* It could be a falcon lying in wait for unsuspecting hares.

He sat perfectly still, concealed behind a clump of purple heather, observing. It stirred again. Tipsy sniffed. Quite a strong odour reached him. What was it? An oily smell… and it seemed to come from that collection of mossy stones in the unoccupied Humanik structure.

A funny noise emanated from the stones. "Churr, chur" it sounded like. *Definitely a bird.* They were always chirping and making funny sounds.

Then it emerged from the crevice. A beak. A head.

Ah, it *was* a bird…but not the scary falcon. It was small and dark with a white rump and was pecking away at something, probably a worm.

Tipsy rambled over to the stone structure and sat looking straight at the bird. The feathered creature winked at him, a sign of friendliness. "Hello…bird. I'm Tipsy. I'm a hare. Do you have a name?"

The bird flapped its very short wings, rearranging its position. "Hey, I can understand you. You know bird talk. I'm a Storm Petrel. My name is Craggy. Just foraging for any bugs lying about. I was here first so you can't have them!"

Tipsy laughed. "No worries. We hares don't devour living things. Eat away."

The bird regarded him with suspicion and puzzlement. "You're joking! How do you survive?"

"Look around you…Craggy. Anything that grows we eat. Hey…you wouldn't be thinking of eating me, would you?"

"Nah…you might taste good, but I'm small and I'd never manage to…you know, overcome you. I wouldn't stand a chance. But if you were dead and I found you…that'd be another story. I'd have a feast then and no mistake!"

Tipsy didn't argue. What happened to your body once you had left it to enter Hare Paradise didn't matter: Whether it rotted or was eaten by another creature had no significance. So Mum had told him. He explained this to the bird and filled him in on the religion of the hares.

Craggy whistled softly. "Gee, that's some God…sorry *Goddess*… you've got to watch over you. Ostara you say. We birds have a different God but she looks after us too. Well, I think she does."

Craggy's beak lowered and his eyes looked sad.

"You think…?" Tipsy queried.

"Yeah, I have my doubts sometimes, and some birds say she's just a fantasy bird-god other birds made up…to make us feel safe and protected."

"Oh, same here", Tipsy said, "I'm told some hares are unbelievers. They lack faith in Ostara…"

"But why?"

Tipsy recalled the guffaws of two macho leverets that never prayed and didn't bother gazing respectfully at the moon for forty heartbeats each night as required by their creed.

"They just want to appear tough…we hares are naturally timid. We don't go around spoiling for a fight. We don't want trouble. But some hares in their youth and late childhood pretend to be stronger than they are, and they think that disbelieving in Ostara makes them less timid. Silly, really…I believe Ostara gives us strength…and looks after us. Some of my friends disbelieve because they claim our Goddess does nothing to protect us. I can see why they might think that…sometimes.

"I mean, when the falcon snatches a baby hare, and I remember how feeble I was when I came into this world, you wonder where Ostara is, why she doesn't see what's happening, or hear his cry for help. If she's all powerful why can't she come down and just kill the falcon? But then I think…maybe Ostara sees things differently. Maybe she waits for the falcon to extinguish the earth life of the hare so she can welcome the spirit leveret into the glory of Hare Heaven, where all hares can expect peace and joy…"

The bird chirped audibly and shook its feathers. "Hey…that sounds like the kind of stuff Storm Petrels say when they talk about mystical things. But how do we really know there's a world after death for birds when no bird has ever gone there and returned to tell us? I've never yet spoken to a bird that actually saw this delightful place where dead birds get to have such a good time…"

"That's because you have to be dead to get there. And if you're dead you can't talk to the living."

"Fine, Tipsy, but what if…" Craggy went silent, his eyes tearful and empty. "…what if the whole thing is a big lie, a story that someone, some crazy bird… made up just to keep us all thinking there's a purpose to all this flying around, pecking, foraging for worms and other scraps, and worrying about being attacked by bigger birds?"

Craggy shivered, barely holding his position on the mossy stone crevice as a blast of wind ruffled his feathers and sent dust swirling around his little beaked feathery head.

Tipsy felt the same breeze but it didn't faze him. "I've thought about that too…some hares I've spoken to about this say they'd only be sure about surviving bodily death if they could see the Other World right now, while still alive, instead of having to wait for a falcon to ambush them, or some mishap…but then I can remember a time before birth…

"I've seen that other place, though the memory of it is almost gone. Father Buck…he's the hare priest around here…he says Ostara demands faith without proof. If we had the proof it would be too easy for us, he says. That's what we hares are taught. That Ostara could easily show herself to us, but then we'd be so dazzled by her brilliance and glory that we'd forget our purpose in life and sit around day and night dreaming about the Next World, and do nothing else."

Craggy shrugged with his wings and raised his beak skyward. "I guess we'll have to wait…and hope for the best.

But I expect to have longer to wait than you; Tipsy. You know most of us Petrels live for almost twice as many heartbeats as a hare. I've heard of one who lived for three times longer than the oldest hare ever.

"It might be just a story. When we get together in the nests and the colonies we tell each other all sorts of stories. We share our knowledge, what we've seen and heard on our travels. Unlike you, and please don't be offended, we have wings. We can fly. You can only run about, and hide from your enemies…."

Tipsy shot back: "But look at how fast we run! And when we hide we live to run again. I'm happy to be a hare. I keep an eye out for the falcon. I won't be caught by that predator. Not me!"

"Happy, are you? That's good. But you know something, you're luckier than hares on the Big Island…over there."

Tipsy glanced in the direction of the far-off land that was only faintly visible through mists from the island. "Have you seen it…the Big Island?" He asked.

Craggy removed a dust mite from an eye and sighed. "Yeah, I've been there. Flew over with friends five sunsets ago. It's full of Humaniks…and other unfriendly critters. One of our group that went was killed."

Craggy shook his head sadly. "You should have seen how it happened. A loud noise from somewhere below. I looked down and saw this bright flash, then a second and third one. It came from this rod a Humanik was pointing up at us. Anyway, my dear friend Turvy just stopped flying…went stiff as a rock in mid flight, and fell. Gutted me to see him…plummeting down, feathers fluttering around him. And there was nothing I could do. I could see little blotches of red where he'd been hit by whatever those Humaniks threw up at him."

Craggy had tears in his tiny eyes. He paused before resuming. "We flew on…we saw strange creatures being poked with sticks by Humaniks, and in a field we saw some of your lot being chased by large and very fast animals whose tongues were steaming as they ran. Humaniks were gathered around and making a lot of noise with their mouths. The hares didn't seem too happy about the whole thing.

"Flying further, I saw frightening shiny contraptions. Gigantic, weird looking things- with Humaniks sitting in them…moving noisily and cutting through fields…hares were also running from these. Birds too took flight. I was a bit distracted by the loss of Turvy but I noticed that those hares looked pretty terrified, though I couldn't hear them above the racket those Humanik things were making…"

Tipsy gawped in horror. "Gee…I reckon the island *is* the best place for us…"

"You can sing it!" agreed Craggy.

"Sorry to hear about your friend, and that you couldn't say goodbye to him because of the way he died…"

"Thanks, and I'm sure the rest of us would have died too if we hadn't changed direction to avoid those Humanik death rods. They are dangerous pests you know...the Humaniks…that's what many Petrels have found. They kill anything that moves…anything they can eat. Yeah, I know I eat small fish and bugs when I find them, but those Humaniks eat everything with a heart beating inside it."

Tipsy silently thanked Ostara that he wasn't living on the Big Island among the Humaniks and whatever other creatures inhabited that awful place. Craggy suddenly flapped his feathers and his tiny body seemed to grow to twice its size.

"Hey…a bug!" he rasped. The bird seemed to have completely forgotten their weighty discussion as he dropped from the stone cleft onto the ground and pecked furiously. "Juiciest bugs ever, yum", he lisped. "Maybe this is Heaven sent, Tipsy…to show me there is a Bird God after all, eh?"

"Maybe" agreed Tipsy, perplexed at how easy it was sometimes to have one's faith restored, but also conceding that the bird may have had a point.

The ways of Ostara were beyond the understanding of any hare in the world. So went the teaching that all hares knew by heart. Trying to fathom the mind of Ostara was pointless and maybe even disrespectful to the great deity. Funny how birds thought they had a god, when everyone knew there was only Ostara, the one true Goddess.

No point in annoying Craggy about that. Ostara will forgive him for that error as I'm sure he's a decent bird. I wonder if Humaniks imagine they have their own god? No…not with the way they behave. Oh thank you Ostara for not sending me to be born on the Big Island.

He resumed his exploration of his Humanik free island, determined to share what he'd learned from the Storm Petrel with other hares.

***

12

Tipsy was tired, though he could run for ten times longer than his playmates. Other maturing leverets; and older hares too, ran themselves into exhaustion in the never ending races that covered the whole island. They threw themselves down and buckled into sleep almost instantly.

Today, each of his twelve competitors had succumbed, leaving Tipsy the only one standing. Still, he was tired enough to want to rest awhile. He also craved a drink. Running always made you thirsty, and the more you ran the thirstier you got. Apart from the running, it was a sweltering hot day. The sun pulsed and burned fiercely, bathing the island in a heat that made hares uncomfortable. A little warmth was fine, but the sun was overdoing it today. And it wasn't even the season for such heat. Sometimes the weather got a bit confused; an old hare had informed him.

Tipsy shook himself. He was drenched in sweat and little droplets of it fell at his feet. Luckily, he was close to the lake, its calm glinting surface visible through swathes of gorse. He scampered drowsily into the lush yellow fodder, pausing now and then to have a nibble, not that he was especially hungry. But his throat was parched.

Forgetting his weariness, he accelerated his pace and found himself at the edge of the lake. The water level had risen, thankfully, after prolonged rainfall the day before that the sun had dried up everywhere else…except here. *Perfect.* Crystal clear water. He could see right down to the bottom: the little pebbles, the crisscrossing patches of purple, dark green and bright orange; the sprigs of juicy moss and the shoals of tiny fish scuttling about.

And then, staring up at him: his reflection. He'd changed since last time he'd studied his image. That was in a little puddle of rainwater near his birthplace. Mum had explained to him that it wasn't another leveret, but himself; that this marvelous ability to see oneself in a flat watery surface was another of Ostara's gifts to creation. His ears had grown quite a bit. His lucid amber eyes were larger, and seemed to pulse and vibrate steadily like his heart. That's another part of him that had grown: His heart. It had swelled and grown stronger. It wasn't visible in the watery image but it beat proudly and prominently behind the reddish brown fur he gazed upon.

Mum had told him hares had mighty hearts. This gave them a big advantage in speed and stamina, she'd said proudly. So his own must be pretty impressive. And yes… he was taller too. *Musn't admire myself too much. Ostara has a problem with self worship for some reason.*

Closing his eyes he pressed his mouth unto the surface and drank deep of the cool water. *The joy of it!* He felt a tingling sensation, followed by a surge of relief and pleasure. Pausing for breath he sipped at a slower rate, savouring every drop. What a contrast… between the refreshing coolness of the water and the sun that warmed his back.

Then he dipped his front paws in the water playfully, splashing about. When he pulled them out he watched the water drizzle, each drop from his paws causing a tiny but perceptible ripple. The drops created a cluster of ever widening circles beneath him. This movement contrasted with the remainder of the lake, or at least the portion within Tipsy's field of vision, that remained placid and undisturbed.

Having drunk his fill, he withdrew his head from the water and again idly fixed his eyes on that image of himself that now wobbled and shape-shifted in the chaos of motion. *How quickly I've grown…* He squinted as the fiery orb of the sun throbbed and scintillated in the lake, encircling and squeezing his own face in the reflection. He adjusted to its intensity, his heart fluttering at the sight of sprightly puffs of white cloud racing across the blue sky like leverets at play.

He marveled at how the sun never ceased to appear, day after day, to sustain life and shine a light on the world. Those clouds were so unlike the ones that lashed the island with rain. Those were dark and menacing. Tipsy yawned. *Time to sleep. Enough running for one day. But…what's that?*

He focused harder on the reflection that still wobbled and warped as drops of water fell from his head into the water. A tiny black dot had appeared just above his head in the likeness. It was growing in size with every heartbeat.

Getting bigger…*or closer? Not a dot. It's…a creature.* It quickly sprouted two flapping wings. *A bird. Getting bigger…or closer.*

Tipsy shook himself. Was tiredness distorting his judgment? He felt rooted to the spot, as if frozen in time and space. *What's happening?*

The wings suddenly disappeared, but the bird kept coming. Now Tipsy saw its ferocious beak, the sheen of its grayish black plumage, and its beady glistening eyes. It vanquished Tipsy's reflection, almost blocked out the sun, and cast a shadow across the lake in front of him. Its wings *hadn't* disappeared. They were closed against its body and it was…swooping.

A voice screamed inside Tipsy's head: *It's not in the water…it's in the sky…behind you….Move…Now!*

Several words but yet all, somehow, one word: *Move!*

Tipsy put every ounce of energy and strength into his sideward leap, a small wind fanning him as he dashed at his topmost speed towards what he hoped was a hiding place.

The falcon kept pace with him and he felt a sharp prodding in his hind left leg. And then a sensation of being dragged back by the tail, but he managed to break free by a sharp frantic effort of will, the smell of something hideous and terrifying assailing him as he tumbled through an opening in a clump of stones.

He huddled inside, pressing himself against a hard prickly wall, the enormous beak pursuing him, snapping at air. He froze, became as stiff and unyielding as stone. The bird shrieked, its beak straining to get closer to Tipsy but in vain.

So close. If the hideaway hadn't extended so far in he'd be bird food by now. The angry shrill cries grew more desperate. Tipsy imagined the falcon pleading. Then he focused. He heard its words: "Damn you hare…how dare you seek to evade me! You are my lunch. Yield to me or you'll suffer even more when I catch you, as I most definitely will!"

"I just want to live a little longer", Tipsy shot back, forgetting that the creature wouldn't be aware of his rare linguistic skills. *Remain still…wait it out.*

The falcon abruptly stopped its shrieking and complaining, falling into a deathly silence. The beak shuffled out of the hideaway, and Tipsy heard the flapping of mighty wings outside. He'd remain awhile, as the falcon might be waiting for him. It could be hovering overhead in readiness for another sky-dive aimed at converting him into an avian dinner.

As he pondered his situation he couldn't help wondering if he'd freaked out the falcon by addressing the bird in its own language. That special gift of his always surprised non-hares. *May as well sleep while I'm here.*

He drifted off in the safety of the cool pebbled abode, relieved at having outwitted the hare's deadliest foe on the island.

***

13

Tipsy gazed respectfully at the full moon, lisping a prayer of thanksgiving. Yes, it was clearly his quick thinking, exceptional speed, and evasive prowess that had saved him, but Mum had instilled into him the need to show due gratitude to Ostara for averted dangers, and blessings bestowed on him. Escaping the claws and snapping beak of the falcon was certainly a blessing and besides, it was Ostara that had gifted him with superior swiftness and stamina.

He was stiff and groggy from spending so long in that stony hideout. The falcon might well have taken to the sky and headed home moments after it withdrew its burrowing beak. Tipsy enjoyed reflecting on the precise moment it stopped poking about, just a whisker from his quaking front paws. Answering the bird in its own language had shocked it, he suspected. He tried to imagine its surprise and alarm at hearing a hare, a creature it probably regarded as nothing more than a piece of meat on four legs, addressing it in perfect bird lingo. He felt a surge of satisfaction at the thought. It must have been the last thing the grasping flesh craving predator expected.

How many leverets, he wondered, had been numbed with fright, frozen into a terror and helplessness they'd never known by that marauding giant of the skies? And yet, each leveret's fear and pain would have been brief. One snap of that ferocious beak and its spirit would be free. *Must tell Mum and Dad about this lucky escape...or blessing...whatever it was.*

The silvery beams of the great celestial light-giver soothed him: So much easier on the eyes than the sun, though both heavenly bodies were equally welcome in the hare's cycle of life. The moon might be deemed the sun's poor imitation by other creatures but hares, Tipsy knew, had a special reverence for it owing its association with their Goddess.

Focusing on it now, he thought he could make out the face of Ostara...yes...the head; and the eyes...a face that was half hare, half Humanik. *Funny that... why Ostara would in any way resemble a member of that species?*

Though his ordeal was over, Tipsy shuddered anew when he recalled the details of the falcon attack and his survival. A strange trembling took his body like a pair of alien paws...and shook it, and he had to quell the shaking by an effort of will. *There. It's stopped.*

It was as if some invisible entity somehow made him shake and quiver...when no threat existed. *Why do we hares tremble and suffer AFTER an unpleasant experience, when the danger has passed?* The more Tipsy stared at the moon the more that hazy white contour seemed to resolve into a face. Was Ostara sending him rays of healing? It certainly felt like it. His breathing had returned to normal. His stressful cogitations had abated.

The moon's glow intensified. *Maybe a sign?* It reined supreme in the heavens, with only a few dissipated fluffy clouds scudding across its benign circle of brightness. And...had she just spoken to him? Startled, he turned around.

"Praying, I see?"

His heart had started racing, but he relaxed when he saw the hare priest sitting behind him, washing his grey whiskers but with one eye turned skyward, no doubt in reverence to the Goddess.

"Oh, hello Father Buck...I didn't see you. So intent on thanking Ostara..."

"Great...mmm...you don't think you might have a vocation...to be a hare priest I mean. Have you given it any consideration?"

"No, Father Buck...but I had a close brush with death earlier, and I'm so grateful to be here, unscathed. If I had moved a fraction of a heartbeat slower I'd be in the belly of the falcon right now."

The old hare snorted. "Ah, Tipsy...then it was not to be...Ostara was looking out for you."

Tipsy agreed. "Oh, and how's Jockser coming along? The leveret who was with you last time we met...on the beach?"

“Oh, fine, fine”. The priest had a wistful look. Grunting affably he quipped: “He’s a living saint among hares. He’ll be taking his final vows very soon. Tell you what...when you get married, as I’m sure you will...it could be Father Jockser who does the honours!”

“Married?”

“Why yes...you’re growing fast. Before you know it you’ll catch the love bug...start your own family. Keep the hare population going!”

Tipsy hadn’t considered this, but he had acquired a fondness for female hares recently, from talking to them and contemplating their alluring shapes, and this attraction had grown a little stronger each day. Perhaps he ought to be on the lookout for a mate. He wondered if he had a mate in that other life, the one he left behind when he emerged into this world.

He had now lost almost all his memories of that wonderful place, but he knew that some day he’d return. Now, though, he had to get on with the business of living in *this* world. He didn’t know exactly what lay in store for him, but he had a feeling deep within his soul that it wasn’t going to be easy.

He walked a little with Father Buck, who could no longer run well due to age, admiring the old priest for his devotion to the spiritual welfare of hares on the island. Many hares scoffed at his simple faith, but even those cynical ones occasionally turned to him for solace. Though hares were by nature solitary creatures, Tipsy hadn’t seen one yet who didn’t appreciate a bit of moral support and company.

Playing with other hares was much more fun than just sitting around on your own, even when your food was delicious, or waves washed ashore in harmony with the soughing of the wind in your ears, or you slept soundly, or when the butterflies swept elegantly out of the sun beams.

Being alone was fine, but no creature deserved *continuous* isolation. *Ostara could never have intended that for us.*

The priest hare waved feebly with his right front paw as his home at the bottom of a daisy studded rocky hill came into view, illuminated by the moon that smiled down at them.

***

14

Tipsy was worried. There was something...*foreboding*... in the tone of his mother's voice.

She'd woken him earlier than usual. And Dad was sitting beside her.

Had he done something wrong? Were they angry with him for almost allowing himself to be taken by the falcon? They'd listened with ears cocked and eyes bulging as he'd recounted his narrow escape. But they hadn't scolded him. In fact, unless his eyes and ears had deceived him they seemed quite impressed...and relieved...at his achievement in dodging an untimely death.

He couldn't think of anything else they might be unhappy or uneasy about...apart from his unusual ability to speak to other animals and birds, his growing reputation on the island as the fastest runner, and his persistence in claiming that he had memories of another life before birth.

But they hadn't shown any marked annoyance with his special gifts, aside from an occasional expression of concern that he'd make other hares jealous if he flaunted his speed and linguistic skills *too much*.

He braced himself for whatever was coming. Mum and Dad exchanged sombre glances. Mum coughed lightly. There was sadness in her eyes. She spoke with great emotion, tears beginning to form.

"Tipsy, Harold and I were discussing this last night. We both love you as our only son, and we treasure your company. You've never done anything to hurt us. But both of us feel the time has come for you to...leave the nest. You have reached the age when a leveret becomes a fully fledged hare and you are now ready to fend for yourself on the island..."

Tipsy didn't know whether to be relieved that he hadn't done anything wrong, or shocked to the core of his being at the idea of leaving his home. He pawed his whiskers thoughtfully. "If you say so Mum...I've got to see quite a bit of the island, and I know where to find food and…where the best hiding places are…"

"Of course you can come to visit us any time. You'll always be welcome…" Mum quickly interjected.

Mum nudged Dad and he cleared his throat. He hopped over to Tipsy and patted him on the head with a firm paw. "Look after yourself son. Don't ever get too smug or forget to watch out for the falcon. He'll be really to get you after that escapade down at the lake. It's great you can talk to all sorts of creatures that share the island with us, but don't get too cozy with them. Treachery abounds in nature, boy! It's hard enough to trust another hare sometimes, never mind those crazy birds and whatever lies beyond this island. And hey… find yourself a mate. There are plenty does that'll be throwing themselves at you!"

Tipsy felt deflated. He wished they'd broken it to him more slowly. Dad was gently ushering him out of the nest. He scampered out past him, turning to say goodbye to him and Mum. Tears were falling from Mum's eyes. "Bye Tipsy", she soothed, "best of luck in finding a new home. Let us know how you get on…and take care."

Tipsy had ventured from the nest many times in his exploration of the island, so he knew the lay of the land, but it felt so different this morning. The rays of the weak sunshine that massaged his body lacked the feel-good warmth of other days when he knew he was heading out for a look around before returning to the snugness and security of home.

The great molten orb seemed to be frowning. The birds that traced patterns in the sky above him and chattered about their perky avian lives seemed to be saying: "You're on your own now Tipsy. No Mum and Dad to go running back to. Big bad world and it's all waiting for you!"

Of course he knew they weren't saying that. If they flew a little lower he'd hear their chirpy talk and maybe answer one or two of them.

"Hello Tipsy!" A tiny voice in his ear. The orange yellow and black butterfly that he'd first seen a few sunsets ago sounded and looked concerned. "Anything bothering you, Tipps?"

"Not really…well, yes…this is my first day of independence from my parents. They cut me loose today and I'm…I suppose…getting used to the idea."

The butterfly sighed, its wings keeping it airborne and hovering at eye level with Tipsy. It spoke wistfully: "I remember my big change. I was a grubby little caterpillar. I slithered and crawled in the earth, always fearing the moment a bird would sink its beak into me. I've seen it happen to many others. Then I died. I mean the caterpillar died. But then I emerged from the carcass and here I am! I dreaded having to give up my life as a caterpillar but now…well, I wouldn't go back to it for anything!"

Tipsy regarded the fluttering creature with curiosity. "I wonder what I'll grow into…or what awaits me."

The butterfly alighted on a dandelion close to Tipsy. After a brief silence it spoke again: "It's funny. When I was a caterpillar I didn't ever think I could be anything better. I feared what would happen after the big change. I had a pretty miserable life but it was all I knew. Now, I'd rather die…I mean *really* die…than go back to crawling along the ground like I used to."

At this it rose gracefully and soared into the air shouting "See you Tipps!"

Tipsy waved a paw at the elegant creature. He admired its unflinching optimism.

He pondered his situation. As he liked seaweed he opted to set up home near the beach. Not on the beach itself, as he'd heard of a hare that was swept out to sea while sleeping in the sand. That hapless buck was never heard from again.

And he'd ensure that his nest would not be visible from the sky. He didn't want the falcon dropping in again on one of his unfriendly visits.

15

Tipsy approached the home of Scutchy, the boxing coach, with a mixture of embarrassment and fervent anticipation.

A few sunsets ago, he'd have scoffed at the idea of seeking advice from the hard-bitten hare famed for his expertise in the art of paw to paw combat. But now he saw things differently.

A hundred sunsets had passed since he left the nest, and though he'd returned several times to visit Mum and Dad, he enjoyed his independence. The initial pain of departure had eased quicker than he'd expected; to be replaced by a new feeling of freedom and adventure...and new *priorities*, one of which motivated his decision to call on the boxing coach.

Scutchy had astounded the hare population, and many a curious bird, butterfly and roving insect, with his uncanny pugilistic prowess. Though getting on in years now, his age only seemed to add even deeper levels of insight to his repertoire of jaw dropping combative tactics and stratagems.

As a greenhorn leveret, Tipsy had viewed him coaching scores of extremely attentive hares. He enjoyed the spectacle, as pairs of hares squared off against each other under Scutchy's keen tutelage. At the time he imagined it was a game, something to while away the heartbeats before or after eating time.

Now he knew better. Hares went to Scutchy to improve their chances of winning a much sought-after girlfriend. Though he knew many hares had sought Scutchy's help, he still felt self-conscious about calling to the old pro. He looked around him: Nobody else visible, apart from a few birds flying overhead. He envied them. They had the sky to themselves, as well as the island.

Drawing nearer the corner of the weed-strewn field, he caught sight of old Scutchy, reclining in his nest and snoring audibly. Reluctant to rouse him from his well-deserved slumber, Tipsy sat and waited for him to wake.

He reflected on the reason for this visit to a quiet stretch of the island he generally avoided due to its remoteness and lack of food resources, apart from an assortment of weeds that weren't to his taste. The coach must be fond of weeds. Maybe they contributed to his toughness, or his tough image.

Though timid by nature, hares weren't supposed to be shy when it came to finding love and female companionship. Another lesson Mum had taught him in one of her late night sessions. She impressed upon him the importance of standing his ground and taking no nonsense from rivals when the time came for him to find a mate. He must use all his strength to assert his honour and win over his true love.

Unfortunately she hadn't elaborated on just how seemingly out of character for supposedly timid creatures the mating ritual could be. As a leveret he had watched goggle-eyed as male hares fought for hours... in the hills, in the fields, in the Humanik ruins, and on the beach. They slapped and thumped and kicked each other as if their lives depended on it.

Tipsy wondered what they were fighting about. Had one hare offended another, perhaps, and then maybe the spat had got out of hand and escalated into this crazy fracas. Or were they fighting over food?

The older hare he'd asked later in the day laughed at his ignorance, explaining that you had to be tough, ruthless beyond belief, to emerge victor in the battle for love. He pretended to understand. He didn't wish to offend the hare, though he still didn't get it. But he understood now.

Over the past twenty sunsets he had grown fonder by the heartbeat of Harriet. Ever since he'd first met her on the beach he'd *known* that she was the one for him.

He'd been nibbling on seaweed, as he did most mornings, when she appeared from somewhere behind him. He thought he'd heard something above the gentle splashing of the waves and the incessant crying of the gulls. He looked around and there she was. She must have been looking at him for some time before he noticed her perched on a rock, the wind rustling her fur and bending her whiskers. Once he spotted her she scampered down to him. She introduced herself. As if caught for words he blurted out: "Do you come here often?"

Tipsy suppressed a laugh. That was, he'd been told, the oldest and most trite chat-up line on the island. But it was better than saying nothing.

Tipsy indicated the clump of seaweed he'd been eating. "Like some?"

Surprisingly she'd never tasted it.

"Try some!"

Delicately she lowered her mouth to the tangled slimy pile and nibbled at a piece. "Oh that's nice...can't believe it tastes so good."

He watched as she devoured the entire pile he had started on, avoiding eye contact with him throughout. He'd felt elated and vindicated that she liked it.

"Thanks for the tip...are you busy...would you fancy a walk?"

Bashful, he'd said "sure".

He turned and began moving slowly along the beach, the relentless, partly soothing, partly monotonous lapping of the waves interrupting the silence and distracting him from figuring what to say next.

She spoke first. "Lovely...the sweet aroma of the ocean...ah it rejuvenates me."

"So you are familiar...with this part of the island?"

"Oh yes" she crooned "...I've dropped down to the beach a few times. Just to get away from... you know...the humdrum of life in the field where I live...near the bird colony. It's a pleasant change."

Tipsy liked the way she looked at him when she rhapsodised about the attractions of the sandy shore and the salt sea air.

Don't hesitate...say it.

'Harriet...do you mind me asking...have you...ah... (he gulped)...a boyfriend?"

She halted in mid step, stared at him and burst out laughing. "You must know it doesn't work that way! Of course I have suitors, hares that admire my...natural beauty...but to be my boyfriend they must prove themselves..."

Taken aback, Tipsy acted dumb.

"Eight sunrises from now, all the hares that fancy me will have an opportunity to make their pitch."

"You mean...show why they're worthy?"

She nodded and resumed walking, looking out to sea as she spoke. "Yes...they'll gather at the old Humanik ruins, and there they will fight for me."

Tipsy swallowed hard.

She continued: "So if you'd like to compete for my attentions...and you are a handsome hare by the way...you'll have to join the fray. And I caution you. It can be rough. My friend Sallyrod told me three hares sustained major injuries fighting for her five sunsets ago. And then, to make matters worse, she decided she didn't fancy any of the remaining five and told them all to get lost."

Shocked, Tipsy stopped in his tracks, kicking sand awkwardly behind him. "Gee, that was a bit unfair, wasn't it?"

"What do you mean? A doe is entitled to change her mind!"

A look of fierce reproach dismayed and silenced him. They resumed their walk. When they'd reached the end of the tide-line and stood at the foot of the high rocky cliff, she smiled. "Thank you for that lovely walk and for sharing your thoughts. If you wish to proceed further and win me over do come along to the ritual..."

Before he could answer she leaned towards him and planted a slurpy kiss that pressed his left set of whiskers lovingly against his facial fur.

"I will...certainly. I'd love to meet again...and raise a family with you....we'd live so happily..."

"Shush...don't get carried away. You have to win me first. Can you box?"

"Ah, no...But I'll learn, I promise."

"You'd better...some of the lads who fancy me are as tough as those rocks on the cliff. They pack a ferocious punch, I hear. I'm off now. Cheerio!"

Without another word she broke into a run. Cloudlets of sand erupted in her wake as she dashed up to the greenery over the horizon. Oh how elegantly she moved. Everything about her was so divine. Was this love? *Maybe.*

A loud snort brought Tipsy back to the present. Scutchy had woken. He heaved a huge sigh, stood and stretched. He shook himself and yawned. Lazily he turned to regard Tipsy with a raised eyebrow. "You looking for someone?"

Tipsy stood and nodded reverentially. "Yes...I was hoping you might be able to provide me with some boxing lessons, Eminent Scutchy. I was told you..."

"Ah, you were told, you were told...didn't the somebody who told you not also let you know that I'm close to retiring... from coaching you guys?"

"No, I'm very sorry, I thought..."

The coach waved a paw. "Never mind...I'll oblige you. Have you any experience?"

"Afraid not; I've watched a few bouts, though I didn't know what it was all about at the time..."

The old hare scuttled over and stood a whisker-length from Tipsy, his wizened eyes sizing up the younger hare.

"Hmm" he murmured, circling Tipsy and pressing a paw in turn against a hind leg, an ear, and poking the back of his neck. "You're a sturdy enough buck; you have it in you to fight, so that's a start..."

"So can you show me a few good moves...so I'll win this amazing doe I've met?"

Scutchy looked serious for a moment, and then burst out laughing. "Ah, you're like them all. You think all you've got to do is learn how to throw a good punch and she's yours. Hey...call back to me...say around this time two sunsets from now. I'll do what I can. Okay?"

Tipsy was elated. "Great! See you, Eminent Scutchy...and thank you, thank you so much!"

Tipsy ran, leapt, and tumbled across the island, not caring which direction he took, running wherever his legs carried him. He felt he was lighter than air.

What is it, this thing called love? He'd never felt like this before. What was it about Harriet that attracted him? She had eyes...a nose...fur...four legs...ears, a tail. No huge difference in appearance between himself and her...apart from her femininity.

But that was everything. *And her alluring ways. How she carried herself. And the twinkles in her eyes.* And the special brand of companionship she could offer.

But would they hit it off? He visualised her, sitting with him on a hillock overlooking the beach, waiting for the sun to go down as the mighty waves surged and frothed and spluttered to cover the sand and the seaweed and all those little oddly shaped shells and stranded creatures washed ashore by the ocean.

Would they have a litter of leverets? *Oh, you're thinking too far ahead. She's not yours yet. Wonder if I'll be able to fight off the competition...*

Tipsy let himself slide through a field of gorse that sloped down a verdant hillside. Normally he'd have stopped to taste the rich vegetation. Now he just wanted to rollick and frolic in it and savour the swish of it against his fur. What would he do to fill the time before he returned to the coach?

Spotting another hare nibbling at the bark of a tree he scuttled over to him. "That's tough on the teeth, ever tried seaweed?" He asked.

The hare looked up, frowned, and resumed eating. "I like it tough. Seaweed is too soft and soggy."

"Suit yourself!" Tipsy quipped, dashing off towards the bird colony. He'd bat the breeze with those scatter brained fliers. Always good for a laugh, or maybe a bit of news from the Big Island. *They see so much from high above the earth.*

***

16

Waxy Bumbleton-Crossbar whistled happily to himself as he reached for the carving knife. He had mixed feelings about chopping up the hare that lay before him on the kitchen table. There was something almost noble about the carcass, he thought, and sad too.

Its running days were over, its fate now to fill the bellies of sportsmen. But the elegance of its reddish-brown form still impressed him. He loved the taste of this animal, but rarely enjoyed its flesh because, well, hares were scarcer in Ireland these days and every one counted.

Coursing clubs were finding it increasingly difficult to make up the required quota for the annual fixture. So no coursing supporter would dream of depriving his club of precious bait by...shudder the thought...killing one for the dinner table.

But Waxy had found a way around that strict unwritten rule of coursing. He didn't scour the countryside in search of a hare to shoot. No. In fact, he didn't have to dirty his boots or hang about all day waiting for one of those elusive creatures to show itself.

He rubbed a forefinger along the left hind leg of the animal. This limb had snapped when the screeching hare became entangled in the net that ensnared him. In his struggle to escape, he had broken his leg.

Foolish animal. He could have gone on to perform at one of the finest coursing venues in Ireland.

Hares were fast, and in some ways attractive,...graceful even, the way they traced those zigzag patterns of flight as they panted and darted at forty-five miles or more per hour to evade the dogs.

But they weren't too clever. If that hare had any sense it would have stayed calm and waited for the supreme privilege of serving his human masters. *But its miscalculation is my blessing.*

Every year a percentage of hares sustained injuries during netting...and injured hares couldn't be coursed. But the coursing club on the Peninsula didn't let those defective ones go to waste. They could be used to help train the greyhounds.

Waxy winced a little at the thought of hares dangling by their back legs from strings for the dogs to play with... blood spraying everywhere, staining the concrete, sprinkling the faces of trainers who stood around slugging beer. But at least they served a purpose, enhancing a dog's performance.

Personally Waxy preferred to eat a hare than feed it live to dogs, whatever about the benefits to a novice greyhound in need of motivation....and the craic with the lads after those hectic training sessions in his converted farmyard. There was a social side to it also, however private those gatherings had to be.

But this hare was for the dinner plate. He chopped the injured leg off with one hefty motion of his arm...then the other hind leg. Off came the front legs, blood squirting around the table and down unto the newspapers that covered the floor tiles.

There would have been more blood had he not drained away most of it a few days earlier after removing the entrails and hanging the carcass upside down.

Always better to leave the hare for about a week before cooking, he'd learned from his grandfather.

Grabbing the ears he sliced the animal's head off with a jagged edged knife. Gathering all the severed body-parts he heaped them into a large metallic jug, which he then placed tentatively in a pan of water on the electric stove.

His mouth watered and his belly rumbled as he envisaged the end result of his cooking.

While the water bubbled and the dismembered hare sizzled Waxy gazed out through the kitchen window. Birds were pecking at remnants of a micro-waved lasagne that had been pulled from the dustbin by stray cats. *Nature red in tooth and claw. Something those blasted antis don't understand.*

He wondered if this year's coursing fixture would go ahead without incident or interference, as any sporting event should. Or would those...people...be there again this year.

The memory returned to irk and taunt him. He had sworn to himself that he would walk straight into the fixture last year. *Don't make eye contact.* That was the advice from HQ to all coursing clubs. *Don't look at the protesters. But...damn it... the temptation was too strong.*

It was a stormy day. Rain poured down as if from giant buckets, lashing the entrance laneway, peppering the rooftops of cars and vans. He had begun running, though grossly overweight, once he alighted from the van. His protruding abdomen quivered like an enormous jelly.

Approaching the entrance he saw them, lining both sides of the laneway. The placards bore insults to his beloved sport. Slogans as such as "Coursing is cowardly barbarism", "Save the innocent Hare!" "A relic of the Dark Ages".

*How dare those idiots...*His blood was boiling at the thought, if not as loudly as the bubbling water in which the jugged hare sizzled and steamed. The chanting of protesters had got to him. Words and taunts that pierced his soul.

His eyes had swivelled to focus on a young woman whose face was contorted with anger, her rain sodden body juddering as she roared at him and the other coursing fans. "How would YOU like to be a Hare...have this done to YOU?"

She was pointing to a cartoon on her placard showing a hare being tossed into the air by two dogs. Ink bled from the rain sodden poster but the image was clear.

Waxy couldn't contain himself. He felt as though she was personally addressing him. He started running towards her, his feet getting stuck in the mucky ground. He felt like one of those slow-motion TV characters.

His friends restrained him before he could lash out at her. His fists flailed at raindrops. Inside the coursing grounds the event went ahead as normal, but even the powerful loudspeaker announcing the results of races and the incessant pounding rain couldn't drown out the sound of that infernal chanting from the picket line.

What did they hope to achieve? They would NEVER end his pastime.

He went back to the cooker. He looked at the wall-clock. Popping open a bottle of red wine he poured a glass for himself; then added some to the jug containing the hare. He dropped in a handful of juniper berries. When the hare was cooked he would mix in the bottle of blood he had drained from its body the previous week.

A lot to this recipe, he considered, but well worth it once the meal was ready.

He laughed, pouring another glass of wine.

Imagine what those anti-coursing hooligans would say if they could see me now, with one of their furry friends all carved up in little pieces.

The lads would be here soon, and what a surprise awaited them. They all loved a hare meal, if not as much as they loved their sport. That came first. Nothing would or could stand in the way of coursing these tasty fleet-footed critters. *Nothing.*

He relaxed his grip on the wine glass. Any tighter and it would have snapped. *Just relax. Coursing is safe. There's nothing to be getting all riled up about.*

***

17

Tipsy sighed. He wondered just what he'd let himself in for. He sat brooding, taking a break from Scutchy's first boxing lesson.

His head swam, not only from the succession of light but still stinging punches the trainer had landed on him, but from the rapid-fire instructions and reprimands that rained on him as he attempted to dodge the old hare's sparring.

Another hare was now squaring up to Scutchy for a similar lesson. It would take the entire day to impart the full series of lessons, Tipsy was told. His spirits lifted at the sight of the second hare.

He fell flat on his back at the first punch, and was moaning, holding his paw to his mouth. Scutchy was standing over him, shaking his head. "You won't win a doe if you go down that fast!" he jibed.

Tipsy had lasted longer, and Scutchy had complimented him on learning so quickly, and "taking it on the chin", as he put it, though he didn't feel that way.

The next hare was fearful, and when Scutchy threw a punch, he shrieked, his ears stood out starkly, and he ran away with fright, disappearing over the ridge of a hill. "He's a good runner. I'll give him that!" Scutchy joked, and both Tipsy and the hare nursing his mouth laughed.

Tipsy approached Scutchy for the next lesson, more alert this time in anticipation of whatever might be coming his way. But Scutchy just smiled. "That first lesson was to give you a flavour of what boxing is all about. You try to hit without being hit…I did all the hitting…now, you go ahead…hit me!"

Tipsy hesitated; then raised his right paw in an effort to strike the tough hare. His paw swiped at air, the wily old head sprang to one side and before he could make a move Tipsy felt the impact of a powerful thump below his jaw. Thinking fast he absorbed the pain and caught Scutchy under the chin with his paw, as he'd seen the trainer do to the previous pupil. Scutchy doddered for a few seconds, staggered back, almost fell but up-righted himself.

Tipsy felt queasy. Added to the stab of pain was a fear he had hurt Scutchy. Had he gone too far? The trainer glared at him. The other hare gave Tipsy a worried look: Then a hearty laugh from Scutchy, who ambled over to Tipsy and patted him on the head. "That's good. You're making progress. Now, listen to me, practice is everything. We'll go through it again, and each time I'll teach you new tactics, and tricks. Okay?"

Tipsy nodded assent, his confidence soaring. Still nursing persistent aches where the trainer's paws had struck him, he steeled himself for the next round of instruction.

Meanwhile, six more hares had arrived for training. All looked nervous, and the sight of the complaining hare, his face screwed up with discomfort, didn't help. They huddled together, murmuring in worried tones and eyeing Scutchy with growing unease. The trainer was lapping water from a small puddle that the rain had created the night before. All that strenuous movement must make him thirsty.

None of them wanted to be here, Tipsy presumed, but for each of them the desire to win the heart of a doe trumped any abhorrence of violence or fear of aches and pains…or even serious injury. He had heard about hares that almost died during fierce mating fights.

A hare who lived down near the lake had assured him this was understandable, and showed how passionate bucks were about winning their sweethearts.

18

Tipsy took a deep breath and sat back against the stone wall, chewing on a plant stalk. Dozens of hares had gathered near the old Humanik ruins for the big showdown. A buzz of lively chatter mingled with the humming of bees and the chirping of birds, and Tipsy had to block out their voices. This was no time for tuning into their babbling, intriguing though it sometimes proved to be, especially when it related to activity on that mysterious Big Island across the sea.

A hare called Rocky, who lived in a cave where he said he guarded a wise old hare, had tipped off Tipsy about the day's proceedings. There were five does present, each seeking a suitable partner.

All the suitors, Tipsy included, had already made known their affections to the does, but today only the successful candidates would secure their chosen girlfriends. The losers would have to resume their search for a mate.

There were eight contenders, including Tipsy, for the affections of Harriet. Two of them were ferocious looking chaps. Right now they were hopping around, punching the air, making their presence felt and casting those intimidating "what are looking at?" glares at everyone else.

Despite the daunting odds, Tipsy was confident. Apart from the praise Scutchy had lavished on him, he knew that he was the fastest hare on the island. He felt sure she would be his before the sun had set on the ocean. But he needed to beat off his rivals to win Harriet.

The first bout was announced. The voice calling the two contenders was familiar, but Tipsy was surprised to see it belonged to Father Buck. Why was the priest officiating at such an event? Wasn't his job attending to the spiritual needs of hares?

Rocky, possibly sensing his thoughts, smirked. Leaning over to Tipsy he whispered: "He's into everything these days. He sees the boxing tournament as an opportunity to get his "we all live on after death" message across to hares who don't normally listen to him."

Tipsy didn't argue. His only concern was winning, and with each passing heartbeat his confidence surged.

The first pair was called out. They faced each other, bowed respectfully in accordance with tradition and then charged, colliding and falling to the ground with a loud thud. Dust, clay and pebbles rose in a squally cloud, spraying the onlookers.

Father Buck stood over the two of them and counted to ten. "Okay, remove them. They are disqualified from today's event! The doe these two fools set their eyes on is free to draw the necessary conclusions from their shabby and lacklustre performance. Next pair!"

Two more hares stepped forward, hopping niftily, waving at the audience, and shadowboxing, their steely expressions evidence of their resolve. One immediately landed a lively punch on the other's midriff. The cuffed hare swayed and his eyes rolled, but he quickly recovered and responded with an uppercut, sending his rival staggering backwards. He collapsed in a heap. It was over in a dozen heartbeats.

The champion leaped for joy, but Father Buck reminded him he still had to beat off other contenders for that particular doe. The next two fighters dodged each other, dancing around and avoiding any contact whatsoever. "Stop fooling, you two. Fight, or get out of my sight!" Father Buck howled.

The two reacted with shock, and immediately became locked in an awkward embrace, neither able to land a punch and yet fearful of letting go of his opponent. Father Buck separated them, urging an end to their attempt to evade their duty as hares in search of love. They resumed, this time peppering each other with probing but inconclusive punches until one managed to leave his rival breathless with a punch in the stomach, followed up with a kick to the groin. Father Buck counted to ten and declared the winner, as the sprawling hare groaned in the grass.

Tipsy was unnerved by the sound of does, who were sitting in a row along the stone wall, giggling and pointing derisively at the grassy arena. They seemed to be enjoying the spectacle of bucks fighting for them.

Tipsy became impatient as pair after pair of love hungry hares fought, each contest bringing triumph to one and crushing defeat to another. Three does walked away with successful fighters. Then, his heart fluttered as the first pair seeking Harriet's affections faced each other.

It was over quickly, with the loser conceding after sustaining several punches and failing to make any headway.

Tipsy watched as the numbers dwindled. Now there was only one left: the one who had beaten off his rivals with ease and Tipsy had to fight him. He braced himself as Father Buck called his name and the name of his opponent: Scraggledy.

This hare was bigger than Tipsy and looked stronger. He started dancing again, and punching the air, as he had done earlier. *What a show-off.* This seemed to unnerve other hares. Understandably, as it showed just how muscular he was and how determined to win his chosen mate.

Father Buck signaled for the fight to begin. Scraggledy immediately rushed at Tipsy, who stepped aside and let him pass unimpeded. Scraggledy wheeled around, leaped at Tipsy and rained punches on him. It happened so fast that Tipsy froze, absorbing the blows. He felt powerless, completely at the mercy of this relentless attack.

A sickening numbness threatened to take hold of his body. He managed to pull back, reeling from the onslaught. His head swam. Steadying himself, he summoned every ounce of strength in his body as the juggernaut returned to finish him off, as he had done so easily with the others.

Don't panic. Hold firm. Don't yield.

Tipsy used his paws to block the rapid-fire punches. Scraggledy raged, his ferocious attack dented. The two became locked in a fierce embrace, from which Tipsy struggled to free himself even as the other tightened his grip.

Neither could strike the other. Was Scraggledy trying to crush him?

Suddenly the two flew apart as Father Buck grabbed them and broke the clinch. This time Tipsy took the initiative. Before the other could make his next move, Tipsy leaped forward, landing on his opponent like a gull pouncing on a fish.

Now it was his turn to pummel Scraggledy. He worked his paws mercilessly. For twenty heartbeats he punched the stronger hare, the latter's shrieks of protest growing less audible. He felt himself being pulled away, his paws still lashing out.

"Enough!"

The voice of Father Buck. The priest was standing over Scraggledy, who was stretched out on the grass like a piece of soggy seaweed, breathing rapidly and groaning. The priest counted…Tipsy waited. When "Ten" was reached Tipsy leapt for joy and hares cheered.

He glanced at the wall, where Harriet sat alone, the other does having been whisked away by their champions. He turned to speak to her but a tap on the shoulder restrained him. "You still have to catch her in a chase. She can run in whatever direction she wishes, and for as long as she so desires…are ye ready, the pair of ye?"

Tipsy sighed. He'd forgotten that part of the challenge. He smiled to himself. *Let's just do this.* He was the fastest hare on the island, so catching her would be no problem. *Better get on with it.*

Father Buck explained that Harriet would be given a thirty heartbeat start and then Tipsy could give chase.

Tipsy sat and waited for Harriet to set off. Scraggledy was on his feet, nursing a sore head…but didn't seem bothered otherwise. He was whistling to himself and smiling. What a decent chap, Tipsy thought, accepting defeat so gracefully. Tipsy watched him hobble over to the wall where Harriet sat. Harriet jumped to the ground, indicating she was ready with a curt nod in Tipsy's direction.

Scraggledy settled onto the wall, occupying the exact spot she had occupied. *What's he up to?*

Harriet bounded forward, and Father Buck counted… "Now!" he shouted.

Tipsy gave chase, easily keeping up with Harriet, but careful not to make it look too easy. She ran through field after field, leaping over the crumbling heaps of stones gracefully as only a mature doe could. How beautiful she was in motion.

Suddenly she veered to the right, disappearing into the depths of thick vegetation that continued all the way upwards to the crest of a hill. Tipsy lost sight of her, following the sounds of disturbance amid the growth, the pungent aromas of plants, herbs and weeds banishing any hint of her scent. His ears made up for absence of sight and smell. Snapping stems, rustling of leaves, and breaking twigs guided him on her trail. Tipsy emerged from the swathes of growth and looked around.

No sign of her.

He ran about the hilltop, surveying the scene on all sides. *There!*

She was hiding behind the little apple tree, just a tip of an ear visible: Enough to give her away. Tipsy half ran, half tumbled down the hillside, joyous at the prospect of soon having a fulltime girlfriend. Harriet leapt from her position and ran at what must be her maximum speed towards the lake.

Tipsy good-humouredly allowed her to increase her lead before dashing to make up ground and bring this silly and increasingly tiresome game to a conclusion.

Harriet was squatting at the edge of the lake, which today looked glorious as sunbeams danced and sparkled on its placid pale-blue surface. *At last…*Tipsy enthused. *She'll be mine in less than thirty heartbeats. What on earth…?* She had just plunged into the lake!

Tipsy leapt headlong in after her. She was certainly making him work damned hard for the privilege of being her mate.

Tipsy swam furiously, Harriet moving elegantly to the other side of the lake. She hopped ashore, shook herself dry, and Tipsy followed.

The chase continued, Tipsy wondering what she was at. This was to be a mere formality, another hare had assured him, just a tradition to be observed…but she was really drawing it out. As he ran, always keeping her in sight, Tipsy realized she was running all the way back to the starting point, which wasn't the standard routine.

Normally, he understood, the runners went in one direction and once they reached the finishing point, they rested and the formal relationship ensued.

Something was amiss…but he dismissed this nagging thought. The race would soon be over, if only because Harriet must yield to exhaustion.

The stone wall came into view. Father Buck was still there, and a few hares who'd watched the bouts earlier were lolling about. Harriet was heading for the wall. Tipsy slowed down as Harriet stopped, seemingly out of breath, slowly hopping along in the grass. Father Buck looked perplexed. The others had all stopped conversing, eating, or exercising and were staring at Tipsy as if he had two heads.

Tipsy's heart fluttered. This was the big moment. He followed Harriet as she strode alluringly towards the stone wall. She halted, and sat at the base of the wall, gazing at Tipsy, but said nothing. Tipsy called out: "Darling…that was a great run. You certainly put me through my paces. Gee, you've got a great quartet of legs. Now I claim your heart!"

He hopped to where she sat, and moved to land the soupiest kiss he could muster upon her fair lips.

"Stop!" She snapped.

"What? What's the problem, apple of my eye…sweetheart of my dreams?"

She avoided eye contact at first, and then fixed him an icy stare. "I don't love you anymore. I love Scraggledy, isn't that right Scragg?"

The hare Tipsy had beaten in a fair fight slid off the wall contemptuously and hobbled over to Harriet, wrapping a paw around her waist. They both gazed awkwardly at Tipsy, who was struck dumb. He tried to speak, but no words came, just breaths of air and incoherent mutterings. "But you can't do this…can they, Father Buck?" he pleaded.

The priest hopped over to his side and patted him on the head. "Afraid they can Tipsy. Sorry for your troubles. You see, though you won fair and square, a doe has the absolute prerogative to change her mind. It's not ideal, and I, as all devout hares on this island know, have always discouraged this practice. But that's just the way it is."

Tears formed in Tipsy's eyes and began streaming down his cheeks. He watched through a watery blur as Harriet turned her back on him and gave Scraggledy a long, twisty passionate kiss that was rightfully Tipsy's. Then they hopped away.

"There, there lad" Father Buck comforted.

Tipsy sank into a deep pit of misery. Shame and disbelief convulsed him. Nothing as horrible as this had ever happened to him, not since he first saw the light of this crazy world after he'd left behind a world of bliss where love reigned supreme and nobody cheated anyone.

This was just sickening… the end of everything: Desolation worse than a falcon's beak closing on a feeble, doomed leveret. If death came now, Tipsy would welcome it with open paws.

***

19

Annemarie Cristobel kicked the bunch of crisp golden leaves, uprooting slivers of clay in the soft earthen laneway through the wood as she did so.

She pounded the ground beneath her with every step, as if this would assuage her heartache and anger.

Taking a walk never failed to clear her head, but not today. It would take more than soothing autumn sunshine and nature's balm to heal the wound inflicted earlier that day. Not a physical wound. *Worse.*

To *suspect* that idiot she loved- and God how she loved him- had been cheating, was bad enough. But to see him practically devour another woman, embracing her greedily as the two of them met outside the post office, was shattering. Only yesterday he had mooted the idea of engagement. A matter of hours later there he was…A bird flew past her from a tree, chirping. What are you so happy about? She almost screamed.

Her second breakup in a year. The last charmer…well at least he was honest. He felt it wasn't working out and they parted. But this latest. She stopped, closed her eyes, breathed deeply, and exhaled…imagining as she did expelling with the spent air all thoughts of that…betrayal.

A moratorium: that's what I'll have…a complete moratorium on relationships. They bring only pain and betrayal.

What was that? She looked behind. Nothing. There it was again. Rising and falling like a siren. An animal in pain. *Must be injured, maybe caught in a trap.*

Her heart fluttering, she stood in the middle of the pathway, straining to hear what direction it came from. It seemed to be somewhere ahead. Quickening her pace, she broke into running. The end of the pathway loomed.

So engrossed had she been in her thoughts she had walked almost the full length of the tourist trail. Emerging from the wood she heard that weird moaning again, now much louder. Also laughter; and men's voices.

This time it was clearly coming from behind a high stone wall to her left. She knew the wall concealed from the public road a stretch of waste ground, occasionally used for handball practice by youngsters.

She stood in front of the wall. It was too high to climb and anyway there were no footholds to get a grip so that was out. Ivy sprouted between the stones. She could grip that but it might come loose. Anyway, she reasoned, if it was an animal in pain, then surely whoever is in there can help the poor creature.

She listened. The wailing or whatever it was had ceased, but the human chatter continued A few swearwords…followed by laughter.

Then it started again. This time it assaulted her ears: a shrill moaning, like an out of tune fire engine, interrupted by barking and yelping.

Dogs.

Standing back from the wall she caught sight of the green decommissioned letter box. The paint was peeling off and rust had corroded parts of it. Smiling, she remembered posting a Valentine card here as a spotty faced teenager. It wasn't much used in recent times, which was probably why they dismantled it.

She was about to walk on when she noticed a chink of light shining from it. Of course… the insides had been ripped out.

Ah, a hole in the wall.

She peered through the slit that had received so many letters and greeting cards. Her field of vision was restricted to a small rectangle of what lay on the other side of the wall, and this was further diminished by cobwebs and ivy fragments.

Still, there was enough to see: A sleek dog, whimpering and snarling, froth bubbling around his mouth…saliva hanging in blobs. He was prancing on his hind legs, forepaws punching air or striving to grasp at…what was it?

A brown shape wriggled and squirmed. She squinted, trying to focus on the limited scene. It was a greyhound, and that was a live animal that somebody was dangling before it. The obese middle aged man attired in mock military style jacket was hollering as he swung the creature which was tied by its hind legs and hanging upside down.

Was it a rabbit? *No. larger. A hare.*

The animal's screeching was unabated, now more like a baby sobbing than a siren wailing.

Annemarie felt faint. Horror froze her. She wanted to avert her eyes but couldn't. Something kept her rooted to the tarmac under her feet. She pressed her face closer to the aperture. The metallic odour of rust and a mossy smell wafted up her nostrils.

The swinging continued, but the sobbing and screeching stopped. The man then tossed the hare, which presumably had died, to the dog. The greyhound buried his snout in its body and began ripping at its fur.

Shining watery strings and lumps of bloody entrails gushed onto the grass as other men came into view. Each of them held a similarly tethered hare, apart from a smirking teenager who was slugging from a beer can. The greyhound she'd been watching turned and sprinted to the right…out of her sight.

A chorus of moaning and sobbing formed a backdrop to an outbreak of animated chatter and chuckling. Her view was partially blocked by a man who abruptly stood with his back to the breach in the wall. She smelt petrol or diesel from his clothing.

She imagined she also caught the whiff of death or decay from the other side of the wall. Something vile that threatened to draw forth the contents of her heaving stomach.

Her view was now limited to tiny flickering glimpses of movement, but the cries of the animals grew louder, almost drowning out the human chatter. She heard the pitiful death screeches through the letterbox and from over the wall, but the visuals were denied her.

She pulled away, stunned and disbelieving.

Did I just see that?

Her heart raced and pounded. Cold sweat broke out on her forehead. What can I do?

The police!

Her hand, trembling, reached inside her jacket for the mobile.

Damn. Of all the times. She'd forgotten to charge it, thanks to that idiot two-timer.

On an impulse, she picked up a handful of pebbles that lay on the roadside, and flung them over the wall, shouting as she did.

"I saw you…I've called the police and they'll be along in less than a minute. Sickos!"

She awaited a response. First a momentary silence as the babble of voices ceased…then a chorus of cursing and shouting and soft rapid footfalls in the grass.

She looked through the cavity again and saw them running in the opposite direction, all but one who was shuffling dead hares into a sack. He then joined his mates in scarpering.

At least they've stopped…but those poor creatures.

She sat down on the pavement, leaning against the wall, her arms folded. She felt nauseous, sickened into immobility. Her head was in turmoil.

Just minutes earlier she'd thought that nothing could rival the stab of betrayal she'd suffered, her seething anger at that conniving heartless cheater who'd turned her life inside out. But it was as nothing compared to this.

Who *were* those people? Why on earth would *anyone* want to hurt such a gentle creature?

***

20

Tipsy did everything he could think of to take his mind off the betrayal. Harriet's heartless rejection of him after his success in beating off all competitors for her was too painful to endure.

He ran to the north, south, east, and west of the island, pausing to reflect in fields he'd never passed through before. He ran along stone walls, moved more slowly amid thick gorse and brambles, and ran perilously close to cliff-edges, heedless of the danger and even scorning it.

He lingered at a steep precipice overlooking the noisy Storm Petrel colony, dark thoughts entering his head. He banished them as soon as they flashed in his consciousness, shocked at their intrusion into his miserable life. No matter how bad things seemed, the option of self-imposed death was never to be considered.

That was a rule that Father Buck had warned all hares about, and his parents had emphasised the value of life. One's allotted span had to be completed before the return to Hare Heaven. Tipsy felt ashamed of self-destructive thoughts, but then, life had given him cause to be upset and disillusioned.

He sat brooding, soothed somewhat by the rhythm of the ocean. He imagined himself as part of the raging surf, absorbed in the endless ebb and flow…at one with its unremitting swell and the righteous rage of the waves that crashed against the cliffs below. Tiring of this distraction he kicked a sod of grass and hopped away from that source of forbidden thoughts. *No.* He would never give in to *that* impulse; come what may.

A familiar chirping roused him from his musings. A small dark bird with its distinctive white rump hopped towards him. A Storm Petrel from the colony below. Tipsy recognized him as Craggy, one of the first creatures he had met in his childhood exploration of the island.

"Hello again" the bird greeted.

Tipsy barely acknowledged its salutation. "Good day" he said curtly, not bothering to look the bird in the eye. Craggy hopped closer to where Tipsy sat on a flat rocky surface.

"Not too happy today Tipsy?"

"No, and I don't want to talk about it."

"Are you sure?"

Tipsy reflected for a moment, and changed his mind. Could it hurt any more than bottling it up upside?

He blurted it out: "The doe I loved, and that I honestly thought loved me deeply, has betrayed me!"

"I'm sorry to hear that. Did you lose her in one of those crazy fights you guys stage? I've seen them…"

"I didn't lose her in a fight; I won her, fair and square…"

"But then…"

"I did everything right. Followed all the advice about how to box honorably…and then what do you think she did…she skedaddled off with another buck!"

Craggy fell silent. His straight bill with its hooked tip was nudging something out of the loose soil beside Tipsy's rocky seat.

Without looking at Tipsy he soothed "I wouldn't let it get me down…happened to me too. She told me…she told me that my beak alone had won her over, even before she saw what a good flier and worm-catcher I was. Oh, she could turn on the charm. I was seduced and I thought bird heaven couldn't be better than being in the company of…that two-timing flapper!"

"So she left you?"

"Left me? I missed her one morning and went around in search of my true love, as I thought she was. I found her with her new feathered boyfriend…hopping from rock to rock down in the bay…the ugliest git in the entire colony, but she said she was in love with his *personality*. Did you ever hear the like?"

"Did it take you long to, ah…recover…from the loss of your girlfriend?"

"A hundred sunsets. That's a lot of heartache and bitterness, but yes, I got over it. I've a new bird girl now. She's the sweetest flier in the bay. I go into a flutter at the mention of her name or the thought of her. Which reminds me…I promised her a juicy worm and I still have to find one… so if you'll excuse me!"

Tipsy arose and continued on his quest to forget about Harriet, his lost love. He felt better after talking to Craggy. Somehow, knowing he wasn't alone in suffering rejection made it easier to bear.

***

21

Tipsy approached his former home with mixed feelings. He liked visiting, but felt more like a stranger calling in recent days and nights than a son returning to say hello. He felt absent and present at the same time when he greeted them, his thoughts wandering to other places and situations. The loss of Harriet still distracted and angered him, despite all his efforts to banish her from his mind.

The sky twinkled with a multitude of stars. Not a cloud to obscure their magnificence. *Wonder if they'll be sitting up marvelling at those heavenly delights.* The nest came into view, but Tipsy didn't notice any sign of his parents admiring the sky. At first he thought the home was empty, until Mum appeared from behind a nearby hill, her fine elegant form silvered by moonlight.

Seeing him waiting by the nest, she quickened her pace slightly and hopped towards him, greeting Tipsy with barely a whimper. This was odd. Usually he got a hearty welcome and her mood was sprightly and radiant. She passed him mutely and began tidying the nest. The grass was all dishevelled and needed rearranging, but hardly right now, Tipsy thought; with him visiting.

He had to break the silence. "Mum...is something wrong?"

She settled herself in the nest of soft dry grass, bidding him to sit beside her. A tear formed in one eye. She spoke with her face averted from Tipsy. "It's Harold...your Dad..."

Tipsy suddenly became acutely aware of his absence. "Oh Mum...has something happened to him?"

You could say that...he's left me."

"What? How could he do that?"

"Quite easily, let me tell you. Two sunsets ago, he returned after what I thought was a rather long run on the beach. I was about to ask him if he'd enjoyed his morning aerobics when he held up a paw to hush me. He had a weird furtive look. He started kicking at the earth, staring at his toes, and muttering. I had to ask him to speak properly. He apologised, and said he didn't know he was muttering. Then he just blurted out: *I came* to *tell you I'm moving in with Sally Scut...I've been seeing her lately. I have more in common with her than I believed possible. Thanks for everything. Give my regards to Tipsy...*then he turned around and headed off to make his new home with this...Sally Scut."

She sniffed. Tears rolled down her cheeks. Tipsy comforted her, his own eyes welling up. "I'm sorry Mum...that was horrible. And I'll tell Dad exactly what I think of what he's done to you..."

Mum pulled away. "No Tipsy...leave it. It's a burden I must bear. I know other does who've lost their husbands too. I spoke to them earlier...they're with the deserted hares group that meets down by the lake..."

Tipsy tried to suppress his anger. He dearly wished to run to Dad and box him for leaving Mum. How could he abandon her as if she counted for nothing? Knowing how hurt she'd be? Irksome memories of the double-dealing doe who'd shafted him after the boxing tournament pushed their way back into his mind. Now Mum had experienced the bitter pang of betrayal. Except that her situation was even more unfair because Dad had pledged in a midnight ceremonial on the High Hill of Matrimony to be her loving husband and the union had been blessed by Father Buck.

Mum changed the subject, pointing to berries she had collected with her friends from the Deserted Hares Group as part of a therapeutic exercise to get her mind off Dad's abrupt departure. Tipsy joined her in a meal and they both ate quietly, though Tipsy found himself taking his anger out on the berries, which he munched fiercely as if biting into Dad to punish him.

They sipped some rainwater from a hollow beside the nest to wash down the berries, and sat for a while contemplating the bejewelled heavens. Tipsy gazed blankly at Ostara's infinite awning, but his mind was on Mum's sad plight and Dad's betrayal. The constellations wobbled and winked through the tears that he couldn't hold back. The quarter moon had a sad lustre about it. Was the Goddess letting him know she understood Mum's heartache? A piece of the lunar orb seemed to slice off, dripping from the sky...his watery eyes warping Ostara's great light giver. He looked away from it and sniffled, and shook his head to make the tears disappear.

"Time to go" Mum whispered.

Tipsy promised to call again, but resolved not to visit Dad. The thought of seeing him with that doe who'd stolen him from Mum made him feel sick to the pit of his stomach. *We hares are timid, and we don't go around attacking other creatures, but we are more than capable of hurting each other...not physically, though we box and spar and argue and a few scratches might result... But inside...that's the hurt nobody else sees or understands, only the ones who feel it.*

He felt *some* of Mum's hurt, but he knew it was only a tiny portion of it. She must be devastated by Dad's leaving. In the days and nights following he visited more often, knowing she'd be lonely, even with her new friends. She was there to greet him and there was always joy in her eyes when he arrived at her new home near the lake. She moved there in the belief that a change of scene would help her forget the break-up.

The pain abated for her with the passage of time. He was glad of that, but she was never the same again after Dad's unfaithfulness.

***

22

"Well…Scabby? Any progress on the hare catching front?"

Scabby looked tense, Waxy thought. But then, nervousness pervaded the small musty conference room of the Hunter's bar, where Ballycrossways Coursing Club was holding a crisis meeting.

The club faced a considerable challenge, but not, Waxy hoped, an insurmountable one: a looming shortage of bait for the annual fixture.

"Cat got your tongue, Scabby? That's not like you…!"

Scabby shook his head and sighed. He raised his pint glass and drained it of stout. Wiping the froth from his lips he whimpered: "Still just thirty in the bag…fifty short."

Waxy nodded to the club gofer to get Scabby another drink from the bar; then cast him a quizzical stare. "How did this happen. By this time of year the holding pens should be brimming with hares. What's the problem?"

Scabby sat forward, elbows on the table, smoke from his cigarette billowing towards the badly cracked and nicotine stained ceiling.

"While you were away on your holidays in Spain at the bullfights, Waxy, we were running into one obstacle after another. Our netting operation has been more like a search for the bloody Golden Fleece. It's the anti-blood sports people.

"You remember that new tactic they started last year, calling to landowners and asking them not to allow hare captures on their land? Right, well, three farmers refused us permission to catch hares for the last season, as you know. We got around that. But now another fourteen landowners have shown us the door. We tried to get them to change their minds. Wouldn't budge.

"Last year, we caught barely enough hares and some of them fell sick. BallyKillMany Coursing Club sold us a few to make up the shortfall…on the quiet, as you know. The rules don't allow that, but we made an exception. No way could we let ourselves be short!"

Waxy drew a sharp intake of breath. This couldn't be happening. Not here on Broc Peninsula…the heart of coursing country.

Scabby wasn't finished. A bitter frown distorted his features. "These antis…they're getting more dangerous. In previous years I know they were a damned nuisance, writing letters to the Gazette and lashing out at us on the radio…but now they've sunk to a new low. Without the consent of landowners we can't catch hares, and if we don't catch enough we can forget about holding the fixture. If that happens, it'll be the first time it's ever been called off since the coursing club's foundation. That would be…unthinkable!"

Waxy motioned Scabby to be silent. He stood up. "No, we can't let that happen. Think! How about that club that sold us hares last year? Can we contact them again?"

Scabby shook his head sadly. "I already phoned them. They have the same problem. The antis are active in their neck of the woods too. I know…it's crazy, but we don't have the same clout with landowners that we used to have."

A hand went up. A small man with frazzled red hair and a threadbare black patch over one eye. Waxy strained to remember his name. He seldom turned up at AGMs but he'd never miss a coursing fixture. The name came to him. "Bowser Skelton…Good man Bowser. Any ideas?"

Boswer was smiling and gesturing coyly towards his empty whisky glass. Waxy snapped his fingers at the gofer again. Bowser spoke haltingly, savouring each word as if it had special value. "I think I know where we might find those extra hares…all legal and above board…if ye're willing to give it a try."

Waxy eyed him with scepticism. The others all pricked up their ears and ogled this veteran member, his eyes closed and his fresh glass of whiskey connected to his lips. He stopped in mid swallow and spluttered, hastily rubbing the spillage off the table.

Waxy shouted: "Tell us Bowser, tell us… Don't keep us in suspense man!" Bowser was a great man for the whiskey, Waxy knew, but he'd never heard of him being gifted upstairs.

Bowser stood, pushed back his chair, and fumbled inside his jacket pocket. He produced a rolled-up sheet of paper. Unfurling it he waved it above his head. Waxy could see it was a map of the Peninsula with part of the ocean visible. Bowser circled the table, pointing to a tiny dot on the map. "Gooseberry Island…that's where you'll find your hares, Waxy!"

Waxy gasped. He knew Bowser couldn't have anything of value to say. Must have been drinking since lunchtime.

Scabby didn't seem as unenthusiastic, but looked as if he didn't want to appear too impressed either. Waxy sneered "you can't be serious Bowser. You mean we'd have to get in a boat and…how far is the island from the coast?"

"Three miles…but not so bad in calm weather. It can be a bit stormy. Ships have been washed up on the island, but that was ages ago, and we could keep an eye on the forecast...set out when we get the all-clear."

"It's uninhabited, isn't it?"

Bowser answered Waxy's question. "Since the late 19th century I believe. I think it has a few old house ruins from an old village, and there was a monastic settlement there way back. Not much left of that either."

"How do you know there are hares on the island, Bowser?" Waxy wanted to know.

"I went fishing around the island five years ago. One of the men on the trawler told me he'd been on the island and that it's crawling with hares. Someone brought a few there decades ago and, naturally, they multiplied. Didn't give it much thought. I mean, we were catching enough till those damned antis starting interfering."

Waxy beamed. "You know Bowser, you might be on to something. We'll need to check a few things though. Make sure there are no protection orders that apply to wildlife on the island. You know the trouble we got into a few years back when we took hares from that bloody bog in County Mayo. No one had told us it was a nature reserve. How were we to know?"

Bowser shushed him. "I can put your mind at rest…The island has no special status. We have a free hand to go there, catch those hares, and use them at our fixture."

Scabby waved a forefinger. "Just a second…that's fine, but shouldn't we be careful. I suggest we keep any plans close to our chests until we're ready to move on this. If the antis got wind of us planning to visit the island they'd go all out to stop us."

"But they can't stop us…the law is on our side. We're entitled to capture those hares, if we decide it's worth the trouble" Waxy countered.

"It's not the law I'm worried about here", Scabby rejoined, "imagine the hullabaloo they'd raise about us…you know…crossing the ocean to…kidnap…their furry friends and all that. Think about it. They'd be there before us, with protests, and before we knew it the whole thing…you know how it works. They'd have it on Facebook, YouTube…"

Waxy nodded. "You're right Scabby. Not a word outside these four walls. Let's think a bit about this. Can we meet again tomorrow night?"

All murmured agreement. Waxy turned to the man of the moment. "Thanks a million Boswer. You may well have saved Ballycrossways Coursing Club from the shame of cancelling our fixture!"

Back home, Waxy made himself another cup of coffee, returning to the large map spread across the sitting room table in his home. It was of Gooseberry Island and the ocean surrounding it, showing key features of the land mass.

It was a hilly place, right enough. Those people who once lived there must have done a lot of climbing. Plenty of vegetation. So those hares didn't ever go hungry. Swathes of gorse and heather, trees...grass growing wild. *Yeah, they'd like that.* And nothing much to bother them, apart from a few falcons and maybe a gull dropping in now and again to scare them.

*Well, hares, you're in for a major surprise when Uncle Waxy comes to your little hideaway. Oh yes, a rude awakening awaits you! You'll serve me well and you'll run as you were born to do...from the best greyhounds in Ireland. But...hold on a minute...*Waxy's mouth dropped. He gasped. *There's no landing pier on the island...how do we get ashore?* Scanning the map closer, his eyes fastened on a little horseshoe shaped opening. *Ah, a little bay...or beach.*

He rose and rolled up the map. He'd study it again later. Yes, they'd go to the island. And, though he didn't relish the notion of a bumpy boat ride, he decided they'd travel by currach.

An engine would make too much noise. Mustn't attract attention. Those antis were watching and waiting for anything to make life difficult for coursing. Okay, there was no law against taking hares from the island, but imagine how they'd present the netting operation to the world. Scabby was right about that. *Perish the thought, but they might follow us and stage a protest...even try to sabotage the hare capture.*

Also, the man who hired out motorboats had a cousin who Waxy long suspected of being a secret anti, a treacherous fool with a grudge against Ballycrossways Coursing Club. Word could easily reach that traitor and in jig time the antis would be on to them.

No...We'll embark at dawn...silently rowing the currachs. We put ashore at the beach, lay the nets...We stay on the island overnight and return to the Peninsula again at daybreak. Must have those hares safely back and in captivity before the antis even know we've been there. Secrecy...so important now that those anti pests are gearing up for an attack on us in parliament. Mustn't give them ammunition to use against us...like film footage or pictures of us netting hares on a quiet offshore island. I can just imagine how they'd twist that...to make us look bad. Pull at the heartstrings of folk who know nothing of our great sport.

He sipped his coffee and took a hearty bite from a muffin. *Have to...what's the expression...Box clever. That's it. Have to be damned cute to outwit those spoilsports who want to ban our beloved coursing and make criminals out of us.*

***

23

Approaching the solitary apple tree in the rocky field, Tipsy was still fixated on Harriet's rejection of him, Dad's betrayal of Mum adding to his dark broodings.

The hare sitting under the tree was happily munching a lovely red-coated apple. Maybe he'd have an opinion on what happened. He found that sharing his troubles helped, if only a little. Even talking to the Storm Petrel, a bird not noted for deep insights, had proved surprisingly uplifting.

The hare was so preoccupied in his feeding that he didn't hear Tipsy's approach. His back was turned to Tipsy so he couldn't see him either. Though a hare's vision took in much of what, for another animal, was considered to be right behind it, that didn't count much when you were focused on sating your hunger or thirst.

Tipsy coughed lightly to get his attention. "Hello there, that apple looks juicy, and the tree-bark too."

The hare froze as if he'd just been caught unawares by a deadly foe. Slowly he turned his head to face Tipsy, dropping half the apple in the grass, and Tipsy saw that it wasn't a he…it was a doe!

Her tension evaporated. She greeted him. "Hello…hey, you're Tipsy, the bravest fighter in that boxing tournament…."

Tipsy, flattered by the unexpected compliment, thanked her. She hopped over to him, her eyes like two rays of warm summer sunshine, her ears two blades of the sweetest soft straw, her leg movements alluring and elegant, her reddish brown breast a picture of feminine delicacy. Before Tipsy could say anything, she had hopped gracefully to him and planted a big syrupy kiss on his forehead.

Almost struck speechless, he motioned her with a paw to move away. This was happening too fast. Awkwardness convulsed him.

"You know it didn't work out…that my sweetheart deserted me…?"

The doe threw her head and rolled her eyes. "Everyone knows. It's been the talk of the island. My sister talks about nothing else. Scraggledy is such a loser, and I can't for the life of me understand what Harriet sees in him. But then love can be very strange. My name is Bumble by the way."

"Pleased to meet you Bumble." Tipsy felt a mild sense of elation at this recognition that he'd been wronged.

"Care to dine with me?" she inquired, indicating the tree that had strips of bark hanging from its trunk and loose apples at its base.

"Love to", he enthused, hopping to her side to share in the nourishing meal.

As they chewed, he on bark and she on apples, Bumble chatted, commenting on everything…the weather, the latest gossip about who was in love with whom; the latest births and deaths, the challenge for coming-of-age leverets to find new homes that were both comfortable and relatively secure from the falcon and sudden storms.

Tipsy savoured the sweetness of her voice. Her words soothed him, regardless of what she spoke about. A question occurred to him. "Do you think what Harriet did is typical of…you know…what happens in relationships?"

Bumble frowned, looked away, and chewed in silence for a few heartbeats. "I don't know how prevalent it is, Tipsy, but I know how I felt when I had to eject my boyfriend from the nest…after I caught him cheating!"

"Oh, I'm sorry to hear that, Bumble…so you're…"

"Single? Yeah, for the past twenty-three sunsets. You wouldn't believe how he pleaded. Apologies gushed from him like rain tumbling from the heavens. He'd never do it again, he promised. I was having none of it. Out, I shouted at him, out…and don't come back. He's living near the lake I believe. Not that I care where he lives, or if he's not living!"

"That was awful. I reckon bucks are as likely to betray as females…"

She had a tear in her eye, Tipsy saw. Remembrance of the betrayal hurt. He certainly understood that.

With a paw she gently wiped away the tear. She shook her head and snorted. "He said he was off on spiritual business…that he was helping Father Buck prepare his sermons for the *Give Praise to Ostara* gatherings. That's why he arrived home so late, he claimed. I swallowed all his lies. Then one evening I went along to offer a prayer or two of my own and compliment Father Buck on his life of devotion to the Hare Goddess. I expected naturally to find my beloved there. Not a sign of him, but another buck told me where I might locate him.

"I followed his directions and hopped along to an old track that Humaniks made on the island ages ago. It led into thick undergrowth. I thought I'd come to the end of the path when I heard laughter. It came from the scrub. Then out from the tangled mass of foliage stepped…my husband, and a doe that was young enough to be his daughter. Oh, the shock I got!"

"He must have been embarrassed…to be caught like that?"

"He started blubbering and talking pure gibberish. He ran to me and said. Oh Bumble, this is not what it seems…I was helping Jillian back there. She got lost in all that gorse and I…was… showing her the way out. You see, Jillian has a bad sense of direction and…wham…I got him in the puss and knocked him into a stupor. He stayed away for five sunsets and then mooched back to the nest and started more of his *oh I'm sorry Bumble* nonsense…"

Tipsy was about to commiserate again when she held up a decisive paw. "I don't want to talk any more about it!"

Then she fluttered her eyelids and smiled. "You are the opposite of that blackguard. You'll make some doe very happy…"

Unable to restrain himself, Tipsy returned the friendly kiss she had gifted him earlier. She grabbed him with her paws. "Oh Tipsy, maybe you're the one I've been waiting for!"

She rained kisses on him and Tipsy, for the first time since winning the boxing tournament, forget completely about Harriet and the smirking Scraggledy running away with her.

***

24

Tipsy was perplexed. Life with Bumble was good. She was a loyal and loving mate, and he should have no complaints. But still it bothered him that tradition was imposing strictures on his otherwise carefree existence.

Well, one tradition. Other hares were happily married, but he, though blissfully paired with a devoted partner, was denied the right to wed.

He'd had it out with Father Buck. Why, he pleaded, couldn't he and Bumble marry? They loved each other, and to all intents and purposes were connubial as Buck and Doe and living in the one nest. But the stubborn spiritual guardian was adamant: Tipsy had not won Bumble in a boxing showdown. To be married in the eyes of the clerical authority, which consisted of Father Buck and five lesser servants of Ostara, he would need to have secured Bumble's paw in marriage via the traditional fights.

Without that seal of approval he and Bumble could call themselves anything they wished…they might be the best couple…the happiest pair, on the island, but they could not be recognised as Buck and Wife.

Most hares accepted couples who found themselves in that position, but some, Tipsy learned, frowned upon what they deemed illicit relationships and looked down their noses at any buck or doe that settled upon such an arrangement. Father Buck stressed that there could be no exceptions.

Tipsy's superior speed, his awareness of the "Other World" from which all hares come to be born and to which they will return, his ability to communicate with other species…these were commendable gifts from Ostara, the cleric conceded, but the same Goddess would take a dim view of hares "living in sin", as he put it.

Tipsy asked Father Buck if there was any higher authority to which he could appeal. Grumpily, the priest alluded to His Eminence in the cave, but quickly added that the Golden Hare, the Supreme Spiritual Leader of the Island Hares, seldom agreed to see anyone. Only on rare and extra special occasions would he even *consider* granting an audience.

Tipsy had heard vaguely of the Golden Hare, but assumed he was just an eccentric buck that lived alone after turning his back on the world. Others had spoken of him with reverence, but he knew nobody who had ever seen him. He resolved to appeal to the Golden Hare, as a last resort.

Not that Bumble would love him any less if they remained technically unmarried. But he knew she secretly longed for that official recognition of their bond. Being unmarried could also have implications for their offspring.

He shuddered at the thought of their first leverets asking why Mum and Dad weren't married like all the other adult hares? How could he explain to them? And he feared other leverets might give them a bad time as they struggled with the challenges of childhood…those first tentative steps into a world that could be hostile to hares.

Well, this Golden Hare might be reclusive and not given to meeting ordinary hares, but he'll listen to me…If I can run faster than other hares I can make my pitch to the Supreme Leader. The worst he can do is say no.

***

25

Tipsy knew that Bumble also wanted official recognition for their partnership. At first she scoffed at the idea of making a fuss about it. She knew other hares who'd formed perfectly happy couplings without having that formal approval or the blessing of Father Buck. Love trumped tradition any day, she soothed.

But in recent evenings she'd broached the subject…casually and without any urgency in the beginning but then, increasingly, there was a more sombre tone. And in her eyes he detected an unease that wasn't there before.

Tipsy had put off calling to the Golden Hare many times. Now, despite his determination to appeal to the Great One, he was putting off the visit again. One more sunset won't make any difference, he reckoned.

Today, he and Bumble had opted to tour the island, or most of it anyway, together. Best do it before any leverets arrived, because then the young ones would command all of Bumble's attention. They ran and walked alternately, covering distance quickly where there wasn't much to see, and slowing down to enjoy the high spots.

Intermittent light showers throughout the morning sent them good humouredly dashing for cover in brushwood, under trees, and beneath the protective canopy of Humanik ruins where overhead branches and crumbling stonework sheltered them, though not completely. Rainwater filtered through in droplets, splashing and making little puddles in a corner.

They helped themselves to sprigs of moss that sprouted from cracks in the earth. It was a strange expanse of rock-hard ground that the Humaniks must have created inside this former home of theirs. How different from hares, Tipsy reflected, who preferred a soft comfortable nest to relax in.

Bumble lapped at the puddle to quench her thirst. She hopped over to Tipsy who was about to eat more moss but he turned away from it when he heard Bumble cough lightly.

He knew she had something on her mind from the way her eyes fixed on him.

"Do you think we've a chance, dearest…with that appeal to the Golden Hare? My sister Rosebud says she's never heard of anyone appealing…they either get married properly or live together without Father Buck's blessing…"

"Oh, well, I'll have plenty to say in the cave. I'll tell that wise hare about you and me and I'm sure our story will touch his heart…"

Bumble kissed him. "That's what I like to hear. Oh you're the best, Tipsy!"

She hopped out of the ruin and exclaimed: "The rain has stopped. How about a run to the beach?"

She had boundless energy. Tipsy never ceased to admire how she ran. Though he could outrun any hare she had such graceful movements. Another reason he'd fallen for her. She was also in love with the island itself. She halted at intervals to catch the scent of a primrose, an exotic wildflower, or a clump of dark green heather, luxuriating in its refreshing aroma, before resuming her dash.

She seemed intent on reaching the beach by the longer route. The shortcut would take you there in scarcely forty heartbeats. Instead she was racing towards the cliff. He followed, the appearance of the sun in its fair splendor after the rain slightly impairing his vision. Not much though. He could close his eyes three quarters of the way and still not miss anything in his wide field of vision.

Bumble ran along the cliff edge, zigzagging to and away from the precipice. Tipsy wished she didn't do that. She seemed to be daring the perilous drop in that fun-seeking style of hers. She glanced back after every twenty heartbeats or so, as if to goad him into even wilder gymnastic flourishes. He accelerated his pace, whooshing close to her and hearing her laugh.

"You have to catch me Tipsy" she called, "and then maybe Father Buck will have to give us his…"

She stopped in mid sentence. The soil gave way under her feet and…*oh no*… She lurched to the left…there was no ground beneath her. Just air.

"Bumble!" He called her name twice.

Her head swiveled. "Tipsy…I'm…I'm falling…!

Tipsy ran faster than his feet had ever carried him. *Too late.*

He stood on the spot where Bumble had slipped, looking down the white face of the cliff. Bumble was hurtling away from him, her wonderful alluring form diminishing in size as she dropped, bouncing off the cliff as she tumbled; her legs flaying nothingness. "Bumble!" he cried, his lungs bursting with a long, painful shriek that issued from the depths of his being.

Her descent was over. He strained to see the tiny remnant of the doe he loved and cherished more than himself. His head pounded. He contemplated the unthinkable, just as he had when Harriet betrayed him. Except that this was worse. Harriet had shafted him and run off with another buck. Bumble was dead. Gone from him.

Then something flashed inside his head. A snippet of knowledge from somewhere in the deep recesses of his consciousness: A hare's spirit stayed around the site of its demise for a short while after death. *If I can get to the beach…*

Instantly he dashed along the cliff edge and reached the beach quicker than usual. He was running so fast he felt himself almost hovering above ground, borne on the strong sea breeze that wafted him on. Sand erupted all him, some of it blighting his vision, as he loped and surged towards the love of his life.

Breathless from the effort, he stood by the saddest sight to assail his eyes since birth: Bumble's body was perfectly still, its reddish brown fur half covered with sand that was blowing around her. A little trickle of blood ran from her nose, mingling with a swatch of half dried sea weed. She looked so peaceful, as if she were just sleeping.

Tipsy muttered a prayer his mum had taught him, an offering to Ostara for the dead. But then he turned his mind to the real Bumble, not the unmoving clump of fur lying in the sand. Closing his eyes tightly, he cried out with all his might: "Bumble, I love you forever!"

His heart beat so loudly he thought his head would burst open. Then, the darkness faded, though his eyes were still shut. Bumble was standing there…surrounded by ethereal forms of faintly visible hares. *I'm okay Tipsy* she said, her voice sweeter and softer than ever. *I'm safe. I'm sorry for being so reckless. I'll see you again someday…It's so beautiful over here Tipsy. I have to go now…*

A bright light enveloped Bumble like a glistening water bubble and her spirit disappeared. The light was dazzling.

Tipsy's eyes flickered open. Though the sun was shining and the waves cascading mightily and barely a cloud was scuttling overhead, the day seemed almost as night compared to the light that accompanied Bumble's departure.

His heart was broken, but a feeling of comfort and relief assuaged his desolation, his crushing sense of loss. A hare's life was short; he'd been told when he was no more than a tiny leveret. This life is full of woes, offset by compensating moments of bliss.

Meeting Bumble was one of those highpoints. Her death was one of those inevitable kicks in the teeth that life held in store for every hare. More for him than for Bumble. She, after all, was now free from suffering. It was he who had to continue his sojourn in the World of Hard Knocks.

He looked again at the remnant. He'd get a few hares to help him convey Bumble's earthly shell into the sea in the time honoured burial tradition for hares that expire on the beach. It's just a body, he reminded himself as he turned away, grieving, to return to his empty nest.

Bumble would wait for him, he was certain, and one day they'd be reunited in a world beyond grief.

***

26

The cries of the dying, tortured hares still ringing in her ears, Annemarie pressed the switch on her PC.

The screen came to life and, her hands trembling, she keyed in the search words "greyhound", "hare", "sport", "live bait". A website in the search list caught her eye…the campaign to abolish blood sports, an organization opposed to cruel hare baiting, among other activities.

The main form of cruelty to hares in Ireland was hare coursing, in which pairs of greyhounds were set upon hares in a large wired-off field. There were more than seventy coursing clubs in the country, mainly the southern-most counties…and yes; one of them was based virtually on her own doorstep.

She paused. She'd heard of Ballycrossways Coursing Club but for some reason had never paid any attention to what it actually did. She'd heard people talk about "the coursing at the weekend" or referring to a particular dog that won a prize, but none of the chatter registered. It was just some boring game that didn't interest her. She had a vague notion of greyhounds being involved, but hadn't thought of live hares being used.

Scrolling down the article her eye snagged the heading "blooding…how coursing folk train their dogs."

Hares have their back legs tied and are forced to run from dogs. Or they are dangled on pieces of string or rope by trainers for the dogs to attack. Where hares aren't available, cats, rabbits or birds are used. The aim is to prolong the process so that the dog is whipped up into a frenzy of bloodlust. Blooding is believed to enhance a greyhound's performance on the coursing field.

At official coursing events the greyhounds are muzzled, though this does not prevent them from inflicting horrific injuries as the dogs maul or forcibly strike the hares. In blooding, the "gloves" are taken off completely and members of the public are not invited to watch. It is a highly secretive activity, technically illegal, but widely practiced within the greyhound industry and an integral part of hare coursing…"

She wondered if any hares were left behind by those…*creeps.* She'd return to the field she saw them in and have a look.

At the end of the article on the website there was a form for anyone wishing to join the campaign against hare coursing. Without hesitation she typed in her name and address and clicked "join."

Human beings…why are we capable of such things? If it's not stabbing each other in the back and cheating in love we're torturing animals… A bundle of fur alighted on her lap, blocking her view of the computer screen. It was Ginger, purring indubitably and making his presence felt.

Looking into his quizzical green eyes she shuddered at the thought that he would ever be taken by those fiends and used as bait. She'd die rather than let that happen.

Stroking Ginger, a feeling of deepest revulsion welled up within her against those people she'd watched through a hole in the wall. Kind of symbolic, she thought, that unfolding of a real life horror show at the other side of a stony divide. It was as if she'd observed an event outside of time, in another dimension.

Yet that stretch of ground existed in her own world, and the people who tortured those helpless creatures to death were flesh and blood human beings like her; not some alien species.

27

Tipsy enjoyed his early morning run among the ruins of the Humanik houses. He never ceased to marvel at how elaborate and painstakingly constructed those old places were. Humaniks needed so many stones to build their homes, and must have taken ages to position them so niftily; piled high and jammed together… *Not like our simple nest in the grass.* He paused to savour that appetising moss that grew between the stones. *Wonder if Humaniks used to eat that? Yum…Didn't know what they were missing if they didn't.*

Tired of running he settled with his back to a pile of loose stones. His eyes wandered skyward. Not a cloud yet. The sun was a fiery ball, its molten gold shimmering. It had set the island aglow, revitalising everything. A light breeze ruffled the bright green blades of grass that tickled Tipsy's haunches, and a butterfly fluttered past, its red and green wings beguiling him with its magical dancing in the air.

Birds flew high above, happily making little patterns as they moved gracefully in and out of the sun beams. Tipsy wondered if any bird had ever flown so high he got burned by that saffron yellow light that Ostara positioned over the world. Hardly, the Goddess would surely have taken measures to avoid that. She could do anything, though banishing tragedy and unfaithfulness from the world weren't among her accomplishments. *But then we're here to cope with all that nastiness and sorrow, and learn from it.*

Strange, he thought, how Harriet's betrayal and Bumble's death seemed to cancel each other out, and Mum's loss of Dad overshadowed both tumultuous events in his life. He must not be held back in his own life by anything, no matter how seemingly overwhelming. He recalled something Mum had told him when he was only a baby: that every challenge met and overcome in life would make him stronger…if it didn't kill him. Perhaps that was Ostara's roundabout way of helping the hares of the world fulfill themselves. He blinked. *Enough deep thinking for today.*

The butterfly was back, silently brushing against his right ear, muttering to itself about a flower it had just vacated as a resting place. Tipsy was about to say good day to it when something distracted him.

A strange humming.

He glanced behind him. The butterfly had alighted on a stone and seemed to be exploring a hidden feature of it. Puzzling. He'd seen many butterflies and had never heard them hum, or make any noise for that matter.

Then he froze. The humming had changed to a buzzing. And it wasn't coming from the butterfly. He cocked an ear to the stone to make sure. Definitely not from the tiny winged creature, who now gazed at Tipsy and quipped: "What are you looking at?"

"Thought I heard something…it wasn't you though."

The startled butterfly stared blankly at Tipsy. "The hare who can talk to butterflies, I've heard about you. What's up? You look bewildered."

Tipsy raised a paw. "Hush. What's that sound? Do you hear it?"

The butterfly shrugged. "I do. Could be a bumblebee…no, it's a bit louder...I don't like it. I'm off!" It spiraled away at twice its normal speed.

Without stirring from his position Tipsy looked all around. No sign of anything unusual: Just the swaying grass and those heaps of stones. But the buzz was getting louder. *Are my ears playing tricks on me?*

Then it struck him. The noise was coming from above him. He glanced upwards. "Ostara help me!" he lisped. Directly over him, about the distance of twenty hares standing back to back…was a weird spectacle: a shiny black circular creature, with four legs outstretched and two extra longer ones protruding from under it.

It was just balanced there, oscillating slightly from side to side but otherwise stationary. It was framed by the fiery disc of the sun. Had it come from the great light-giver? Had Ostara sent it?

Tipsy shivered. Fear convulsed his whole body. But he dared not budge. Was it some kind of hostile bird…one hungrier, faster, and more dangerous than the falcon? Was it sizing him up, deciding whether to swoop and take him off to its nest to eat later?

Do I run…or sit still and wait for it to move on…if it hasn't already decided to attack?

The thing was getting bigger…or drawing closer. *Not sure which. If I stay it'll catch me easily…if I run… Ostara help me but it's about to pounce…I'm sure of it.*

Tipsy bounded from his spot and ran towards a sheltered Humanik ruin, one he knew had a roof of tree branches that kept out even the small birds. If he could just squeeze in through the brambles that blocked its doorway, he'd be safe. He'd covered half the distance when he heard the buzz grow louder, change to a hum, and then back to a buzz. He felt something swishing over him.

A nervous glance to one side and overhead revealed the black creature pursuing him…at a steady relaxed rate but easily staying close to him. As the fastest hare on the island how could anything keep pace with him like that?

Tipsy darted to the entrance and collided with the tangle of branches and leaves. With every ounce of strength he could muster, he squeezed through the foliage and dropped onto the soft clay inside the Humanik abode.

Relief. His heartbeat slowed. He thanked Ostara. Turning around, he tried to see if the thing was still watching him. It was impossible to see anything through the foliage and the sky was blocked off by the branchy ceiling. He strained to hear. The buzzing had stopped. It was humming again, but the sound was fading fast. *There.* He cocked his ears. *Gone.*

But would it return? He'd wait. Usually, with the falcon at least, if you waited long enough in hiding the bird would move off and try its luck elsewhere.

***

28

Waxy waited for the chatter to abate before commencing his introduction. The club members fell quiet, their attention fixed on their special guest speaker.

"Gentlemen, you are all familiar with the wonderful Doctor Patsy Callaghan, an honorary member of Ballycrossways Coursing Club who has in the past donated generously to hare catching and dog training events. He has also, as you all know, conducted a survey of the hare population that just happened to favour the pro coursing side over the anti coursing one. Thanks ever so much Doctor. Over the past week, Dr Callaghan has operated a drone to take a close look at Gooseberry Island. The result of this undertaking will help us no end in our quest to harvest hares from there. He's done a stellar job. Dr. Callaghan?"

The small bearded bald man stood and took a bow, to a standing ovation. Waxy's heart pulsed with pride. This man would lend a new respectability to the club's endeavours. Here was a man of science who appreciated the value of hare coursing.

The lights were dimmed and the large computer screen sputtered to life. A breathtaking bird's eye view of the island appeared. Mighty waves crashed around the landmass as the drone zoomed towards it.

Dr Callaghan spoke. "Now, as you see, the island is prone to harsh and occasionally violent Atlantic storms. That's something you'll have to watch, especially if you intend to go there in currachs, which I personally wouldn't recommend but I appreciate the value of tradition and the old ways..."

Waxy blushed. He was adamant that currachs would be used, even if this meant rowing in foul weather.

"Now, you see, the island is inaccessible to boats except at this stretch of beach..."

He pointed at the horseshoe shaped inlet that Waxy already knew about, the only one on the island. The film showed high chalk-white cliffs and the ocean pounding their sides.

Then the scene changed to extensive swathes of purple heather and other brightly hued vegetation, this in turn giving way to a scattering of fields bordered by crude walls of loose stones. The drone swept on to reveal clusters of buildings, or rather, Waxy corrected himself, ruins of buildings.

"The old village..." the doctor remarked, as the drone hovered over...*yes...a hare running. Must have seen the drone.*

Then a second, third and forth hare appeared, seemingly from nowhere. They scurried for cover, their heads sporadically swivelling skyward at what to them must be a mysterious object. The drone continued on its flight path, revealing more hares.

Waxy beamed. Though he couldn't see the faces of the others in the darkened hall, he knew they were thinking the same: the place was crawling with the wily runners. *They'll soon be running for us, from the best greyhounds in Ireland.*

More stone buildings showed up. The doctor explained: "Monastic ruins...dating to when the island played host to holy men who prayed that Ireland would always be a saintly and devout nation...but I won't bore you lads. I know that it's hares you're after, not, ah...spiritual solace..."

The lads tittered and murmured assent. Further patches of green interspersed with stone walls appeared and then a lake, around which dozens of Storm Petrels fluttered. These took flight as the drone flew overhead.

More fields, a few trees spread thinly across the island, and then...another hare, this one sitting calmly at the entrance to what looked like a cave. The camera zoomed on this creature, and Waxy gasped.

He heard the other palpable intakes of breath around him. It wasn't just that the hare didn't run when the drone approached. He calmly looked up at it, and it was then that Waxy and his colleagues saw this strange...*aberration*:

Its eyes were electric blue...not brown as a hare's should be. And its coat was a glowing golden hue.

Also the tips of its ears were not black as they ought to be. Was this some trick achieved by computer enhancement or digital editing?

Waxy rose to his feet. "Dr Callaghan? Can you explain? How can this be?"

Others were interrupting, also querying the anomaly. The doctor waved his question side. "It's a genetic mutation, found nowhere else in Ireland, or in the world. But let's not get carried away. You may be aware of a legend, just an old wives' tale really...concerning this hare. It's reputed to have special powers, and anyone who approaches it with hostile intent...or displeases it in any way, will come to grief shortly afterwards.

"Don't worry lads, it's only poppycock...a silly story told at bedtime to scare children in the old days. Anyway, when you go to the island you'll not be including this particular hare in your catch. It wouldn't help your cause if opponents of your...magnificent...sport could say you took the Golden Hare from the island and had him running from greyhounds. And if the creature were to be killed or injured...that would be to your considerable disadvantage...I mean from a public relations point of view of course..."

Waxy remembered. He had heard the fairy stories about a magical hare on the island but didn't realise there really was this...*mutant*...with its strange colouring. Dr Callaghan had frozen the image of the Golden Hare staring defiantly up at the drone. *It has no fear. Astonishing. Hares are afraid of their own shadows. But seemingly not this...genetic mutant.*

A guffaw from the back of the hall. "Be jeepers we'll see if old Blue Eyes is so brave when he's running from Scruffy's Patch...the fastest dog in County Kerry!"

Another shouted "We'll put manners on that cheeky puss. Who does he think he is?"

"Leave him alone I say" a tremulous voice intoned close to Waxy. "I've heard about that latchico. There's a curse on anyone that as much as looks the wrong way at him. He's a jinx. I'd stay well out of his way."

Waxy raised his voice an octave: "Let me remind ye lads that this is the twenty-first century, and we shouldn't be swayed by fairy stories...especially not ones about hares that can harm humans. There isn't a hare on this earth that wouldn't run like crazy from a dog or a human...and he's no exception..."

Waxy walked up to the computer screen and tapped his finger on the image of the Golden Hare, its fierce blue eyes gazing hypnotically and fearlessly at the drone.

"This fellow can do nothing to us. But I agree with Dr Callaghan. The last thing we need is bad publicity. The antis would go into overdrive if we captured or coursed this jumped-up bundle of fur. So he's strictly off-limits when we get to the island."

29

Playing safe, Tipsy waited until nightfall before emerging from his hiding place. A flurry of movement stopped him in his tracks as he approached his latest home at the foot of a small hill: hares had gathered in clusters near his nest. He heard their lively chatter in the moonlight. Silvery rays bathed them; wisps of frosty breath forming little clouds over them as they conversed in worried tones. Seeing Tipsy approach, someone shouted "Did you see it?"

A second hare loped up to him, mild panic in his eyes. Before Tipsy could relate his own sighting the other hare was babbling like a giddy leveret: "It was a giant wasp. I was lucky to escape. It chased us…I ran from one end of the island to the other. I was too clever for it, but boy was it moving fast!"

"It was no wasp", another hare countered. "Definitely a bird…wasps are never that big!"

Hares were speaking all at the same time, making it difficult to hear properly. A hare close to Tipsy rolled his eyes, indicating the others. "That's all nonsense Tipsy. I reckon it's one of those shiny Humanik things that fly higher than birds…they leave white trails across the sky…"

Another hare scoffed. "No, they never fly that low, not like this thing!"

An older hare looked doubtful "I've never seen a bird like that and no wasp or bee could be that big…"

A real bird startled them all as it landed on a nearby rock. Tipsy recognised him in the moonlight. It was Craggy, the Storm Petrel. "Hey, Craggy, did you see that weird creature this morning?"

Hares cried in unison: "Tell us his answer Tipsy…what did he see?"

Craggy looked unfazed, and, as usual, seemed happy to have his opinion sought. He waited until the curious hares had formed a circle around him, and then directly addressed Tipsy, the only hare who understand him.

"It wasn't a bird, Tipps. It's a Humanik contraption. They make all sorts of gadgets to perform tasks for them. Like the rod that flashes and kills. And the monstrous noisy things that make grass disappear on the Big Island. That flying creature as you call it…It's not a creature at all! I was flying over the Big Island last week and I saw three of those accursed gadgets…a wise bird told me the Humaniks direct them to fly above an area if there's something they want to have a look at."

Tipsy translated for them. An older hare guffawed. "You mean the Humaniks were taking a look at…us? Maybe they just wanted to see the island?"

Craggy shrugged. "The gadget didn't spend much time watching us Petrels. Barely flew past. Hovered for a few heartbeats… then kept going. But from what I've been hearing it had a big interest in you guys."

Tipsy paused for a moment, thinking it might be better not to translate this, but felt impelled to continue. They were entitled to know the truth.

"Yes" a nervous hare grunted. "I and my five brothers and two sisters were followed by it. When we tried to hide it hovered over us, buzzing and humming, humming and buzzing…we were petrified. I feared it might dive and sting us to death, or that a mouth of some kind would open and devour us. Harmless it turned out to be. Nothing to worry about."

Tipsy had heard enough. The gadget, as Craggy called it, didn't harm any of them, but it was certainly spying on hares for some reason, and this unnerved. A strange unease arose deep inside him. Evil was afoot. It could be just a silly notion, but all too often his gut instinct had proven right.

Basking in a lustrous moonbeam he looked towards the faraway cliff and listened to the faint sounds of the waves washing ashore: A familiar echo that soothed him. But something niggled. He couldn't shake off the feeling that the island hares faced a terrifying threat… from some malevolent force or entity. What could it be?

Somehow, he felt, this shadow of foreboding had been cast from across the ocean.

***

30

The journey to the island was long enough without this, Waxy moaned. But not audibly. He'd warned the others they must be strong. The crescent moon provided the only light, its silver rays faintly illuminating the raging surf and the yellow oilskins of the rowers. Swirling black clouds hung over the five vessels that Ballycrossways coursing club had acquired for its hare-catching mission.

The howling wind almost ripped its way into Waxy's body, despite the heavy raingear and the hood secured firmly around his head. The salty water had encrusted his eyebrows. It lashed his face and his fingers felt like icicles as he pulled the oars with all his might.

It was worse earlier, when the storm was at its height. Mountainous waves had almost consigned his boat to perdition, raising it effortlessly, spinning it sideways, and then dropping it back with a casual contempt onto the raging ocean. His boat, and the others, had risen and fallen like roller-coasters, their oars redundant as the currachs seemed possessed by forces beyond human control. His bones had jarred and rattled with each impact.

They should have paid closer attention to the sea area forecast as Dr Callaghan had warned them. Waxy had expected this to be hard work, but he hadn't banked on the phenomenal effort required of him.

The other four men in the currach were groaning and cursing, the oars moving nonstop. The island was still at least a mile off. "Are you sure about this Waxy…I mean…not questioning your judgment, but…"

"Shut your mouth and keep rowing or by God I'll toss you overboard. No slacking. I'll personally see to it that you are expelled from the club if I hear another word from you!"

The reprimand hurt Waxy. Not emotionally, but physically. When he opened his mouth he realized his lips were cracked and sore, and he spat briny water as he spoke.

Tommy Spiddle O' Toole went quiet and stopped even the muffled swearing. Waxy grunted. He strained to see if the dissenter, who was one place ahead of the man directly in front of him, was showing any further signs of impudence. He had to be firm. Any show of weakness and that fool would infect the others with his defeatism.

"Not much longer now", Scabby shouted, a forced note of cheeriness in his voice. A murmur of approval ran through the currach, even as a wave lashed them all and Waxy took his right hand from the oar for an instant as something struck his face. A tiny fish. It dropped wriggling into the boat. He threw it out.

He stopped thinking, focusing completely on the repetitive, monotonous but essential routine. His arms stung and every muscle in his body ached, crying out for sympathy.

Waxy gritted his teeth. *Just keep rowing…* Glancing to his left and then to his right he saw that the other boats were proceeding doggedly, the lads not giving an inch to the hostile elements. The boats were holding up well, but then they were built to resist and withstand the forces of nature. Waxy shuddered at the thought of what might have happened had they used less formidable vessels. A lovingly wrought latticework of ribs, laths and tarred canvas made each currach a robust and seaworthy craft.

The sky was brightening. Dawn couldn't be far away. Above the surge of the sea, Waxy heard the cries of gulls and then saw them… wheeling haphazardly and being tossed about by the wind like hares on a coursing field. The clouds were losing some of their gaunt muckiness, little shafts of light appearing at their edges. *Good.*

The storm too had abated, and while the winds still whistled and roared and the boat rattled Waxy felt a calmness approaching. Stars were reappearing, twinkling momentarily only to switch off again within seconds, as if unsure of themselves or their purpose. Swathes of purple diluted and slowly washed away the darkness, the sky in turn yielding to shades of deep blue and fluffy whitish grey clouds.

The emergence of sunlight raised Waxy's heart. Just being able to see made the rowing easier. Men in the boats on either side waved to him. He returned their salutations. After what seemed days, but could only have been a couple of hours, Waxy heard a voice from one of the other boats. "The island…up ahead!"

Waxy had not been looking in front of him for several minutes, so intent was he on the rowing. The outline was familiar to him from the maps and the drone footage: The high, chalk-white cliffs and hilly terrain were shrouded in a half-light, and a grayish mist gave them a filmy appearance.

He removed a hand from an oar to reach inside his oilskin for the binoculars. His hand, the numbness thankfully gone from it, shivered slightly as he focused on the horseshoe beach. "Almost there, lads…just a little to the left."

He was keenly aware that the small beach was their only way on to the island. It was sheer rock-wall otherwise, all the way around. And this would be no climbing expedition.

No wonder its human inhabitants had long since deserted it. I just hope those damned hares are worth this trouble. By God but they'll run well for us or pay one hell of a price. If those pussies had the slightest notion of the lengths we go for coursing they'd bow before us.

***

31

Tipsy lay down on the beach. He felt tired. He'd deliberately run himself into near exhaustion. It helped overcome his recent bouts of insomnia. He'd known that dawn was approaching as he traced a familiar safe route across the island. Though his eyesight was sharp, he took care to avoid cliff-edges at night, except when a full moon cast its loving glow on the landscape.

Darkness was fading fast. Scudding rain clouds became visible. Flickers of orange and red signalled the beginnings of a new day.

He yawned, idly contemplating the waves washing ashore. The heavy rain and stormy winds that sent him scurrying for cover earlier had thankfully given way to a calm, unruffled daybreak.

Time passed lazily. The sun grew in prominence. Its weak rays lacked the warmth of late mornings and afternoons. But it still cast a benevolent soothing spell over the island.

Thoughts of his beloved Bumble had intruded now and again in recent days, but he thanked Ostara that the pain of loss decreased with every heartbeat. Not, he kept telling himself, because he was losing interest. No, his love for her remained constant, even to the extent that he vowed never to form another relationship. What kept him strong was the certainty that he'd meet her again in the afterlife.

He nibbled on a piece of seaweed, pulling purple strings of it from a soggy heap, his paws pressed down on the succulent mound in the sand as he sunk his teeth into it. Having eaten his fill, he belched and sat up, shaking off grains of sand that had blown into his fur. He'd head back to his nest and, hopefully, get some sleep, now that tiredness had finally taken hold of him.

He was about to turn towards the pathway up from the beach when something caught his eye...out there on the ocean. He strained to see in the dawn-light. Tiny dots bobbing on the surface. *What on earth...*

He focused, with some difficulty as his eyes wanted to close. With each heartbeat the dots grew larger.

To get a better view he climbed up the sloping beach to the beginning of the pathway that led from the cliff down to the strand. Now he saw them as wooden structures of some kind: Large hunks of wood getting closer, floating and surging forward unremittingly...towards the beach.

Tipsy's tiredness whittled away, replaced by alertness and a rapidly growing unease. There were creatures in those wooden containers: Pale forms with patches of different colours on their heads. They had eyes and mouths and noses, but not like any he'd seen.

Humaniks!

The description matched the stories he'd heard from old hares and the tales mum told him as a leveret. Mum had cautioned about these creatures. Like the falcon and other large swooping birds they posed a mortal threat to hares. But they rarely showed up on the island. Just the odd few of them came to walk about.

He recalled Craggy the Storm Petrel's warning that Humaniks used long sticks that spat fire and death. But Humanik visits were as rare, Mum said, as snow in summertime. And that was so rare that no hare worried too much about them. But here they were...and getting closer.

Tipsy felt sleepy again. He'd covered half the island on his run, he reckoned, so was entitled to doze off for a while. *Not too long.* He yawned. A pleasant and dreamy feeling washed over him. He drifted and swayed.

A sudden jolt awoke him. He looked around. What am I doing on the beach? *Oh yes, eating seaweed. How appetising. Better than leaves I think, whatever the others say. Well, they've all got their own tastes. Some prefer brambles and grass, others crave tree bark. But this is much nicer. My taste buds must be different.*

He shook himself fully awake. He froze.

He was rooted to the spot, startled by the sudden appearance of the Humaniks. He'd forgotten about them and those wooden containers they'd been squatting in, the restless ocean bearing them to the island.

Tipsy withdrew himself from the exposed position he'd been sitting in, retreating further up along the pathway.

Now they were on the beach, some of them pulling the wooden contrivances further through the sand, the wind fluttering those stringy patches that covered their heads and seemed to grow from them.

A Humanik made angry noises as sand peppered his face. He rubbed his eyes furiously. Others carried those strange giant cobwebs his mother had told him about: Humaniks used them in the past to catch fish from the sea around the island.

Nothing for a hare to worry about, she said, unless you got entangled in it. Some of these silly things had been abandoned by Humaniks on the island and it was annoying to find yourself in a knot if you stumbled into one.

They weren't real cobwebs of course, as no spider Mum had ever seen was powerful enough to spin one that large. Usually a spider's web was tiny, and only flies got trapped in them. Humaniks must be able to spin those huge cobwebs to catch fish.

***

32

Alighting from the currach, Waxy's body ached and his feet sank into a soft moist carpet of sand. He extracted himself and took a few steps. His boots felt heavier than usual on this yielding surface. The rest of the netting team moaned and grumbled as they heaved themselves out of their boats.

The sky was brighter than he expected it would be at this point. The sun had risen, throwing a mantle of light over this neglected piece of Ireland's national territory. They'd taken longer than planned to reach the island, but they still had more than adequate time to complete their hare-catching operation.

The beach was drier further in. It was a pleasant stretch, apart from unsightly driftwood, twisted fragments of rusted corrugated iron, and those hideous clumps of seaweed that Waxy had hated since childhood. He disliked even more the notion of eating the stuff, as health food loons advocated.

A bewildering array of shells dotted the strand. He imagined it would make an ideal holiday destination if it didn't happen to be positioned on this forsaken offshore island. He stretched himself and spat salt water from his mouth, before pulling off the oilskin coat and hood. He felt warm, whether from the long exertion or unseasonal weather he wasn't sure. Gone was the wind that had lashed him for almost the entire crossing.

The others likewise removed their raingear. One was examining a starfish as if it were a rare jewel. Another had a shell to his ear, and a silly smirk. Daylight was quickly asserting itself as Waxy turned and helped the others pull the currachs further in from the tide-line.

Satisfied that all the boats were safe from the hungry ocean, he reached for the map. Parts of it were soggy and he cursed his neglect in not wrapping it in plastic. Pointing to his left, he directed the hare-catchers to a mossy path that, according to the map, led up to the ruins of a village located near a monastic site.

From there, they would have easy access to areas of dense vegetation where hares usually set up home. The map indicated clearly the locations of all the suitable target sites, so Waxy knew he could save time by avoiding stony moorland, caves, various inhospitable parts of the island, and the bird colonies.

The ruins of houses he wouldn't overlook: Those could be overgrown with weeds and other growth that hares might take a liking to. The twenty-five men gathered around him, some with rolled-up nets under their arms or slung over their shoulders, others holding hare-boxes, and all, including Waxy, wielding long sticks. These would be needed to beat the ground once the nets were laid…propelling those pussies into the care of Ballycrossways Coursing Club.

With the map in one hand and using the stick as a walking aid, Waxy led the way up the path. It was a steep climb, like ascending a stairs or ladder made of moss and grass, with hard rocky earth underneath. The effort had Waxy panting and wheezing. His eyes recoiled from the sight of his belly flapping and quivering, threatening to break through his shirt and pullover as he forced one foot in front of another. He groaned with the effort.

"Okay Boss?" Scabby sounded concerned.

"Fine, keep moving, lads" he gasped.

His arms ached from the rowing. Every bone in his body protested. And now this…After what seemed like ages, Waxy stepped onto a rocky surface. Loose stones and pebbles covered a wide area that contained the shattered remnants of nineteenth century hovels. In the distance a crumbling round tower loomed.

Waxy sat on a large rock. The others all seated themselves, the older men winded like Waxy and wiping the sweat from their brows. "Before we go any further, let's have a bite to eat."

His suggestion elicited broad grins and hearty gasps of gratitude. Lunch boxes flicked open and the first humans to alight on the island in decades devoured ham-sandwiches and cold sausage.

Bits of tangled discarded tinfoil rattled in a soft breeze amid the stones and chubby tufts of grass, the only sound apart from the munching of teeth into thick slices of brown bread and the slurping of tea from flasks. An abrupt cacophony of shrieking above him distracted Waxy as he started into his third sandwich. Gulls were circling warily; their beady eyes fixated on the hare-catchers.

Their hunger and thirst sated, Waxy roused the men and re-issued his instructions. They'd endeavour to complete the operation within a few hours. Take as many hares as they could trap… then wait. A weather forecast indicated the sea would be calm later. They'd return home at dawn, reaching the Peninsula before any nosey folk were up and about.

Under no circumstances was this visit to the island to become public knowledge.

***

33

The Humaniks panted and wheezed, and muttered angry noises from their mouths as they ascended the grassy slope from the beach. Tipsy shuffled back a bit to avoid being seen, but ventured to peep down at them.

Carrying those vast cobwebs must be slowing them. How could they expect to catch fish up here? They must know that fish can be found only offshore in the water.

The lake. Maybe they think there's fish in the lake. They'll be disappointed. Craggy told me the Storm Petrels and the gulls don't bother with the lake any more. No fish worth talking about in it, he says.

Tipsy waited until he saw their feet, shielded from the weather like the rest of their upright two legged bodies by coverings that hid their flesh. Their soft footfalls in the sand belied their menacing presence and dubious intent, Tipsy felt. He didn't trust them an inch.

He cursed his curiosity. He blinked and squinted as a Humanik foot kicked sand into his eyes.

As he shook away the grains a loud roar almost split his skull. They'd spotted him. He saw them clearly, standing and staring at him. For a moment he froze, petrified. He couldn't take his eyes off them: Must be dozens of them, cold cruel eyes fixed on him.

A Humanik edged towards him.

Move, Tipsy, move his inner voice screamed.

Slowly at first, he turned around…A quick backwards glance revealed a Humanik dashing at him, long legs pounding the earth, arms outstretched. The creature leaped.

Tipsy sprinted sideways just in time to avoid being squashed under the Humanik who landed on his belly in the long grass, screeching with annoyance or pain, Tipsy didn't care which. He kept running. Passing a heap of stones he spotted two hares nesting quietly, their eyes glazed and half shut.

"Run" he shouted, "they're coming this way…Humaniks. One tried to jump on me. I escaped. Run!"

The two hares rose lazily. One yawned: "Are you okay Tipsy? Were you dreaming? There are no Humaniks on the island. You know that!"

"Tell that to the ones who are right now heading this way…!"

The second hare was gaping worriedly at him. "Are you sure? Where did you see them?"

"On the beach. Look, can you spread the word. They may wish to harm us. Tell every hare you meet to hide in the usual places. And to stay there until those creatures leave the island. They have fishing webs. Could be it's only fish they're after, but I've got a bad feeling about this…"

With that Tipsy resumed his frenzied run…

***

It was midday. Tipsy could tell by the position of the sun. How long would these intruders stalk the island? What did they want hares for?

He'd seen seven so far being manhandled by those frightening creatures. They'd pulled the hares from those webs after his unsuspecting brethren had become ensnared in them. He almost stumbled into a web himself, avoiding it at the last moment when he spotted the evil trap.

Now, he heard the Humaniks hollering. Then he saw them, their heads jutting above the crest of a hill. He hid again, for the umpteenth time since these hostile creatures stepped ashore, sinking into a shallow hole full of leaves that covered him nicely. Pitch darkness engulfed the cramped space.

He was a bundle of fear, his breathing frenzied. Terror tightened its grip. When running, fear tended to give way to the urgency of escape. Now he'd more time to fret.

A tiny pinpoint of light shone down through the leafy shield. He saw movement. And smelt the Humaniks too. A distinctive odour, unfamiliar before today but this was the second time he'd noticed it. Neither pleasant nor offensive: Just different from any other on the island.

Loud Humanik sounds...That strange shouting and grunting again, getting louder by the heartbeat.

Bang! Something struck the leaves overhead with great force, scrunching them and narrowly avoiding contact with his head. *Close,* he thought. Had they seen him?

He now had a clear view of the sky, as the object crashing down had swept away some of the leaves. He caught sight of…what was it: a long stick it seemed…the Humanik was holding it. He used it to beat the ground close to Tipsy's hiding place, but no…the Humanik hadn't spotted him.

The creature moved on, and the whacking sound of the stick beating the earth continued, growing less distinct as the intruder's smell faded.

Tipsy breathed a long sigh of relief... but dared not stir. Mustn't budge until he was certain the danger had passed, whatever that danger was. What did they want?

He recalled Craggy's tale of those rods that spat fire and death. Had they come to kill him and the other hares? A shudder went through him. Perhaps that stick thing the Humanik used to beat the ground was one of those killing contrivances.

Perhaps... and the thought sickened him... they used it to *kill* the hares once they retrieved them from the webs?

Silence had returned, apart from noises in the distance that Tipsy assumed was caused by the Humaniks and their scary behaviour. He ventured a look, slowly raising his head, shaking off crispy leaves that fell around him, tickling his mouth and nose. Cautiously, he swivelled his head around, taking in the terrain with intense deliberation.

Just the swaying grasses…the heather over there…and. *What on earth?* Two hares came bounding towards him. He was about to signal to them, but they raced past him, one on either side of the hole. They hadn't seen him. Were they running from the Humaniks? He'd ask later.

34

Watching from the cliff at dawn, Tipsy waited until the last of the Humanik vessels had left the beach.

Then, to be absolutely sure they'd gone, he waited a little longer. Only when the wooden craft were bobbing up and down on the ocean, mercifully fading from sight, did he venture to turn around and leave the cliff edge.

The danger had passed. He'd avoided capture. But what of the others? His heart sank at the thought of what the invaders might have done to them...the ones who hadn't been so lucky.

He hadn't eaten for ages, so he feasted on moss and berries and sipped water from a puddle that had formed in a cracked pathway. He rested awhile, letting the light of morning grow stronger before opting to inquire further into the great calamity that had befallen the island hares.

He ran from one to another of the known abodes of his friends…and of hares he'd never spoken to but had noticed on his travels. Some knew nothing, apart from the fact they'd instinctively hidden from the strange creatures and emerged from hiding when neighbours sounded the all-clear. Others had narrowly avoided capture but were still recovering from the shock of the experience and could barely speak.

Scaling a slope strewn with old Humanik homes Tipsy spotted a hare known for his vigilance. Only part of his left ear was visible above the pinnacle of a crumbling stone wall. What was his name? It came to him… "Crafty!" he called out.

The hare peeped over the wall, but didn't answer. Tipsy shuffled to his abode. The hare was shaking, and had a strange furtive look. All hares were careful and alert and timid. But this wasn't just nervousness. His big orangey eyes bulged with fear.

“Hey Crafty…it’s just me. What’s happening, do you know? I saw those Humaniks on the beach at sunrise and I hid all day and for most of the night too. I saw them spreading out across the island. Where is everybody?”

Crafty motioned Tipsy to sit near to him. The fear in his gaze subsided and his breathing grew less frenzied.

He spoke in staccato bursts: “I hid too…here…but I had to move fast when they arrived. They were everywhere, Tipsy: Beating the ground with rods and sticks, and shouting the way only Humaniks do.

“I was asleep, in the middle of a happy dream, when this crazy racket woke me. They were heading straight towards me, whacking the earth as if they were angry with something that lay beneath the grass. In front of them ran at least a dozen hares. I recognised some of them. There was Banjo from the far side of the island…Fozzie from the cliff…Scamper from near the Storm Petrel colony…and Dolly who’s little more than a leveret.

“I turned and ran. I don’t know why I did it, some instinct I reckon or maybe it was Ostara guiding me- but instead of dashing away in front of them as the other hares were doing, I turned sideways and ran to the purple heather. I glanced back after I’d gained some ground and my heart missed a beat: All but two of the hares in full flight from the invaders were wriggling in those horrible webs. It was the saddest sight ever…worse than watching the falcon take one of ours because…well, what would the Humaniks do with them?”

“Did you not see what happened to them, what the Humaniks did? Did they eat them?”

“No idea. I was too busy escaping. There was nothing I could do. If I tried to help I’d surely have been caught too. I ran to the far side of the island. It was safe there in the rocky terrain where food is scarce. No Humaniks… though no hares either. A lonely stretch of land, but safe... Thank Ostara. I returned here when I supposed the Humaniks would have gone, and it seems they have…”

Tipsy looked around him. He saw another hare tentatively nosing the ground in the distance, along the cliff edge overlooking the beach. Another scampering across a field in a zigzag pattern, as if making up for lost exercise.

Tipsy felt the world contracting and darkening about him. His lips quivered, fear and anxiety mingling to conspire against everything he held dear. "So what do you think's going on Crafty? I've seen seven empty hare abodes so far. Broken homes. Wonder what the Humaniks have done with them…*to* them?"

A deep sadness enshrouded Crafty. Tears fell unto his palpitating chest and streamed to his feet. He avoided Tipsy's quizzical gawp as he spoke: "I only know what a giddy, half hysterical leveret told me. The young fellow says he saw the Humaniks remove the captured hares from those webbed contrivances…and put them into square-shaped four-sided rocks they had with them…."

"Rocks?"

"Well, not really. He didn't know what they were, or what to call them. Hollowed-out rocks of some sort he thought they were, with openings in them. Anyway, he saw hares being forced into these weird...shapes... held by the Humaniks. The leveret said the hares could look out through one side of these confining shapes and they all looked desperately frightened and helpless. He ran along at a safe distance behind the Humaniks and saw them carry the captured hares down to the beach. Later, at daybreak, they got into the wooden craft- there were five of them if the leveret can be believed- and left the island with…I don't know how many hares."

Tipsy nodded. "I saw the vessels leaving, but in the weak light of dawn I didn't see the hares in them." He shivered momentarily, but not with the cold, though there was a sharp nip in the air and a strong breeze was fanning the island from the sea. "I wonder where they've taking them…and why they went to all the trouble of catching them. I must ask Mum about this. She's very clever- no offence meant Crafty- and she'd know something..."

The other hare sighed. "The leveret lost sight of them when they departed the beach and the waves carried them forth...but he saw them heading that way."

Crafty indicated the general direction of the Big Island. Not an attractive prospect, Tipsy thought, recalling what the Storm Petrel had told him about Humaniks with flashing rods that killed, four-legged creatures chasing hares, and other grim surprises.

Tipsy turned and set off at a brisk pace towards where Mum could usually be found, desperately anxious to hear her explanation for all this alarming Humanik activity on the island and the likely fate of the captured hares. Red yellow and orange leaves rustled as he crashed through the heaps of them that lay scattered in his path. It was the season where trees shed their crisp tasty foliage.

No time to eat leaves now. Through carpets of damp gorse he bounded, increasing speed as though he needed to get there quickly to avert some unnamed horror. He accelerated as he drew near her mossy domain by the lakeside, the wind caressing his face and fanning his whole body; his heartbeat also speeding up. A feeling of worry nagged him, increasing with every leap forward.

He slowed down when Mum's familiar grassy abode came into view. He sensed that something was amiss. She wasn't at home. She might be close by...but normally she stayed put by day and moved about by night, like most hares on the island.

Tipsy cast his eyes around. No sign of her. He began to consider if he ought to explore further when a hare he knew as one of the oldest on the island appeared from somewhere behind him. His eyes were wise and his reddish brown coat was speckled with grey. His movements were slow and hesitant.

"Hello there Tipsy...looking for your mother? Bad news I'm afraid. She was among the captives. I was lucky...I was hiding and I saw her...she got tangled in the Humanik web. I followed them to the beach. They had at least twenty hares. I'm sorry to be the one to tell you, Tipsy."

Tipsy's heart sank. He had to force himself to answer the old hare. "What...what do you think will happen to her...what do you think the Humaniks will do to her...to the others?"

"That's a question some of us plan to put to the Golden Hare tonight. He has access to the Higher Worlds and, occasionally, to the mind of the Goddess Ostara herself, may her name be blessed. We're meeting at the Cave of the Most High- and His Eminence, we hope, will enlighten us. Please pass the word to every hare you meet. Cover as much of the island as you can Tipsy and tell them: We meet when the light is almost, but not quite, drained from the sky and shadows still sweep the land."

"I'll be there" Tipsy confirmed, setting off to alert the others to this rare meeting with the Golden Hare, Ostara's earthly messenger on the island and, hopefully unknown to Humaniks Tipsy reflected, also spiritual leader of hares on the Big Island to which Mum had been taken.

***

35

Waxy rubbed his hands together. He was shivering despite being wrapped in winter gear, and it was only late October. The dew drenched field extended in front of him, enclosed on four sides by chain-link wire fencing. To his right was the slipper, holding on to a black and white Border collie by a leash. The sheepdog looked a little confused.

No wonder. This wasn't his usual workplace, or what he'd been bred for. From a little wooden box behind the slipper a hare popped out and began his run down the field. The collie was unleashed, and the hare easily outran him, making its way to the escape hatch at the end of the field.

The hares had to be trained to run in a straight line to the escape, and the first of the two competing greyhounds to turn the animal from this straight run was declared the winner in each course. But in training the hares it was important not to kill or injure any of them at that stage.

Hence the collie. Waxy scoffed at how some coursing clubs used greyhounds in the training phase...it risked harming the hares *before* coursing day, a pointless and self-defeating exercise. Once training was over, it didn't matter how many hares got the works. All that counted was a high standard of chasing, with as many hares as possible being "turned" by the dogs.

He watched as the collie almost cried with frustration: he hadn't a hope in hell of ever catching up with a hare, let alone damaging it. Waxy noted with interest that the island hares were outperforming, in terms of both speed and evasiveness, the ones captured on the Peninsula or purchased on the black market from other coursing clubs. Must be all that gorse and seaweed they'd gorged themselves on.

He'd ensured that tiny symbols were added to the ear-tags of those particular hares to identify them. They'd fetch a good price- the surviving ones- from other clubs once the coursing event was over. Not less than two-hundred Euro apiece. Hares were scarce on the Peninsula, but scarcer elsewhere in Ireland.

Thank God for the island, but he wouldn't be sharing that piece of good luck with other clubs. They'd pick it clean of hares if word got around: Bad enough having to contend with the antis and their sentimentalist twaddle...he was keenly aware that on the ruthless dog-eat-dog coursing scene it was every club for itself: the ones with the best and biggest stocks of captive hares ran the best fixtures.

The clubs with fewer hares had to re-course them far too many times, meaning that the animals performed less impressively with each rerun. He'd observed that wretched scenario at Ballycrossways in past seasons: Tired hares getting caught too easily by the dogs. They had to be dispatched on the spot or reserved for blooding.

The training ended. The collie was led away and the handful of observers dispersed. Waxy waved to the veteran group of hare handlers as they exited the field. All but one carried two boxes apiece containing the animals. The exception was the club's number one hare catcher.

Barty the Gob had been a star on the island, netting those evasive runners with the greatest of ease. He approached Waxy, a robust looking hare held in a tight arm-grip. "Jeepers but these are athletic pussies! The dogs'll have their work cut out!"

Waxy whistled approval. Barty passed by Waxy on his way to the hare-holding compound, his pockmarked face with its wandering eye and split lip a testimony to his brawling days as a wayward youth. He was a great asset to the club.

The hare's eyes bulged with fear. Its whole body quivered. It had cause to be afraid, Waxy mused. If he didn't perform for Barty he'd wind up as bait in a blooding session. Not a nice way to leave this world. Even for a fur-ball.

But that wasn't likely in this instance. The Island Hares wouldn't let down Ballycrossways Coursing Club. Waxy was more concerned about those interfering politicians who'd hitched their fortunes to the anti wagon. He'd be ready for them too whenever they posed a real challenge to his sport.

***

36

Annemarie drove through the entrance gate, suppressing a queasy feeling she'd had since she'd started the car engine to drive out of the village.

Her research had given her every reason to feel fearful and uneasy about attending this event. It had come as a shock to her to learn that the act of cruelty she'd witnessed during her walk on the day she broke up with her boyfriend was not an isolated incident, but part of a bigger picture that included the whole practice of hare coursing in Ireland.

Around ninety coursing fixtures were held annually between the October 1st and the end of February. The one at Ballycrossways was among the largest: three days of hare baiting. One or two-day events were the norm, but the Peninsula was a notorious black-spot for this relic of the Dark Ages.

Following an arrow daubed on a paper sign, she parked the car alongside others in the field. Seagulls circled and squawked overhead, a reminder of the venue's proximity to the edge of the Peninsula. Lucky birds, free to soar above the earth untrammeled by humans.

She had no sooner opened the car door and stepped onto the closely cropped grass when she felt scores of eyes focusing on her.

Some fans stood about chatting; others were washing down greyhounds alongside high-powered vehicles or small battered vans. A strong smell of whiskey or some other drink wafted up her nostrils. Small groups huddled together munching sandwiches and drinking tea or coffee from plastic cups.

All of them seemed piqued in some unaccountable way by her arrival. And it wasn't just paranoia. Suspicion was etched onto those faces attached to heads that were swiveling on obese bodies to take in her presence. What did they think she was…an alien disembarking from a UFO?

She pretended not to notice, walking briskly towards the entrance to another field behind hundreds of men and women attired in winter gear. Nearing the entrance their wellingtons squelched in muck, the sputtering of their feet dimming their voices and the nonstop wheezing and coughing that reminded her of a Church in mid winter, though this was autumn.

She cursed herself for not allowing for how these people dressed. She must have stood out garishly. She wore boots when everyone here had wellingtons. She was dressed casually- blue denim jeans with matching jacket and an old *I Love Bono* T shirt. Her appearance was all wrong for the setting. The coloured streaks in her hair were seriously out-of -place among these diehard traditionalists: A pathetic giveaway. She'd know better next time.

Chancing a glance to either side she noticed they were still watching her: To her left stood two elderly men with narrowed eyes, Russian style hats warding off the cold and cigarettes butts hanging from their lips.

To her right a group of men in their twenties slouched forward parallel to her, all looking straight ahead but with their eyes fixed sideways on her. A boy of about nine who had an odd manly appearance stared at her, mimicking an adult demeanor, his face screwed up with mortification.

She tried not to return his discomfited gaze but couldn't help notice him pulling a mouth organ from his pocket which he put to his lips and played jerkily, still keeping an eye on her. She quickened her step, blocking out the feeling of being something akin to a rare specimen in a test tube. Paying fifteen Euros to a man at the gate, she said thanks for the ticket but he said nothing: Again that disapproving leer. She relaxed as she made towards the front of the crowd that stood facing another field, this one fenced in by a large enclosure.

She felt shoulders rubbing against her on both sides. But this time no funny looks. They were too focused on the enclosure. Off to her right inside the grassy amphitheatre a man attired in red jacket and white jodhpurs clung to a pair of muzzled greyhounds that strained at the two-pronged leash, their tongues lolling and steam rising from their teeth.

A voice droned self-importantly over a crackling public address system: "First course: Scraggy's Chain Link versus Danny Boy Crapper."

Then, from a little box a hare emerged, briefly looking around him before dashing down towards the opposite end of the field.

She traced his progress to her left. He had covered a quarter of the distance to the hatch at the other end when the two greyhounds slipped free of the costumed fellow, who had trotted a few paces with a dramatic flourish before unleashing them.

The hare was over halfway to the hatch, which Annemarie knew to be the supposed life-saving "escape" exit, when the dogs caught up with him. The terrified animal dodged and swerved, the pursuers almost literally breathing down his neck. But he managed to evade them, and with yards to spare, shot through the escape hatch, leaving the dogs in a fury, snarling and salivating…shaking their heads in frustration.

A minute later, another hare covered the full distance of the running ground, again making good its escape. The loudspeaker announced the winning dog's name. Annemarie breathed a sigh of relief, which fans on either side of her seemed to hear or sense.

Quizzical expressions bore in on her. Somebody nudged her right shoulder…a suntanned man sporting a cowboy hat with feathers protruding from it. He was chewing a long straw and peering caustically at her. "You from around here, girl?

"Ah yes, from the village" she replied nervously.

He removed his hat momentarily to reveal a freckled bald head. Replacing the hat and setting it in place he mumbled: "You wouldn't be planning on causing any trouble for us, would you?"

She forced herself to laugh. "God no", why would you say that?"

"You don't have an events card, not a betting woman, eh?"

"Just dropped in to see…the coursing" she said, almost in a whisper and averting her eyes.

He nodded, gave her a last optical rundown, and grunted, before belching loudly and spitting on the ground in front of him. "No troublemakers wanted here" he muttered, without looking at her.

He seemed to forget about her as the next race got underway. She followed the hare's graceful dash, still thinking about the gruff man beside her, and allowing her mind to wander a little.

Then it happened. Her whole body shuddered as the hare miscalculated and ran straight into one of his pursuers. The dog struck him forcibly and tossed him high into the air. The hare landed on his feet but stumbled and keeled over. He struggled to his feet to resume his run but the second dog pounced on him with astonishing speed.

A deafening roar erupted from the fans, mingled with laughter and jesting words of encouragement to the rival dogs.

Annemarie froze, not daring to show a reaction as the hare, obviously injured, was mauled by the two dogs.

A blood curdling scream rose from the field, defiling the crisp Autumnal air, followed by that sobbing that tore at the heartstrings. She closed her eyes, willing it to stop, but the sounds pierced her eardrums.

The loudspeaker was cracking and droning, static breaking through the emotion-free announcement: "Hare being attended to, next pair of dogs please!"

Attended to…what a euphemism. You'd think he was receiving medical care.

A man was casually striding over to the wrestling dogs and their vanquished prey. He bent down and separated the dogs from the hare, wringing its neck to huge applause from the crowd.

Annemarie wanted to leave, but stayed put. The man with the cowboy hat was now staring at her, a triumphant grin forming, his hands conspicuously clapping. "Great dogs Miss, what do ya think?"

She couldn't respond. Words died in her throat as the urge to express her true feelings clashed with a grim resolve not to betray a searing abhorrence. Someone was tapping her left shoulder from behind. She turned to find a small man with a head of bushy red hair and a wandering eyeball. It floated like a goldfish in a bowl. He raised a whiskey flask. "Care for a slug?" He rasped.

"Ah no, but thanks, I'm okay" she said, forcing a smile.

"Sure? It's chicken broth? Warm your insides."

She felt a sudden urge to retch at the smell of washing up liquid mingled with the soup, borne to her nostrils on a wave of whiskey breath. Turning away she thought she heard him mutter "fancy bitch!"

Was he referring to herself…or a greyhound?

She remained for another half-hour, during which she saw seven more hares have their necks broken after the dogs had crushed their bones or mauled them.

Not all the fans cheered the cruelty. A boy, who clung to a man, presumably his father, kept pulling at him and saying he wanted to go home. The man ignored him, his attention fixed on a betting card.

When a hare was sent spinning skyward and began limping from the dogs, the boy lurched forward, streams of green and yellow liquid spewing from his mouth onto the grass: A fitting and honest response to the "sport". More honest than her own reaction, she thought.

A clatter across the neck sent the boy reeling. He lost his balance, emitting a low shriek as he plopped into his own vomit. "Up, you pup!" the man wheezed, striking the boy with a closed umbrella.

Other fans were busily ogling their betting cards as a pair of dogs was readied for the next chase. The dispatcher was furtively stretching an injured hare behind the straining dogs, his back turned to the crowd. He resembled a man playing an accordion, the dying hare his instrument. Over the whistling and static of the loudspeaker and the chatter of fans she heard the animal's death cries.

She'd seen enough. She shuffled through the clusters of fans, the loudspeaker spluttering out dog names and reminders about a fundraising dance. She felt sick to the core. Her stomach heaved.

She'd already known how it worked, and what to expect, but being physically present at such an exhibition of man's inhumanity was different. She felt doubly helpless. Each hare that screeched in agony seemed to be calling to her personally to help…to intervene, to somehow ease its sad plight.

This was the third and final day of the annual event. Next time, next year… she'd bring a camera. She'd record the whole sickening charade that some of the most powerful people, including politicians, lawyers, and business tycoons, felt drawn to like strings of iron filaments to a magnet.

Film footage was rare enough because cameras weren't allowed unless by permission of the club and in the strict understanding that pictures must comply with the rules. These included that no stills or video footage could show coursing "to disadvantage".

But she'd find a way: If she could secretly film the cruelty that would help the cause. Joining a public protest outside the venue, like the one organised last year, wasn't an option. She'd been advised that to speak out against coursing on the Peninsula would amount to "career suicide"; that clients of the accountancy firm where she worked had high profile coursing fans as clients.

Her boss wasn't aware of her anti-coursing views, but she knew he'd be none too happy if she spoke out. Their influence extended into every sphere of life in the district.

Many villagers, she knew, disapproved of coursing, but there was an unwritten rule that you didn't make your views public.

You didn't "make waves" about those well-connected people who turned a patch of peaceful countryside each year into a little piece of hell.

***

37

Tipsy arrived at the meeting place. He'd first seen it shortly after he entered the world. Mum had taken him, but he had not entered the sacred abode of the Golden Hare. She'd told him almost in a whisper as they stood outside the entrance, partially concealed and blocked to keep predators out; that only on rare occasions did ordinary hares venture inside the cave to consult His Eminence.

Some great event or emergency might justify calling to him, and those didn't arise too often on the island. His own plan to seek the Great One's blessing for his unrecognised marriage to Bumble had come to nothing. He wondered what the response would have been; not that it mattered now.

The last rays of the sun were fading. Tipsy observed the great orb descend below the horizon. He imagined it was sinking faster than usual, as though in homage to the gravity of the situation. He heard low voices, teeth grinding, and soft purring.

To his left and right hares appeared and, without acknowledging him, entered the cave. He noticed that the camouflage and obstructing rocks had been rolled away. He followed the others inside.

Immediately he entered a larger than average hare blocked his path. "Name" he demanded.

"I'm Tipsy" he replied meekly, "Is there a problem?"

"Where on the island do you live?"

Tipsy gave his current address as the form located twenty leaps, a scamper and two shuffles from the High Tree on the purple heathery hill.

"That checks out...we've heard you were coming. You may pass!"

He waved Tipsy in, attending to the next hare in the queue. "Name!"

Tipsy looked around him. The cave was quite spacious, if a little dark apart from the light cast by dying sunbeams.

Hares were standing or sitting all around, some chatting; others deep in thought. *Probably looking for answers, like me,* Tipsy presumed. Some were little older than leverets. He figured their mothers were missing too.

The Golden Hare appeared from an opening in the glistening rocky wall that must have led into another tunnel. A flash of light dazzled Tipsy. Had he been struck blind? He had to cover his eyes to avoid the sudden brightness.

Slowly he let himself see. The others seemed not to be struggling with the unexpected glare. Adjusting to it, Tipsy saw a seated hare facing them encircled with a radiance that equalled that of the sun as it slowly dipped into the ocean. It glowed and flared with a dazzling orange luminosity.

The Golden Hare himself was unaffected by the light that enveloped him. All the hares were stunned into silence, apart from two that stood on either side of him. One of these was the tough-sounding hare that took all their names at the entrance.

He stepped in front of His Eminence, surveyed all present and said: "Now...my name is Bouncer. As you know, Ostara's Representative on Earth will shortly address you on the great calamity that has befallen us. You will not interrupt. When he has spoken you may ask questions: One at a time. Interrupters will be ejected from the cave. My decision on ejections will be final and not open to appeal."

Charming fellow Tipsy thought, but he could see why order had to be maintained.

"Good evening, fellow hares." The Great One spoke. There was something otherworldly about his voice.

"Good evening Your Eminence." A communal zealous response.

"I said no interruptions!" Bouncer shouted, his voice echoing around the cave.

His Eminence motioned him to be silent. Bouncer grumpily sat, his eyes fixed reverently on the Great One.

"You are asking what has happened. Why your loved ones, friends, acquaintances were taken from you? Where are they?

My dear flock, after I heard of the invaders and the traps set by them to capture many of our brethren I spoke to our beloved Ostara herself..."

At the mention of the Goddess the radiance momentarily shone even brighter, with little light orbs spraying like tiny bubbles outward from his body, causing Tipsy to again shield his eyes, though the others didn't seem affected.

The Golden Hare continued: "In a deep trance she made herself visible to me. I was shown a vision...in it I saw the Humaniks and heard them speak, and their language became known to me. Brethren, they took the hares for their amusement. On the Big Island, Humaniks force hares to run and dodge in front of four-legged creatures that crave the taste of our flesh. But eating us is not the purpose of this strange and terrible practise. The creatures they use to pursue us have their mouths blocked to ensure that their teeth do not make contact with us when we run from them.

"So...they can pin us to the ground, throw us high into the air, to spin and gyrate like leaves in the wind, or they break our bones. The Humaniks in this recreation of theirs do not aim to kill us...instead they wish to see us suffer a living death, a slow and painful demise.

"You all know of the falcon that has taken some of our younger hares on this island? Some of you may have seen that dreadful bird swoop on and kill a beloved leveret? But even the falcon did not prolong the anguish of his victim. His quest was for food. That bird was our foe, yes, but his motive was hunger, and maybe he needed nourishment, not for himself, but for young birds.

"The Humaniks, I have been told by Ostara, enjoy the taste of our flesh like the falcon. But they rarely indulge that craving. On the Big Island the Humaniks want us for that evil game...If they come again to the island, know that you must do everything you can to avoid capture..."

His Eminence fell silent. Bouncer stood, looked reverently at the Golden Hare, who nodded, the radiance around him now easier on Tipsy's eyes but still bright enough to illuminate the entire cave. A hare in the front row was on all fours. "Your Eminence. I marvel at how our Goddess Ostara has revealed so much to you. We now know why our beloved fathers, mothers, brothers, sisters and cousins were captured. But is there not something we can do? I mean, apart from hiding better next time...if there is a next time...the Humaniks come for us?"

Other hares murmured agreement and purred their approval of this question.

The Golden Hare spoke, more slowly this time, and the regret in his voice deepened. "That is a matter upon which I will have to consult our Goddess. She cannot intervene physically to save us. That you must accept. But if there is a way to help our captured brethren and outwit the Humaniks she will, I am confident, reveal it to me. This meeting is concluded..."

***

38

The last of the injured hares had stopped kicking. Waxy leaned towards it. Not quite dead yet. It was exhaling frantically and its eyes bulged. Blood dripped from its mouth unto the plastic sheeting spread across the concrete. Its death-throes vibrated the taut line from which it and the six other injured or substandard hares had been suspended.

The blooding had gone off well, Waxy thought. And the trainers had left the venue satisfied. It was messy at times, but still a darned sight more effective than conventional training.

No matter how many hours a trainer devoted to his dogs, nothing could beat a good blooding session. A tantalising taste of live hare flesh in a controlled setting gave any dog a serious edge over its rivals...that extra motivation on the track or field.

Gruesome it might appear to weaklings and those unfamiliar with the inner workings of the coursing tradition, but all true aficionados understood its value.

God, just imagine if one of those anti idiots dropped in and saw this. Shudder the thought! But they'll never catch us on that one. Better cut them down.

Striding across the plastic sheeting, his booted feet crackled. First he went to the hare that hadn't expired. He took the head in one hand by the ears, and tightening his grip with the other around its neck, he pulled. A faint screeching emitted from its quivering mouth.

He saw and felt saliva and blood trickle from the dying creature as he wrung its neck. Letting it go, the freshly killed carcass swung like a furry pendulum, blood splattering from side to side to stain the plastic sheeting.

Opening his penknife, he cut down the hare. It fell with a plop, brushing against his leg as it did. He repeated the procedure with the others. He winced at the sight of one animal from which a back leg hung loose. A dog had partly chewed it off. Another hare was missing an eye. Not a pretty sight.

With all the blooding bait piled grotesquely before him, he gathered up the plastic, folding it around them. He then carefully tied a big knot with a piece of rope. The carcasses would have to be incinerated. If the antis found any of them they'd make a song and dance. They'd howl with indignation.

Yet, the hares had served a useful purpose. Their injuries or weaknesses made them useless to the club. Hares had to be in top form to run. But as bait for training they were doing their bit to benefit the human race.

Anger shot through him. *If only those antis understood that we love the hare, in our own way. Those people see only the chase. Never how we feed and water those animals, building the finest holding compounds for them. Six Thousand Euros the club spent on our new facilities. State of the art lodgings you might call them... for hares that might otherwise have just lived boring lives squatting in a bloody field listening to the wind whistle or maybe eating the bark off trees on private property.*

*The Devil makes work for idle minds. Well...*he sniggered...*those seven chappies won't be chewing any bark. Ah sure, they're out of their misery anyhow. Their injuries weren't going to heal. They'd have died slowly in the wild if we let them go.*

The sounds of barking and yelping and the shrieks of the tormented animals echoed inside his head as he placed the bundle of quenched lives into the open boot of his four-wheeled drive and slammed it shut.

The loud clang partly quelled his memory of the blooding session. Little taunts of partially suppressed conscience burst like bubbles inside his head. Unease niggled. *Must push that from my mind. That's what turns people into antis: Weakness intruding when you need to be strong. The great ancient tribesmen who hunted the hare buck naked for their grateful wives back in the caves didn't get weak at the knees at the sight of a little blood and the cries of a few tethered bunnies.*

Retreating to the house, he raised a slightly shaking hand to the drinks cabinet, fetched a half bottle of whiskey, and poured himself a glass. He downed it in one gulp.

Ah, that's good. The Water of Life. Washes away crass misgivings. Restores strength. Get a grip. They were half-dead when I tied them up. Probably in shock, or unconscious, so they didn't know what was happening when the dogs...

Sitting by the fireside with the bottle, he poured himself another drink. He felt better already.

***

39

Tipsy settled into his grassy nest to sleep. It had been a long day, and even longer night. There was so much to mull over.

His eyes were drowsy. His whole body felt like dead weight. Yet the terrible events kept him awake even as his eyelids drooped and sought to dim his sight.

Slivers of cloud sailed past the crescent moon in slow succession, reminding him of those Humaniks in their wooden craft sailing away with his mother across the sea, his beloved mum who had brought him into the world.

She told him it was a sunny day when he arrived; that his eyes sparkled with curiosity and his ears registered the sweet sound of birdsong, the music of the friendly fliers. He vaguely remembered his first heartbeats in the earth world, but what he did recall was tinged with happiness and a sense of safety.

Mum was there, and his father, reassuring presences that added to his feeling of contentment and security. Only when he had aged by twenty sunsets had mum, as he snuggled beside her in the purple heather, broached the subject of predators. Well, one predator...the falcon.

She hinted at others that hares faced beyond the island, but she didn't pay too much heed of those. The island didn't have to bother with them. And she'd only heard about those creatures in stories passed down from older hares and hares that had crossed over aeons ago to Hare Heaven.

The falcon, and there might be more than one of them stalking the island for prey, was the hare's enemy, though once you remained alert for him you could hide or run to safety. The greatest fear among hares was to be caught in short grass, with no refuge or escape route in sight...and the dreaded juggernaut hovering on the breeze.

You knew he saw you, and he'd swoop. You might outrun him, but he flew like lightning. Leverets were most at risk, because they didn't understand the danger. How could they? They were just babies and hadn't a clue. The falcon took full advantage of that, and many a baby hare had been swept upwards in that predator's tight claws, never to be seen again.

He had cheated the falcon, but others hadn't been so fortunate. He shuddered when he imagined the leveret disappearing inside the bird, frightened and dying as the falcon devoured him, crunching his bones. *Ugh, the thought of it!*

Still, that only happened if you were careless enough not to be on your guard. Every hare knew the danger and allowed for it. But nobody had allowed for those damned Humaniks! Mum had spoken of them darkly in his babyhood, but always sought to dispel any fears he might have, since, she said soothingly, those creatures rarely came to the island and then only to catch the fish that swam beneath the waves. That was bad for the fish, but not the hare's problem.

Oh mum...how could you not have known how dangerous they were...that they would come and take you?

Tipsy drifted into slumber. The dreary world faded and he was a leveret again, gambolling in the summer sunshine, mum looking on wistfully and the Goddess Ostara casting her protective invisible shield around the joyful domain of the hares.

***

40

Waxy peeled back a fold of the semitransparent canvass covering on the side of the disused hay barn. Normally utilized for blooding sessions, it would serve today as the venue for what he hoped would be a successful meeting with a man revered by fieldsports people nationwide. But would he undertake the task Waxy had in mind?

There he was… crossing the yard after letting himself in through the rusty gate, as Waxy had instructed him to do. He didn't want him calling to the front door. This could be dicey if things went askew. Plausible deniability was essential to the success of many a coursing-related enterprise. That applied especially to blooding, but today's issue might require a spot of innovative dissembling too. Hopefully it wouldn't come to that.

Catching sight of Waxy The Poacher O' Dea waved and a big smile cracked open his granite face, with its jagged purple birthmark across his left cheek that resembled the shape of the Peninsula itself. Waxy held aside the canvass to let The Poacher in, looking both ways to ensure there was nobody snooping around the yard. That included even greyhound owners or coursing fans. Today's business at the barn was for nobody's ears but his and the Poacher's.

"You wanted to see me about…a delicate…matter, you were saying Waxy?"

"Delicate is the word, and I have to ask right now for your solemn promise that you'll not breathe a syllable to a solitary soul of what I'm about to discuss with you?"

The Poacher spat on his right hand, clasped it to the breast of his nicotine-stained fake flak jacket, rubbed in the saliva vigorously, and shut his eyes. "On the grave of my nearest and dearest!" he intoned, his face crunched into a distorted clump of flesh in which only the nose and lips were recognizable.

"Take a seat!" Waxy indicated an old wooden stool that stood in a corner of the darkened barn, into which weak yellowish light struggled through holes in the canvass. He pulled over another stool and sat facing The Poacher, just inches separating them. Waxy picked up the bottle of Paddy Whiskey he had brought along for the meeting. He handed The Poacher a glass and filled it for him.

"Gosh, thanks Waxy. It must be a hell of an important job you have for me."

The Poacher grimaced as he downed the half-glass of amber liquid. "God…that was good", he gasped.

Waxy sipped at his own glass, the heady malt aroma distracting him slightly. He laid the glass on the ground beside the stool. *Must keep a clear head for this.*

He got straight to the subject. "Poacher, I know you're the best shot in these parts, and I have a special request to make. There's a troublesome bird…well, maybe three or four of them…that I want taken out."

The Poacher laughed. "No Problem. God, I thought from the way you spoke on the phone that I'd be handling something really damned complicated. Birds?"

The Poacher rubbed his hands together playfully, spat to one side, and clenched his teeth. Leaning towards Waxy he crooned: "Crows giving you trouble, or those bloody jackdaws? What a racket they make in the mornings. Or is it the magpies? Can't stand the sight of them meself!"

Waxy shook his head slowly, motioning The Poacher to let him explain. "No…they can be a nuisance right enough, but that's not the problem I wish you to solve. Poacher, you know about those hares we harvested from Gooseberry Island last year? Well, we'll need to revisit the island in the coming season. The place is full of them. There's just one thing that bothers me. Those damned falcons! You see…the island hares have no real predators to contend with… apart from those birds. The falcons kill leverets with the greatest of ease…lots of them."

The Poacher raised a hand, "Just a minute Waxy. Hold it there…You're not asking me to…to shoot the falcons? Hell man, they're a protected species. I'd be cooling my heels in

Scrubs Ball Prison if I got caught…and anyway, the hares here on the Peninsula have even more predators than the island ones…foxes, stoats, other birds of prey. That's just nature taking its course man. You can't change the way nature works!"

Waxy had to suppress his irritation. "Look Poacher. I understand all that, but this is how I see it. The falcon is competing with us for those hares, and the island hares are precious to us. Without them we can't have our coursing events. If we can take those birds out of the equation there'll be more hares for us. I know it's illegal to shoot a falcon, but look Poacher…I wouldn't ask you to do this if I didn't believe it was in the best long-term interests of Ballycrossways Coursing Club."

The Poacher gazed thoughtfully at the straw-speckled ground, bloodstains from the most recent training session still visible on the grey concrete. He massaged his stubbly chin, then his birthmark, before looking Waxy straight in the face. "I'll do it…but only because it's you doing the asking, Waxy. I owe you one since the day you tipped me off about Scarecrow's Fancy, the dog that won the finals back in ninety-seven. Made a fortune on that."

Waxy stood and leaned to clap the Poacher heartily on the back. He then grabbed his hand, shaking it with great relief and emotion. "Thank you Poacher, I knew I could rely on you…"

The Poacher pulled away his hand delicately and turned his eyes to the heavily cobwebbed galvanized ceiling. "Ah, I'll need a rifle with an effective range of a mile or two, Waxy. I don't expect to be able to creep up on them in their cozy little nests on the cliffs…or wherever else they hang out. I'd be happier aiming upwards. They fly over and back between the island and the Peninsula early in the mornings…"

Waxy walked to the other end of the barn and pulled the discarded tablecloth away from a shining black rectangular case. He handed it to the Poacher.

The wily shooter laid the case down on the stool reverentially, and flicked it open. He whistled softly, removing the sleek grayish brown rifle from its casing. He held it in both hands, savouring the feel of it. In the gloom it mirrored the diluted sunlight. He examined the weapon in silence before speaking slowly, deferentially, as though it were a sacred object. "Nosler Model Forty-Eight…Long Range rifle… Guaranteed Maximum Accuracy. And it's weather resistant. It'll need to be, out there in the Atlantic…"

The Poacher raised the rifle and cocked it, taking aim through the telescopic sight. "I'll need to do a few adjustments…but this is definitely the gun for the job: A beautiful piece. I'll be needing a motor boat. I'd prefer to be as far away from another human soul as I can when I…do the business. I don't want them falling anywhere on the Peninsula if I can help it. Best have them drop in the ocean. Otherwise the Wildlife Service will be probing around. It wouldn't look good for the gun clubs, you understand?"

Waxy threw out his hands in a gesture of submission. "Do it any way you wish Poacher and here…you said on the phone that you'd take no payment, seeing you were returning that favour and all, but Poacher…you can keep this weapon as a token of my gratitude."

Poacher's mouth gaped and his eyelids flickered in the gloom. "Gee thanks Waxy" He fondled the rifle, rubbing a hand along the stock and the glistening black barrel. He raised the weapon again, aimed at the barn ceiling, touched the trigger and mouthed a wordless *bang!*

"Another one?" Waxy posited, grabbing the whiskey bottle by its neck and raising it over his head like a Communion Chalice. The Poacher returned the rifle to its case and held out his glass for a refill. Waxy joined him in a toast to the upcoming coursing season.

***

41

Tipsy felt helpless. He was sitting on the cliff edge that offered a panoramic view of the ocean. He nibbled on moss as he took in the sprawling swathe of earth, sea and sky. The sizzling euphoric swell of the sea fixated him. How it seemed to have a life of its own... as if all the water splashing and spraying and surging forth was directed by one mind. Ostara perhaps?

And he always liked to watch the slow movement of clouds, some fluffy, some of them vast sprawling receptacles of rain in the making, some ethereal and others shaped...*like hares* he thought.

But that was an illusion. Shapes could fool you sometimes. *Is Ostara playing tricks to amuse us?*

Gulls maintained their constant shrieking, flapping and diving at the bottom of the cliff in search of food, fighting each other in the process.

He savoured these familiar sights and sounds most mornings after sunrise. Today, though, his gaze shifted fearfully to that far-off green stripe on the horizon with those humps and peaks protruding from it at intervals.

Some days it was invisible, shrouded in fog or concealed by mist or rainfall. But today it was starkly visible, below the shimmering sun: The Big Island...the land of the Humaniks. That sinister and frightful place where Mum was held captive, along with the other hares they'd snatched with their evil webs.

He swallowed a clump of moss, but then stopped eating. He wasn't that hungry this morning. In fact his appetite hadn't been the same since the Humaniks violated the island's relative contentment.

He'd experienced a sense of foreboding when the Storm Petrel told of his flight...over there. How a friend had been wrenched from the sky by a flashing rod. And stories told by the older hares sent chills up and down his spine.

But now those obnoxious creatures had brought their terrifying ways to the island. Life could never be the same again.

He thought of what the Golden Hare had said...but drew no consolation from it. Was there really nothing they could do but plan to hide more cleverly next time the Humaniks came? Or run faster?

Anger grew within him. *Why are we so timid? Why so afraid of everything? Look at those seagulls down there? Ruthless and determined to get what they want. They'd kill any other seagull that tried to stop them. And the falcon is afraid of nobody. Even the Storm Petrels in their colony on the other side of the island go about their lives with less fear than we do.*

Mum said we are born timid. We do no harm to other creatures. That is our proud heritage; bestowed on us by Ostara in her divine wisdom and we must live up to it. Other animals and birds may behave differently, and see the world through different, more belligerent eyes, but not us.

Great! So we just allow everything with a heart ticking inside it to push us around and get away with it.

Tipsy fumed and his own heart beat faster as he stared over at that green patch of horror, separated from the island by a tempestuous ocean.

If only...if only there was a way to help Mum and the others. I'd forget about my duty to be timid. I'd make those Humaniks suffer and pay them back.

Tipsy averted his gaze from the Big Island, now partially obscured by cloud, and began running. He dashed back through grassy terrain and up the steep slope containing the old Humanik dwellings.

Entering one that consisted of four stone walls and the remnants of an overhead tree-branch covering, he visualised Humaniks standing about inside, and what he'd say to them. Though they wouldn't hear or understand.

He'd like to rush at them with a blazing audacity…so that they'd turn and flee. If only...but he was a hare. Running and hiding were his options in the face of adversity. Gazing up at the sky he raged "Ostara, why did make us like this? Please...can you not give me the strength...the power...to save my mother and the other innocent ones? And when I've sorted out those Humaniks I promise I'll be timid again...more gentle than a new born leveret?"

His anger subsided. He relaxed and felt sleepy.

***

42

Tipsy luxuriated in the sand, letting the incoming tide splash over him. He rolled over and over, savouring both the refreshing balm of the cleansing water and the caressing hush of the never-ending waves that advanced and retreated with comforting regularity.

So much in a hare's life was unexpected, sudden. But the great surge of the ocean was constant and unthreatening. True, the Humaniks had come to the island aided by that same stretch of water, but that wasn't the sea's fault. Tipsy shook himself dry and prepared to go home for a sleep.

A cracking sound distracted him. It was far away and he thought it came from the direction of the Big Island. He scanned the horizon from left to right and then back again. Nothing but the heaving swells of the sea. *But wait.* There was something: A tiny dot bobbing on the water. Yes, and little darts of sunlight bounced off it.

He waited. Was it heading for the island? Many heartbeats passed and the object didn't get any bigger or closer. Then, as Tipsy decided to leave the beach, another crack…and another: It sounded like reeds snapping when you stepped on them.

This time Tipsy gaped awestruck at the zigzagging movements of a bird that was flying towards the island and would soon, he estimated, be right above him. *The falcon!* He'd better get himself out of sight. *But wait…something's amiss.* The falcon didn't fly like that…in a clumsy, chaotic fashion…as if half asleep or being pulled hither and thither by an invisible force.

Tipsy was so riveted by this out of character conduct that he remaining sitting in the sand, watching the bird's progress. There it went again…the cracking in the sky, or at least it seemed to come from up there. The sound seemed to affect the falcon. At each crack his flight patterns altered…his whole body reacted. His flying became more haphazard and Tipsy heard him shriek.

Did the cracking frighten or discommode him in some way? He reminded Tipsy of how a hare behaved when struck by a bout of madness that sent him into a sudden foolish flurry. The falcon's wings flapped wearily, haphazardly, as if he'd lost interest in being a bird and now…was he swooping on a gull…or a leveret he'd just spotted?

But no…normally the falcon closed its wings for that deadly swoop. This time he was falling but not diving…tumbling, twisting and turning randomly, occasionally regaining some control and still flying or fluttering awkwardly. He then continued his awkward descent.

Tipsy followed the falcon's disordered downward trajectory as it rallied slightly and flew unsteadily in the general direction of the island, before again reverting to a distorted swoop. Somehow, it didn't seem like the bird was on a killing mission. *But wait.* Was this a deliberate ply, a new tactic aimed at gulling his intended prey? They'd see him flying or falling about in a clumsy manner, seeming not to care where he was going or on which part of the island he might land. Then…just when the target creature had let its guard down he'd revert to his deadly routine, descending like the wrath of a hail storm, beak ready for snapping, claws poised to crush and rip.

Tipsy felt inclined to rule out that theory as the falcon passed directly over him, still alternating between falling helplessly and struggling to rise again. Now he was falling more than rising. Tipsy watched as the huge bird that struck fear into every hare disappeared from sight, further inland. Had he been bluffing…or was he at this moment in the final stages of an attack that would end the life of a hare or some unlucky small bird?

Before long, Tipsy would hear of its fate from other hares. He might be listening to yet another sad tale of a leveret snatched from the world of the living, swept up into the heavens by the mightiest and fastest bird hares ever had to contend with.

He didn't have to wait long. No sooner had he reached the cliff-top when a dozen frantic hares- adults and leverets- came running and leaping to him, shouting excitedly. "Did you see it Tipsy?" one hollered.

"He's got what he deserved…at last. Let's dance on his miserable carcass!" Another cried out.

"Has Ostara answered our prayers and brought down the predator?" a leveret queried.

Tipsy ran with them, the frenzied group led by a hare who loudly and giddily proclaimed to have seen the body of the falcon.

Tipsy joined his fellow islanders at the top of a small hill near the lake. A collective cry of astonishment went up from the assembly at the unprecedented sight. Beneath them, slumped amid a weed patch of orange white and green, with crushed vegetation peeping from under him; was the most feared bird on earth.

The falcon was spread out pathetically on his back, both wings stretched to either side, attempting to flap but succeeding only to flutter feebly, as if struggling to retain a miniscule part of their once mighty potential.

Tipsy was surprised by its colour. It wasn't black, as it seemed when you saw him flying high: More of a bluish grey. His under-parts were a glowing white, speckled with a lattice of black bars that swelled and contracted with its breathing. But the striking plumage was marred by a garish blotch of red on its breast. Somehow, that didn't seem to belong.

Tipsy ventured further down the hillside. As he neared the stricken bird a chorus of voices hollered warnings. One hare scampering right behind Tipsy whispered in his ear: "Watch him; he might be feigning injury to fool us. He might be planning to eat us all."

Tipsy didn't agree. Inching closer, he heard the gasping breaths and saw the glazed look in its shining black eyes. Its bright yellow beak was opening and closing slowly. And that red mark on his breast wasn't part of his plumage. The circular spot oozed blood that ran in tiny rivulets from the whiteness into the bluish grey feathers, spilling unto the flattened grass and flowers.

Tipsy's heart gathered pace and hammered inside him as he drew closer. Curiosity trumped fear. Now he saw the blood falling in opaque drops from its beak, moistening and discolouring the bird's fluffy moustache.

Its eyes swiveled to regard Tipsy. He moved tentatively to its side, nervously watching for any sign of a trap, though that seemed a remote possibility. Tipsy turned and signaled to the others, all gathered in a semicircle on the hilltop, eyes fixated on the great heaving clump of avian half- life below them. "He's no threat anymore. He's dying!" he hollered.

Never before, Tipsy knew; had hares on the island seen a falcon brought low like this. They knew that falcons must die at some point, in accordance with the laws of nature, but no-one had seen a dead or wounded falcon. Their only sightings of the dreaded foe were above the island, circling in triumph and dominion, patrolling the skies, blotting out the sun…ready at any moment to pounce.

The hares exchanged glances. Tipsy read a variety of expressions: puzzlement, relief, skepticism, curiosity. But all these reactions quickly morphed to a single emotion. "Let's pay him back for all the grief he's brought us" a hare shrieked.

"Yes…I lost my brother to him; and my uncle…"

"He killed my dear sister, and devoured my mother!"

All the pent-up fury exploded, and down the hill the hares ran, fell, slid, tumbled or leaped. Tipsy stepped aside to make way for what he feared had become a collective craving for revenge.

The hares encircled the falcon, quietly examining the mysterious king of the skies, prodding him at various points along his wing spans, pressing paws against his quaking black hood, his fierce but redundant beak and intimidating blood stained moustache. A strange silence held them in its grip. Then, a hare howled: "The Humaniks must have done this to him…no other creature could. Good on the Humaniks if they brought him down!"

A maturing leveret leaped unto its panting breast, crying out in rage: "Die you monster, for your crimes, die!"

The others followed, kicking, punching, and spitting. Tipsy felt sickened. Yes. The falcon was *his* enemy too, but what was the point in attacking the bird as he lay dying? Earsplitting roars of hatred almost drowned out the falcon's desperate whimpers of pain and pleading.

"Stop it…Stop it…immediately!" The commanding voice of Father Buck.

Tipsy saw him, standing atop the hill, disgust convulsing his features, his grayish wizened frame shaking: a dignified figure silhouetted against a rain threatening sky. In keeping with this dark moment, Tipsy thought. The hares withdrew, though reluctantly, from their full-blooded attack on the falcon, muttering insults and still getting in the odd kick at their fallen foe as they moved away.

The priest heaved his way into their presence, motioning them to stand further back. They ogled him with a mixture of reverence and resentment.

He roared "What are you doing? Are you not hares? Did the Goddess not confer on you the sacred gift of timidity? We do not engage in violence like this, except maybe in the mating contests, but even then we don't aim to kill…or seek revenge. Vengeance is un-hare like. It is sinful…And how on earth can you praise Humanik viciousness, even if it is directed at your enemy? Have you so quickly forgotten your brethren…cruelly snatched from the island?"

A hare stepped forward. He took a deep breath, and Tipsy saw the suppressed rage in his eyes. "Father, with due respect, that monster has taken many of our family and friends. We're just sending him to Ostara so she can kick him into the place of punishment reserved for bad dudes!"

"Punishment for what?" The priest retorted. Casting a sad look at the ailing, mutilated heap, its feathers all bloodied and its breathing reduced to a low hiss, he intoned: "That creature lived by different rules to us. We cannot judge him, Only Ostara can…"

"And she'll torture him for all eternity" scoffed a hare hidden from sight.

"Tipsy!" Father Buck shouted, "Come here!"

Tipsy hopped to the priest's side. "Can you commune with this…creature…see if he repents his crime against the hares of this island? Let him know that we are not hateful beings, but that he needs to account for himself…at the hour of his death!"

Tipsy felt awkward. Why did he have to be selected for this disturbing task? But he felt honoured too. It was a big occasion. The impending death of a falcon was an event you didn't get to witness every day.

Adjusting himself mentally, he tuned in to the bird's thoughts and complex avian lingo. "Falcon…my colleagues were angry. They acted out of hurt. Can you understand this? You have killed and eaten many of their loved ones. When they saw you prostrate here…helpless and vulnerable…after all you've done to the hare population, they vented their hurt and anger on you. Can you understand this? Why it happened?"

The great hulking mass of pulsating feathers heaved its mutilated head, which had been facing skyward, and turned to look Tipsy in the eye. It was an unpleasant sensation: Its gaze, even in the midst of its agonizing death-throes, was unnerving. Tipsy felt those inscrutable black orbs piercing his very soul. The bird spoke haltingly, every word seeming to hurt…a thorn pricking its body. "I have never disliked, let alone hated, your kind", he groaned, spitting blood.

He spoke rapidly, his beak trembling, as if anxious to say his piece before his heart stopped. "We falcons happen to feed on the flesh of other creatures. Not because we are nasty or hateful or monstrous. We take hares to assuage our hunger. We eat to live…to survive. I understand your antagonism. And I understand why hares hate me so much. If hares could fly up into the sky and take us as food we wouldn't be too happy about that either. But it doesn't work that way.

"Look…I'm dying. Shortly I'll be with friends in the world beyond this one. I'm…I'm sorry…for the grief and pain I've caused all of you. But I'm not sorry for being a falcon, and for living as a falcon does. The creator of all things, the cosmic flier in his nest made of stardust, ordained that all creatures would have their place in the world. I acted how I did because…otherwise I would not be who I was."

He paused to spit globules of blood into a cluster of flattened daisies. Tipsy winced at how it stained the flora. Curiosity prompted his next question. "What happened…what inflicted this terrible injury that pulled you from the sky?"

The falcon turned away, again looking straight up…this time at the ever-thickening rainclouds that moved furtively across the heavens. "I saw the Humanik…he was in a craft on the ocean. He raised that…killing contrivance they use…and instantly I knew I was in danger. Many birds have fallen to this Humanik method of killing…I tried to dodge but the death rod is faster than any bird on earth."

"What's he saying, Tipsy, tell us!" a hare interrupted.

Tipsy recounted what the falcon had told him. Ridicule, swearing, and loud guffaws erupted.

"He's sorry now because he's leaving this world" one mocked. "Are we supposed to shed tears for this killer bird? I say: well done to the Humanik who felled him!"

Tipsy translated for the falcon. The bird let out a sad sigh and closed its eyes. "I had a magnificent life…soaring above the earth, faster than any other species of bird…and on land no animal was a match for me: How I loved being caressed by the thermals as I flew high over land and sea…and oh…the joy of gliding…and the satisfaction of a scrumptious nourishing meal of flesh and blood.

"With my talons outstretched I delivered the killing blow at the end of each hunt. The sharp claw of my hind-toe was the last thing many a bird and leveret felt before…and how I savoured the prize. I dined on cliff-tops and slept soundly in my nest. Never once was I troubled by a guilty conscience. No offence, but I preferred hare any day to those stupid gulls. So tasty. The gulls were hardly worth the effort. I thanked the great bird god every time I gulped down the last piece of…of one of you guys. I'm sorry…ah… the pain is easing. The world is fading, but another beckons. The time has come. Just a few heartbeats left…"

Tipsy wished him well in the afterlife, though he wouldn't let the others know this, and was about to turn away when the bird raised a wing, with excruciating effort. His feathers swished softly. The wing brushed off Tipsy, startling him.

"Yes?"

"One more thing" the falcon rasped, his voice scarcely audible. "You said your friends felt like celebrating…my death…at the hands of the Humaniks. There's something you should know. It came to me in a flash of enlightenment after I felt the stab of the death rod: The Humaniks have killed me for a special reason. Not because they dislike falcons…or wish to save you from us. No. They want to save you because…because they want you for themselves…"

"How do you mean…for themselves? For what?"

No answer. The falcon's distressed eyes had shut. Its head slumped to one side and the quivering of its vast body stopped. It lay perfectly still. The once feared bird had a peaceful air to it, Tipsy reflected. He was struck by the dignity and majesty of his composed hooded head, his proud blood-spattered breast, and the prominent beak that faced upward…towards the sky that had been his unchallenged domain.

Tipsy translated his final words, which were greeted with a grim and stunned silence. "They want us for themselves" Fr Buck repeated sombrely, "like the dear ones they snatched and took across the sea…"

The simmering hostility towards the falcon had abated, giving way, Tipsy thought, to concern about what those enemies on the Big Island had in store for them. One by one, they departed the death scene quietly; heads bowed, and reverted to their homes… in the hills, in the fields, on the cliffs, by the lake, in the stony ruins, and in the caves on the far side of the island.

***

43

There was gritty steel in the eyes of the grossly overweight bald sweating man, weightier even than Waxy, who stood to address the meeting of coursing clubs.

He wore a black suit, in keeping, Waxy thought, with the bleak solemnity of the occasion. His lower lip and his flapping jowls quivered as he surveyed the large attendance.

Clearing his threat, he spoke at first in a low, sombre, wheezy voice. "As you know ladies and gentlemen, our beloved sport of coursing…our right to take those runners designed by God to perform for us and keep us amused…enthralled...in the winter months when otherwise most of us would be bored out of our minds and at risk of losing our sanity in the wind and the rain and frost and the snow…this great sport now faces…a clear and present danger, as they say in those Hollywood films."

He paused to quench his thirst with a half pint of cider. He slurped loudly, the microphone amplifying every swallow.

He continued, raising his voice: "Except this is not a silly episode from a movie. This is real. Ignorant people, idiots who care nothing for our cherished traditions, want to stop us from setting greyhounds, those fine elegant dogs we love so much, after hares. They moan and whine about how the …the poor hares they call them…get knocked about or killed. They wring their hands about the screams of the hares.

"I ask you…in a world where wars rage and famine abounds and the price of beer and cigarettes may be increased in the next budget, and we're expected not to have a few drinks when we drive…among other calamities, why would any sane, right minded person be worried about what happens to a few bloody hares?"

Loud cheering, wolf whistles, and banging of feet on the floorboards greeted his words.

He motioned for silence. "Only complete spacers…hippies…bunny huggers of the most ignorant sort would take away our God-given right to make hares pay their way in this world. Why, my trusty colleagues, should hares not serve us, us hard working men and women, instead of just sitting around all day and all night washing their whiskers... idling their useless lives away...staring in front of them...sleeping by day and mooching around like pookas by night?

"Did you know that hares die of boredom? Oh yes. I've heard that in countries that don't have coursing they've been seen jumping from cliffs and lying in front of cars, craving an end to it all. They've nothing to live for, no challenge to make their lives worthwhile. We give them that challenge! We, the coursing clubs of Ireland.

"No Irish Hare ever even *contemplates* suicide. Why? Because he knows that we have a job for him…that he was put on this earth by the great God above to outrun, or be dispatched by, our dogs. If hares in other lands heard about our coursing…why they'd raise their furry paws to Heaven and BEG to join their Irish brethren on the coursing fields of this land!"

Thunderous applause: Chairs overturned, glasses of beer crashed to the floor, splintering. Shards flew and lodged in the smoke stained ceiling. Thin streams of blood trickled from foreheads and ruddy cheeks. But nobody complained about the small cuts inflicted.

Waxy covered his ears to muffle the high octave clamour of euphoria. He'd heard all this before. Rabblerousing speeches were fine. But beyond the confines of this hall, he knew, others were watching and waiting for the big showdown in parliament: Devious enemies who'd stop at nothing to deprive these decent folk of their pastime.

A man in front of him leaped to his feet and shrieked; his fist clenched: "Let the politicians hear that, by jeepers…then they'll see coursing is here to stay!"

Another roared "The hares want coursing. If only hares could talk...they'd kiss our asses for what we do for them. The politicians must be told this…that we are the best friend the hares ever had. They love us! And they love coursing!"

Waxy rose, and tried to make himself head above the babble of voices. The chairman roared: "Silence...let Waxy speak!"

"Thank you!" Gesturing towards the assembly he spoke slowly, his words suffused with sadness: "I admire your passion, your love of the game...but listen, you need to let the lads up in Dublin see how much you care about coursing, and how much the hares appreciate what we do for them. You must fight the antis at every turn..."

He halted, his voice choking with emotion. Then he continued. "None of us believed, in the halcyon days of our sport, that our opponents would ever gain ground. But they did. We laughed at them, at their tattered placards and their foghorns…their insulting slogans…as we passed them on our way to and from coursing. We laughed because we knew they were talking nonsense. But others, including at first a few politicians, started to listen to them.

"And then they visited the schools, poisoning the minds of our young with their bunny-hugging propaganda. And yes…they made progress. And we continued to ignore them…we toddled along dreamy-eyed, thinking they would just go away. Well, we see where that attitude has got us…to the point, where, unless we can, if you'll excuse the expression, pull one mighty big rabbit out of the biggest hat in the country, hare coursing in Ireland could be tossed onto the rubbish heap like the other great sports of the past.

"Without us, hares will expire like withered leaves. With no greyhounds to chase them, they'll go completely mad first, attacking humans, snatching babies from prams, invading our towns and cities like Space Aliens. But that burst of activity will be short lived. When they realise that coursing is gone forever, they'll pack it in, ladies and gentlemen. The Irish Hare will become well and truly extinct, like the Dodo. Will you let that happen?"

A thunderous boom erupted again. It seemed to rise from the very bowels of the earth itself. The floorboards creaked loudly, glasses and newspaper supplements were flung at the walls, and chairs toppled over as the entire assembly rose in a surge of outrage.

"Never...never...never!" They roared with one voice.

"Bloody ungrateful hares" another howled, eliciting more cheering and back clapping. A stampede mentality quickly seized the gathering and stewards had to slap the faces of frenzied delegates and douse them with water to calm them

Waxy sighed. How could it have come to this? And what was all this talking going to achieve? Hot air was fine for pumping up balloons, but it wouldn't save coursing when those anti politicians made their move in parliament.

The next speaker, a thin red-faced man with a patch over one eye, was on his feet, shaking a fist, ashes flying from his cigarette onto the floor.

He repeated most of what the previous speaker had said, ending with: "A great monk… or maybe he was a saint…anyway, he prophesised…that if coursing was ever banned in Ireland, the end of the world would quickly follow. And those damned anti-blood sports hippies would be to blame…"

Cries of "Dead Right", and "No Way" filled the hall.

A man two spaces to the left of Waxy rose. "Those politicians always backed us in the past when coursing was under attack, why should it be any different this time?"

The microphone crackled behind the rostrum as the chairman took control of proceedings. "Now, now, my dear sporting colleagues...patience. We may yet win the vote. We must keep lobbying. Don't stop making phone-calls. Visit your local politicians, in every part of this gorgeous country of ours. No let-up. The antis have got to this point by lobbying. We must now show that we can do it better..."

Waxy was only half listening at this stage. Already four high ranking officials of the National Hare Coursing Association had addressed the concerned coursers from all over Ireland in a desperate effort to motivate them to campaign even harder against that accursed Bill.

Oh yes, there had been other Bills in parliament introduced by crazy politicians in an effort to ban hare coursing. *Misguided idiots!* Those Bills had all been defeated: Easily rejected because a majority of the members of the Irish Parliament had favoured setting fine Irish dogs after those wily hares. They'd seen and appreciated the skills of the dogs and understood that hares were created by God to be chased at Irish coursing events.

So, yes, the politicians opposed to hare coursing had ranted and raved about cruelty and compassion and said all sorts of nasty things about this great sport. But when it came to a vote in parliament the anti side always lost.

But that was all about to change, unless...*unless what?*

Waxy added up the numbers again: 75MPs would vote for a ban on hare coursing next week, 74 would vote against the ban. Unless two politicians could be persuaded to switch sides it was bye-bye hare coursing. The thought of that cut through him like a knife.

***

44

Tipsy sat facing the Golden Hare in the strangely illuminated cave. It ought to be dark, as black as the night sky. Yet the walls exuded a faint but perceptible glow.

And then there was the shimmering aura that radiated from His Eminence. *What could he want with me? Did I break some rule when we all gathered for the meeting? Maybe I inadvertently jumped the queue. That hare standing guard was so strict. He might have lodged a complaint.*

Tipsy had been escorted here by two hares who'd disrupted a nap he was having down on the beach. He loved nodding off to the soothing backdrop of waves washing ashore. What a lovely rhythm of nature. *So peaceful.*

The two lads refused to answer his questions. "Orders" one had rasped, "the Divine One wishes to see you...immediately!" The terseness and their grim silence as they traversed half the island to reach the sacred place reinforced his concern that he'd done something wrong. Nervously, he opened his mouth to apologise in advance. Before he could utter a word the Wise One harrumphed. Tipsy held his tongue.

"You wonder why I've summoned you?"

"Ye...yes, Your Eminence..."

The faint trace of a smile lightened the Great One's countenance. "Be at your ease...I called for you because you, Tipsy, are a special hare. I have known of your importance since your emergence into this world..."

He paused. Tipsy couldn't restrain himself. "In what way am I special? I mean, Your Eminence...I am just a humble hare..."

The smile widened a little. "Tell me, Tipsy; is it not true that you can, with ease, communicate with other creatures on this island...the birds, the butterflies...even the fish that live in the ocean?"

"Yes...that's true." *Where is this going?*

The Great One gestured with his front paws, his snow-white teeth flashing momentarily. "Apart from myself, there is no other hare...on this island, or anywhere in the entire world, that has that ability."

"I didn't know that, Your Eminence."

"It marks you out as special, unique, but that is not all. You can see the aura that surrounds my earthly form?"

"Yes, and I saw it when we all gathered here to meet you about the Humanik invasion."

The Great One raised a paw pointedly. "None of the other hares could perceive the radiance. To them the cave was as black as night and they had to adjust to its darkness in the normal way. My aura is visible to you, Tipsy, because you are partially clairvoyant. This enables you, in certain circumstances, to see with your inner eye…."

Tipsy recalled his glimpse of Bumble's spirit after she fell to her death from the cliff. And occasionally he'd noticed bluish wisps in the vicinity of recently expired hares.

The Golden Hare continued: "You have other powers, as yet undeveloped, that could in the near future prove beneficial to you and other hares. I will enlighten you further on the subject at our next meeting. Right now, I want to show you something. I want to share with you the knowledge of our proud heritage."

The aura beamed brighter, tiny effervescent globules popping at its edges. His voice took on a more solemn tone. "Hares have been on this planet for a very long time and we have endured the toughest of trials...."

He averted his gaze and indicated a small pile of different coloured berries to Tipsy's left. "Eat those and wait for them to take effect."

Tipsy shuffled over to the red, yellow, and green orbs. He had never seen such berries. They must be rare ones that grew only in the vicinity of the cave. No sooner had he digested the last berry (they tasted a little bitter but not unpleasant) when everything went hazy.

"I can't see or feel my body!" he cried with alarm.

The partial illumination vanished. Darkness enveloped.

The great one spoke: "Tipsy! Listen to my voice. We hares are timid for a reason...so we can learn the lesson of fear...what it is and how, if we wish and make a supreme effort, we can overcome it. Very few ever do. The obstacles are enormous...the world unforgiving and too cruel...

"You and I, and the others on this island and the Big Island across the sea, are Irish Hares. We go back a long way, Tipsy. Look!"

The darkness faded, slowly morphing to a vast whiteness. Tipsy felt himself swaying, but he didn't fall, which was just as well he thought as everywhere around him was...*ice and snow.* A blizzard was blowing, like the one the older hares said had swept the island many heartbeats ago. But this didn't look like the island. Was he dreaming?

You are not imagining.

The voice of the Golden Hare was loud and distinct. It seemed to resonate inside his own head and yet come from somewhere outside also...from the sky that was barely visible through the white snowflakes that swirled about so thickly, accompanied by a cheerless whining and whistling of winds.

The ground underneath him swayed and vibrated. It was slippery and shiny and he saw his reflection in it. He was standing on a rocky surface, though it felt icy.

Then, through a maelstrom of howling winds and splattering snow a clearing opened up. As he watched awestruck it gradually widened as if part of the blizzard that seemed to convulse the whole world was being peeled back.

Through the cavity he saw that he was perched on top of a promontory or a hill that stretched high into the sky. And he was peering over the edge of this ...through the hole that had appeared in the whirligig of searing whiteness.

The opening widened to create a 360 degree view for him. What he saw took his breath away... though he wasn't aware of himself breathing in this strange trance or dreamlike condition.

Beneath him and stretching on all sides around the hill or raised surface upon which he sat were enormous sheets of slowly moving ice. His eyes swivelled to take in the all-conquering power of this advancing glacial menace that swept away living creatures and living space.

The great icy invaders, though they had no sentient life of their own, creaked and hissed and stirred nauseatingly and seemed to whisper up to him. "You defy us...you are timid and yet you survive!"

Tipsy felt elated at the compliment from that terrifying force of nature that held the world in its grip. He steadied himself to ensure he didn't slip from his perch. If he lost his balance, he feared, he'd plunge headlong down. Be swallowed up by that earth-shattering transformation unfolding below and around him.

Funny that he didn't feel cold, with all that snow and ice and howling winds.

The Golden Hare's voice intoned: *This was home to our species countless heartbeats in the past, so far back that Humaniks were fewer than today and lacked the power to hurt us. They had yet to make their appearance on the large island of Ireland, where your ancestors hail from, Tipsy. Yes, they lived on the great island before some of them were taken here on a ship.*

"A ship"?

Yes, you saw the boats? A ship is a very large boat that Humaniks travel in when they wish to cross the waters of the world to reach other places and other Humaniks.

The scene around him speeded up. The ice melted quickly as if the sun had suddenly appeared. Its rays must have banished it from the earth. Humaniks were strutting about, wearing dead animals...or was it the skins of animals...as they skulked forward awkwardly?

The scene changed again: Hares that had been sitting around a mountainside munching on sallies and pincushion moss suddenly dropped to the earth and remained still. Little rods or sticks protruded from their bodies.

Observe and learn, the Wise One intoned.

Tipsy saw Humaniks approach the hares and sling them over their shoulders, blood dripping from the limp bodies. How awful! Tipsy moaned. He saw Humaniks turning the dead hares over a blazing fire, flames licking at the roasting flesh.

The scene speeded up. This time hares that were peacefully grazing suddenly tensed and collapsed. Humaniks then picked them up. They'd died from some unspecified ailment. Each death was accompanied by a sharp cracking sound.

"Enough!" Tipsy pleaded. "Why are you showing me all this, Why are those Humaniks doing this to us?"

There's more, announced the disembodied voice.

A loud clip-clopping sound pounded in Tipsy's ears. Another weird vista: Strange powerful four-legged creatures that Tipsy had never seen before dashed across a landscape dotted with fields, ditches and stone walls. Humaniks were mounted on them, attired in blood-red coverings.

Not all. Some were draped in black and their head patches were enwrapped. Then, Tipsy saw dozens of smaller creatures running in front of the ones bearing the Humaniks. These were yelping and howling, louder than the island birds.

And way out in front of them all a solitary hare ran; his motions frantic and frightful.

Tipsy saw him up close. The hare was terrified. His eyes bulged. His head throbbed.

Well, that's no surprise, Tipsy thought, *with that many creatures after him.*

"Why"; Tipsy asked, "Why are all those creatures chasing him? Do all those Humaniks and those peculiar entities think they can get a piece of him to eat?"

Not to eat thundered the Wise One. *Humaniks do this because it makes them happy.*

"Happy? You mean like when we play in the fields, chasing each other?"

Observe, the voice commanded. The hare, tiring of the chase, slowed down and the creatures caught up with him, their tongues lolling and their jaws snapping at air in anticipation of a kill.

One snatched at his tail and another sank its teeth into his back. The hare wailed. Several more of the creatures fought to reach the hare, whose screeching abated.

It must be dead, Tipsy thought. He could no longer see the hare, as his view was obstructed by the predators that seemed to be locked in a mad frenzy, vying with each other to devour the body.

"I don't understand", Tipsy gasped.

The voice explained: *Those creatures are what Humaniks call dogs. They use them to attack us for their amusement.*

"Now I've definitely seen enough", Tipsy cried, "Can I go home?"

There's more, grumbled the Golden Hare.

A hare emerged from a little square wooden structure and darted across a field. Two creatures- those dog things again- appeared seemingly out of nowhere, quickly closing on the hare. The dogs wore funny masks over their mouths. But this didn't slow them down. "Run faster!" Tipsy shouted at the hare, but the creature couldn't hear him across the immensity of time and space.

One of the dogs nudged the hare and he seemed to take flight, soaring into the air like a bird, but, unlike a bird, he fell back to earth again. Finding his feet, the hare resumed his frantic dash, and Tipsy thought he might elude his pursuers.

But alas...the second dog gained on him and nuzzled him to the ground. The hare was injured, but limped along. Both dogs began to maul him. A Humanik suddenly appeared, separating the dogs from the hare. He sprinted away from the dogs, holding the still live hare by the back legs.

The scene switched to a patch of ground behind the wall that skirted the field. The Humanik was beating the hare against the wall. Tipsy heard a muffled thud with each impact. The hare stopped screeching.

Tipsy tried to shut his eyes against the unfolding horrors. But he couldn't. Then he remembered: He wasn't in his body. This was some kind of dream.

Not a dream said the Wise One. *This is what Humaniks do to hares. It was necessary for you see this, Tipsy. Here on the island you have to stay alert for predatory birds. Just one enemy to contend with; and it's the helpless leverets that the falcon mainly takes. On the large island, there are others: dogs, wild dogs called foxes, more predatory birds, and worse of all, the Humaniks. Or to be precise, Humaniks using other creatures to help them in their quest to hurt us. Being torn between dogs is a truly painful way to exit this world.*

We can die quickly if the fire-spitting rods are aimed properly at us, I have learned, though when this doesn't happen a hare suffers a prolonged and horrible death. We have scant influence in the world. Humaniks rule and they do what they wish to us.

"Humaniks!" Tipsy objected, crying out in his trance-like state, his voice inaudible to himself. "They must be the most evil creatures on earth. If only they didn't exist."

Tipsy heard a sigh...

Not all of them.

"You mean there are good Humaniks?"

It's complicated...there are Humaniks who want to protect us hares...to stop the cruel stupid ones from tormenting us. I have been granted a vision of these compassionate ones. They struggle to make themselves heard. They try to persuade the Humaniks who control the large island called Ireland to ease our predicament.

In our next session Tipsy I will explain why I showed you all this. You are a special hare, as I've told you. You have a purpose in life. A mission. One that can, if you succeed, change the way Humaniks see us and maybe how they treat us as well.

45

Waxy rose slowly to his feet and the microphone was passed down to him. Every pair of eyes at the latest *Save Hare Coursing* conference was fixed on him.

Good. He had their undivided attention.

A spontaneous round of applause erupted, and some delegates broke into cheering.

"Thank you...I appreciate your sympathy and support. Like all of you, I am today staring into the abyss. If this Bill succeeds a whole way of life will be gone. A tradition handed down to us by generations of coursers and hare-catchers will be tossed on to the rubbish heap. Never again will we stand shoulder to shoulder and watch those sprightly greyhounds put the fear of God into those lithesome hares.

"Never again will we place bets or drink whiskey on a frosty winter afternoon as dogs pursue hares in accordance with the will of the Saints and Angels in Heaven who all, Father Flynn has assured me, support coursing from on-high..."

More shouting and cheering. Waxy motioned for silence. This was his moment. There was something they needed to hear, and understand.

"Those politicians...the ones who plan to vote for a ban on coursing. I wonder just how committed they are to that course of action..."

The chairman interrupted. "It's on knife-edge Waxy, but we know that most of the 75 anti coursing MPs are determined to see it through. They've made that clear in correspondence and in response to phone-calls. There are three of them who aren't as strong-minded about the whole thing, but they've said they'll be voting for the ban.

"They know how strong our case is...we've told them a hundred times in the last three weeks, from the day we heard about the Bill to ban hare coursing, that Ireland will never be the same again if they back the antis. We've made it clear that the hares themselves enjoy being chased. It's what both God and evolution equipped them to do. But so far there's no sign of those lukewarm politicians converting to our cause..."

"So far..." Waxy intoned, putting great emphasis on the two words.

He held the microphone closer to his lips. "Tell me, delegates, have any of you ever known a hare that didn't smack his lips when a juicy carrot was dangled in front of him?"

Every man shook his head vigorously.

"And did any of you ever see a politician's response when a carrot..."

The chairman's microphone crackled: "Now, now Waxy...careful there. We have a reputation to uphold. Any lobbying we do must be above board. We must win over the MPs by cogent argument and the strength of our case for coursing...."

Waxy apologised. "Yes, delegates, we must pray to the Patron Saint of Hunting, and...and...make further polite phone-calls to our politicians, in the hope that they'll see sense and abandon this daft notion of banning coursing..."

Deafening applause.

When the meeting ended, Waxy didn't stay behind to chat with coursers from others parts of the country he hadn't seen in years. Summoning three fellow members of Ballycrossways Coursing Club, he swept out of the hall and the four of them boarded a four-wheeled drive parked outside.

A light sea breeze unsettled his hair, causing him to gaze momentarily in the direction of the island. He smiled to himself.

Those idiots can lobby all they want, or put their faith in the power of prayer. I know exactly how to save coursing from the chopping block, and it's not by using honeyed words to persuade politicians how marvellous we coursing folk are. There's another language they understand much better, one that was in vogue long before speech itself was invented...

***

46

Tipsy was more relaxed this time as he made his way, accompanied by two hares, to the cave.

For some reason his escorts were less taciturn than last time. Bouncer and Sedge: The hares who stood guard at the entrance to the most exalted hare; not just here on the island, but possibly in all of creation.

They weren't exactly the brightest, Tipsy noted. It was their brawn... their superior physique; that elicited respect from all the hares on the island. Not that they were bullies or moronic fellows. They cherished their role as Guardians of the Golden Hare.

They chatted affably with Tipsy, joked about near misses with the falcon, the silly fishes that allowed the gulls to grab them from the sea when they could easily elude them underwater and the behaviour of their unbelievably demanding hare girlfriends in recent days. Every subject and whim was explored and remarked on...except the purpose of this meeting with His Eminence.

He had a vague idea that it would be a continuation of what the Wise One had discussed and shown him via that weird vision on the previous occasion: The long, meandering, action-packed, never a dull moment history of the Irish Hare...our purpose in life and all that.

Important stuff, no question about that...but all I really want to do is live happily here on the island, hopefully find a suitable girlfriend like those two guys, and become father to a family of sprightly leverets.

Somehow, though, he suspected that the enlightened hare of hares, he who dwelt in that shadowy sacred cave and communed with Ostara day and night, had other plans.

He told me I was special. Yeah, that's nice. But what does Ostara, or the Golden Hare, have in mind for me? What can I possibly do to change things...to make life better for hares? I can't force the other hares to act...or think...differently. I can't transfer my own superior speed to them, or my ability to talk to all other creatures except Humaniks.

"Gone all quiet on us, Tipsy?"

Sedge's voice pierced his skull.

He laughed. "No, just wondering what he wants from me. It's an honour to be called, but the suspense is getting to me!"

The two escorts stopped their chattering and looked away, embarrassed smiles distorting their features.

Bouncer quipped: "That's not for us to know, Tipsy. He must have a high opinion of you. That's enough for us to know. He doesn't wake up every day and summon a hare to meet him. He goes hundreds of sunsets without even speaking. He says nothing...He stirs and moves his lips only after several hundred dawns have passed and the same number of twilights. Hey, you must be special, like he says..."

Tipsy cuffed Bouncer playfully. "Maybe he's going to promote me to assistant head honcho on the island. You'd better be nice to me!"

Bouncer laughed, but a shade nervously and without any visible enthusiasm. Sedge chuckled: "If you do...get promoted...put in a good word for us Tipsy. Don't get me wrong. We're grateful for our positions...but, it's always nice to be appreciated. Ostara willing, we might progress further...become super hares like His Eminence."

Bouncer scowled. Sedge reverted to his natural timid nature. "Sorry, I was getting a bit carried away there. I'd never dream of taking over from the Golden Hare. I mean...all that responsibility. No. I like being a common Irish Hare in a place where no Humaniks dwell...apart from that awful time."

He fell silent. They approached the cave, the entrance to which was bathed in moonlight. It was almost as if the great Lunar Orb was lighting the way to his future...to whatever the Great One inside had in mind for him.

The cave looked different this time. Yes. It had that faint pulsing illumination from the walls. Tipsy noticed it when he drew closer to the inner chamber where His Eminence dwelt. But the additional light that normally radiated from the Golden Hare was missing.

Not entirely. But it was much weaker. Instead, tonight, the Great One had a gentler aura that exuded soft swirling colours and shades that vibrated at a slower rate. And his normally austere countenance had mellowed to a benign, compassionate demeanour.

Tipsy felt rays of love and deep understanding wash over him as he approached the hollowed-out Rock of Divinity upon which this mysterious creature was seated. He hadn't seen the throne before, probably because of the brilliance of the auric kaleidoscope within which the Great One normally sat like a miniature sun or shining star. Now, the atmosphere was less formal.

Was this a good omen? Tipsy had his doubts. Here goes: "You wished to see me, Eminence?"

A broad benevolent smile cracked and smoothed its way across the Russet Brown face, a purple halo suffused with flashes of gold appeared around his head and those penetrating eyes shimmered and twinkled like drops of deep watery blue from the ocean.

"Tipsy. Welcome. Have some berries. Don't worry. Those won't draw you into trance. Those are for taste and sustenance."

"Thank you" Tipsy edged to the little pile of berries. He had never seen ones like them before. He took three in one gulp. *Delicious!*

Digesting them, he moved back into position, facing his hallowed host. The halo had gone from purple shot through with flickerings of orange to almost pure gold, but was still semitransparent, the luminous cave wall behind being clearly visible.

His Eminence nodded graciously. "Tipsy, on our last encounter you saw, with a little help from me, some of the highlights of the long journey of the Irish Hare, our unique species, through the ages. We are the great survivors. Other creatures have succumbed to the whims of nature and the relentless interventions and never-ending malevolence of the Humaniks. We have survived despite our timidity; the very trait that, according to other creatures should have doomed us to extinction.

"We Irish Hares, like hares all over the world, are renowned, though also scorned, for being gentle, non-aggressive. We run or hide to avoid danger. Humaniks prey upon us as other creatures do, but for different reasons. On the Big Island, hares have to outrun, and hide from, foxes, stoats, even cats...though cats rarely cause us trouble. They'd like to eat us but we're too strong for them!

"On the Big Island, hares have, as elsewhere in the world, evolved ways of fending off those predators. But one predator we have not managed to elude. The Humanik. He has power over all the species in the world, and he abuses that power gleefully and at the slightest whim..."

The Golden Hare paused, lowered his mouth to sip at water that flowed from a crevice in the cave wall into a slit in the ground at his feet. Tipsy wondered where this talk was going. It was interesting hearing about how hares had survived the manifold threats to their wellbeing down the ages, but what had any of this to do with him?

His Eminence continued. "You remember what the Humaniks did to us? Your mother was among those taken into captivity when they came in their wooden vessels to the island. This brings me to why I summoned you. You, Tipsy, are endowed with special abilities. You are aware of some of these: You outrun every other hare on the island. Your speed is known and spoken about equally by young and old among us. It draws gasps of admiration and disbelief. Not only can you run faster than the others... You can leap higher, see over vast distances, and with greater clarity...is this not so?"

"Yes...I haven't given much thought to it, Great One, but it's true..."

"And there is your truly remarkable gift of communication. You can converse fluently with all other creatures, except Humaniks..."

"True, I appreciate that gift. I thank Ostara for the privilege..."

The Great One purred audibly. "Before twenty sunsets have blessed the island, other skills and powers will be yours. Foremost among them will be the ability to render yourself invisible to predators who threaten you. You will achieve this by making direct eye-contact with them. From the moment you gaze into the eyes of an adversary, he will not be able to see you for one hundred heartbeats. You will create a blind-spot around your body for the duration of the spell. Also, you will soon be capable of receiving messages and visitations from me...in lucid dreams. You will always heed my counsel and act upon it..."

He paused again, and Tipsy took advantage of this to speak his mind.

"Your Eminence... I will treasure these gifts from above, but will it be necessary to deploy such abilities? I mean, apart from falcons, and at least one of them died recently, we have little to fear from predators..."

"On the island, yes, we are fortunate. But beyond this, our home, the opposite is true, as I have already emphasised. Tipsy, you have been gifted with these special powers for a reason. I have to tell you that the Humaniks who brought grief and terror to the island...will return. In a vision I have been shown this calamity. As before they will land with their vessels, encroach on our homes and feeding places, and, as before; they will take hares away to the Big Island..."

Tipsy's heart fell. He felt a sickening rumble in his stomach. Thoughts of his mother's abduction returned. Of the long despair and grief that hovered over the island like the blackest rain-cloud for so many sunsets afterwards.

Slowly, sombrely, he said: "So, your Eminence, I'm presuming I would be expected to help the others evade capture...or somehow thwart the Humaniks..."

The Golden Hare's demeanour changed. A sad frown replaced his benevolent pensive gaze: "To thwart the Humaniks, yes, and to help your fellow Irish Hares...but not here on the island. No. The Higher Spirits...hares who have long since departed this troublesome world, have decreed that you be tasked with a mission, one that will take you beyond the island. You must go to the Big Island. There you will be shown a way to strike a blow for the oppressed hares of that land. In doing so, you will of course be helping the island hares too. This mission is of the utmost importance, my guides assure me. They stress that it could fail, but that it stands a reasonable chance of success..."

Tipsy saw a major snag. "If I could, I would gladly act on behalf of the hares on the Big Island, but I cannot reach that place. My special powers do not include the ability to swim that far. I would drown before I reached my destination..."

"This is the difficult part Tipsy. You are free to opt out if you wish. The plan is that you allow yourself to be captured when the Humaniks return. When you arrive on the Big Island you will know what to do. I will send you guidance as required or where possible. You will have the prayers and blessings and divine invocations of saintly hares in the spirit realms. Certain events will unfold, I am told, on the Big Island. I do not know what those developments will be, as they involve the Humaniks and their alien ways, but my guides insist that *you* can play a role in some crucial turn of events that will ease the plight of hares on the Big Island..."

Another pause, this time accompanied by a tear dropping from the left eye of the Golden Hare, giving the eye the appearance of a little pool of blue water. *Strange, never thought of him as having emotions...*

"Tipsy, my guides say that you have been chosen by Ostara herself, to help deliver her beloved ones from the terrors and unnatural enslavements that Humaniks inflict on the hares of Ireland...and on those stolen from our own island. You are not under any obligation to accept this mission. Should you opt not to; I will respect your decision and never raise the matter again with you. You will be free to live the remainder of your life here on the island, like the other hares..."

"I accept."

Tipsy couldn't believe he'd just said that. *Damn it.* He couldn't say otherwise.

***

47

Waxy sat disconsolately with Bonzo and Slapper, facing Joey the Fixer Lannigan's mahogany desk. Their reflections gazed back at them from the freshly polished front surface.

They'd been waiting in the consultation room of the politician's clinic, located on the edge of the Peninsula with a pleasant view of the ocean, for more than twenty minutes. They whispered, fidgeted and sporadically glanced at the clock on the wall, listening to its relentless tick-tocking in the otherwise unruffled silence.

The secretary had let them into the room and asked them to be patient, explaining that the parliamentary representative for Broc Peninsula and the Islands, was a busy man. He'd been delayed on his visit to needy constituents and the official opening of a fake fur-shop on the opposite end of his electoral district.

Waxy had looked uneasily around as the three muttered nervously; a bit like those fellows in the back row of the church who couldn't wait for Mass to end. He suspected the room was bugged, and that the whole aim of keeping folk waiting was to record what they said, so that Lannigan would know what people really thought of him, the idea being to enable the wily politician to change his policies and adjust his speeches and sound-bites accordingly to ensure his continued popularity and guarantee his re-election.

But part of him scoffed at this suspicion, reasoning that Lannigan wouldn't be that devious, whatever about his famed political skills and charm. He had a knack for seeming to be everybody's friend, which was why the hare coursing fraternity was incredulous when he indicated he'd be voting for the abolition of their sport.

If Mister-All-things-to-all-Men-Lannigan was prepared to vote against hare coursing, then the sport was in serious trouble. But Waxy knew Lannigan wouldn't be comfortable about voting that way. The antis must have hoodwinked him into believing there were more votes to be won by opposing the sport than backing it.

And he might just be right. A survey of people in the *Broc Peninsula and the Islands* constituency a few weeks earlier found that a narrow majority of respondents favoured a ban on hare coursing. But the narrowness of the margin would have Lannigan dithering somewhat. Waxy was sure the politician could at least be persuaded to abstain in the parliamentary vote, and he would have been happy just a few days ago to see him do that.

But now that wasn't enough. The numbers intending to vote for and against the anti hare- coursing Bill had tightened, and coursing fans faced the alarming prospect of a knife-edged result, with maybe an exact number on both sides, or a win by a margin of one or two for the pro or anti-coursing side, allowing for last minute defections from either camp. Uncertainty and anxiety had coursing fans nationwide on tenterhooks. Lannigan must not be let abstain. He must take a stand.

Waxy felt the nudge at his elbow. Bonzo whispered: "What if he doesn't go for it? Or if...he reports us?"

Waxy groaned: "He won't. He's a politician. There's a risk. But what choice do we have? Our necks are on the block. We need his vote or the antis just might...*win*...this time. It's going down to the wire, lads. Even with Lannigan's support we may lose, but without him hare coursing is finished, and if that happens Ireland itself will be finished."

Waxy reminded them again of the martyr who predicted that if coursing were ever stopped here, the island of Ireland would be submerged seven years later in a flood. Nobody would be spared.

Slapper whistled softly. "God, we can't let that happen, lads."

Bonzo said nothing, just stared up at the clock. Waxy was about to pontificate further on the geomorphic and scatological implications of a coursing ban when the doorknob squeaked and turned slowly after a curt knock.

Waxy and his two colleagues straightened their ties, dusted off their jackets, and assumed sombre expressions. *It's now or never*, thought Waxy, uttering a quick prayer to the Patron Saint of Hunting without moving his lips.

Lannigan was shorter and more corpulent than he appeared in his election posters, Waxy thought, when the politician entered. He cast a shifty glance at his three constituents before slowly turning around to close the door behind him.

Lannigan had gained weight since Waxy saw him last at the hare coursing fundraising disco and buffet two years earlier. He hadn't attended last year's event- cute operator- to avoid offending the anti-coursing lobby.

He was sweating and puffing, as though he had just finished a lively sprint to his office, though his huge mop of bushy brown hair was perfectly sprayed in place. He looked tense and uncomfortable.

In those few seconds when he turned to shut the door, he was probably already scheming and sizing up these...to him, gullible fools. Politicians were always sizing up people and situations to deduce where their own personal advantage lay.

Well, *they* wouldn't be the fools today if Lannigan took the bait.

The tension and furrowed brow disappeared when he ogled the three of them from behind his desk and pulled out his seat. A broad smile and hearty laugh sent waves of warmth and friendliness towards the lads. Waxy felt better already.

"Great to see ye...Waxy, you're looking great. And Bonzo... is the used car business still thriving? Gosh, Slapper, I'm sorry I missed your daughter's wedding last month. You know how it is, I can't be everywhere. If I could, I'd be like that saint...what's his name...he used to say mass in two places at the one time. Anyway, what can I do for ye?"

Lannigan slumped into his black leather swinging chair, his podgy laced fingers moist from the sweat. His beady watery green blood-shot eyes had narrowed to slits. They focused uneasily on Waxy at first; then switched attention fleetingly to his two colleagues, before fixing Waxy with a slightly worried look.

Waxy knew well that Lannigan knew why they were there- and what would be on offer- but he opted to be tactful. Clearing his throat and leaning towards the desk, he spoke reverentially. "Well, Joey, It's about the vote in parliament...on the anti-hare coursing Bill..."

Lannigan interrupted with an emphatic cough, closed his eyes and sat back, raising his hands in exasperation. "Lads, I can save ye a lot of time. Forget it. I've given my commitment to the Animal Welfare League and the Society for the Abolition of Blood Sports. I have to support the Bill."

His eyelids fluttered, fresh beads of sweat breaking out on his forehead and cheeks and seeming to drip in tiny rivulets from around his ears. His hands shot out as if about to catch a ball.

"Now don't get me wrong lads. You know I have great sympathy for coursing. I remember those long nights in O' Gorman's and the all the other pubs on the Peninsula, singing the hunting songs and...and ye do remember I bought drinks to beat the band. I launched those benefit nights for coursing..."

He stopped abruptly, as if he had run out of breath. A tuft of his hair had broken loose and was hanging recklessly over one eye. He tried to blow it back but it kept falling down. His tongue clicked. "That was then lads, but this is now..."

He hung his head, as if in shame, Waxy thought.

Avoiding eye-contact, he continued: "Times are changing lads. Coursing has been banned across the water...who thought the British would ban it? And above in the Six Counties people in all the political parties who seldom agree on anything...came together to end...such a lovely sport. Sorry lads."

Lannigan snuffled and Waxy saw the tears begin to form in his eyes. Slapper stood and extended a paper tissue to him. "Thanks" he lisped, I'm okay, give me a minute..."

Waxy shifted uncomfortably in his chair. *What a born conniver. I wonder if he had a slice of onion ready for that little act!*

After blowing his nose, a spray of snot narrowly avoiding his constituents, and wiping away his tears, he held up his hands: "I'm okay now. Look, lads, there are times when a politician has to vote for things he would never in a month of Sundays want to support...but that's politics...The folks out there...not just in the big cities and towns...but now, even here on the Peninsula, don't want hares running from dogs in wired enclosures any more. I know...it's a smaller majority for the antis here in this neck of the woods, but it's still a majority. And lads, I don't have a choice but to go with the feelings of the people who...the people I represent. It's not that I'm afraid of losing votes, God no. It's that I have to respect the views of the majority..."

Waxy leaned forward. He forced himself to adopt a respectful tone. "Joey, we appreciate your position. It's a desperate dilemma right enough. You know I've always voted for you Joey and all the lads in the club have too. And our friends and relatives. And we voted for your father and grandfather when they stood for the party. Can I ask you something, Joey, and this is in the complete confidence of this clinic, you understand?"

Lannigan nodded, a hint of suspicion clouding his features.

Waxy continued: "The election next year will be a close run thing...You've read the surveys and predictions. Your seat will be at risk whether you back the anti-coursing Bill or not. Support for your party is lower in the opinion polls than it's been for decades. So, what I...*we*...were wondering is...could we do something to make life easier for you...you know...cushion you against the bad times that may be coming down the tracks?"

Lannigan slouched in his chair, puzzlement written all over him. Waxy suppressed a smile. Lannigan knew well what was coming. Could it be that he was hoping for it? That he had no notion of supporting the anti-coursing bill when he could so easily abstain if he feared the animal welfare head-bangers? *Careful though. Don't want to offend him. Too much at stake.*

Waxy looked demurely at his two colleagues, then at Lannigan, and gave a delicate cough. "What I have to propose...eh...is strictly confidential. No question of it ever getting beyond these four walls."

Lannigan still looked confused, or pretended too, Waxy surmised, for a moment before directing his attention to his secretary, who was busily typing on a computer to his right, her back turned to them. Lannigan quipped "Ah you wouldn't mind leaving for a while...Susan...take a break. You deserve one. You've been typing all morning. I'll call you when I've completed some delicate business with these gentlemen."

Susan rose; a broad grin enhancing her bright and cheery appearance as she curtly left the office with a sheaf of folders under her arm. "I'll leave ye to it", she chirped.

Waxy was careful to say nothing further until she had gone.

When the door closed, Lannigan relaxed, throwing out his hands. "Well, I'll listen to anything...I'm sorry I have to disappoint you on the coursing lads, but I have to move with the times, and the times are not favourable to the old dog and hare lark..."

Waxy suppressed a strong desire to roar at this...*this Have it Every Way slippery populist.* No time for losing the rag. He forced a smile and concealed his contempt skilfully. He hissed "We...the lads and I here... have a delicate proposal and we make it in good faith. Nobody else knows anything about our proposed arrangement. Not a soul. Definitely nobody on the Executive of the National Coursing League...."

"Lads, I have a busy agenda. Could you maybe...not rushing you now...but could you get to the point?"

Waxy spoke rapidly: "We're anxious to make a private donation to you, Joey. Not to the party, but to you. We feel you deserve it. As I said, things are not looking great for you come the next election. Wouldn't it be nice to have...you know...a little nest-egg to tide you over the lean years that may lie ahead?"

"That's a delicate proposition alright."

The politician fidgeted, opening a drawer and pulling out a packet of cigarettes, removing one for himself and offering the packet to Waxy. Waxy declined; the others also.

Lannigan lit up and began inhaling deeply, blowing smoke at the three of them.

Waxy waved aside the blue wisps, wondering if Lannigan was trying to distract them as he calculated how to respond to what was coming. "We have something for you Joey...and we urge you to accept our...contribution...Bonzo?"

Bonzo reached into a satchel that lay between his feet on the floor and pulled from it a large bulky brown envelope, its contents bulging as if desperate to break through the flimsy paper secreting them. Bonzo handed the envelope to Waxy, who clung to it lovingly as if it contained treasures beyond value.

Lannigan's beady eyes opened wide, and seemed to have increased in size, though Waxy thought that was a mere illusion. His mouth was opening too and his lips quaked.

Waxy stood and opened the envelope. He was poised to let the contents fall unto the desk when Lannigan rose abruptly.

"Just a second." He turned and closed the Venetian blind of the window to the left of the lads that overlooked the main street. Returning to his seat, he raised a trembling hand. "Go on...you were saying..."

Waxy shook the upside-down envelope and onto the desk spilled fat bundles of One Hundred Euro notes.

Lannigan covered his mouth and stared at the cash that lay scattered across his desk as more of it fell from the envelope.

Waxy resumed his seat, and cupped his hands under his chin, moving his tongue thoughtfully between his lips.

Lannigan was staring at the money but not with the kind of enthusiasm one might expect. A tense silence filled the room, eased only by the perpetual distant clamour of seagulls outside and the ticking of the wall-clock.

Nervousness was rising in Waxy. He saw his colleagues too were on edge.

Lannigan then broke what seemed like a long silence but was, Waxy knew, only a few seconds of quiet. As if he'd suddenly resolved a perplexing equation he removed his elbows from the desk and pulled open the top drawer. He made room in it, fidgeting with unseen documents.

Standing to his full height, and without making eye contact with any of the lads, he leaned over the desk, stretched out his arms and began scooping the wads of cash towards himself. They made a soft plopping sound as they dropped into the capacious drawer.

When the desk was clear, he gently pushed the drawer shut. He fixed an uneasy gaze on Waxy.

"Please do not misunderstand...I have accepted a donation. Nothing more. But in fairness I can see how much the outcome of the parliamentary vote on hare coursing means to you. Yes, lads, on reflection I...cannot...in conscience...support a Bill that would...rip something precious from the very soul of Ireland..."

He bowed his head, placed his hands over his face, and looked up, his eyes twinkling. "By God I'll not be the man who kills off a mighty tradition...I'll be absent on the day. I'll have nothing to do with that attack on the greatest sport that God in his infinite wisdom, bequeathed to the Irish nation. Now, lads, if you'll excuse me I have to attend to a dozen commitments...no rest for a servant of the people. You know how it is!"

He began to rise and shake Waxy's hand across the desk, But Waxy didn't move.

Tersely, he said "Ah, Joey, just a minute. Abstaining on the vote would give coursing a slightly better chance, but the Bill might still pass by the narrowest of margins. It could go either way. You wouldn't consider taking a stand...no offence mind...and making sure that the Bill is killed off as it deserves to be...like a lame hare?"

Lannigan had barely opened his mouth, his hand still held in readiness for a shake, when Waxy turned to Bonzo and quipped: "Never let it be said we don't appreciate and reward our friends..."

Bonzo produced, not an envelope, but a large squarish bulky shopping bag. He upended it, and out spilled at least three times more wads of cash than had fallen from the brown envelope.

Lannigan rubbed his forehead and whistled softly. Grinning like a child who's got a new toy, he pulled open a second drawer with a loud squeak and began scooping the money in. He had removed just a few wads from the little cash mountain when Waxy sprang to his feet and pinned Lannigan's hands to the desk.

The politician looked startled and offended. His face reddened. Waxy eased his grip, and let go. Lannigan stood staring at him, raising his eyebrows. "Can I take it Joey that you WILL be voting against the Bill?"

Lannigan said nothing for a few seconds. He switched his attention from one to another of the three men; then looked Waxy straight in the face. Waxy's heart raced. Was this buffoon going to let him down?

Then Lannigan exploded laughing. "Of course I'll oblige ye...take your hands away like a good man Waxy."

Waxy slid back into his chair as Lannigan resumed scooping. He had to open a third drawer to accommodate the remainder of the generous "donation."

When it was all stashed away, he closed the drawer, pushing at it stubbornly. It was creaking, full to overflowing with cash.

Waxy was sure it would burst if Lannigan pushed it any further. "You might need a bag...or other container, Joey..."

Lannigan was puffing with the effort. A final heave and the drawer shut, though with a splintering protest. *Good*, thought Waxy, *that's the sound of our generosity. It's too kind we are.*

Lannigan, relieved, took his hands off the drawer and smiled broadly. He gave a little friendly titter, and then, like an actor changing roles on stage, assumed a grave expression. Leaning forward, Waxy saw his beady eyes narrowing to slits.

Fresh beads of perspiration had broken out on his forehead and shiny cheeks. His hair was leaking grease. He peered to his side at the window as if to double-check that the Venetian blind had been fully closed. His voice quivered and his right arm trembled as he wagged a finger towards them. There was real fear in his voice.

"Do I have your absolute assurance that this ...donation...will *never* be spoken of...to another living person? You do understand that an inference might be drawn that I was influenced in my voting intentions by an inducement. Aside from the fact that the anti-coursing brigade would twist and misrepresent your...big-heartedness... and my support for your cause, the other parties would have me...and my party...for breakfast if this got out...and was misconstrued."

Waxy dismissed his concerns with a flourish. Rising, along with his two colleagues, he used a forefinger to make a zipping gesture across his lips. "We called to lobby our friendly local parliamentarian. And he was moved by the strength of our case for hare coursing. Lads; did either of you see any money change hands in this office?"

Bonzo guffawed, shaking his head.

"Not a cent" lisped Slapper.

Lannigan rose and stepped away from his desk. Hearty handshakes followed. He ushered the men from his office as if their presence posed an immediate threat to him.

Opening the door, he waved them out. "You can count on me lads. Having listened to your heartfelt plea for coursing, I saw the light. Yes, today I had my Road to Damascus conversion. Bye now, and safe journey to ye."

Before closing the door, Lannigan craned his head around to survey the approach to his clinic as if to ensure nobody saw who was emerging from it.

Waxy smiled as he climbed into his van. Bonzo and Slapper were ecstatic. They had every reason to be, Waxy told them, after switching his mobile phone back on. He'd had it powered off during their meeting with Lannigan. Now, he saw that ten minutes before entering Lannigan's office he'd received a text message, which he read with a relief he hadn't felt since his successful hare-netting mission to the island last year. The message from a top national coursing official (using an agreed pseudonym) revealed that four other non-committal politicians had undergone a similar change of heart to Lannigan's and would now be voting against the anti hare coursing Bill.

Each of them had proven just as greedy and unethical as Lannigan, their principles (if they had any) counting for nothing once all that alluring dosh was dangled, like a juicy carrot, before them.

Pity it had to be done that way, Waxy thought, and a lot of money had to be raised in a short space of time to secure the support of those crooked politicians. But a small price to pay to save hare coursing from the chopping block. The politicians were unethical anyway, so why not avail of that...*weakness*...of theirs...in the pursuit of a greater good: the survival of a proud tradition without which Ireland would be a mere shadow of its former field-sporting self?

Slapper started the engine and as the van hummed to life, Waxy muttered a prayer to the Patron Saint of Hunting: *Please try to understand...and explain to God if you don't mind...that there was no other way.*

***

48

Tipsy shivered. The season was changing, or rather; he corrected himself, about to give way to a new one. The signs were all around him. The sky was a swirling mass of angry grey and black clouds. Sand blew in great swathes across the beach. Tipsy had to shut his eyes tight or cover them with his paws to avoid it. Fallen leaves on the island had rotted and were now freezing as evening approached.

The sea breeze that soothed him and the other hares in the warmer time now had a cool sharpness to it, and it whistled a direful tune. The winds that shook the branches and leaves of the trees further inland made them shake more vigorously, and there were suddenly far less leaves to be shaken.

He remembered this same change happening before. When was it? Mum had explained the four seasons to him. This would be the second cold season of his life, when it finally arrived in full force to cast a pall of snow and ice over the island and diminish the heat and light of the sun. Rain too it would bring, but that didn't bother him, as rain could fall anytime. It might be heavier and more prolonged, but it was just a question of finding shelter, under a tree, in one of the Humanik former dwellings, or in a cave on the far side of the island.

The cold season would, he expected, be even colder and more miserable for some hares: The ones who had lost family or friends to the Humanik incursion. There was so much that hares forgot: the countless everyday chores, the familiar sights and sounds, the thoughts and impressions that flickered momentarily in their heads. But not a single hare on the island had forgotten those terrifying two-legged creatures that came ashore in their wooden craft, fanning out across the island with their giant webs to take precious loved ones into captivity.

Though the Golden Hare had assured Tipsy he was "special", endowed with powers unknown to other hares, this didn't banish sorrow from his soul, or make him immune to the concerns that dominated the minds of his island brethren between sunrise and sunset. The sun never sank beneath the horizon without Tipsy having asked himself, at least once: "Where are you, Mum? Will you ever return?"

It irked him that despite his special status, he couldn't get an answer to this question. Telepathic communication didn't work for him over such long distances. He could only commune with creatures he could see. The Big Island, to which Mum had been transported, was completely out of range. It might as well be up there among the stars. Tipsy squinted at the sky through a haze of sand cloudlets that the wind was tossing about, distorting his view of everything. Best get off the exposed beach and back into a cosy protected setting. No point in suffering when comfort and security beckoned.

Tipsy set off for his new abode. He'd lost count of how many times he'd moved house since leaving the loving nest where Mum and Dad had pampered him and listened to his latest exploits, recounted with bated breath, as he familiarised himself with the island. Wherever he went on the island to start anew he met no hostility, apart from the odd grumbling hare in a bad mood, or some creature that, unknown to him, had already settled on the same patch or the same spot amid the old Humanik ruins.

Gambolling leisurely along a dusty clay path fringed by swaying high grass and even taller yellow weeds, he passed two hares heading in the opposite direction. Both greeted him cheerfully. He returned their salutations. He knew their apparent high spirits belied their heartache and crushing sense of loss. One sorely missed his brother, the second his father. They'd scoured the island after the Day of Terror, when the invading Humaniks had departed. They found not a trace of their treasured kith and kin. They prayed for their safe return, not knowing whether to mourn them or show never-ending patience. But how patient should a hare have to be? It was the not knowing about Mum that perplexed Tipsy. At least with Bumble he had the certainty of her transition from the world and had come to accept her absence.

Ah! What was that? A sharp pebble had struck his forehead. Another stung his left ear. Suddenly he was being showered with them, each eliciting a stab of pain that made him jump. His whole body felt the irksome pebbles. No, not pebbles. *Hailstones!* : Another unpleasant feature of that harsh season that seemed intent on making its appearance a little earlier than expected.

The ice-cold particles from the sky pounded the earth, bouncing off the clay and flattening the grass and weeds to either side of the path. Tipsy instinctively dashed to the piece of shattered wall he knew to be situated not far to his left. It was really only a clump of disintegrating mossy stones. He made straight for the hollow he had dug many sunsets before for just such an emergency, one of several around the island.

He should have made it bigger, but there was enough space within. He turned around slowly in the cramped alcove, still smarting from the impact of the hailstones. He sat watching the storm batter the island, wondering if many other hares had been taken unawares by it. The poor leverets he felt sorry for. Some of those hailstones were so large they could kill a baby hare.

Then again, refuges from the elements were never too far away, unless you happened to be caught on the beach, where there was no shelter and you'd be drenched from the rain or aching from the bitter stings before reaching cover. The hail eventually abated, but the sky retained its malevolent glower. A few birds dared to chirp, hoping he supposed like himself that they'd seen the last of it.

In the distance he saw a hare shake himself after emerging from under a ditch that had turned an ugly greyish white with the hail. To avoid another ducking, tipsy opted to remain for a while in his temporary shelter. The balm of sleep crept up on him. He felt himself swaying, and a peculiar dizziness began to take hold inside his head. Had the hailstones inflicted some injury?

Suddenly the dark, restricted space of the stony hideaway had gone, as was his view of the hail-pummelled ground outside his little refuge. Tipsy was sitting instead on an emerald green surface that seemed to stretch to infinity all around him. The grass shone and glistened as if alive. The sky was no longer threatening or unsightly. It had the most tranquil sunrise he'd ever seen, brighter and deeper, devoid of clouds; with glittering reds, blues, yellows and soft purples vying for dominance, all suffused with a golden light that pulsed like a gentle heartbeat and emitted pure benevolence.

And then the landscape that seemed featureless at first began to sprout flowers and luscious vegetation. Daffodils fluttered in rows, rosebushes appeared and lines of hedges materialized out of nowhere. And now also a stream appeared some distance in front of him. It ran all the way to his left and right. He edged towards it to investigate. The stream split the whole pastoral picture in two, he deduced. And there...was that a *bridge* spanning the stream?

He approached the crossing. As he did the stream widened until, Tipsy thought, it was almost as broad from one side to the other as the lake on the island. And as it widened the bridge also grew in length. He ventured slowly to the bridge and stepped unto it. The water beneath was crystal clear and gurgling melodiously. No weeds were visible on the stream bed, nor any ugly twisted weeds. It was pure delight, pure to the taste also, he imagined, and somehow not of the world as he knew it.

Something else caught his eye. On the other side of the stream lights shone and danced. Circular orbs like miniature suns. Tipsy felt an overwhelming sense of peace...but part of him disbelieved and tried to shake off the whole experience. Was it a dream? He tapped his feet on the bridge to make sure it was really there. *Seems sold enough.* It was made of wood, and as his feet rested on the boards the love and strength of the trees from which the wood derived washed over him. He heard and felt their song of empathy deep within.

The lights visible on the other side of the stream multiplied. Some of them rose tentatively from ground level and floated effortlessly above the others, soaring high into the glorious firmament and then casually returned to rejoin the other orbs.

Then, as Tipsy strained to understand what they were, some of the lights began to assume shape, to become...hares! Hares of all sizes and ages...male, female, wizened grey hares and sprightly leverets that leapt giddily in the sparkling green meadow that extended behind them in undulating swathes to a remote horizon.

Vast numbers of them stood, sat, lay sleeping, or moved slowly, or grazed...or darted about with astonishing energy, iridescent across a landscape that had increased in heart-warming splendour since Tipsy had first glimpsed it just moments ago.

And all basked in a glow of contentment that was brighter and balmier than earthly sunshine at its best.

Tipsy felt drawn further along the span, and the stream beneath now looked even wider than the island lake. Up ahead, some of the hares were taking a break from their frolics and directing their attention to him, sending blissful thoughts and support to him. Dozens, then hundreds of them were gathering on the other side of the stream, with the heaviest concentration close to where the bridge started. He heard a murmuring of intense glee and expectancy.

The immense outpouring of love and compassion pulled him further towards those happy hares like an irresistible force. But he stopped abruptly. Just ahead he beheld a sparkling soft bluish band that looked like a break in the bridge. He could see straight down through it at the beguiling waters below. He now felt a conflicting pull of emotions; one urging him on across that dividing line, to meet those wonderful beings that emanated such an all-encompassing welcome; Another, equally compelling emotion or inner voice seemed to be crying "Stop! No further!"

Perplexed, he stood still, wondering which way to go: forwards...or back to his starting point. As he pondered, a hare emerged out of the assembled throng and stepped onto the bridge from the other side. The radiant being half walked, half glided towards him. When she drew closer he almost cried for joy: "Mum! Is it you?"

She stopped less than a paw's distance from the dividing line whose soft bluish glow had turned to a vivid luminosity. Mum was recognisable, but far lovelier than ever he had seen her. Not a blemish detracted from her perfect reddish brown and white form.

Then she spoke, her voice a gentle harmonic hum: "Tipsy, you've been worrying about me. Stop your worrying! I'm safe now, where no Humanik can ever harm me..."

Her voice was the same as he'd remembered it. But her magnificent appearance called to mind a most brilliant sunset, and her eyes were two twinkling stars plucked from a glitzy night sky over the island. Thus far Tipsy had gone with the flow of this strange experience, not bothering to question or analyse what it meant.

Now it hit him. "Mum...you're speaking to me from across the divide...is this the divide between earthly life and Hare Heaven? Does this mean that...you've died?"

Tears welled up, if tears could fall here, or at least he had a sensation of rising grief in this dreamy or spiritual milieu. Mum sent him waves of solace and strength. Her soothing voice pierced his consciousness. "Tipsy, death is just an illusion, as you know. It hurts only those left behind. Not we who have made the transition. Do we look unhappy?"

Tipsy didn't need to think about the question. He felt the boundless jubilation of all those hares on the other side of the stream. They certainly didn't seem bothered about leaving behind the miseries of earth. Still, Tipsy had to know: "Mum, how did it happen...I mean...what event ended your life on earth?"

Smiling, she held up a paw and instantly a translucent bubble appeared within her grasp that instantly moved away from her, floating to hover above the dividing line on the bridge. Within the bubble a scene unfolded. Tipsy saw Mum's earthly body hanging upside down alongside other hares, blood dripping from her head and front paws.

Humaniks were standing about making loud ugly noises. Four-legged creatures were howling, their mouths salivating and their teeth showing prominently as they snapped at dead or dying hares. The eyes on Mum's earthly frame closed and her spirit departed; unseen by the Humaniks.

The bubble dissolved into effervescent dots and disappeared.

Tipsy was horrified, and yet there, right in front of him, was Mum, looking better than ever. He fumed: "I detest Humaniks, I hate them more than any creature on this planet...I..."

She motioned him to hush. "No hatred Tipsy. You will fight back, but in a way that will help all hares and hurt nobody."

Tipsy wanted to hug his mother, and was about to step forward...across the Great Divide. "No Tipsy, it is not your time!" She held up a restraining paw. "You have much to achieve. When you have completed your great task, you will join us here...all your friends and kindred who have crossed to the world of spirit. Look!"

A dazzling orb appeared beside Mum, resolving itself into another hare.

"Bumble!"

Tipsy was ecstatic, but an invisible force restrained him from embracing his lost love. Like Mum, she pointed to the dividing line, from which little sparks of light were rising in a lustrous vapour to block his passage. The two hares on the bridge began to fade.

Bumble spoke softly: "Not yet. We await your arrival, dearest. Go now and complete your mission!"

Tipsy sent his love on waves of thought to Mum and Bumble, and to all the gentle beings that looked on from the Other Side.

49

Annemarie placed the pink and blue ribbon wrapped bottle of champagne on the coffee table beside her, admiring its sparkle, and sat back in her sofa in front of the TV. She felt entitled to a little self indulgence. It wasn't every day she had something to celebrate. But this was a unique occasion. Rather, she corrected herself, was *likely to be.*

Excitement had been mounting all week as the big moment drew nearer. She mentally checked the numbers again. Seventy-two members of parliament had declared in favour of the Bill to ban hare coursing, with sixty eighty opposed. The rest were abstaining. Okay, that would be a narrow majority, but that didn't matter. A win would be a win, and never again could hares be legally captured in the Irish countryside by coursing clubs for use as live bait.

The parliamentary debate on the Bill had concluded. She'd watched it for almost two and a half hours on the politics channel. Passions had raged; raised voices crackling with emotion as the arguments went to and fro. Advocates of hare protection pitched their case eloquently, countered by impassioned pleas from pro-coursing politicians. The Parliamentary Chairman had been compelled to intervene several times to quell angry hecklers in the debating chamber who sought to shout down speakers or distract them.

All week, pro and anti-hare coursing protesters had gathered outside the House of Parliament in Dublin's Kildare Street... each day between noon and two pm to pile pressure on the politicians. A lot was at stake. The vote would either end the persecution of hares or safeguard the "rights" of the people who made life hell for them. Now, the debating chamber was empty, Annemarie noticed, apart a few politicians hanging about in groups of three or four, whispering furtively, hands waving frantically, heads nodding above folded arms, feet tapping the floor.

Impatient for the big decision, she switched to the news channel. Just five minutes to the Nine O' Clock news. She reckoned the vote would surely have been held by then. It was supposed to be all over by eight-fifty. She crossed her fingers, tension mounting within her. The Nine O' Clock news logo filled the TV screen, accompanied by the signature tune. She raised the volume. The chirpy female newsreader highlighted the main events of the day.

Odd... no mention of the vote yet. Ten minutes passed. Still not a word, though just about every other news item, even minor ones... had been covered. Then...Annemarie leaned closer to the TV, fingers tightly clasped, teeth gritted. The newsreader was accepting a note from someone hidden to her left in the studio. She put it away and announced tersely: "The vote on the widely anticipated and highly controversial anti-hare coursing Bill was delayed owing to last minute deliberations, but has taken place within the last two minutes. Over now to our parliamentary correspondent: Stephen, can you bring us the latest?"

The burley bushy-haired male reporter, standing at the entrance to the House of Parliament, had to shout to be heard amidst a throng of cheering and booing, amplified by megaphones. "Yes, Susan...It really went down to the wire. As you know, the expectation was that the Bill would pass, but there was always a possibility of things not going as predicted. The Bill was defeated by seventy one votes to sixty-nine. It's believed an eleventh hour conversion by some politicians produced this shock result. So it seems that hare coursing has survived... for the time being..."

Annemarie's stomach heaved. She rose abruptly, grabbed the champagne and almost threw the bottle back into the fridge, slamming it shut. She raised the remote control to switch off the TV but she couldn't press the button. She was riveted to the ongoing commentary. Beside the reporter a familiar face smirked, flashing a set of shining white teeth. Joey Lannigan. He'd sworn blind just a fortnight ago that he'd back the Bill, but there he was... sporting a "Coursing is our pride and joy!" badge, and swathes of arms were heartily clapping him on the back.

The reporter held the microphone up to him: "I have here with me the representative for Broc Peninsula and the Islands. Ah, Mr. Lannigan, can you tell me....up to last Wednesday you were clearly in the anti camp. What prompted you to change sides?"

The wily politician adjusted his oversized multicoloured tie and touched his mouth delicately: "Well actually, it was a hard decision. I like hares. I genuinely do, and I'd be the last man in Ireland to take pleasure from the sight of any hare...you know...getting into difficulty...at a coursing event. But then, I've got to know some of the finest coursing men in my time. Great chaps. And when it came to the vote, I just couldn't bring myself to...ah...snub their wonderful pastime. Having said that, I've noted the concerns of the anti-coursing lobby and I'll keep their views in mind. Animals are great...and I love wildlife. I really do. Sure the rural districts wouldn't be the same without hares running around...and the birds...and the rabbits. But...yes...I have to be honest...I couldn't betray a fond old Irish tradition...a bucolic field sport."

The reporter abruptly ended the interview, ushering Lannigan out of his way, the space quickly filled by a well known anti-coursing campaigner. Annemarie listened through a pounding headache, her anger rising. The tears rolling down her cheeks distorted the TV screen as the blonde pony-tailed woman, her features contorted into a deep frown, spoke: "Yes...it's a huge disappointment...though we were never one hundred percent sure of success. But on a positive note, this Bill had more supporters than any of the previous three parliamentary Bills tabled over the past thirty years. The most recent one before today's was defeated by one hundred and sixteen to twenty...so today's result, while a setback, shows that we're edging closer to the ban on hare coursing that most Irish people support. We're gutted. No denying that. We came here daring to hope...that our politicians had finally found the courage and the compassion to face down the blood sports lobby. But I'd like to assure your viewers, and the people of Ireland, that our campaign will continue. We'll not stop until the Irish Hare is protected. Our day will come!"

Annemarie switched off the TV, and was about to rise from the sofa when her slightly overweight but frisky cat Ginger leaped up onto her lap, purring noisily and pawing for attention. She hugged him, welcoming the distraction. She'd better get him some food. Dropping him on the carpet she went to the fridge and removed a tin of Kitty-Cat. Passing by the mirror above the empty fireplace she stopped.

What on earth?

She rubbed her eyes and looked again. It was gone. Must have been the tears that caused her to see...or imagine she saw...a radiant creature...a hare...sitting on a patch of grass. The fleeting scene had appeared in the mirror as if the glass had become an alternative TV screen. For that fraction of a second. Or it was it a momentary hallucination...brought on by thinking and fretting too long about the anti coursing campaign?

She pushed it from her mind, scooping the gooey mess onto Ginger's plate. The grateful cat purred his thanks and helped himself to the meal. Annemarie reached for her coat and woolly cap. She'd take a walk. Clear her head. But she'd be visiting that coursing fixture at Ballycrossways again. It was just a few months away.

And she'd film it this time, if only to show what a twat Joey Lannigan was, and those other politicians who'd given the thumbs-up to that so-called "bucolic field sport."

50

After Tipsy's encounter with Mum on the Ethereal Bridge, the seasons passed him by dreamily, as if the otherworldly ambience of the visitation had persisted. He viewed life differently. Everything was sharper, more alive. The blades of grass shimmered in their intense greenness, snowflakes in the shivering season glistened and sparkled as they fell and settled on the fields, pathways, rocks, or melted into the beach. The sand granules on the seashore he could perceive separately, if he focused...not just as a gently undulating soft spread.

All the hares he met seemed more alive too: their eyes shone, their moist whiskers gleamed in the sun and moonshine. And anything they had to say, however trivial it might once have sounded, now had meaning. Nothing was *without* meaning.

In the season of renewal, when the cold days and freezing nights receded, vegetation returned and the frosts disappeared. He felt less despondent about his mission, though not less aware of its immensity and how it might make or break him. The season's bright optimism was infectious, bringing new hope to the island hares amid nature's joyous rebirth. The revival of flowers, absent or dead during the long cold season, tugged at the heartstrings.

Primroses were pushing up where the soil favoured their growth, mainly inside the Humanik ruins and in odd sheltered nooks across the less habitable parts of the island. Tipsy loved the sight and sweet scent of this flower, which, Mum had told him, augured a happier climate after so many days and nights of discomfort.

The small birds sang louder than usual, a cheery tone entering their chirpy voices. They were relieved no doubt at the passing of those chilly winds, and the frozen earth that refused to yield to their pecking. As the season progressed, the permanently resident island birds were joined by returning migrants that had fled during the cold spell. The chorus of tweeting and whistling at dawn grew sweeter with each passing day. Tipsy enjoyed the melodious birdsong.

Butterflies were back, in all their multihued splendour, merrily greeting him as they fluttered around his nest. The lake seemed to be cheering itself up too. Gone were the icy sheets from its surface, and the dead foliage skirting the great reservoir that quenched the thirst of every islander. Frogs croaked and grunted to each other in their grumpy lingo at the lake's edge. Tipsy didn't bother attuning to their exchanges, respecting their fiercely asserted privacy, though he could see they were busy caring for their offspring, the spawn that didn't look like a living species at all... wrapped chaotically in strings around aquatic plants.

But the jollity and exuberance of others sometime saddened him. He felt a pang of loss at the sight of hares seeking mates. He halted in passing by Sparring Hill upon which more than a dozen bucks were gathered for a boxing tournament. In the previous days, many a doe had sought his paw in marriage. Tipsy had politely declined their approaches. It pained him to do so, especially when the prospect of a contented life with a family of sprightly leverets dangled itself temptingly. But he couldn't begin a relationship now, only to have to say goodbye to a despairing doe when the Humaniks captured him. He'd have to leave her and the leverets: An unthinkable scenario. But he couldn't share that thought with other hares.

One of the hares on the hill, spotting him, cried out: "Hey Tipsy...aren't you joining us? We know you miss poor Bumble...but life goes on, no matter what. Want to fight for a doe?"

Two hares were engaged in a ferocious bout of sparring, urged on by a frenzied cluster of bucks. But some eyes were directed at Tipsy; curious hares awaiting his response. Tipsy waved a dismissive paw, shouting back "Not this time...I've other things on my mind!"

"Suit yourself...you're missing some lovely does!" the jaunty hare retorted.

Tipsy felt the weight of his destiny. Love and romance would have to wait until after his mission, assuming his earth life wasn't cut short by this...*assignment.* Not that he feared death: quite the opposite. It would mean meeting Mum and Bumble again, and returning to a far happier state of existence. But he hoped, and prayed, that the end of his earthly term didn't come *before* he had accomplished his great task...whatever it proved to be.

When the hot season came he exulted in dashing across the beach, the warmth of the sand always a pleasant sensation, almost equalling the pleasure of running through the gorse and high grass, or half-falling, half-skidding, down the slopes of the little hills. The trees had their leaves back, and he loved the pungent aromas that wafted to him from the hedgerows: The sweet scents of wild honeysuckle and dogroses. Creamy flowers bloomed across the island. You could admire their prettiness, or eat them...or both, depending on your mood. The birds continued with their happy harmonies, chirping and pecking and chatting among themselves, and occasionally with him, in the pleasant balm of that laidback season.

But his appreciation of this normally happy time, when the sun made hares lazy and inclined to forget danger, was tempered by a deep niggling at the back of his mind. He felt the approach of the next season, the one that last time around was marred by the Humanik terror. It would bring another calamity this time, for his fellow islanders, and he'd be tested to the utmost.

As his Day of Destiny drew nearer, he found that time itself seemed to behave in strange and erratic ways. Some days it seemed to slow down, when he wished it to hurry along...and he tried frantically to stretch out happy experiences. A pointless effort, as time gobbled up the heartbeats faster than a hare gulped down a clump of juicy seaweed. But whether time moved slowly or at an accelerated pace, it always moved in the same direction, and was bringing closer with every heartbeat the Day of Challenge.

Leaning against a crumbling mossy wall, Tipsy raised his eyes to the full moon, savouring its benevolent sheen. The effulgent rays, easy on the eyes unlike the burning midday sun, cast a gentle lustre over the island. Ostara's celestial orb illuminated patches of the familiar terrain that Tipsy knew he'd have to leave behind. But not yet.

Other hares were mooching about, and he greeted them heartily as he embarked on one of his nocturnal forays across the island. Wherever he went, hares were active, some nibbling on plants or tree bark, or munching gorse. A few concentrated on the ripening blackberries, sloes, and elderberries...anxious to get their teeth into them before rival hares...or hungry birds... reached these emerging tasty foods.

Other hares Tipsy saw sitting under moonbeams with eyes shut tight, whispering prayers to Ostara. Leverets frolicked in the moonbeams. His heart sank. Some of the older ones, he feared, could be among the victims on that direful future date. Humaniks didn't take newborns as they'd serve no purpose, he'd learned from His Eminence.

Hares called him by name, praising the warm weather and top-class food they'd partaken of, saying how happy they were in their new matings, or how the young were growing so quickly. Others again gave voice to their innermost hopes and wishes, and a few expressed thanks for getting through another day without falling prey to falcons. Though the feared birds had been absent from the skies for quite a while, their reappearance was deemed inevitable, as the Humaniks couldn't kill every falcon in the Universe.

But NO hare uttered a word about the invasion, or the prospect of a recurrence. Tipsy knew it wasn't because they didn't *think* about it. No...It was such a terrifying and appalling vista that they tried to pretend it wasn't there. They buried it deep inside their heads, as if ignoring the horror would make it go away. He didn't blame them. A mind convulsed with fear didn't alter the future; it just added to the sum-total of suffering to be endured.

Tipsy ran faster, to take in as much of the island as he could during this spell of glorious moonshine. Climbing to the peak of a high hill, he rested. His panoramic view took in great swathes of terrain. Bathed in the lunar luminescence hares lived their simple lives: eating, frolicking, sleeping, playing...timid and unthreatening as always... troubling nobody. Other, less benign creatures would trouble *them.* Though that was in the future. *We must live in the present.*

Right now, he fancied a swim. He descended to the beach, guided by the moonlight, and ran along the warm sand, luxuriating in its softness as the frothy waves lapped forwards to meet him. A surging breaker thrust Tipsy backwards, whirling him into a momentary giddiness. But undaunted he leapt back into the surf, all four paws propelling him into the mighty ocean. Its coolness on such a warm night soothed him. He dived underwater, re-surfaced, and plunged again into the depths. Sated with the joy of swimming, he allowed the tide to sweep him back onto the beach.

Shaking himself dry, he paced the sand, the lunar rays even brighter than earlier, shining down on him. As he prepared to ascend the slope to take him home, an intuition came to him...a spark of knowledge that somehow fizzed inside his head for a mere fraction of a heartbeat: But he grasped its significance and held the thought as he retraced the meandering course to his nest: *The sun will rise and set ninety times more before the Day of Challenge arrives.*

He felt a surge of relief. *That's a little eternity in the life of a hare. Life is for living*, he sighed, *and living in fear is not living at all.* Trepidation gave way to a casual acceptance of whatever the future might bring. Inhaling the invigorating sea air, he brimmed with a giddy confidence.

In the days that followed he allowed the weight of the coming invasion to fade from his mind. As the hare at the boxing tournament had hollered: *Life goes on, no matter what!*

***

51

Waxy and his group of twenty-four hare catchers stood about in the frosty predawn air, well insulated against the cold and in high spirits. The stars had begun their retreat from approaching daybreak but still dominated the chilly heavens. The sea was calm. The black-grey froth of the Atlantic mirrored moonlight in sporadic unruffled patches. No winds. No rain either: A perfect absence of climatic challenge.

At Waxy's command the men set about retrieving the five currachs from the long rectangular pens where the upturned craft lay anchored. He admired the skill of the locals who'd built the pens from stones and pebbles for the sturdy boats. Not that they knew exactly what the boats were for. That was known only to club members, who'd been warned, as they had been last year, not to breathe a word about the netting on Gooseberry Island.

The hare-catchers hummed and whistled in the half-light, three of them moving faster than the others, already carrying a currach over their heads towards the nearby pier. Everything was going as planned for this second visit to the island. They were better equipped this time, with the best of waterproof jackets and trousers, buoyancy aids to greater safety, and a generous supply of tea and ham sandwiches. Better quality nets also to capture those elusive critters.

The sea area forecast was a godsend. No storms waiting to dash them back and forth or maybe send them to the bottom of the ocean. Best of all, and the main reason the lads were so upbeat, was the fact that these currachs, unlike the previous ones, had small outboard engines. There would still be some rowing to do, but the boats would move more smoothly and the burden would be eased on men who were, after all, hare-coursers: not sailors or fishermen.

Yes, Waxy reflected, all was well. So why the unease? It had taken hold of him almost from the moment he awoke two hours before. He'd had enough sleep. No snags he could think of. Why the nagging, persistent feeling that something was amiss? Again he went through all the steps…the boats were tried and tested. They'd go all the way to America he'd been assured. The food was packed…nobody outside the club knew about their little expedition. The Poacher O' Dea had taken out three more falcons that threatened hare stocks on the island.

Everything is fine, he repeated to himself, catching a glimpse of a faint smattering of yellow and orange on the far horizon: incipient sunlight to keep the moon company up there. But though he sought to reassure himself, the strange disquiet was tightening its grip: An intuitive sense that something was amiss, somehow *out of joint*. But he couldn't pin down its source or meaning.

His right hand shaking slightly, *probably from the cold*, he reached for his hipflask and took two mouthfuls of Jemsen. He winced as it gushed to his stomach, stinging his throat along the way. The discomfort quickly turned to mild euphoria. Had that done it? He felt better.

"Let me help you with that!" he rasped, offering to shoulder a currach with five of the lads, all of them aglow with appreciation of their loved/feared boss chipping in. Minutes later, stepping into the first currach off the pier, he shut his eyes tight and made a quick reconnaissance of his mind. Yes, that vague blur of uneasiness wasn't as distracting now; thanks maybe to the whiskey… but it hadn't gone away.

The boats embarked on the journey, engines switched off until they were out of earshot of possible early risers on the Peninsula. As they rowed, Waxy's brooding continued. He talked more than usual to distract himself. Cracked jokes, made upbeat remarks about the club's fixture planned for later that month. The prize money would be increased to attract more entries and faster dogs. The lads nodded, sharing his enthusiasm.

That helped. But whenever he stopped talking or the others fell silent the strange ominous niggling inside his head resumed…accompanied he fancied by a persistent pulse that beat in time to his heartbeat. He felt it now too as an ache of reproach… or was it *foreboding…* in the depths of his being. *Must be a bug I've got. An early symptom of the flu coming* on…

He relaxed his grip on the oars to knock back another helping from the flask. *Pull yourself together Waxy…don't let the lads see you moping like that. Bad for morale.*

He forced himself to start singing a ballad, urging his four boat-mates to sing along. He wasn't known for crooning or balladeering, but it helped to repress the internal agitation, or whatever it was that gnawed at him. As he sang, the indigo infused half-light seemed to affect his vision…or had the whisky gone straight to his head? He thought he saw an ethereal glowing figure brush past to his left, gliding along inches above the water.

The man behind him nudged. "Okay boss?"

Waxy stopped staring, shaking his head. "A gull maybe" he muttered. *White lie*: It was unmistakably a hare, that nimble wraithlike form, feet pressing delicately on air as it raced in slow motion… before dissolving into the starry gloom.

But that was impossible. Must be all the talking and thinking about the upcoming coursing event. *Mind playing tricks. But how vivid that image was.*

He clenched his teeth and fists, squeezing the oars until his palms hurt. *Let's get the real hares into these boats and back to Ballycrossways.* He forced a reassuring laugh and lightened his grip on the oars. A gentle breeze ruffled his hair as the currach continued towards Gooseberry Island, the engine now propelling it. Waxy found its low hum soothing. It was just audible above the surge of the mighty ocean.

Then the unease returned…

***

52

A day of terrors, and it's only beginning. Tipsy's heart sank at the thought. He'd known this day was coming, and he'd promised the Golden Hare that he'd let himself be captured by the ghastly Humaniks. He hadn't allowed that unsavoury knowledge to trouble him unduly in the intervening period. He had a mission, a divine purpose. But this wasn't just about *his* life or destiny. Before giving himself up to captivity he must alert the others.

This time, the invaders had come with greater stealth. He wasn't on the beach to see or hear their sinister vessels heaving ashore. He'd been sleeping later than usual, thanks to overindulgence in this season of the fallen leaves. He'd joined dozens of hares who'd rushed to the hedges that sagged under the weight of blackberries and crab-apples. These delicious fruits grew only in a few select patches on the island, each well-known to the hares; and from the moment they appeared every hare sought to feast on them.

Many missed out, finding hedges picked clean when they arrived to partake. Not that food was scarce on the island. There was plenty for all, but the inhabitants liked an occasional treat and didn't miss an opportunity when nature presented it.

Tipsy was dreaming about crab-apple juice when a series of whistles awoke him. He wasn't in his home nest near the beach, having dozed off further inland on the High Hill of Matrimony, scene of many a happy wedding. It was the swallows that roused him. Hundreds of them circled overhead, warbling and chattering. He knew they were intent on abandoning the island for a while...preparing for their periodic flight to a far-off land. Eyes half open, he gestured up at them to stop the racket and let him rest.

But one swallow that he knew by name; having conversed with him in the previous season, fluttered down and, hovering in air, shrieked: "Tipsy, haven't you heard...or noticed...your enemies have landed. They're coming this way. Better move yourself, pal."

The giddy creature rejoined the swirling horde aloft and all the birds flew towards the cliff and out over the ocean as if drawn by some invisible force. Tipsy had leaped to his feet instantly, shook his weary head, and surveyed what lay within his field of vision.

The swallow was right: Humaniks were skulking across the island. Singly and in small groups they mooched about, some wielding long sticks as before, others carrying those accursed webs. Others again he saw kicking through gorse, kneeling in fields or on dusty paths, laying those traps that hares never saw until it was too late.

Now, he pondered how to respond. Surrendering immediately wasn't necessary. He must help the others, lest all of them succumb to those harbingers of death and woe. The marathon eating session would have left many of them lazy and less responsive to the unfolding threat. The falcon's apparent demise had also made them careless and smug...feeling safe from any prowling predators.

Tipsy didn't share their confidence. Nor did a hard core of astute colleagues who remembered the dying falcon's warning: His defeat wasn't a gift to them. The Humaniks wanted the hares for themselves. And here they were: back to bring misery to the island and snatch as many hares as they could lay their grasping paws upon.

Tipsy scanned the patchworks of walled fields, leaf-strewn paths, swathes of green yellow and orange foliage and the blue-grey rocky terrain. Humaniks everywhere... sneakily laying their invisible traps...others standing about, seemingly observing the webs they'd planted. A few startled hares, having spotted them, were fleeing, but most, he knew, would at that moment be dozing blithely in their nests, ignorant of the malign presence.

There! He spotted a hare wriggling in the corner of a field close to a crumbling stonewall. He'd clearly got caught in a Humanik web. The hare's struggle was toppling stones and clay from the wall onto the grass. He must have walked straight into the trap after climbing over the wall or through a hole in it. Tipsy dashed at breakneck speed to the pitiful scene, knowing there was little if anything he could do for the entangled creature.

Before he'd covered half the distance he spotted three more hares, moving at a leisurely pace towards the wall and, he presumed, intending to enter the same field where the web was laid. He shouted at them as he ran: "Stop! Wait!"

They sauntered on, heedless and unsuspecting. Drawing nearer, Tipsy repeated his plea. The hares stood facing the wall. One began his ascent of it, followed quickly by the others. Tipsy hollered: "It's a trap...don't go in there!"

Their heads swivelled around as Tipsy arrived at the wall, panting. One of them guffawed: "Tipsy. What's up? We're just popping in to visit a friend who lives in there."

The hare who'd climbed to the top of the wall was sitting, and staring down at the grass inside. Before Tipsy could begin his spiff, the hare's ears juddered like windblown leaves; he gasped in horror, and gave a sudden shriek. "It's Bobtail...he's...he's crying. He's trying to break out of something. The web! But how?"

"Humaniks. They're back," Tipsy snapped.

The three hares went rigid as stones. They stood at the base of the wall, staring at him, their lips stirring but no words escaping. Tipsy raised himself to his full height. He must show leadership and gain their trust. He broke the stunned silence, catching the unmistakable smell of fear from the three of them. He tried to sound positive, or at least not panicky. "Look, we know from last time that once you get caught in that thing you can't break free. You don't even see it until you're caught. Bobtail is captured. But listen...all the plans we made after last time are meaningless unless we spread the word that the Humaniks are here..."

Two of the hares responded simultaneously in giddy and almost incomprehensible tones. At a signal from Tipsy one stopped babbling to let the other speak: "But how can we warn the others on the island without being captured ourselves. If we can't see the webs we risk being caught with every step we take!"

Tipsy nodded sympathetically, but held up a restraining paw. "You're right. If all the hares knew the Humaniks were here the best strategy would be, as we agreed, for each hare to sit still, preferably in hiding, and not move from his or her position until the Humaniks depart. That way, we'd avoid the webs. But that plan is irrelevant because the Humaniks have crept up on us without warning. So, we who know what's happening must alert as many hares as possible. Yes, there's a high risk of capture but it's a risk we must take. I suggest that we split and go in different directions; spreading the news whenever and wherever we can ...otherwise the entire island hare population, all of us, will be wiped out!"

The group exchanged morbid glances, nodding hesitant, worried acceptance of Tipsy's proposal. Each chose a different route and set off to sound the alarm. Tipsy inwardly applauded their courage. Hares were timid, but not cowardly, he reflected. He mustn't tell anyone about his own mission. . Deliberately getting caught wouldn't make sense to them. It didn't make a lot of sense to him either but he trusted in the wisdom of the Golden Hare and the higher entities that inspired His Eminence.

Hearing a startled wail somewhere behind him he hastened towards the sound. A hare was frantically striving to disentangle himself, tumbling over and over but making his plight worse. Two other hares, that Tipsy recognised as the Bramble Brothers from the lakeside, looked on, helpless and grieving the loss of their friend. Tipsy wished them well in eluding the same fate, and moved on. How ironic, he thought, that he hadn't yet been ensnared, given his intention to get caught...but he was happy to be able to warn any hare who hadn't yet been appraised of the invasion.

Having traversed most of the land to north, south, east and west, he opted to descend to the beach. Not likely to be any hares there as they'd have been the first ones in the path of the Humaniks when they swept ashore. The grass gave way to rocky terrain as he approached, at a brisk pace, the path leading from the cliff to the strand. A sigh of anguish, or was it exasperation, halted him mid-sprint, his hind legs scattering dust and pebbles.

He looked around him. *Listened.* There it was again. A faint low moan. It wasn't the wind because there was scarcely a breeze blowing. He was about to shrug it off as imagination when he detected a bundle of greyish-white fur close to the cliff edge, partly concealed by a jagged moss-covered rock. He approached the creature hesitantly. It was a hare...an old one, his breathing jerky and his whole body quivering. Tipsy braced himself for the telltale sign of the web that must be constricting him.

But there wasn't any. The hare, his back turned to Tipsy, rose awkwardly, walked untrammelled for a few heartbeats, and then flopped down again. He couldn't move like that if entangled. "What's troubling you?" Tipsy asked.

Slowly, as if it hurt to move his head, the hare stood shakily and turned around. Tipsy almost fainted with alarm. "Father Buck...it's you. Are you injured? Did the Humaniks...?"

The old priest hare sat, with great difficulty, his eyes fluttering open and closed, his grey-white breast heaving. "I was hearing confessions near the lake...a few hares felt guilty about eating all those crab-apples and leaving none for their neighbours. That sort of thing. Dawn had broken and the first rays of sunlight illuminated the landscape.

"I had barely completed the blessings, thanking Ostara for all her beneficence, when I saw them...the invaders. Menacing forms. Eyes of malice embedded above pink snouts. Radiating terror and loathing... *Run,* I shouted to the brethren, and they vamoosed quicker than I ever saw them move. I watched and waited until they were safely out of sight.

"Then I did what any normal hare would do in the circumstances. I turned and ran myself...as fast as my feeble legs could carry me. Oh how it hurt. I haven't run for ages. Haven't needed to. Predators haven't bothered me. Until this morning. Loyal hares brought food to me when it wasn't within reach...."

He stopped, winced from some ache or a stab of pain, and continued. "I didn't want any hare to see me run...I'm supposed to give leadership, guidance, and spiritual comfort. I waited for the penitents to be gone before I cut loose. I mean...what would be the point of letting those Humaniks take me? But it doesn't matter now. I...I'm dying, Tipsy."

"What? You can recover. You don't seem too badly hurt. Unless internally..."

Father Buck groaned, globules of spittle falling from his lips. "That's the problem...my heart is old. It's been ticking longer than anyone else's on this island... apart from that of His Eminence in the cave. He's been there since...for longer than anyone can remember. But a hare's mortal heart has to stop sometime, so that the spirit may pass on to...a better place. My last resort to speed and evasion in this world of sorrows was cut short, Tipsy, by an ailment that doesn't often afflict hares on the island, but I've known a few who've fallen prey to it. It's called a heart attack. It can happen when we're frightened out of our wits, or forced to perform beyond our natural endurance. My race is run, Tipsy..."

Tipsy understood. He knew that hares occasionally died of fright. Some situations were just too stressful and overwhelming...and Father Buck had succumbed to such a calamity. He sat alongside the dying old hare. The spiritual adviser whose word had been law for so many seasons was weakening by the heartbeat, and that mighty life-giver inside his chest had slowed to an almost imperceptible pulse.

Tipsy drew closer, to comfort him with a caressing front paw. At Father Buck's breast he felt only the faintest of rhythmic throbbing. The old hare struggled to speak again, his words so low Tipsy had to strain his ears to hear. "There's something...Tipsy... I'm sorry about that day on the beach...when I first met you. About how my anger took hold when you spoke of that other world...the one you remembered from before your birth...the world I will shortly be entering. I shouldn't have upbraided you. I...I have a confession to make, I who have heard so many confessions from contrite hares.

"I was *jealous* of you that day Tipsy. Jealous, because you had precious memories...and knowledge... that I didn't have...I, a priest. But I know that His Eminence has great confidence in you and your special gift. My sight grows dim. I feel my heart reaching the end of its tick-tock voyage across the Sea of Time. Goodbye Tipsy."

His eyes opened wide and for an instant he smiled feebly and the orbs of vision shone bright. Then the lids closed, never to open again. His heart fell silent. The greyish-white head drooped and fell to one side, whiskers pressing on the dark rocky surface of the cliff-edge. Tipsy saw the glowing blue wisp emerge from the remnant, and watched as it flew out over the beach, continuing to the far horizon above the sea like those migrating swallows he'd seen earlier. *Father Buck is migrating too, from a world of sorrow to a land where suffering is unknown.*

The Golden Hare had referred to him as a simple character, well-meaning but prone to arrogance and a fondness for throwing his weight around. But Tipsy had seen another side of him: On that day when the mob stood poised to rip the dying falcon to pieces. Father Buck had shown great strength and compassion. He'd intervened to prevent an act of bloodthirsty revenge that, he rightly stressed, would be un-hare like behaviour. And keeping the falcon alive a little longer also enabled the hated, misunderstood creature to reveal that the Humaniks had killed him so *they* could seize the hares for themselves, as they were now doing.

Tipsy wondered how the hares would take Father Buck's death. Morale would be pretty low as it was, with hares being trapped all over the island. This could crush their spirits. Though they would, he hoped, accept Jockser as Father Buck's successor, assuming he wasn't ensnared; and they'd draw solace from knowing that the Golden Hare still prayed for them in his cave and would, if he could, find a way to thwart the Humaniks.

Tipsy sighed. It was time to do his duty...to get it over with. He set off for the beach, leaving the body of Father Buck where it lay... in accordance with tradition: to be feasted on by gulls and insects. Once the spirit had departed, the remnant served no purpose and should be returned to nature as quickly as possible.

His ears prickled. Humanik voices again. He peeped over the cliff-edge. The enslavers were strutting about in the sand, some of them carrying hares, others holding up containers into which the hares were placed, wailing and sobbing as their captors mishandled them. Other activity distracted him from somewhere to his right. He saw two hares struggling near the old Humanik ruins. *Webbed, no doubt.*

From every part of the island, as if his hearing had suddenly sharpened, sounds of lamentation and desperation reached him...unanswered cries for help, Humanik chatter. Telepathic snatches of thought whispered in his ears, fear the dominant theme. He felt it...and smelt it too. Then momentary images flashed within his brain, of hares running, wriggling in webs, dropping dead from fright, or clawing to escape from those green containers.

Tipsy gritted his teeth and shut out both the sights and sounds of Humanik cruelty. He pressed on reluctantly to the beach.

***

53

The dirt-track from the cliff to the beach was normally unobstructed, a pleasant sloping route that wound its way to that lovely stretch of sand upon which the great ocean lapped rhythmically, day and night. Today Tipsy found it blocked. He halted just in time to avoid capture.

The webs, while difficult to see, were not quite invisible, though you only saw them if you focused very carefully, which a hare couldn't be expected to do when in full flight or thinking wistfully about other things.

Tipsy stood at one of the extremities of the evil device, tentatively pawing its ingeniously woven strands. If he'd walked on a little more he'd have become entangled. Others had not been so lucky. Their twisting forms became visible to him when he sidestepped the pathway and climbed up onto a high protruding rock to his right. He now had a full view of the path down to the beach and the beach itself.

He shuddered as multiple cruel scenes unfolded. At intervals along the slope, hares were hopelessly resisting their capture, kicking and pawing and shadowboxing to break free. Sobbing and shrieking.

Anger welled up in him when a Humanik came lumbering up the slope and reached down to extract a hare from the web. He held the hare tightly, grabbing him by the ears and underbelly. Tipsy recognised the victim. It was Bouncer, one of the sentries that guarded the cave of the Golden Hare.

He was a tough one. Or always seemed to be when he stood at the cave entrance and vetted every hare that approached. Fiercely loyal to His Eminence, he'd gladly die defending him.

Tipsy surveyed the landscape to his left and right. More hares wriggling in the horrible webs like the fish that Humaniks caught in the sea many sunsets ago. Except that hares were not sea creatures, and the catching today was right here on the island. *And the purpose of the exercise is not to catch us for eating.*

Not that the hares were aware of that. All they knew was that Humaniks had again invaded the island and were snatching them.

Tipsy understood the terror...the numbing dread that gripped the struggling captives. But he didn't share the panic that the aggressors instilled. Savouring his last moments of freedom before he joined his comrades in captivity, he closed his eyes and mumbled a prayer to Ostara.

Oh Divine Goddess, the Golden Hare has assured me I will go with his blessing and protection. Forgive my lack of faith but doubt niggles at my heart. Grant that I can survive and accomplish my mission, which has yet to be made known to me.

Humanik hollering shattered his musings. Raucous noises so loud they almost pierced his eardrums. His eyelids fluttered open to take in a heartbreaking scenario: All the hares had been retrieved from the webbing on the slope and were being carried to the beach.

He leapt from the rock onto the cleared path and drew closer, concealing himself behind a cluster of weeds. He saw those green containers again, now close-up. Each had an orifice through which its captive could see.

Hares already boxed in these strange receptacles were being conveyed to the vessels, around which water lapped as it surged to mingle with the sand on the beach. But two Humaniks were not so occupied. They stood staring up at him, pointing and making those weird disharmonious sounds with their mouths peculiar to that species.

He figured they were annoyed at having missed him. Wishing they could reach out and grab this elusive one. *Well, I'll oblige them.*

He granted himself one last run. Steeling himself, he ran back up the slope, across the cliff-top, through barren soil, leaping over rocks and dashing through yellow gorse, all the way down to the beach from another route.

He saw the two Humaniks who'd been watching him, standing near the waterline, their backs turned. He could still change his mind. He was concealed from their view by a pile of soggy sea weed. It felt and smelt so tasty he was tempted to stay and have a luscious meal. It was what any hare would do.

But he wasn't just any hare...*unfortunately. Why do I have to be the one selected by someone up there in Hare Heaven to pull off some...divine stunt...?*

The two Humaniks seemed to have forgotten him already. They were cackling and tossing their arms about; and one was drinking from a little container in his hand. They looked like giants, but that was only because he now observed them at ground level. Humaniks were much taller and stronger than hares, though they could never run as fast.

Let's get this over with. Am I really doing this? Here goes.

His heart pounding and a feeling of wooziness threatening to topple him before he reached them, he moved at a brisk but not fast pace towards them. Their ugly frames grew larger and more menacing the nearer he got. Then, suddenly, both of them turned their grotesque faces in his direction. Tipsy halted, and stood facing them.

The one holding the drinking vessel dropped it in the sand, and both of them began walking towards him. He remained rooted to the spot. He knew they must expect him to run. It's what hares did. This must be confusing to them. He should have been with the others earlier. It wouldn't have looked as odd as this.

When they stood just the length of two hares from him, one of them pounced. With the foul smelling Humanik covering his body, Tipsy thought he'd be crushed. The invader's weight was unbearable. If he pressed down any harder he'd crush Tipsy's bones.

The weight lifted. Tipsy felt his ears being gripped tightly and pulled and his whole body was swinging upside down for an instant. Then he saw the world swaying around him...the sand...the waves lashing the beach...the vessels full of Humaniks and hare containers...the sky that was overcast with angry rain-clouds...and the covered feet of the Humanik that held his body, and his life, in those callous paws of his.

The queasiness in Tipsy's stomach worsened. So did the aches and pains that racked his quivering body as the sea-craft drew near. Humaniks squatted in the vessel, along with those green containers.

The craft had been resting on the beach. Now it was bobbing up and down and from side to side in the water. *I could still escape and get back to the island, by swimming, if I could break loose. But No. I have to go to the Big Island.*

The Humaniks were clutching long wooden poles, like tree-branches denuded of foliage. He closed his eyes to blot out the pain and humiliation of capture. It ripped at the core of his being.

He felt himself being wrenched by another pair of paws. When he looked again, he was being lowered into a container like the ones that enclosed the other hares. A cover slammed shut on it. It was dark on three sides but there was that opening he'd noticed earlier, crisscrossed with hard lines of a substance he'd never seen or felt before. Some Humanik contrivance he surmised, to enable sight of the outside world and yet also prevent escape.

All he could see was the wooden edge of the vessel and the water splashing beyond it. The sky appeared intermittently, as if to reassure him it was still there. There was scarcely room to move in this space, but at least he could sit, and scratch, if only just about.

A strange discordant humming started, drowning out the low sobbing of trapped hares similarly confined. The hum was produced by the craft, he suspected, as it reminded him of no animal or bird sound, or any resonance of nature. He felt a sickness, a sense of utter hopelessness and sadness as the Humanik vessel began its journey to the Big Island.

He settled as best he could and willed himself to sleep. This was a new phase in his life. He was leaving behind the island that had been his home since birth. For all its drawbacks, he loved every patch and stony particle of it. Okay, the falcon was an ever-present threat, at least before he'd been downed by a Humanik death rod. Hares there had their quarrels and personality clashes, and adverse weather took the lives of leverets now and then. But that was just life.

He'd miss the daily routine: The many choices of food and those friendly birds that more than made up for the falcon and the screechy gulls.

What adventures...*untold horrors*...lay ahead? He wasn't sure...only that he'd be tested to the utmost, and that, if he held his nerve and followed his Inner Voice, he'd be triumphant. He might fail. The Golden Hare had emphasised that.

But with a fierce resolve and the guiding light of Ostara, he hoped to survive and strike a blow for the hares of the Big Island, where his fellow creatures awaited deliverance from the loathsome Humaniks.

***

54

The body may be trapped, but the spirit is never enslaved.

Tipsy comforted himself with hopes of future peace and freedom. He soared over the landscape as only a bird could do in the physical world. Memories of the vision in the cave flooded back. Those enormous ice sheets creaking and crunching in the dim distant past…hares looking down from the highest altitudes, defying the cataclysmic changes wrought by nature while other species disappeared without trace.

The Wise One had shown him that to remind him that hares could battle the odds and triumph. They might be shy and retiring in the estimation of other creatures but Ostara compensated for that drawback by conferring on them a flair for survival.

Other aspects of the vision loomed also…the cruelty of Humaniks, something he didn't need reminding of after what he'd seen on the island and the dream encounter with his slain mother …the heartless way they'd stolen so many hares, without a care as to how that would impact on their distraught loves ones.

They may as well have killed them. The pain of loss and absence could be worse than death. And at least with death there was certainty. By stealing them, the Humaniks had ratcheted up the levels of suffering and despair the hares on the island would have to cope with.

On the far horizon, as he flew on thermal currents, gigantic tapestries depicting Humanik ill-treatment of hares rose from the ocean, each displaying a different form of cruelty: hares falling to death rods, being chased endlessly across bleak landscapes, or being ripped to pieces by other creatures controlled by Humaniks. Their cries filled the world…

Then, this panoply of horrors faded to be replaced by a heavenly scene: hares in the afterlife, grazing in pastures that exuded the loveliest of hues and fragrances, and where a peace beyond earthly understanding pervaded as hares of all ages and sizes frolicked under a smiling summer sun.

A voice in the clouds boomed: *When life's journey ends, the hare will bask in glory...but first you must learn the lessons of earth.*

He envied the hare spirits. Their running and hiding days were done…they cast sorrowful looks at him across time and space. Then they vanished in a blinding flash, accompanied by a shrill grating sound. It reminded Tipsy of the wrenching apart of a tougher than usual piece of sea weed between your teeth…

Happy hares gone. Heaven a long way off.

His dreaming ended with a crash and a bump to his head. His whole world had upended. But his body could barely move so how could that be?

Fully awake he realized it must be the wooden structure enclosing him that was tumbling about. He felt himself spinning, banging off the walls of the container. His head ached from repeated collisions, but worse than the dull throbbing was the dizziness. It distorted his vision, not that he could see much in his present predicament: Just whatever appeared intermittently in that slit for his eyes. He felt like vomiting but overcame the urge. Didn't want to be swilling about in *this*! *So restricted.*

His bones ached. Every one of them pulsated and cried out for relief. And his fur itched all over. Scratching was difficult. Scarcely enough room to move a paw sideways or in front. How long had he been trapped in this accursed thing? It seemed eons.

Thousands of heartbeats had passed since he'd seen the full light of day on the island. Little beams of light had penetrated the space that contained him. Between waking and sleeping he'd caught fleeting glimpses of sky and droplets of rain had splashed against the tiny opening, forming pools around his feet. Straining his head to reach them, he'd sipped those precious drops.

He thanked Ostara for quenching his thirst. His body was shaking all over. It was as if someone was rattling his bones to shake them out of his body. He could no longer see the sliver of sky.

Now it was Humanik legs with their coverings that swished and flapped against the opening. Someone was carrying him. He saw the ground underneath the Humaniks too…in snatches. Yes, and then he spotted, for a fraction of a heartbeat, a Humanik holding a similar structure to the one containing him, with two eyes staring from it. Another terrified captive. *We must have arrived at wherever those cruel entities are taking us.*

Suddenly the movement ceased. Everything went black. He checked that he hadn't shut his eyes. They were wide open. Up to now there was at least that slit through which he could see, reminding him of the outside world that still existed and of which he was still a living part. Total darkness, without even the stars or the comforting lunar beams, was frightening.

But he must hold his nerve. This was but another phase in his journey, another steppingstone to the completion of his special mission.

Strange odours assailed his nostrils: *Unfamiliar territory.* Unlike the island smells. Then a deafening noise, like a hundred raging gulls shrieking in his ear. He shook like a leaf in the wind inside his confined space. Everything was rattling and clattering but he somehow managed to remain in a sitting position.

Adjusting to the darkness, he saw the opening, and through it a shadowy wall of some kind that shone hazily. He had a sensation of moving, though by what means or to where he'd no idea.

Just wait, he reminded himself. *All will be revealed.* The unpleasant noise abated, dwindling to a low humming. Humanik voices erupted, harsh on the ear and disharmonious as always. What was it about those creatures? They seemed to go against the flow of nature and turn contentment into viciousness.

A loud scraping sound and again light filtered into his confinement, quickly covered by glimpses of Humanik activity. He was being carried again, swinging back and forth, unable to see anything clearly as the movement obscured his vision.

Fleeting images vied for his attention: Humanik feet in their coverings, a wet grassy surface, and Humanik paws clutching other hares in those containers. Many Humanik voices sounding at once, some low, some loud and menacing, others consisting of gasps or whispers, and all of these interspersed with inarticulate outbursts of the kind he'd heard on the island when he'd seen those creatures with their giant cobwebs.

It was the sound that Humaniks made, according to an old hare, when they wished to express joy or supreme satisfaction without resorting to language.

***

55

Waxy rubbed his hands together at the counter of Dick the Miller's pub in the village square. His pint of Guinness was readying itself, awaiting the addition of the final flourish that made it a world-renowned Irish beverage.

The music had started, with accordions playing and tin-whistles belting out old Irish tunes. His head was clear. Not a trace of that crazy brooding that had taken hold of him as he set off on that sea journey. Must have been a bug he'd caught. Sometimes those ailments affected the mind. But once he hit the island his mind healed completely.

He imagined himself on a par with Columbus discovering America. His own discovery wasn't as spectacular, but of immense value he believed because it solved the club's hare-shortage problem. What a godsend Gooseberry island had proved to be: The hares were there for the taking and by God he took plenty of them.

A sudden shrill croaking jarred him. A man who thought he could sing but couldn't had started to murder a ballad. But his disharmonious airs didn't faze Waxy. Things were looking up. The hares were all safely locked and bolted in at Ballycrossways. The contingent from the island made up the numbers again, as they had last year, and nobody apart from himself and the club officials knew where they'd come from.

Important to keep their origins under wraps. Those antis and the lunatic Greens would make a song and dance about meddling with the island's ecosystem and all that rot. Okay, a few hares had keeled over and one or two had to be given the chop due to injuries, but the club would have plenty runners thanks to that handy little stock of pussies from the island.

The boat trip wasn't too bad, thanks to the outboard engines, though two of the lads had puked when their currachs were tossed a little. But he persuaded those sissies that a true sportsman and lover of the Peninsula's prized traditions didn't shun a few high waves, the odd gust of wind, or the healthy ocean spray lashing his face. He straightened them out, reminding them that this was no time for weakness.

Coursing had survived a major attack by its enemies, and to ensure it continued to brave the storms of ignorance and misguided opposition they must remain steadfast in the faith-as hard as nails. If he heard as much as a whimper from any of them, he'd warned, he'd lay the culprit flat with a broken jaw. That shook them.

The barman pushed the completed frothy pint of Guinness across the counter to Waxy, and a large whiskey alongside it. "The large one is on me", he winked.

Waxy downed the yellow liquid in two gulps and lovingly grasped the pint. Someone clapped him on the back as he moved cautiously to a stool near the musicians, who were playing a lament for Ireland's patriot dead. "Ye'll have great coursing tomorrow Waxy!" the man yelled to be heard above the music.

"We will" Waxy agreed, wishing that the out-of-tune man would kindly take a break from singing and that the others would play something less despondent.

He was on a high about the big event tomorrow, and this grief-stricken melody was pulling him down. As soon as the crooning ended, he'd ask them to play *Master McGrath,* the ballad of the great coursing greyhound; and by God he'd stand and join in. He'd reason to celebrate.

Fixing himself on the stool, he took his first sip of the pint, savouring the creamy lather that formed on its legendary "head". He sighed with a deep satisfaction. He had helped to save coursing from the chopping block last year. Now he'd rescued his own club yet again from the shame of not having enough hares for the annual fixture.

His reflection gazed back from the long rectangular mirror behind the counter. The fluffy froth speckled his lips and hung like a little beard from his chin, reminding him of the bubbly foam that dashed and cooled his head in the currach.

***

56

Moving again. He was being carried. He caught glimpses of sky, grass… and all manner of fleeting images and shapes unfamiliar to him. Then his whole body shook as the container alighted on a hard surface.

A hatch opened and something or somebody beat the sides of the container. He stepped out of it. The sudden flare of sunlight dazzled him. He squinted, glancing to either side. Humanik feet shuffling about in their coverings, and more of that awful racket they made with their voices.

A Humanik foot kicked him lightly in his rump. He took the hint, which he assumed it was, and scuttled forward. Adjusting to the daylight after so long in that restricted space, he saw another hare emerging from a similar container, and looking about in confusion. Then another hare darted right across in front of him. More hares appeared, as if Ostara had decided to create them all in this one location.

He was in a field, except it wasn't like any field or stretch of grass he'd trod upon. On the island fields were enclosed by vegetation or those stone walls that Humanks had built in the distant past. Here the grassy earth upon which he and the others sat or walked on was hemmed in on all sides by a high barrier that was neither foliage nor stone. It was something stringy and shining that was somehow transparent.

Two hares were already at the edge of the field staring through the barrier. He rushed over to join them. He tested the barrier with a forepaw. The strands of which it was composed were as hard to the touch as stone, but smoother. The barrier was cold and featureless. It smelt of…he sniffed carefully…*nothing.*

But the spaces between the glistening filaments made it easy to see what lay beyond: Strange dwellings or constructions that only Humanik understood. Mosses, tiny flowers, and other assorted growths sprouted from rock just outside the barrier. This was *their* world, where no hare belonged.

Humanik voices prompted him to turn around. A Humanik was walking about holding a vessel from which he removed what must be food. Hares were devouring bits of it where it fell. He sat still, as the Humanik approached him and the two hares that flanked him. The greenish and orange fragments that he tossed towards them smelled okay, but Tipsy had never seen food like it.

The hare to his left nudged him. "Carrots and lettuce. It's fine. They have to feed us. We're no use to them starved." The other hare laughed nervously.

Tipsy was hungry. Where the food came from didn't matter, so long as it was nourishing and tasted good. He bit off a piece of carrot. *Juicy. Not bad.* He grabbed some lettuce. That wasn't as tasty but he wouldn't complain. He'd have enough to complain of in the not too distant future, he suspected.

All around him hares nibbled, chewed, munched and…yes, there was water to drink too. He sipped from a shiny circular container, quenching his thirst. His throat was parched from the long trek across the sea to this place of captivity.

Most of the hares seemed engrossed in their eating and drinking. But he noticed a few that were less focused on their food. Their eyes revealed a deep unease as they sat staring through the barrier, as if waiting for unknown terrors; or perhaps ones they already knew of. He approached one of them. "Nice food, eh?" he quipped.

The hare regarded him with a cynical air. "Food… I've been here before. They feed us to keep us strong for their enjoyment. This is where they hold us before dog-dodging day."

Tipsy felt a twinge of recognition. He recalled the vision…the use of large four-legged creatures to chase hares.

"Dog-dodging?"

The other hare nodded sadly. “It’s the big Humanik game, and we’re the playthings.”

Tipsy swallowed hard. He knew that this crazy Humanik game was part of the reason for his presence here on the Big Island.

***

57

Tipsy yawned. He stretched himself, sat up, and looked around him: Still confined an all sides. Except above, but hares couldn't fly so that didn't count. He squinted at the lacklustre ball of fire that these days wasn't radiating much warmth; saw bloated banks of dull grey cloud lazily passing, causing the sun to wink mischievously.

Was the mighty source of life and growth signalling him? Letting him know quietly that things would somehow be okay, despite the pall of gloom and unease that hung like a malevolent fog over this place?

Several sunsets had come and gone since his arrival on the Big Island and his delivery to this confining structure. He'd lost track of how long he'd been here, but he was sure the Humaniks weren't holding him and the others for any benevolent purpose. Already, he'd been taken out into another venue, where the Humaniks had set a shaggy black and white creature after him. A dog, another hare informed him.

He had easily outrun the creature, only to be subjected to another chase. It only dawned on him second time around that he was supposed to run towards a hatch at the other end of the field. The dog almost collapsed from exhaustion pursuing him around the field, and the angry sounds emanating from the watching Humaniks indicated Tipsy wasn't doing what they wanted. So *that* had been aim of the exercise. The idea was to run towards the open hatch and then straight through it.

Only two of the hares in captivity knew exactly what was happening and they explained it to Tipsy. One of them, a wizened fellow called Snuffles, had just told Tipsy that the shaggy dog was a breed normally used by Humaniks to achieve control over other animals, and wasn't especially hostile to hares.

The Humaniks wanted hares to run to that spot at the end of the field only because it suited them. It was part of their plan to make the hares run in such a way as would give pleasure to Humaniks at a later stage...members of that species who enjoyed watching animals chasing, frightening, and possibly killing each other.

A hare sitting close by, hearing this, quipped: "But that won't happen because that silly old dog is too slow to ever catch us!"

The hare sounded as if he spoke more to reassure himself than put the others at ease. Snuffles shook his head sadly. "I was here many sunsets ago, when the leaves had fallen and the daylight was frail, just like today, and I saw what they do..."

Hares quickly gravitated to Snuffles to hear, though Tipsy already suspected what was in store for them all. The hard-bitten hare seemed to relish being the centre of attention. He puffed up his chest and surveyed his little audience.

Wisdom glowed in his countenance, his ears straightened, and his whiskers gleamed in a fading sunbeam as he spoke. "They've been training us...preparing us for the run of our lives. The dogs they'll set on us...out there... will be the fastest in the world. I was lucky last time, and I hope I'll be lucky today."

"What...what's it like?" a nervous bundle of fur muttered somewhere to the rear of the gathering. Snuffles raised his bleary eyes to the sky.

"Like nothing you've ever been through. You must run with all your might. When free from Humanik control, we all run...we hide; we bluff. We remain still and hope Humaniks or other predators won't see. In the great Humanik game we can run but we can't hide. And if the dogs are cleverer, or catch us..."

He stopped. A hare blurted: "Finish it Snuffles...what happens if we don't make it to that hole in the ditch?"

Snuffles waved them all away, refusing to elaborate. The second hare who had survived the Humanik game in a past time also sang dumb when queried. The refusal of the two veterans of the game to divulge its true nature, or what hares could expect, only exacerbated the all-pervasive fear and tension in the enclosure.

Another cause of anxiety was the mystery of the disappearing hares. At least they *seemed* to have vanished. There had been seventy-five when Tipsy arrived. Now there were sixty-two. So where were the others?

Rumours abounded. Some hares speculated that there could be a hole in the ground that opened at night and swallowed up any hare sitting in the affected spot. Others wondered aloud if Ostara had taken them to Hare Heaven in physical form, something Tipsy knew never happened: You had to die to qualify for a trip to the Afterlife. One hare swore he had seen his missing friend waving down at him from the moon. A trick of the light, Tipsy had corrected him, adding that if his friend had indeed "crossed over" he'd meet him again in the afterlife.

Though Snuffles had fallen silent on the question of how the chase might work out for them, Tipsy queried him about the missing hares. Snuffles tut-tutted. "Haven't you worked it out? The Humaniks come in when we're sleeping and take them."

"Take them where?" a sprightly leveret who was almost an adult asked.

"They take the weaker ones; the hares that they know won't run very well or who show signs of illness."

"And what do they do to them?" The leveret asked; his face contorted with a mixture of curiosity and incipient panic.

Snuffles shrugged. "Who knows? All I know is that when the Humaniks did the same last time, the missing hares were never seen or heard from again."

Tipsy felt light-headed, the vision of Mum's final moments on earth flashing inside his head. She had an injured foot last time he'd visited her, and that was just three sunsets before she was captured. So that was it. The weak ones who couldn't run were fed to the dogs.

Despite knowing Mum was safely in the afterlife, he shuddered at the thought of what Humaniks had done to her. Should he share this knowledge with the others?

No. If any of them met a similar fate nothing could be done about it. If they didn't it wouldn't matter anyhow. No point in giving them further cause for alarm in this oppressive place.

Tipsy rested, not that he should feel tired since he was confined to this miserable spot on the Big Island and couldn't run far in any direction. And yet fatigue had overcome him. Must be a weariness of the head brought on by too much fretting. It was different from the effects of strenuous physical activity but the result was the same. You wanted to doze off or lie down and let the world slide past. Around him hares snored, mumbled to themselves, grinded their teeth...or gave out low troubled purring. Some nibbled on carrot or lettuce remnants.

Then Tipsy sprang to his feet, startled by the abrupt appearance of a Humanik who had stepped into the cage through an opening. The tall creature, draped in a dark blue covering, stood looking at them all for a while. Then he stooped and grabbed a hare, whisked him off his feet, turned and exited the cage. The others exchanged frantic glances that quickly gave way to relief that it wasn't them leaving in the arms of that creature.

Tipsy shared the general sense of reprieve, but knew instinctively that all of them would get his turn. Snuffles raised a paw... "Guys...this is it...when they come for you, don't panic. When they take you for the game, just run as if your life depended on it, because it will..."

Nobody asked him to elaborate this time. Tipsy assumed they accepted that their lives might be coming to an end, and had quietly resigned themselves to it. One hare broke the silence: "Could it be any worse than being banged up in here? Maybe they let us go if we put on a show for them...running or whatever?"

Snuffles rolled his eyes as if to say *you've a lot to learn*. Another hare began to speak but his words were stilled by a great roar that surged high into the air and swept over them like a wave.

Tipsy tensed, and he saw other hares trembling. Some sat immobile, ears cocked, their bodies rigid with fear. "Humanik voices", Snuffles murmured, "it's their show of gratification..."

Tipsy recalled the vision...how Humaniks sought pleasure in the suffering of others. The clamour abated, declining into a buzz of chatter and babbling. Then that opening of the hatch again and the Humanik had another hare in his grasp. He had him held by the ears and front-legs, eliciting shock and alarm from the others as their friend was snatched. "Ostara go with you!" a hare shouted as the Humanik turned his back to leave.

Tipsy felt helpless. He could do nothing to prevent what was happening. Moments later that hollering resumed, punctuated by whistling and odd cackling noises...then another sound...a pitiful wailing. All the hares cocked their ears, their eyes turned pleadingly to the grey troubled sky.

Tipsy's heart sank and he shut his eyes against the world. The Humanik clamour had subsided, but the screeching of the hare out there continued...rising and falling like a sad sighing wind that blew across the island. Then it stopped abruptly.

Had the hare died? Or lost consciousness?

Before Tipsy or any of the others could recover their wits another hare was leaving the pen, squirming and protesting as the Humanik took him to his fate.

Tipsy braced himself. The cage was emptying of hares. After each departure came that sickening roar from the Humaniks, followed by a lull before the next surge of Humanik bellowing or the death-screech of a hare. Tipsy felt a presence beside him where no hare sat, and a voice within soothed: *Don't fret. Be calm but alert.* The Great One, far away in his cave, was sending him thoughts of strength and reassurance.

The grotesque routine seemed to go on forever. A hare close to Tipsy was wrenched from his brooding squat by those cruel Humanik paws. It was the maturing leveret. He didn't make a sound, surprisingly as he had been the jumpiest and most panicky of them all. A Humanik face devoid of compassion under a weird head-covering glowered as Tipsy met the young hare's eyes and wished him to live...or die quickly.

Tipsy waited. Two-hundred heartbeats passed and he heard the roar. But no screeching ensued. The maturing leveret was safe, at least for the time being. Tipsy lisped a prayer of thanksgiving. Other hares smiled and were grateful. Their jubilation was short-lived, interrupted by the re-appearance of the Humanik.

Tipsy shuddered as the misshapen intruder skulked towards him. A sudden sickness threatened; a visceral urge to vomit that he couldn't act upon. His world contracted. Evil loomed, more menacing than the outstretched wings of a falcon poised to swoop. But he felt relief too. The waiting was over.

This is it. What's the worst they can do to me? If I die, I'll be with Bumble and I'll see Mum, and others. But I won't die...if I can help it. I'll show these monsters that we hares have as much right to live and breathe as they have.

Tipsy felt himself drifting into a strange faintness as the Humanik hoisted him up by the ears and the creature then grasped his hind legs. He caught a stench of unfamiliar dizzying odours, carried to him on vapours from his captor. He was powerless, completely at the mercy of this hostile being. The whole world seemed to rock back and forth, the sky and the earth and the stirring of two-legged creatures around him merging into a blur as his body moved through space in the clutches of the Humanik.

He felt himself being lowered, but he didn't alight on grass or clay. He was being pressed into a wooden structure; a bit like the one he had been crammed into when he was captured on the island. He felt trapped and confined in this wooden contrivance. His eyes sought the light behind him, which was partially shielded by the Humanik's large paw that had just pushed him further in.

The light was dwindling. Then a deafening thud made his bones rattle. He smelt the dark wood squeezing him from all sides. The light was gone and he had a queasy sensation of day turning rapidly to night.

***

58

Annemarie pushed the mini camcorder inside her jacket.

She was keenly aware of the strict prohibition on what coursing clubs called "unauthorised photography" and the reason for the ban: After the close-run vote in parliament, coursing clubs were more alert than ever to footage or stills that exposed their "sport" to adverse publicity.

True, such damning footage had been recorded in the past, but its value diminished with time. In the present coursing season, attempts by activists to record the cruelty had so far been rebuffed. Coursing officials and fans had an uncanny knack for recognising outsiders, people unfamiliar to them or who didn't have that quintessential coursing look about them.

Last year she might as well have advertised her presence with her trendy outfit. Anyone on a healthy diet or who wasn't overweight was suspect, as was any woman with an overtly modern hairstyle or a "hippy" demeanor. Nose or cheek studs were instant giveaways.

Annemarie thought she had an edge in this regard. She had acquired a secondhand racing jacket at a charity shop and retrieved her late father's wellingtons from the garage. She'd pushed a cushion under the jacket to lend extra weight to her appearance. Just as importantly, she had practiced, six mornings in a row in the bedroom mirror, that uncaring cynical beady-eyed look typical of the female coursing fan.

Would it be convincing enough to fool the hard bitten "old hands" who had been spotting infiltrators for decades? *Maybe.* The biggest challenge of course would be when she produced the camera. She'd resigned herself to the inevitability of being asked to stop filming at some point.

But she hoped to be able to record enough footage to aid the campaign before being rumbled. She'd promised the campaign group that she'd pass on any significant evidence to them.

She opened the garage door and unlocked the car. Then, as an afterthought, she went back into the house, out in the garden and scooped some clay into her hands. She daubed her face with it. May as well complete the makeover, she reflected. She reviewed her appearance in the car side- mirror as she started the engine.

She grimaced and bared her teeth, narrowing her eyes. Yes. She reminded herself of a coursing fan she'd seen pictured in the Observer a few days before, the wife of a prominent pig farmer who assisted him in his work. She might even be mistaken for the same woman.

Ideally, she'd be accepted as a legitimate coursing fan who was recording the action for her own private edification. She wasn't known as an anti-coursing campaigner locally- another advantage- so maybe she'd pull it off.

***

59

Tipsy shivered inside the little wooden box.

Complete darkness. It wasn't just the cold weather, though he'd felt a distinct chill earlier in that other field, the smaller one with that strange see-through wall around it. You could see though it but couldn't get past it. There was no apparent escape.

He braced himself in the darkness. This was part of his mission. There were things he had to experience- and this chase about to start was one of them- before he could break free from the cruel Humaniks.

He waited...They'd already boxed him in like this...must be two sunsets ago...when he was chased by that large, very hairy and rather slow-moving dog. He had easily outrun and outwitted the creature, leaving it with its tongue lolling and steaming and a sad expression on its snout.

But he knew that was just a test. Several Big Island hares had alerted him. Next time, they warned, there would be two fast-moving dogs, and to be caught by *them* could mean injury or death.

Steady yourself Tipsy...focus. Remember...When you make eye contact with a creature you can make yourself invisible to him for twenty heartbeats. Steady...Focus!

The voice of the Golden Hare: Had he just recalled it, or was the mysterious Wise One communicating?

Doesn't matter which...mustn't let my guard down...

A tiny vibration shot through his body. Something scraped against the roof of the box. Then its front shot up. The cold autumn sun momentarily dazzled him as he darted from the box and alighted on the frost-covered grass.

It was an immense field, and enclosed on all sides. No escape except the one the Humaniks had created, directly in front of him, but far away. And the grass was so short it was if the earth were merely coloured green to give the impression of grass growing.

He skidded but quickly recovered, running straight for the opposite end of the field where he knew he'd find the hatch through which he could run to safety. The hatch was a mere speck in the distance, growing larger as he ran with all his might.

Then, a sudden outbreak of Humanik shouting and roaring assailed him. At the periphery of his vision he saw the two sleek dogs being unleashed by a Humanik draped in red and white. They were heading straight for him, closing the distance with every heartbeat.

Another backward glance revealed their straining hungry eyes, their long salivating tongues, their powerful bodies eating up space between him and them, and their mouths...as in the vision they were covered by some weird webbing. It had been easy with the shaggy old dog. He'd been slow, unable to keep up with Tipsy. But these...these were super-dogs. The hatch loomed larger now. He'd be there in forty heartbeats.

Something brushed past him. He felt a rush of air against his right ear. A dog had caught up...*Swerve. Avoid.*

Tipsy darted to the left, avoided him and then got behind the dog, leaving him confused. The dog, in spinning around, tumbled and fell on its back, its legs flaying the air, before up-righting itself. But then it fell again, this time unable to get back on its feet. It was limping and seemed to be in pain.

Tipsy was about to resume his dash to the hatch when the second dog passed him, swung around and aimed his snout at him. He missed, and Tipsy managed to get ahead of him, closer to the hatch. He fixed his eyes on those of the oncoming creature. For a fraction of a heartbeat.

Instantly, the dog stopped in its tracks.

More noise from the Humanik throng...anger this time, Tipsy thought.

He was about to run under the opening at the hatch, but a tiny voice whispered: *Not yet...*Tipsy looked in amazement at the two dogs that he'd feared would kill him. One was limping and yelping and a Humanik was running awkwardly towards it onto the field. The other dog was staggering about in a daze as if it had lost something and its attempt to find it was proving acutely frustrating.

Tipsy couldn't resist it. He really had rendered himself invisible to the dog. He ran up to the bewildered creature, passed under its legs and then leaped over it, before heading for the hatch and sanctuary.

He found himself in another confined area, with six other hares. One shrugged. "You made it, but they'll force us to run again tomorrow."

Another hare was agog with excitement. "I saw that...I...how did you do it? Has Ostara laid her hands upon you? That's not supposed to happen! You made those dogs look stupid, and the Humaniks too!"

***

60

Waxy rubbed his eyes with a sleeve of his jacket. *Am I dreaming? This can't be happening.* He closed them tight and then looked again at the coursing field. The hare was still prancing three-quarters of the way down the field around the confused greyhound who seemed either oblivious to his presence or unable to see him. *Impossible!*

He had observed hundreds of courses...thousands...and never had he seen a greyhound that ignored a hare like this. But the hare...its behaviour was astonishing! Had it lost fear of a dog that could kill it? Or...he glanced to either side of him. Was he hallucinating? He nudged the man next to him. "See that?" He awaited a response anxiously. The man's mouth was open wide, his face blank, twisted into a grotesque silent parody of a question-mark.

"What's going on?" he lisped.

Waxy whooshed "Thought I'd lost it for a second there!"

The man resumed gazing at the bizarre scene... "A miracle...must be a miracle..." he muttered.

Waxy didn't believe in miracles, but this spectacle was severely testing his sceptical nature: An injured greyhound being carried off the field, a second darting to and fro in search of something it couldn't see, and the hare seemingly mocking its pitiable plight.

But wait...the hare was now giving up its impertinence. It was running to the escape hatch...and, just as it dashed to safety, the dog snapped out of its weird reverie.

Yes. He had caught sight of the hare again, and was chasing the out-of-reach animal...but too late to get even close to it. It was as if the dog had temporarily lost its bearings, or its eyesight, but that didn't explain the hare's odd behaviour.

As the next pair of dogs were prepared and another hare was about to be released from its box, Waxy spotted a woman checking her camera.

Camera! Unauthorised Photography was strictly prohibited. *Must be one of those damned antis.* Had she recorded the incident? A hare making a complete fool of a greyhound: The media would go to town on that.... more ridicule and hostility to contend with. He squinted: She was furtively fiddling with the camcorder, little frosty puffs of breath escaping from her nose and mouth. *How misguided people can be...searching for ways to hurt our great sport.*

The girl was well wrapped up for the winter...red duffel coat, thick woollen neck scarf, and a green bonnet pulled down around her head that almost concealed her face. *These people will stop at nothing.*

Waxy nudged the coursing fan next to him again, pointing to the girl. The man nodded, signalling to another man and the three of them headed towards the unauthorised photographer.

***

61

Annemarie trembled with excitement. She'd captured the most astonishing footage with her camcorder...the earlier recording of the two hares being mercilessly pummelled; flung high into the air like paper toys was disturbing, but exactly what she needed to strengthen the case against coursing. Her hands had almost dropped the device.

It was difficult not to react to such abuse of those gentle creatures. And then there was the so-called "dispatcher", as the coursing club called him. She'd filmed him with his back turned to the fans, wringing the injured hare's neck. That footage she'd upload to YouTube later. It would add to the sum total of the evidence against hare coursing and boost efforts to have it banned.

That was good...*but this*...this was beyond belief. A hare had not only outwitted the two greyhounds unleashed against it. The animal had left one dog limping and yelping in pain, and the other in a state of total bewilderment. She thought she might be dreaming. It seemed so unreal...The hare had performed the weirdest acrobatics that resulted in the first dog becoming injured, moving at speeds that seemed unnatural...like a cartoon animal or computer-generated fictional creature.

But it happened right here...on a field in the heart of rural Ireland. With hundreds of gawking coursing fans gob-smacked by the little animal's defiant gymnastics. The first big gasp from the crowd came in response to the dog stopping in its tracks and wandering about foolishly while the hare ran ahead of it. Sharp intakes of breath turned to cries of disbelief when the hare also stopped, turned around and scampered back towards the dog, seemingly taunting it...and the dog appeared oblivious to its presence, as if it had been struck blind.

She adjusted the buttons and checked that she'd gotten the footage. *Perfect.* Everything was there. God, what a sensation this would be when it went online later that evening. The coursing event wasn't over. An hour at least remained, and she saw another brace of dogs being led up to the starting point. But she had enough. *Best get moving before...*

"Hey you...stop right there...you with the camera!" The shouts came from behind her. A backward glance revealed three men shuffling through the crowd, pushing others gruffly aside. Red-faced and fuming, they were heading her way, cursing and shouting warnings that she couldn't quite make out, but she heard "bitch" and several indecent words above the chatter and murmurings of the fans.

She moved quickly to leave the venue, excusing herself as she brushed against men in heavy winter clothes and coughing amidst clouds of blue cigarette smoke that warmed the frosty air.

"Stop her!" The roar came from behind. Fans began to notice her and a rakish man with an ugly scar on one side of his face grabbed her, twisting her left arm behind her back.

"Let me go!" she shrieked. The three men caught up with her, panting and wheezing. The largest of them stood directly in front of her, glaring down at her. His head resembled a large turnip with sprigs of hair protruding from it. His eyes bulged in his half purple face.

"Where is it...hand it over!" he hollered.

"Where's what?" she asked, her arm hurting where the wiry fellow gripped it.

"The camera.... Let's have it. You know photography isn't allowed unless you have special permission in writing from the club secretary. Hand it over!"

"That man will break my arm!"

At a signal the man released his grip. She began to move away, but the three of them blocked her path. The large man rushed at her, pushing roughly. She fell to the ground. The cushion she'd used to make her look chubbier lay beside her, eliciting jeers from the men. Before she could rise, she felt a hand searching in her jacket inside pocket, and the camcorder being wrenched from it. Her head throbbed and she felt blood on her face. Unable to think clearly she lashed out with her arms. "Give me that...you can't just..."

"You'll get it back when we've deleted anything you've recorded here. Lads, remove her!" She was suddenly lifted off her feet and half-carried, half-dragged all the way to the entrance gate. They threw her out into a half congealed heap of dung.

When she recovered from the sharp aches and cleaned the blood from under her nose, she cried. Tears flowed like little streams as she thought of the precious footage she'd lost. If only she'd moved faster...before those heavies spotted her; if she hadn't wasted time checking the device. That could have been done later, once safely out of the coursing field.

But her tears gave way to another feeling. One of defiance. Tomorrow was the final day of the coursing event. If she could do something to help those hares...

The image of that brave hare putting all those coursing fans to shame returned. She hadn't got the film but she'd seen what happened. Was it a sign? She reckoned it wasn't just a chance event.

It meant *something.*

***

62

Tipsy sat on the hard clay surface of the new Humanik place of detention.

No grass growing beneath him this time, but tufts of straw and a scattering of loose weeds compensated. He was with the hares that had, like himself, outrun the dogs and survived...his every nerve and fibre tensed up, his heart still racing after his success against those dogs that sought to catch and maul him.

He was glad to get a corner. It was a favoured vantage point. Every hare felt safer having his back protected, though in this case any feeling of protection could be illusory, he knew, with the Humaniks in control. They had the power of life and death over hares. At any time, they could kill them if they wished. They could do it with fire rods, or by unleashing dogs at them. If dogs were to enter this enclosure not a single hare would survive.

The ground was solid and unyielding to his paws, unlike almost any part of the island, apart from the rocky cliffs or the frozen fields in winter. This called to mind the bad place that some hare mums warned their offspring they'd be sent to in the afterlife if they didn't behave here on earth. The opposite of Hare Heaven. They hadn't reckoned on it being right here…on earth, instead of somewhere else…underground, or in some far distant part of the universe.

Tipsy tried to shield his ears from the moaning at the opposite end of the evil structure that enclosed them. The lamentations were issuing from a cluster of hares that were gathered around a hare that was drawing his last breath.

Two others had died earlier, and the same ritual followed this latest death: Hares related to the dying one; that had known him, were praying for his spirit, grieving his passing from this world to another. Tipsy didn't know any of the victims. They were not from the island. But he thanked Ostara for letting him see those faint bluish wisps leaving their bodies at the point of death and soaring into the heavens like happy birds.

And why wouldn't they be happy, freed as they were from this truly awful place to which the Humaniks had taken them. They would now be with loved ones in a world without pain or predators.

Above the moaning and sad purring he heard the now familiar chorus of Humanik voices, exulting in the terror of another hare fleeing from a pair of dogs. The Golden Hare had shown him similar instances of these supposedly superior beings, creatures who ruled the world, making hares suffer for their amusement.

Tipsy shuddered. A sudden grating sound pierced his consciousness. His eyes flashed open. A Humanik had entered their hellish abode. All the hares ran over to where Tipsy sat, away from this feared intruder. Had the creature come to take them for another round of chasing?

They cowered in terror, their bodies trembling, their eyes bulging with fright. Tipsy was less frightened but still deeply apprehensive. Okay, if it was time to die...to leave this horrible world, he was ready. He'd gladly embrace the unconditional peace and bliss that awaited all hares, even if so many doubted or had never believed in the first place. But not knowing what to expect...or *when* it would happen, was unbearable.

The Humanik didn't seem interested in them. Or at least not the living hares. He was bending down and picking up a dead hare. He dropped the body into a large pouch of some kind he was carrying. The body made a muffled sound as it hit the bottom of the pouch. He then reached for the other two bodies, likewise disposing of these. He then stood staring at all the hares that sat in a cluster, watching him intently.

He dropped the pouch on the ground and began hollering...What was he at? If he wished to frighten them he succeeded.

They all, Tipsy included, ran to the opposite end of the enclosure to avoid him. All except Grasshopper, who remained where he'd been since he was taken here after he'd survived the chase.

The Humanik kicked him lightly, eliciting a low sobbing from the hare. The Humanik then reached down and grabbed him, holding him by the ears and hind legs. Tipsy gazed in horror as the Humanik pulled Grasshopper as if he wanted to stretch him.

Grasshopper cried louder. The Humanik removed his paw from the hare's ears, using both paws to clutch the hind legs. He began beating Grasshopper off the ground, making strange gasping sounds as he did so.

The hare's sobbing ceased. His body swung from the Humanik's paw as the hostile being held it up close to his cruel eyes. Tipsy could see Grasshopper had died, though the body twitched as if still resisting. A hare's mortal body sometimes did that when the spirit had departed.

The Humanik added Grasshopper's body to the pouch and exited the enclosure. The hares eyed each other with blank expressions of horror.

Tipsy noticed Bouncer wasn't moving as freely as the others, who were dispersing around the pen. Tipsy approached Bouncer: "It's awful, I know, but the rest of us must remain strong, within the limits of our natural timidity..."

Bouncer's face screwed up with anguish.

"Hey, you okay?" Tipsy queried.

Bouncer moaned "Didn't want the Humanik to notice. Seen what he did to Grasshopper. We're no use to them if we're injured. Another hare told me that earlier. I pretended to be in good health, but I'm not...I'm dying, Tipsy."

Tipsy felt tears welling up in his own eyes as he beheld the sadness in Bouncer's pulsating orbs. The tough hare who had served as a sentry for so long at the Wise One's cave had been reduced to a shaking disconsolate shadow of his former self.

His breathing was irregular. He rasped "I could have let the Humanik kill me, like he killed Grasshopper...but...the pain is getting worse...I wanted to die in my own good time, not at the hands of that monster!"

He collapsed from his sitting position to lie on his side, breathing rapidly. Other hares began to gather at the spot. He lisped: "Thank you Tipsy, and forgive my impatience with some of you guys when you came to hear the Wise One. Nothing personal. I just had to keep things orderly..."

"We hold nothing against you Bouncer" another hare blurted, giving his reclining colleague a friendly rub with his head. Hares not from the island stood further back, but showed equal reverence to yet another casualty of the Humanik torture session.

Bouncer fell silent, but his pain seemed to diminish. "Not hurting so badly now" he said almost in a whisper.

Tipsy moved closer and murmured: "You'll be free of all pain Bouncer...I'll see you again when my time comes...."

Bouncer's eyes flashed open again. He was smiling, his words barely audible: "Tipsy...it's real...This is awesome. Fields of gold…hares without fear. Someone is beckoning me."

Gradually his eyes closed and his body relaxed. The heartbeat slowed, and then stopped. The assembled hares moved away. They had troubles of their own in this oppressive Humanik den.

Tipsy observed Bouncer's spirit quietly depart his body, an exact replica (though purplish blue and transparent) of the mortal frame that now awaited collection by that creepy Humanik with his pouch.

Unlike the others, Tipsy envied Bouncer. He knew that death wasn't the end. How harrowing it must be to cope with death when you either didn't know about an afterlife or refused to believe in it out of ignorance or stubbornness.

Then again, he reminded himself, he had an advantage in being able to see spirits taking flight from earth and having knowledge of all things spiritual imparted to him by the Golden Hare. Without these special insights he might be as dismissive or sceptical of life after death as the ones who professed, or pretended, not to believe.

***

63

Dr. Callaghan rubbed, and pulled at, the stubble on his beard. He turned away from the large computer wall screen to regard the small gathering of coursing club committee members. He removed his glasses, wiped them with a tissue and replaced them.

He spoke calmly but Waxy thought there was an undercurrent of nervousness in his voice. "The hare is noted for his evasive skills, as you all know. Physiologically and genetically he can handle any predator when it comes to speed. His 360 degree vision and stereophonic hearing give him a huge advantage in outwitting the fastest and cleverest foe…but, gentleman…"

He paused and looked from one to another of his listeners. "No hare can make himself *invisible,* and that seems to be what's happening here. Let's play that again Waxy. From the beginning."

Waxy adjusted the controls and the film started from where the strange hare was released from his box.

"Slow it down!" the doctor snapped.

Waxy reduced the hare's run to a crawl.

"And zoom…on its head…that's right…"

Waxy stared as an eye grew larger within the patch of reddish-brown fur. Then he saw it…reflected in the eye was the form of a woman with the head of a hare, and she was glaring. *Surely a trick of the light. Or a defect in the film.*

Callaghan grabbed the control from Waxy and further enlarged the image. "I don't believe it", he gasped. "It's a representation of the mythical Goddess, Eostre; a protector of the hare in legend, also known as Ostara…"

Waxy mumbled: "But how did that appear…?"

Callaghan seemed entranced by the mind-blowing image that filled the screen. He spoke almost in a whisper: "That legend about the island and the hares…it states that the Goddess looks after them, and that the Golden Hare can, with her intervention, confer powers on mortal hares. All poppycock of course, but how on earth did that perfect form get inside a digital camera? Wonder if the girl did this to play tricks on us?"

"Impossible", Waxy rasped, "We took it from her on the field…less than a minute after we saw that hare mesmerizing the greyhound. She had no time to do anything with the camcorder, let alone alter the footage."

The doctor's mouth drooped. His normally firm ruddy complexion paled. His lower lip quivered.

"Okay doc?" Waxy felt spooked. The little audience was chattering in low troubled tones.

Callaghan's eyes remained fixed on the image. He spoke more slowly, his voice quavering and a strange nervousness distorting his features. "The legend says too that the Golden Hare will, with Ostara's blessing, bring grief to anyone, human, animal or bird that meddles in the affairs of the Island Hares."

Waxy guffawed. "But that's just more malarkey, right?"

The doctor shook his head forebodingly. "That's what I always thought. I mean…the old stories. There are tall tales about hares, in all cultures. You know…passed from father to son down through the generations. No substance to them. Just stories people told to fill in the time around the fires in the long winters. But you wonder sometimes…if there might be a grain of truth in some of these legends."

Waxy laughed nervously, and the club members echoed his response with a few halfhearted guffaws. No raised voices though, he noticed, or vigorous putdowns. He fixed his attention on the screen again. "You're not suggesting…?"

Callaghan avoided Waxy's gaze. He looked oddly distracted, as if straining to perceive something beyond the range of his vision. Now he spoke in a faint undertone, fear and hesitation besmirching his fluency.

"Waxy…I've been a keen patron of the club for…twelve years now. But I'm calling it a day. I have a bad feeling about this. Even now, as I speak, I feel a weird tingling in my spine. And a sense…of nauseous…*foreboding*. I won't be at the

AGM next month. Do pass on my apologies. I'll draft a letter setting out my reasons for relinquishing my honorary position of Club Scientific and Heritage Adviser."

Waxy was gob-smacked. Before he could respond, the doctor was reaching for his Armani coat and walnut silver topped cane.

"Good bye Waxy, apologies gentlemen!" Without a backward glance he swept towards the door, opened it with his typical flourish, and shut it behind him with what Waxy imagined was an unhealthy emphasis.

Waxy stood bewildered.

"What does this mean?" Scabby was asking.

"Are you sure you have the right piece of film?" another lisped.

"This meeting is concluded!" Waxy shot back. "Someone is trying to spook us. Off to your homes lads!"

The room emptied, some of the members eyeing Waxy with concern as they exited. Left alone in front of the screen, he stood squinting at the hare's enlarged eye and that weird Goddess, as the doctor had called her, staring back at him. He shuddered. *Had she…no…*he thought he detected a smile on her ethereal lips. *Nonsense!*

Now he had to return the camcorder to that confounded girl. He'd intended to delete the potentially embarrassing footage but first he'd copy it. He'd show it to the others. Maybe consult a photographic expert. Get alternative opinions. *Callaghan must be on some medication that's blurring his judgment.*

He switched off the computer. The screen went blank. *Just a silly image…like seeing a face in a cloud, or in piece of wood. Mind playing tricks. You'd think he'd have more sense!*

***

64

Annemarie tossed and turned in bed, unable to sleep. Her ejection from the coursing grounds and the confiscation of her camera still preoccupied her. She felt she'd failed, that she should have stopped filming sooner, before attracting attention. She despaired of getting any rest. But then, suddenly, she felt a strange drowsiness. She was drifting into slumber. *Good,* she said*, at last...*Darkness gave way to a drizzly yellowish/orange light. *Have I left the lamp on?*

She went to reach for the switch but found herself immobile, unable to stir. Her eyes were open, but the walls of the bedroom had disappeared. The familiar patterns of the wallpaper had gone...and the ceiling above. That was gone too. *Must be dreaming. But this seems so real.*

She felt a light warm breeze and where the ceiling should be she beheld a pleasant blue sky with birds of all shapes and sizes fluttering and tracing lithesome spirals overhead. She was still in bed, or at least reclining, but she couldn't perceive the bed. It was as if she were floating like a weightless bubble in some outdoor location. But she didn't feel threatened.

Switching her attention from the sky she perceived a landscape of indescribable beauty stretching before her: A lakeside with daffodils dancing on its edges like in the poem, misty bluish-grey mountains in the distance, and a gently rolling effulgent meadow in the foreground. Something was moving amid the white, red and yellow flowers that dotted the green sward.

A rabbit?

It was scampering over to her. No, it was a hare, but of an unusual colour. Almost golden...how strange.

The creature hopped over and then sat directly in front of her. It seemed to be positioned in midair, as she couldn't perceive any ground beneath it. Its eyes were bright blue. *Must be dreaming about a hare after what happened today.*

She felt a peculiar sensation...as if a mild electrical current had passed though her. As she pondered the significance of this, the hare opened its mouth. Astonishment gripped her.

The hare was talking.

No, this couldn't be. But words were coming from this oddly coloured creature. "Hello Annemarie!"

"Hello", she replied, not knowing what else to do but play along with this bizarre state of affairs.

"You are in the afterlife sphere of the Irish Hare. All hares pass to the Other Side, but we Irish hares have our own special place..."

"Are you dead then...a spirit, or what?"

"Not dead, though my days on earth are drawing to a close. No, you don't need to be dead to meet in this wonderful afterlife realm. You can visit it in dreams, as hares (or their spirits I should say) do every time they sleep, though few of them realise it. Humans, normally, don't come here, unless by special dispensation, when Ostara permits it."

"I don't understand. If humans aren't supposed to visit this...realm...then why I am here? Or is this just a silly dream?"

"You are here for a reason. Annemarie, I am the Golden Hare of the Island. I know everything about what happened to you. You are a blessed Humanik, one of those who try to help us hares in our modest quest to live our short earth-lives in peace. I know what those Humaniks did to you. You have suffered a setback in your efforts to help us. But don't despair. There is something you can do that will make a difference. There is a special hare. You saw him earlier today. He is what you might call magical...he has rare abilities."

Annemarie felt a surge of elation. "Yes...he dodged those dogs and even seemed to be invisible to them!"

"He's one in a million. Right now he is with the other hares in that shameful cage built by the Humaniks, awaiting another Day of Terror."

Annemarie knew the final day of the big coursing event was due to be staged tomorrow. But what could be done now? Morning must be only a few hours away. It was too late to prevent the fixture from going ahead.

Seemingly reading her mind, he continued: "Dawn is three hours away, by Humanik time. There are no Humaniks guarding the cage, but they will return later. You can release my dear friends if you go there immediately. May Ostara bless you!"

She was about to plead with the hare, but, like a light being switched off, the vision disappeared, to be replaced instantly by the familiar walls and ceiling, the closed curtains, and the alarm clock ticking on her bedside locker.

***

65

Tipsy steadied himself. He had been running frantically up and down the length of the large cage that held him and the other hares. The others were restless too. They had evaded the dogs and were alive, but suspected that their troubles hadn't ended.

Suspicion hung in the frosty air. Tipsy could see fear in the little puffs of breath that emitted from their nostrils. He saw it in their eyes too, even in the darkness that was punctuated by weak moonbeams reflected from the silvery walls of the cage.

Being nervous and ill at ease was nothing new to hares of course, and after being chased by those dogs they had every reason to be suspicious of the Humaniks. But Tipsy was feeding the additional frenzy and near panic among the captives. Pausing, and trying hard to get his thoughts together, he pondered the vision he had received earlier, just before sundown.

His Eminence the Golden Hare had appeared in all his resplendent majesty, his aura flickering and shimmering in the semidarkness. None of the others had seen or noticed anything, so the manifestation was for Tipsy's benefit only. But the message was for the benefit of all.

The gist of it was that a female Humanik who liked hares, which must make her a very odd Humanik indeed, would attempt to free them from captivity. Tipsy was to prepare them for her arrival. She would perform some deed before dawn, following which Tipsy would signal them to follow him and do as he ordered.

But His Eminence had stipulated that they must not be told of the plan until the last possible moment. If she failed to turn up, the disappointment would be overwhelming and might destroy their already low morale. It was in the hands of Ostara. So Tipsy hadn't told them...well, not everything, but he had hinted that things *might* go their way...if they prayed to Ostara. Who knows, he asked, a miracle might happen, to which some hares responded with guffaws and sneers, others with pious reflection and new expressions of hope. He regretted even hinting now, as it had them all on edge.

Suddenly, everyone stopped and remained still as rocks. Tipsy glanced at the sky. It was still dark, with clouds obscuring the moon. It wasn't time yet. Three Humanik forms materialised. A bright light dazzled him. It illuminated the hares, who sat fearfully in clusters, all staring at the swivelling light.

Tipsy squinted, trying to make out the forms. Could any of them be the sympathetic Humanik? No, he decided. He had seen those same ones earlier. They were watchers, ensuring no doubt that no hares could escape.

The light disappeared and he heard the Humanik footsteps, growing fainter with each heartbeat.

The silence continued for a while, giving way to another round of frenzied running, leaping, and scampering in the cage. Tipsy shivered. It wasn't just the frost. He wished dawn would break and this mysterious Humanik would arrive... if she existed. He felt guilty about allowing such a blasphemous doubt enter his heard. But what if His Eminence was mistaken?

Okay, Ostara was infallible, but that didn't mean the Golden Hare always got her messages correctly, and *he* never claimed to be infallible, just a channel for the Great One who watched over all the hares of the world.

I sometimes misunderstand what another hare is saying, or trying to say, and hares are liable to act on false or half understood info occasionally. But surely not His Eminence. He wouldn't give me false hope. He must be sure of what Ostara told him. Yeah.

For the hundredth time, he began tracing a path around the perimeter of the cage, wondering again how they could find a way out of this accursed place.

***

66

Annemarie felt a surge of elation as she stepped out of her house, her mind firmly fixed on following the instructions of...*of who...or what?* That magical, mysterious creature...the Golden Hare. But was he...*it*...real?

He certainly seemed so. Dreams were different. They had a certain muddled reality, but upon awakening they vanished like puffs of smoke, and as the day progressed they faded from consciousness, apart from little wisps of remembrance that lingered for a few hours. But this...*experience*...was different.

Closing the small cast-iron gate behind her, she stepped onto the road, guided by the rays of a crescent moon and the streetlights. There was nobody around, naturally. She had to walk. Taking the car wasn't an option. The coursing club would be hyper-alert for any unexpected or unusual sounds or the presence of strangers in the vicinity of the compound. Hares had been released at other venues. Not here at Ballycrossways, but the club wasn't taking any chances.

God, what would people in the village say if she told them a hare had appeared to her in a vision? Probably laugh till they cried. Or call the fellows in the white coats.

The hours before dawn didn't see much activity in the village, apart from late-night antics at weekends like cider parties in the fields and a drunkard or two staggering home. Exiting the village the street lighting gave way to a more complete darkness, thankfully relieved by the waning but still bright sliver of moon that hung tremulously over the Peninsula.

A feeling of mild euphoria grew stronger as she walked on; drawing nearer every second to what she knew would be an act of sabotage.

She shuddered at the thought. If she got to carry out the plan, she'd be breaking the law. The weight on her back of the knapsack wasn't too bad, but it had the feel of a burden about it. Not a physical but rather an ethical one.

The wire-cutter was old and rusty. It hadn't been used since her father had died three years ago. But she'd tested it quickly in the shed on an iron rod and it worked perfectly. The rod had snapped after she pressed hard. She hoped the padlock on the coursing compound wouldn't be any tougher or thicker.

The ethics of it? She had no problem with the idea of damaging the compound, or of trespassing by entering land marked "Private Property". Under normal circumstances she respected the laws of the land, she reminded herself. But this wasn't a normal situation. It wasn't every day that a Golden Hare appeared to you and told you to go out and save other hares from a truly shocking form of animal cruelty.

And she knew that if she didn't act those hares at Ballycrossways would be put through that same Russian roulette ordeal as they'd undergone yesterday.

Her heart missed a beat as a car honked. She pressed herself against the ditch on her right and froze. Walking in the dark wearing dark clothes was something she didn't do too often. The car cruised past. The driver obviously hadn't seen her.

She heard rather than felt the sighing of an ice-cold breeze, and shivered more at the thought of it than the prickly sensation on her face.

A weird furtiveness replaced the elation she'd felt setting off. If caught, she'd end up in court and possibly be saddled with a criminal conviction that would hurt her career prospects, and maybe affect her current job as an accountant's secretary. Being in trouble with the law didn't help smooth one's path in the world.

Funny how she had to break the law to save animals from ill-treatment: Laws were peculiar. Hare coursing was legal here, but a criminal offence a few hundred miles away in Northern Ireland and in many other jurisdictions.

Chosen. Imagine...to be chosen like this by a supernatural entity.

She halted at the crossroads and turned left. She slowed her pace, and reached into the pocket of the duffel coat for those socks. She pulled them on over her runners. An old trick she'd read about...to stifle the impact of her footfalls.

Burglars did that, though she abhorred the comparison. She wasn't a criminal, even if the law would say otherwise. She wasn't going to steal, or hurt, or terrorise...just bend the rules a little bit.

***

Annemarie cast a fleeting glance at the sky. The moon was struggling to shine through thickening clouds.

Good and bad. Useful not to have too much light so anyone mooching about couldn't see her. Not so helpful as she might have difficulty seeing her way around when she reached the compound.

Right...I cross this field, and the next, and the one after that contains the compound.

She took the tiny torch from her pocket and shone it at the ditch in front of her. *Can't see any gate. Where's the gate?*

She switched it off; fearful of giving herself away. The black sky was beginning to leak reddish-purple streaks, complementing the weak moonlight. She shuffled alongside the ditch, straining to see in the gloom. *Ah, there it is.* She climbed over the iron-gate; alighting in a half-congealed heap of cow dung. The socks would be smelly. *Never mind.*

She jogged across the field until she reached a low ditch that separated it from the meadow where stood the big hare prison. There was no gate allowing access to the meadow. She crouched, peering over the brambles and manmade obstacles that straddled the ditch. Though the ditch was low, it had tangled masses of barbed-wire running along the full length of it. The razor sharp fronds mirrored the faint moonbeams and the first flickering of dawn. She hadn't reckoned on this. *They must have installed it a few days ago, to prevent someone like me from getting into the field. Damn.*

She'd be ripped to pieces if she tried to climb over that. Frantically she ran along the ditch, hoping to find a breach or a spot sufficiently less daunting to let her through.

Hey. She stopped, her right foot stickily landing on a piece of wood. *A rotten plank.* She bent down and grabbed it. The plank was twice her own height; but not too heavy. She let it fall across the tangle of spiky viciousness. It sprung softly on the strands, before settling like a ladder. Was it sufficiently strong to take her weight? *Have to take a chance.*

She positioned a foot on it, and began her ascent, wobbling and maintaining her balance like a trapeze artist with hands outstretched. *Don't stop to think. Just do it.* She felt the board fall under her as she ran down the other side, stumbling as she landed in the meadow. *Hope I can find it on the way back.*

Her heart raced as she squinted and made out the dim shape of the compound ahead. No sign of light or movement. The watchmen mustn't be around. The vision was right. Unless...there *could* be someone on guard at the other side of the compound; or watching from further off through binoculars...

Just keep going. What's that? A car engine! She froze. *Where's the road?*

She waited two or three seconds. *Nothing...just passing.* She ran soundlessly towards the compound that loomed larger and more menacing the closer she got.

No! She halted, swaying and just about managing not to lose her balance, flapping her arms about. *Torches...* Beams sweeping along the grass in front of the cage...forms strutting to and fro...voices... laughter... and wisps of breath caught in the torch beams...hares within the compound illuminated: some sitting still, others darting about, startled by the intrusion.

She lay flat on the ground, facing downwards. The grass was only inches high, not enough to shield her if they shone a torch in her direction. But they wouldn't have heard her.

She lay still, breathing fitfully and trying to blow a blade of grass from a nostril. It tickled her and she had an overpowering urge to sneeze. She muffled it, but...had they heard anything? She turned around and lay on the flat of her back, wincing at the discomfort of the wire-cutter pressing into her flesh.

She focused on her icy breath. Pinpoints of weak skylight intermittently pierced it from behind unfurling ribbons of cloud. The blackness had changed to a velvety hue as night underwent the gradual transformation to a new day. *Just don't change too fast.*

Averting her eyes from the heavens she caught sight of the watchmen. She could see their legs stirring, a torch beam swinging about as they chatted in low tones. Her eyes had adjusted to the gloom.

The torch flicked off. Daring to rise a little, she saw the figures growing smaller as they moved further from the compound, hopefully away from the field to wherever they lived. She strained to hear. *Not a sound.* The voices had ceased.

Hardly daring to breathe, she counted to twenty, gazing at the velvety cloud-scudded curtain with its pulsing but fast disappearing diamonds.

Are you up there God? Give me strength. Let me succeed. If what I'm doing is a sin, though how on earth can it be, you can sort it out with me later, but not right now, okay?

She rose slowly, soundlessly, glad of the socks that muffled her presence. She edged forward, expecting at any instant to have to make a run for it. *No point in getting caught if I can't pull this off. At the first sight or sign or sound of humans I get the hell out of here.*

She felt a hammering in her forehead that seemed set on matching her galloping heart-rate as she drew close, the ghastly structure now clearer. Through the holes in the chain-link she caught sight of movement. Little forms scurrying to and fro. Blobs of fur in the murky predawn shadows amid the dark carpeting of clay and straw that constituted the floor of their prison...

Her heart pounded as she stood facing scores of hares that sat, lay sleeping, or squatted there. Some were tensed up, eying her inscrutably. Others had an indifferent or casual demeanour. Possibly they saw her as one of the detestable, exploitative humans who enslaved them.

She felt a surge of pity. This was it. She reached behind her for the wire-cutter. It seemed to weigh heavier than earlier when she packed it. Her hands and arms vibrating like jelly on a plate, she grasped the cutter and opened the jaws at either side of the sturdy half-rusted padlock that dangled from the entrance. She pressed with all her might.

So unyielding. God, this was thicker than the rod she'd tested the cutter on in the shed. She took a deep breath and braced herself. She pressed harder, squeezing with every ounce of her strength. The urge to relent, to let go, was immense, almost overpowering, but she persisted. *A last effort. Keep squeezing.*

Snap. The jaws met in a metallic crunch. *Thank God.* She wrenched off the broken lock and pulled across the latch. She swung open the gate. Standing aside, she waited. Nothing happened.

What on earth? Don't they know they can run out?

She used the wire-cutter to bang on the cage beside the open hatch that swung creakingly in the chill night air, moonshine conveniently tracing a path away from it.

Then, tentatively, one hare hopped out through the opening, followed by two more. The animals looked about them; then bounded straight ahead. Others followed, some unhesitatingly, others as if they might be safer remaining behind. She banged the chain-link again. "Hey, come on, you guys. I'm trying to help you, here" she urged, though not daring to raise her voice.

Gradually, after what seemed like hours but really couldn't have been more than a few tension-racked minutes, the compound was empty, though a few hares still seemed undecided on what to do once they got outside.

"Shoo, shoo", she hushed, careful again not to alert those watchmen who might return at any moment. They could still be guarding, from near or far, this oppressive place of detention. *There's nothing more I can do. Those poor animals are on their own now. Hope they survive.*

She slipped the wire-cutter back into the knapsack, zipped it up and retraced her steps, her footfalls again mercifully muffled by the socks, now mud caked, wrapped around her boots. She broke into running, stopping only to scale the plank over that accursed barbed-wire obstacle into the next field.

The sky was lightening by the minute, sunshine struggling to erase the velvety atmosphere. She thought she heard sounds behind her: *Could be voices. Or cows. Or distant traffic.*

She dared not look back. She might have been spotted, but turning around wouldn't help. A pursuer might then identify her. *Keep running.* Awkward with that blasted wire-cutter pressing against her spine. It reminded her of athletics at school, but that hadn't been in the dark and after getting on the wrong side of the law. And there were no dire consequences if she didn't run fast enough.

Exiting the last field she felt a surge of relief once she stepped onto the road. If she'd been caught near the compound or in an adjoining field she'd have had difficulty explaining her presence there...and then she'd have been easily linked to the sabotage....not having the vaguest notion of any excuse that she, a known opponent of hare coursing, could offer for being in the vicinity of a hare-holding compound.

She wasn't completely in the clear yet. Just being out so early, dressed in black and carrying a wire-cutter would still look suspicious...if somebody saw. *Not likely to be cars about at this hour. Or walkers either.*

She carried on towards the village, soothed somewhat by the whistling and warbling of songbirds. A few tentative chirps to begin with, warming up quickly to a Dawn Chorus. White-throated sparrows, thrushes, chaffinches, and robins flew around her from all sides, heading for their singing perches in trees, bushes, or on telephone wires.

Their sweet music cheered her, especially one melodic bird whose notes rose above the lyrical concord. She'd been meaning for the past five years, since before leaving school, to listen to this wondrous miracle of nature, though not in these unusual, furtive circumstances.

***

67

Tipsy's patience was wearing thin. For the umpteenth time he raised his eyes skyward. Definitely, the pitch darkness was giving way to a metallic grey, and the scudding clouds illuminated by the fading moon were now brighter, thanks to the first tentative sunbeams. The great molten orb was still hidden, but the thin struggling ribbons of light signalled its inevitable emergence.

So where was this Humanik? If only he could be as confident of her arrival as he was of the great sunrise. "Before dawn" was now...Surely the Golden Hare knew what he was talking about? But from which direction would she come? What if she couldn't see them in the dark?

He scampered in turn to each corner of the cage, excusing himself as he brushed against sleeping or disgruntled hares, or hares so tensed up they looked like they might explode.

"You expecting someone?" an old hare asked, fear trumping curiosity in his frantic demeanour. Tipsy restrained himself.

"Something on my mind...hey; Try to be calm. Trust in Ostara!" he soothed.

"Yeah, that'll help!" the hard-bitten one responded sarcastically.

Nothing out there, he said to himself, surveying the stretch of darkened grass. Nor there, he moaned, checking the opposite side of the cage. *How am I to know where...what's that?*

Sounded like movement out there. He stopped in his tracks. Others had heard it too*: Footsteps. Faint, almost inaudible, but we hares don't miss much when it comes to hearing.*

There it was again: The smallest of twigs bending and snapping. The crunch of earth, the contact between blades of grass and those things Humaniks wear on their feet. Though the sound it made was softer than usual.

He ran to where the sounds seemed to emanate from. Others were heading that way too, to investigate. *Yes.* A form was moving in the dim light. *Just one.* So it wasn't the Humaniks who'd checked on them earlier.

Standing at what he deemed a safe enough distance, Tipsy fastened his eyes on the Humanik. From the shape he deduced it was a female. None of the Humaniks he'd seen thus far had those contours.

She was difficult to make out, attired as she was in materials darker than the fading night that was changing to morning with every heartbeat. She was holding some contraption and applying it to the cage, making low squeaking noises.

Instinctively, Tipsy knew the time had come. He turned around to face the hares that were all gathered about in one big cluster behind him, wondering what the Humanik was up to, murmuring quietly among themselves and speculating, he presumed, as to what their persecutors had in mind for them now...at this unearthly hour.

"Friends. He hollered, "Ostara has heeded your prayers. Do as I command, and follow where I go!"

"What do you mean? What's happening?" Several cried out at once.

"Ostara has smiled upon us, and devised a way to save us from the Humaniks!"

"Are you mad? That's a Humanik out there...look! Unless my eyes deceive me it's one of them. They're no friends of ours!"

Tipsy shot back: "No time for arguments or explaining. Just follow me when I tell you!"

68

The hares reacted with a mixture of scepticism, shock, and intense curiosity to Tipsy's appeal. Scores of amber eyes scrutinized him. Then his heart missed a beat. A sudden *snap* from somewhere behind jolted him.

He turned to see the Humanik female pushing at the side of the cage. A sharp jangling accompanied her movements, followed by the abrupt appearance of a hole in that confining structure. The Humanik stood where she'd opened the hatch, gazing upon the captives. It had to be her. *Yes.* She was the liberator.

Tipsy got in front of the others and addressed them. *No time to lose.* "Okay lads. All of you. Follow me!"

He darted out through the opening, halting momentarily to look at her, this rare creature who'd come to free them. He transmitted a quick "Thank you" to her, not knowing if she'd received the thought. Telepathic communication only worked between him and other animals and birds. Humaniks weren't included, he understood, but you'd never know.

He didn't wait around to see if she'd got the message. A backward glance revealed only two hares following. But the Humanik was banging on the cage, probably to frighten them into leaving.

How stupid we hares can be sometimes. There we all were, bemoaning our captivity...and now some of us hesitate when freedom is handed to us like a tuft of grass or a clump of delicious seaweed. Ostara, help me!

Prayer answered! Out they came, hesitantly at first but then jostling to get past each other, sweeping by him...running and leaping...congregating in three clusters halfway down the field, awaiting further advice.

He joined them, calling the hares to gather about him. They formed a circle. "Listen...no time to hang about. We're free...but we don't know what dangers we face. It's every hare for himself. But at least we've got a chance. Those Humaniks were going to make us run from the dogs again, and any who survived would end up as food for dogs... or Humaniks. Any of you who were injured, that even got a scratch, would have been...I saw this in a vision...dangled *live* before dogs. Your guts would have been ripped out while your hearts still beat inside. So...go where your feet...or the will of Ostara, takes you. Go alone, or in pairs, or larger groups, as you wish."

Tipsy knew that each hare had his buddies and confidantes. They stuck together. Others were born loners. He didn't wish to impose on any of them. "Let's go!" he hollered, darting to the end of the field. "Not here" he cautioned, signalling the others scampering behind him.

That little light of guidance flashed inside his head. Was it the Golden Hare? Without pausing to think, he added "Sharp impediment, killer thorns prepared by Humaniks...avoid!"

They heeded his warning. They raced along parallel to the long ditch that bristled with those shiny meshes of barbed fronds. A dead bird was speared on a spike, eyes staring blankly, blood dripping from its tiny carcass. The same could have happened to any of the hares. *Who will warn them when they haven't got me to alert them?*

Plenty spaces in the next ditch. Hares dashed underneath, and vanished into the gloom, now partially drained of darkness by brightening sunbeams. The stars were quietly signing off; a deep blue spreading across the heavens to banish the velvet canopy under which Tipsy and his fellow captives had spent a fitful night, what many had feared would be their last.

Tipsy thanked Ostara that two hares remained with him. He was resigned to accepting her divine will if she decreed that he go it alone, but support was always reassuring. Okay... hares were solitary creatures by nature, but when you faced the unknown it was comforting to have others with you.

"Where to now?" Lockjaw asked.

"Does it matter!" quipped Cupid, the other hare.

Tipsy knew neither of them as they weren't from the island. Lockjaw gave Tipsy a guilty look. "Don't be offended. I'm very grateful to you for helping us escape, but I'm heading off that way...alone. I think there's a good hiding place I've seen before. Only room for one though. Sorry friends...it's just a feeling I've got. The Humaniks will be hunting us and I reckon their dogs will smell out three of us easier than one."

Awkwardly he turned; eyes averted from Tipsy and Cupid, and had disappeared into the half-light within five heartbeats. Cupid exploded. "Well of all the lousy...you selfish git!"

"Leave him" assuaged Tipsy, "he's right...and I won't blame you if you go it alone too, though I'll value your company..."

Cupid sighed. "Let's go Tipps...Lockjaw would have been useful. He's from around here. We'll just have to take our chances..."

***

69

Darkness had give way to weak sunlight as Annemarie pressed her hand on the little gate in front of her house. Nervously, she looked around, dreading early risers or insomniacs who might be about, or peering at her from any of the houses opposite. She felt a huge burden, a rapidly acquired weight of responsibility.

Not of guilt, though she knew she'd broken the law. There was the damage to the compound... the broken lock. She wasn't sure about the legality of releasing the hares, but there was the matter of trespassing on land declared "private property."

She quickly entered the house, closing the door gently so as not to arouse the neighbours. She hoped they hadn't noticed her leaving or returning at such odd times. That could tell against her if the police called. But why would they bother? It was hardly a major crime when one considered...well, murder, burglary, assault; drug-dealing. *No. Still, mustn't leave evidence lying around.*

She'd tossed the wire-cutter into the crumbling depths of the local dump, which she passed on her way back to the village. It wouldn't be noticed amid all that scrap-iron and bits of old fridges and car parts.

The clock on the mantelpiece said five am. She must get some sleep. She had to be up at eight to be ready for work at nine. She'd be less efficient at the accountant's office without adequate sleep. *Well. It's just one day. But can't call in sick: investigators would notice that.*

Rushing to change her clothing she gasped. Her two knees were visible, mud stained and with tiny cuts, through her jeans. They'd been ripped, probably when climbing over that barbed-wire. Those pieces of material could be traced to her...but only if they could be matched with her jeans. She'd have to ditch those. Even as she said it she scoffed at the idea. *Why would the police be bothered with this anyway? Still, better be careful.*

She'd add the jeans to a bag of stuff she'd planned to give to a local charity shop. She'd drop the bag outside the shop on the way to work. Fingerprints weren't a problem. She'd worn gloves to keep out the cold. *Footprints?* She'd add the boots to the bag for the charity shop.

Wonder if they had hidden CCTV at the compound? Oh forget it. My face was mostly covered by the hood and it was so dark. This thing won't be an issue anyway.

Undressing to enter the shower, she gasped. Those cuts on her knees: The police could test the blood samples in a laboratory, match it to hers and she'd be caught. DNA evidence had put away many a bad dude.

Oh, what am I thinking? I haven't hurt anyone or stolen anything...what's the worst that could happen? It's only when a series crime is involved that those forensic people are called in... I suppose there's the job. The accountancy firm mightn't be all that happy about having a convicted criminal working in the office in the middle of the village. No...but that's only if I'm caught. I won't be, if I can help it. If any police come knocking I'll just deny everything. Make them prove it...and they can't.

Shutting her eyes she let the refreshing hot water splash over her, daring to think it was washing away all traces of her daring stance against hare coursing. Soap and sudds could make everything clean.

She yawned. *Must get sleep and act normal in the morning. Try not to think about what happened at Ballycrossways. Just turn up at the office and breeze through the day. Ignore any comments. No furtive, guilty looks. Just be calm...*

70

Waxy had dozed off again. He'd been up late keeping an eye on the hares at Ballycrossways. No need really: The more militant antis wouldn't dare show their balaclava-concealed faces around here.

The ones with the placards occasionally ventured into the village, just a brief appearance on opening day of the coursing season, to hand out a few leaflets. Though there were people for and against the sport on the Peninsula, those with anti sentiments kept their heads down. They knew what to expect if they made any serious waves. This was traditionally a coursing stronghold, and would remain so regardless of what those idiots said or did. *God. I hope I didn't catch a cold, or worse, punching in my turn standing guard.*

Rising from his chair beside the rayburn cooker he stretched himself. He went to fill the kettle to make coffee. He placed the kettle under the tap in the sink and let the water splash into it. Before he could replace the lid, his mobile boom-boomed inside his jacket, and chimed its distinctive Tennessee Waltz tune at high volume. He left the kettle in the sink, reaching for the Nokia. As he raised it to his ear the landline began ringing. Whoever it was could wait, or he'd ring back.

"Yes?"

The person on the other end was blabbering at a frantic rate, spluttering and half shouting. Waxy couldn't make out a single word.

"Slow down, man…Jimmy, is that you, What's up? I didn't catch what you said."

"Waxy…Waxy, Oh God above all Hell has broke loose. We're finished. What are we going to do?"

"What is it? What's up?"

"The hares! They've broken out. Escaped. God protect us but could this be the end of the world?"

Waxy's grip on the phone weakened. He had to force himself to keep holding it. He felt faint. This couldn't be happening. Hares didn't escape from Ballycrossways. The man must be raving… or on the bottle…

"Listen...carefully, have you been drinking? Have you seen the compound yourself? Or did someone tell you this?"

"Ah cripes Waxy, I've seen it alright. I'm not in the better of it. I was in a healthier state when I heard my father died ten years ago, or when I lost a thousand euro on Scraggly's Fancy at the coursing last year. Mikey and Jimmy-Joe were keeping watch. That was after you went home. Then they took a break. Just a twenty-minute break for God's sake…and when they returned to the compound…it was empty. They couldn't believe it!"

Waxy, still refusing to credit or take on board what he was hearing, asked: "Was it deliberate…or did someone leave the hatch open? Maybe the hares are within catching distance…they might have just wandered out but they could be in the next field. I've known that to happen. They might come back to where they know they'll be fed…"

"Waxy…you're not getting this. The hatch was swinging in the wind…and not a single hare was inside. The lock was snipped. Oh God, Waxy, it was no freak accident. Those hares didn't do that on their own. They'd never do that to us. Never. Ballycrossways has never had trouble from hares. It was a crime, Waxy. Can you imagine anyone doing something like that? This is the worst crime to hit the Peninsula since Michael O' Keeffe was flogged to death by the Redcoats here in 1798. No…no it's worse than that. Far worse!"

"Look, my other phone is ringing like mad. Can I call you later? But tell me. Have you contacted the police?"

"The whole club is down at Ballycrossways and the police are all over the place: Uniformed and special branch. There's a police helicopter flying over and back above the Peninsula. There's a battalion of soldiers due there within the hour. One of the lads at the club phoned Interpol but them boys it seems don't care too much about coursing. They told Benjy they have other priorities and that the hares won't have crossed any international borders. Benjy swore the man was being sarcastic."

"Could well be. Look, you've done your best. Bye...I'll answer this."

Waxy ran to the landline, grabbing the receiver.

"Yes?"

Heavy breathing followed by a terse disciplined voice: "Detective Chief Superintendent Malachy O' Neill here…Mr. Bumbleton Crossbar, we're doing everything we can to apprehend the culprits. You don't have to tell me…people are shocked to the core. The national flag is flying at half-mast on government offices across the Peninsula. We expect to make several arrests. Emergency laws will be invoked. Every anti trouble maker on the Peninsula and in the counties bordering our own will be picked up. Don't worry! We'll catch whoever is behind this attack on all we hold dear. No effort will be spared. In no time at all they'll cooling their heels in a maximum security prison."

"Yes, of course, I don't doubt you." Waxy had to raise his voice above the whirring of a chopper over his house. "But catching the culprits won't get those hares back safely to us. Today's coursing will have to be deferred…or cancelled. We can't catch enough hares at such short notice…"

"I'm sorry Sir, but as you know police aren't trained to catch hares. That's your department. I'll have a word though with General McNulty. He may be able to spare troops to aid you in searching for the missing hares. I'll impress upon him the need to use the very latest technology to track them down…"

Waxy's mobile was ringing again, and from outside the house came a clamour of panic-stricken hollering. He thought he heard a woman scream. That would be Mrs. Hackler, wife of multi-award winning net-man, Paddy the Joker. She was devoted to coursing. She'd be in bits, the poor woman.

Saying thank you and goodbye to the Chief Superintendent he reached for his mobile. Too late.

Rushing to the window, he beheld scenes of terror and hysteria. Men were calling for vengeance, waving shotguns and cudgels. Doctor Ryan was holding Mrs. Hackler in his arms. She had obviously swooned. *Unless she's got a heart attack.* Anything was possible.

Waxy opened the front door. No sooner had he appeared on the doorstep when the group of more than thirty men and woman surged towards him like zombies lusting for their daily feed of blood and guts. He feared they'd trample him underfoot as they pressed him, wide-eyed, yelling and stammering incoherently, shaking their fists. One man was foaming at the mouth. The owner of last year's winning greyhound at Ballycrossways. Waxy embraced him. "It'll be okay, Podge, It'll be okay!"

But Podge was inconsolable. He looked like a man who had contracted Rabies. "I'm dead if those hares aren't caught Waxy, I'm dead. I'll swing for those bloody hares." Podge was gently pulled away from Waxy's embrace by Fr. Holohan, whose corpulent form had suddenly materialised amid the growing throng that was blocking the street.

The priest hollered: "Easy there Podge…the rest of you…get off the street. Gather at the parish hall an hour from now. I've called an emergency public meeting to discuss this terrible event in our community."

Waxy had to usher three unfamiliar men out of his house. They were lolling about in the kitchen eating his freshly made ham sandwiches. They must have slipped in while he was preoccupied consoling Podge and assuring others that somehow the hares would be recaptured.

But even as he said it he knew his consoling words were hollow. If the hares had been deliberately freed, they could be miles from the compound, or dead on the roads if they got caught in traffic. The coursing event would have to be deferred. An unheard of situation, but the club and the wider community would have to come to terms with this…what was it that old English judge said years ago…*Appalling Vista!*

Calls to make. What on earth do soldiers and police know about catching hares? He punched in the number of Hawker Brandon, the number one poacher on the Peninsula. Normally a mortal enemy of coursing clubs because he snatched the hares before they found them. He might prove to be an ally, for a price, in the quest to recapture them.

***

71

Tipsy reckoned they'd put a fair distance between themselves and the Humaniks. He imagined them raging at the loss of their captives. Morning had come, the sun melting the frost that had covered much of the grassy and hard surfaces and the leaf-strewn woodland that Tipsy and Cupid trod upon. It had chilled Tipsy's feet but now he felt the warmth return to his body.

They'd been on the move almost without pause, traversing swathes of forest, fields with grass so short you couldn't get your teeth into it, and those Humanik built stretches of hard surface that were devoid of vegetation and, according to Cupid, *life threatening* due to a crazy Humanik contraption that moved along them at high speed and could crush any living creature beneath its underbelly.

Tipsy hadn't seen any of them yet but he'd heard strange faraway noises that Cupid cautioned were made by those monstrosities. They'd crossed another of those featureless Humanik pathways and entered yet another big field when Tipsy felt Cupid's paw pressing the back of his neck. "Shush", the other hare lisped.

Tipsy stopped and immediately followed Cupid's line of sight. *What's this?* A strange looking furry red dog with a swishing bushy tail.

It wasn't *all* red, Tipsy corrected himself, as it raised its peculiar flattened head a little. The lower part of its face and most of its underside was whitish, though discoloured with splashes of mud or clay. *Must have been digging.*

It was smaller and stockier than the greyhounds. They'd been sleek and rather bald looking. It had a wistful, intelligent gaze, its triangular ears protruding sharply upward and its snout busily darting from side to side as if it were sniffing something.

"It's not a dog", Cupid whispered, cowering behind a fuchsia brush, "It's called a fox. They're very clever...and very dangerous!"

The fox had a wily, furtive demeanour, edging along towards their hiding place, sniffing the ground as it went. Then, abruptly, it raised its head and cocked its ears...Its beady eyes were focused directly on the spot where they sat watching it. Its eyes closed tight and it emitted a sharp eerie bark.

Cupid lost his nerve, bolted and ran. "Don't move!" Tipsy had started to plead... too late. The fox bounded forward and the chase began.

Tipsy quickly caught up with Cupid and they both reached the opposite end of the field. A backward glance revealed that their pursuer had either lost them or just wasn't fast enough to keep up.

"That wasn't so bad" Cupid rasped, catching his breath.

"Hold it". Tipsy's inner voice had sounded caution. "See that crumbling wall yonder", he quipped, "it's low enough to leap over."

Cupid shrugged. "But the fox is gone..."

Seemingly from nowhere the red menace reappeared, moving from a ditch to their left where it must have been sneaking by quietly. The two hares dashed to the wall, bounding over it. Alighting in a field of lush vegetation they ran in and out between the clumps of green leaves that Cupid called *cabbages*. Hot on the trail came the fox, seemingly determined to catch them, probably for food.

Tipsy rasped "I don't fancy being his dinner."

Cupid laughed. "Me neither!"

On they sprinted, the landscape a blur as they re-enacted an age-old hare's run for survival. Tipsy's hearted fluttered. "In there!" he gasped. He'd almost passed the circular opening into one of those Humanik contrivances that went underground. Cupid scuttled in first, barely small enough to get through the orifice. Tipsy followed him, squeezing in with no time to spare.

He felt the breath of the fox on his neck and smelt it too. At the periphery of his vision, he saw its nose and long mouth and a pair of brown piercing eyes that gleamed in the semidarkness.

Pushing further into the tunnel, the two hares were easily out of the fox's reach. Tipsy managed to turn his head to see its jaws snapping harmlessly. He heard the deadly gnashing of its fangs and a whiff of carrion from its breath: *The smell of death...its last victim no doubt.*

They waited. Tipsy strained his head to check at intervals. After what seemed an eternity of heartbeats, the fox withdrew its jaws, seemingly tired of the standoff, and light streamed into the tunnel.

"Think he's gone?" Cupid asked.

"I reckon so."

Gingerly, Tipsy shuffled back to the tunnel entrance, cautiously jutting his head out to survey the terrain. "Not a sign of him, let's go!"

They dropped onto the grass beneath the opening, their eyes swivelling in all directions to ensure the deadly predator wasn't still around. It *could* be lying in wait. But they'd have to take a chance on that.

They proceeded towards a line of trees. Cupid beamed. "Forest in there" he enthused; "Might be an idea to rest awhile. It ought to be quiet and peaceful."

As they set foot on a path strewn with crisp leaves, pebbles, and nuts, Tipsy thought he heard something. What was it? Cupid heard it too...a mournful but somehow menacing sound, rising and falling in pitch. For a moment Tipsy wondered what class of creature it was...but then his inner voice cautioned*: It's the Humaniks!*

Cupid had a worried look. "Have you heard it before?" Tipsy wanted to know.

Cupid nodded grimly. "It's a kind of signal the Humaniks make when they set off to hunt down and kill for their amusement. "It could be us they're after, unless they've caught sight or scent of other prey."

The sinister doleful racket grew louder. Whatever they were chasing they were getting closer. Tipsy scampered into the midst of the forest, anxious to put some distance between the approaching Humaniks and himself. Cupid kept pace with him.

Tipsy spotted another of those Humanik structures, similar to the old ruined houses on the island. It was just a collection of mossy stone walls, open to the sky and almost completely congested with tall thick stringy plants and weeds. It looked like a decent hiding place. Cupid agreed it was as good a refuge as any.

"Food" Tipsy gasped when they entered through the little doorway that was almost blocked by a tangle of thorny bushes. The shrubbery was delicious. They both nibbled it. Not as succulent or tasty as seaweed, Tipsy thought, but he wasn't complaining.

Cupid was snorting with pleasure as he munched and chewed and digested leaves that lay scattered in thick clumps beneath their feet.

Tipsy froze when something stirred nearby in the tangle of foliage. He relaxed as a tiny speckled bird hopped up to him from behind a stalk, brushing aside leaves in its movement. Attuning instantly to its lingo Tipsy said: "hello bird...searching for food?"

"Yes...hey...how can you speak sparrow?"

"A long story... and I'm sure you're anxious to get on with your foraging."

"So what are you doing here? You guys are hares. I know about you. You don't hurt anyone, apart from fighting among yourselves."

Cupid was incredulous: "Hey, what are you saying? Are you talking to that silly bird?"

"Yes, he's surprised too...but I want to ask him something...." Reverting to bird talk, he resumed his chat: "Did you fly in just now...did you happen to see any Humaniks heading this way?"

The bird scoffed, fluttering its tiny wings. "Oh...you mean those crazy ones galloping on those huge beasts and the loudmouthed smaller beasts running ahead of them? God, what a bunch of crazies. Humans are loud and dangerous at the best of times, but when they go in for that stunt they really show themselves up..."

Tipsy thanked him. "But are they coming this way...are we safe...*here?"*

The bird spat a piece of something and chirped. Casually he said: "Could be...depends on where the fugitive goes. Where he runs, they follow..."

"Fugitive...Some creature they're chasing, you mean?"

"Yeah, I was pretty high up when I saw them all, so I'm pretty sure they're chasing something, but I couldn't make out what it was. From my vantage point it was just a blob shooting ahead of all those humans and their four-legged slave collaborators. The noise they made...I could hear it way up in the sky. They must be desperate to catch that creature, and boy was he running... like his life depended on it...anyway, leave me alone you guys. I haven't had anything to eat for hours!"

Tipsy and Cupid sighed. Cupid resumed nibbling on a juicy plant stalk. Tipsy helped himself to some brittle leaves that broke up and dissolved nicely in his mouth. As he dined he wondered where this wandering about in strange, unfamiliar land was getting them. Would they end up back in Humanik captivity... and what then?

His Eminence (how remote he seemed now, far away in that cave back on the island) had assured him that his mission would be revealed when the time was right, but right now he couldn't figure what he could possibly do to help the hares of the Big Island. It was challenging enough just keeping himself alive. How could he alter the plight of hares that lived, (or hid or were held captive) in this vast land to which he'd been taken? Correction: that he had *allowed himself* to be taken to. He felt a craving...to be back on familiar territory, close to the sea and the undisturbed hills and meadows where no Humaniks dwelt.

What's that? Cupid's mouth was open wide, a half-chewed twig dropping into the weeds at his feet. Tipsy slowed his chewing and went directly into intense listening mode. It was that Humanik mournful sound again, like an animal crying aloud...but this time interspersed by howling and barking and snarling. "Dogs!" Cupid groaned, "And they're getting nearer."

"Do we stay here or start running?" Tipsy asked the bird, who answered promptly, and Tipsy translated for Cupid. "Says we should stay put. The foliage in this old building, he says, is too thick for dogs to break into...but perfect for small creatures to hide in."

"Makes sense" Cupid agreed nervously.

Before Tipsy could ask the bird anything else, the chirping bundle of feathers was inching his way out of the ruin.

"Where's he going?" Cupid asked.

The bird, having extricated itself from a tangle of shrubbery, rose swiftly into the air and fluttered momentarily, blinking at them. He chirped: "I'm off...having wings does give you that additional option...no point in hanging about to listen to that racket. Best of luck, hares!"

The mournful clamour grew louder and drew nearer, as did the cacophony of canine shrieking and yelping. Tipsy tried to make himself small, Cupid doing likewise.

"Just sit tight...let them pass by", Cupid suggested.

The noise from the Humanik contrivance stopped, but the frenzied howling and barking had reached almost deafening levels, and now the dogs were in the wood: Tipsy heard the crushing of twigs, the scattering of leaves, and the splashing of water in those little pools left by rainfall. Then, Cupid gasped "We've been discovered"! He was shaking like a windblown leaf.

A small furry dog was forcing its way through the foliage, cursing and yelping in pain as thorns cut into its flesh. He saw its face. Not a dog, Tipsy saw...*the fox!*

Cupid turned around and set about exiting the ruin. Tipsy had the same idea, but the fox rasped: "Don't flee. I'm not going to hurt you. Okay, I would have back there...earlier...But only because I was hungry. Those dogs...you hear them?"

Tipsy felt the ground shudder and vibrate with the pounding of heavy footfalls, the pattering of smaller feet, and the raucous voices of the Humaniks. The fox pleaded: "It's me they're after...just let me hide here awhile, until they've gone, and I promise I won't eat you!"

Tipsy, separated from the panting fox by the length of a whisker, wasn't going to argue. If they bolted, the dogs or the Humaniks would hunt them down. If they stayed the fox might not keep his promise. But they didn't have a choice.

Suddenly they were surrounded by the dogs. It was as if all the four-legged blood-lusting creatures had morphed into one monstrous being that sought to close in and annihilate anything caught within this hiding place.

"They know- or suspect- that I'm here, though they can't see me", the fox wheezed. He seemed to be exhausted and completely out of breath. Tipsy felt repulsed by an overpowering smell of perspiration, mingled with one of extreme fear. The fox added, its eyes beady and gleaming, and its tongue lolling: "They'll be after your scent too. Anything that moves they're out to kill it!"

A flat silvery solid shape began beating down on the mass of plants and weeds that shielded the three of them. Tipsy felt the pressure of thick vegetation and prickly stalks pressing down on him.... a thorn pricked his head. He winced, but didn't budge from his position. Cupid was cursing and praying at the same time.

"This is going to end badly" the fox moaned..."unless, hey, they don't know how many of us there are, only that something giving off a strong scent is in here . Look, I'm beat. If I brake out, I haven't the energy to run. They'll rip me in two and pull my guts out like they did to my mother last autumn. But you guys...*any hare*... can outrun a foxhound. I've seen it many times. Could one of you distract them...It'll give me time to escape?"

Several of those silvery shapes attached to sticks were now beating the greenery, the dogs were howling even louder, and the Humaniks struggled to be heard above the noise as they shrieked and hollered and stamped their feet around the ruin.

Tipsy quickly agreed. To remain wasn't an option anyway as the Humaniks and dogs would eventually break through. "You stay here, Cupid. I'm breaking out...All going well, I'll be back soon!"

Eying a suitable breach in the vegetation, he eased himself through; narrowly dodging the snapping jaws of a dog, whose long flapping ears drooped around his sweating, snarling, terrifying face.

A Humanik foot swiped towards him, brushing snappily against Tipsy's left ear. He felt a sharp sting from the assault but kept running.

The fox had said the dogs pursued by scent. So invisibility wouldn't be such a great advantage, and the Humaniks would still see him anyway. He felt the menace and the aggression and the bloodlust closing on him as he ran around trees, squeezed through or underneath bushes, and leaped over fallen twisted hulks of rotted wood that lay dispersed throughout the forest. Instinctively he ran towards the shafts of sunlight to his right. *Must get out of the forest.*

The cavalcade of ill-intentioned chasers remained on his tail. Over a ditch and into a long wide field he leaped. *Soft short-cut grass:* and no frost, unlike the stretch where the greyhounds chased him. He doubled his speed and had covered half the length of the field when he noticed the noise had died away. Perhaps they'd found another scent and were happily chasing that.

Cupid mightn't have made it if he'd run the gauntlet. A hare might outrun a dog but there were so many of them.

Doubling back to the forest, he halted abruptly as he spotted in the distance to his right the long meandering line of galloping beasts bearing Humaniks and the dogs under their control.

It rekindled a memory: Yes, The Golden Hare had shown him such contrived Humanik games. They used those other creatures to bring pain and suffering to creatures hostile to Humaniks, or ones they just didn't like, or that they enjoyed chasing and killing. Was there any escape from the Humaniks and their evil ways?

He waited until the last of the loud, aggressive creatures had disappeared over the horizon, and then scurried back to the old ruin. He fretted: *The fox...he's with Cupid.* He felt sickened at the thought. The fox had pledged not to harm either of them if they helped him elude the dogs and Humaniks, But could he be trusted?

His heart sinking, Tipsy eased his way into the depths of the greenery, fearful of what he'd find. He braced himself for the sight of Cupid with his guts spilled on the ground in front of him. Heart fluttering, he called him.

A cheerful retort assuaged his concern. Curled up in a ball of red and white fur, partially concealed by ferns and squashed wild flowers, his bushy tail wrapped around him, lay the fox, and Cupid was stretching himself lazily next to the wily creature. "Glad you've returned Tipsy. Can't understand a word this fellow's being saying. I reckon he thinks I know his lingo cos you do!"

The fox was snoring, all tension gone from his body now that the immediate threat from the Humaniks and dogs had passed. Cupid whispered: "He was rattling on about all sorts of stuff; then he nodded off, a big wry smile on his face."

"Let's get far away from here" Tipsy suggested, "he could be dreaming about his next meal, which could be us if he changes his mind. He was desperate when he made the promise not to harm us. Hunger has a way of overtaking other obligations and priorities...let's go!"

Cupid sighed. "Does it matter where we go? Dangers are everywhere. Why did we even bother to escape?"

Tipsy didn't answer, as they emerged from the forest and edged along the side of a pathway that vibrated with loud humming and hammering. A large shining dark green object came spluttering around the turn in the pathway, circular shapes spinning underneath as if conveying the monstrosity.

They instantly leapt over a low ditch to their right; narrowly avoiding the strange contrivance that Tipsy was certain would have crushed them. Tipsy coughed, a foul smelling bluish-grey vapour from the speeding object having wafted up his nostrils.

"More Humanik craziness", muttered Cupid. "Just imagine...they travel about in those things!"

72

Annemarie cuddled her large cat, Ginger, her mind again focused on the fallout from her one-woman attack on the coursing compound. Mental images of hares dashing to their freedom as she banged on the link-wire, and the entrance hatch swinging on its hinges in the predawn gloom, were seldom far from her consciousness.

She re-ran the sequence of events over and over, marvelling at the idea that she'd done such a thing. Almost a week had passed and with each day she felt safer from the long arm of the law that seemed to be reaching in all directions on behalf of the coursing club…except hers.

She'd turned it over in her mind a hundred times since the night she got back to her house after the daring exploit: The pros and cons of her predicament. Yes, there was that shred of clothing and those tiny blood stains that could, if analysed in a laboratory, place her at the scene of the...*crime...to them*: But only if they bothered to conduct a painstakingly thorough investigation.

I mean...this isn't a murder case, or anything remotely serious as lawbreaking goes. And she hadn't made any serious waves about coursing...just behind the scenes stuff. And yet it bothered her that others were paying the price of what she'd done.

Yes, it was an act of compassion. Those captive hares were facing another round of contrived baiting. Some of them would have suffered broken bones or other injuries and been finished off by that creepy dispatcher guy. Others would have been mauled or battered to death. Others again would die days later from stress-related ailments arising directly from their torment.

So sure, it was worth it. She'd do the same again if a similar situation arose. But...those arrests. Thirteen people, dedicated campaigners who'd devoted a huge portion of their lives to the ban hare coursing campaign, had been snatched from their homes, a bit like hares abducted from their habitats, and subjected to gruelling police interrogations.

Though innocent of any involvement in the sabotage, they had to endure the embarrassment and stress of being awoken at their homes and taken away by squads of special branch officers and uniformed police in full view of neighbours.

One of them was three years younger than herself. The girl was badly shaken up by the ordeal and receiving counselling. Her insistence that she only ever handed out a few anti-coursing leaflets had been greeted with derision by her interrogators, who demanded information on the people she "knew" carried out the raid at Ballycrossways.

Another woman told Annemarie she feared well-known campaigners in other parts of Ireland would also be arrested and grilled in the coming days and weeks. She claimed the coursing clubs were exploiting the incident to set the police like dogs on anyone who spoke out against their "sport". Annemarie was troubled.

And if the police were so unrelenting in their questioning of those campaigners, what could *she* expect if they picked up that forensic evidence from the barbed wire in the field and opted to view her as a suspect?

***

73

Waxy answered the phone: He didn't recognise the voice.

"It's me, Doctor Joe…"

Callaghan. What does he want? "You sound…different."

"Waxy, listen to me…drop the coursing. Drop it now. I've been having these…nightmares. You wouldn't believe. I'm walking along a lane, and this giant hare blocks my path, and when I try to turn back and run, I can't. I freeze to the spot. Then he lunges at me and with one gulp he swallows me."

"Doctor, for heaven's sake, I'm surprised at you. Get a grip!"

"No Waxy…there's more. Dreams …well…I'd have put it down to maybe drinking and eating cheese sandwiches before bedtime. My wife almost hit me over the head with a frying pan when I told her about the dreams. There's the other stuff..." The line went quiet.

"Are you there Doctor?"

"Yes, yes…God above...when I think of it... I was out walking the dog yesterday evening…the sun was still up, birds whistling in the trees, people waved as they always do when I walked past them. Then, as I got to the edge of the wood, just about to enter along that little path, he was there…Oh God Waxy, he was standing there, as clearly as I'd see you standing in front of me….glaring, mocking me…"

"Who, Doctor...who was there…?"

"That...monster. The giant hare, just like in the dream, but this wasn't dreaming. He started to move towards me. In desperation, I tried to unleash my dog. He's just a border collie, but used to chasing anything that moves. I thought he'd deter this…thing…"

"And did he?"

Silence. Then weeping.

"Are you okay there Doctor?"

"I'm anything but okay…dear God, when I went to cut the dog loose, he was already gone. Out of sight. The lead was gone too. I didn't notice him running off. I turned and ran as fast I could. I'm not very athletic, but God I made my legs work. I dared not look behind…but as I neared my house, people were standing gaping at me as if I had two heads. I could feel the thing behind me, closing in. I felt its breath, like a breeze against my neck.

"Shaking like a big lump of jelly on a saucer I managed to insert the key in the front door. As I got inside and was pulling the door shut I caught sight of the monster. It was standing outside, staring at me, its eyes swivelling and its ears standing up on its head, blocking out the sunlight.

"It was a hare Waxy…and before the door had slammed shut I heard the words…not in the normal way with my hearing…but somewhere inside my head. *Give up coursing or I'll be back,* it said. I was chilled to the bone. I finished the bottle of brandy, Waxy…"

Waxy felt a chill shuffling its way up his own spine, but scepticism won out, as it always did when alleged affairs of the supernatural poked into his life.

"Just a second Doctor, are you still there? Did anyone else see that thing?"

A deep sigh down the line. "That's the crazy part. No. There were people on the street when I ran back into the village. They saw nothing."

"So you imagined it then. That's obvious, isn't it?"

"I don't know…it's ever since that episode with the hare at the coursing and how it looked in the camera footage...the dog losing sight of him and all that. It's what prompted me to resign as patron. But I hadn't intended turning my back on coursing completely. Now I must. Waxy. If you had seen…and felt…what I did, you, even you, Waxy, with all your loyalty to the game. You'd be gone from it quicker than…than a hare from a greyhound!"

***

74

Tipsy cursed his carelessness. He and Cupid had somehow lost each other. It happened after both had stopped to sip at a stream in the wood where they'd met the fox. Cupid had wondered off to explore the wood, curiosity getting the better of him as he heard some silly little birds whistling in a bush. Tipsy had himself then stepped out of the wood into a vast field which, thankfully, had long grass and a smattering of unfamiliar weeds.

Thinking Cupid would return to the stream shortly he reckoned he'd have a run in the luscious swatches of swaying grass and maybe a brief nibble. The field was right outside the wood so he'd be back inside within a few heartbeats.

But when Tipsy returned Cupid was nowhere to be seen. He waited awhile, before giving up. Cupid would have to go it alone, unless he teamed up with other hares, whether escapees or free-living Big Island ones. Tipsy was about to re-enter the sprawling field when a loud noise made him quiver. He shook with fright. *Calm...panicking never helps!*

Bang! *What's that?*

There again...Bang! Loud sharp irritable noises echoed across the countryside, the intervals between them getting shorter as Tipsy listened. Like thunderclaps but harsher on the ear and not as long drawn-out.

He winced at each menacing bang that seemed to carry on the wind. Edging closer to the high ditch separating the wood from the field, he sought an opening through which he could see whatever it was that made those sounds, without revealing himself. The shrubbery didn't afford much chance to observe. He ran along the ditch in search of a spy-hole, moving fast but furtively parallel to the tangle of briars and berries...*there!*

Sunlight squeezed through to dazzle him a little. He peered at the light, which grew dimmer and easier on the eye with each heartbeat. He beheld an expanse of tasty green pasture, a different field from the one he'd visited earlier.

Then, pressing closer to the ditch, he saw lines of fur in the grass, stretching from the top end of the field to almost halfway towards where he sat watching. Focusing, he gasped "Fur? Those are hares!"

They all seemed motionless. Were they sleeping? He'd never seen a hare sleeping that didn't show some signs of movement. *Must take a closer look.*

At the opposite end of the field a Humanik sat on a stile, vapour wafting from a tiny stick that hung from his mouth. He seemed to be guarding all those hares. *Might be dangerous to enter that field, with the Humanik sitting there, but I must see if there's anything I can do...*

Squinting, he tried to get the scene into focus, but it was difficult to make out clearly from this distance. He'd have to get nearer. *Those hares must be ill, just lying in the grass like that. Hares don't sleep in that posture, on their sides with their legs thrust forward and all head to tail in row upon row. Something's not right.*

Curiosity proved stronger than fear. Tipsy ventured further along until he reached a gap in the ditch blocked only by a wooden barrier that was easy to slip under. With the grass so short he risked being spotted by that Humanik who sat in a little cloud of blue vapour, but he felt compelled to press on. He broke into a run, making towards the lines of motionless hares. There were five lines, each separated from the other by thin strips of flattened grass. He ran parallel to the first line, slowing as he did so to have a closer look.

He stopped and edged up to the first hare in the line. He nudged him, whispering: "Are you okay...wake up!" The hare failed to respond, or even register the slightest movement. Tipsy circled him...and stopped in horror. Blood streamed from the hare's mouth and the eyes were lifeless. Parts of his fur were matted with dried blood. The red blotches were more prominent on the white underbelly than the auburn hued parts of his body. Flies buzzed over the creature's head, competing greedily for the meat.

Tipsy turned away, running breathlessly to the next hare. He too was dead and speckled with red dots. Tipsy ran along the entire line. *All dead.*

His nostrils caught the unmistakable stench of decaying flesh. It was overpowering. He felt sickened and revolted. Tears welled up. His heart hammering and his head splitting with anger, he saw hare after hare laid out, all empty shells whose spirits had gone to...

Bang!

The crack startled and almost deafened him. He froze, and saw the vapourish man on the stile aiming a long smooth rod at him. *Danger. Must be that death stick the Storm Petrel told me about.*

Tipsy darted back to the high ditch without a backward glance. He quickly reached the gap...and safety. He ushered the horrors of what he'd seen...and smelt... from his mind. *Must warn the others, when I find them.*

Bang!

More cracks, exactly like the one the Humanik made with his rod. Tipsy felt a whooshing sensation as something brushed past him, just inches from his left eye, followed by a second, third and fourth zapping of sharp gusts all around him. *Keep running.*

The banging ceased. Another field loomed. His heart missed a beat. Over the low ditch he saw them: A line of Humaniks with their backs turned to him, standing a little apart from each other and moving slowly through the grass. And each of them had a rod similar to that wielded by the vaporous man in the field with all the dead hares. Some had their heads covered with strange Humanik materials.

At intervals as they walked, one or more of them raised his rod to make that cracking sound. When two or three did this at the same time the noise was amplified and the vibrations made the earth tremble. *Best get out of here...before one of them turns around.*

Tipsy turned and was about to put his powerful hind legs into action, and get far away from this depressing scene, when he heard a loud cry...the unmistakable screech of a hare. It came from somewhere in front of that line of Humaniks, further down the field they were trawling in that creepy coordinated movement.

The cry rose and fell, punctuated by more cracks and Humanik chatter. Then another cry...and another: a chorus of hare screeches.

Tipsy's heart swelled with rage and sadness. They were killing the hares. *So that's it. They're killing them like they must have killed all those hares displayed so neatly and bloodily in that other field. But what can I do? I can easily escape. None of them has seen me. Their eyes are averted and they can't see what's behind them. But...I run faster than any hare on either the island or this bigger island of the Humaniks. Can I distract them from their killing game?*

A quick backward glance revealed a landscape free of Humaniks or any life apart from gentle creatures grazing...the fleecy black-footed ones. He could make a run for it in that direction. But no: He must help those hares.

Instinctively he ran straight at the line of Humaniks. Normally when he ran it was fear that propelled him forward, or the promise of food or a meeting with others of his species. Anger drove him now. He dashed against the leg of a Humanik, eliciting a yelp from him.

The creature instantly pointed his death rod at Tipsy, and a loud bang erupted, but Tipsy felt nothing. Instead, another Humanik roared and fell to the ground. He writhed and rolled about, holding his leg.

The other Humaniks rushed to their fallen comrade, fussing around him and making strange panicky noises. Tipsy's attention was diverted from this bizarre scene by the sight of several hares running about the field, ahead of the advancing Humaniks. And by the bloodied clumps of fur...more dead hares, scattered around in front of him.

Seeing the Humaniks preoccupied with their injured companion, he dashed on, calling out to the scampering and seemingly disorientated hares: "Get out of this field...they're trying to kill you...Don't sit still...they see you...leave this field or you'll die!"

The startled hares got the message. Scores of them dashed to the end of the field, others running to either side in search of escape routes. Within a dozen heartbeats all of them had vacated the field, leaving their dead comrades on the sward, bleeding and dead...or dying.

Tipsy knew the wounded hares were lost. Hares didn't recover from serious injuries. Those ones would soon be basking in the glory of the afterlife. *May Ostara take them into her warm embrace.*

Bang!

Tipsy jumped. Humaniks running straight at him, little flames darting from their accursed death rods, accompanied by clicking and banging. They were roaring, their faces contorted and even uglier than usual. He diverted from his run to the far end of the field to a tiny gap he spotted to his left in a low ditch. He passed through it to an almost deafening chorus of cracks and loud Humanik mouth noises.

Berries and thorns struck or scratched the side of his head as he clambered through the small opening and heard those breeze-like whizzing noises all around him before emerging on the other side. He quickly surveyed his surroundings. *A Humanik free zone!*

A white grazing creature eyed him blankly, and then stepped aside meekly to let him pass. "Thank you!"

"Don't mention it" the unthreatening creature with its comfy looking fleecy fur replied, "Those Humaniks are playing their silly games again, turning live hares into dead ones!"

"I know, I'm trying to avoid becoming a dead one, and I think I've saved a few others too."

The creature looked mildly surprised, but not shocked, by Tipsy's linguistic prowess. "Keep running, hare...if a Humanik sees me talking to you I could end up dead!"

Tipsy didn't wait around to consider the advice. A ruffling of leaves and briars startled him. A Humanik appeared behind him, raising his fire rod. Instead of running away from him Tipsy felt impelled to do the opposite: His heart raced. His head pounded. The Humanik's paw was pressing on to something attached to the fire rod.

Bang!

No pain. So I'm okay.

A clicking noise from the fire rod, that was now again pointing directly at Tipsy. He leaped at the Humanik, who opened his mouth wide and emitted a low gasp as Tipsy made contact, bouncing off the hostile creature. The fire rod fell to the ground beside Tipsy, the narrower end pointing at the Humanik.

Bang! Tipsy went deaf for a second or two. *What an explosion.* He shuddered and felt dizzy as he clambered to his feet to flee. But the Humanik was falling...*Best get out of the way...fast.*

Tipsy watched; astonishment banishing fear, as the Humanik collapsed in a big heap across the gap. Humaniks were bellowing somewhere near. But this one just whimpered. He lay where he fell, stretched out like the hares in the other field, his head covering detached, crumpled in the grass. Blood poured in thin streams from the Humanik's paw that had held the death rod, and from one of his legs. His eyes pressed shut, he was sobbing.

Tipsy coughed. A foul vapour issuing from the discarded fire rod had wafted up his nostrils, irritating him. He shook his head and the sensation disappeared. *Have I hurt him? Hares don't hurt Humaniks. We don't even eat animals that other animals kill. No time for brooding...*

Three Humanik heads peered out over the ditch...fierce reddened faces, spitting and growling and staring straight at him. Tipsy ran sideways, loud voices ringing in his ears as he sprinted to safety.

Bang!

Death rods in action again: A succession of bangs followed and he felt those whooshing zaps above and to either side of him as he raced at top speed. The bangs grew fainter and the whizzing sensations less frequent as he put some distance between himself and the Humaniks. *Do they blame me, I wonder, and was I responsible for his injury? All I did was punch him with my body, like the greyhounds punched those hares. But a Humanik is far bigger and stronger than a hare, stronger than a dog even. How could I have done that?*

Tipsy half ran, half skidded down a hill dotted with sweet scented white and yellow flowers, leaped over a gurgling stream at its bottom, and into a stretch of woodland. No Humaniks in sight, but no room for complacency either. *They turn up when and where you least expect them.*

Tipsy sat under a tall beech tree and pondered his situation. He was tired but dared not sleep. What if a Humanik crept up on him with a death rod?

"Tipps!" A familiar cry from somewhere behind him. A quick backward glance revealed Cupid, scampering towards him in a carefree manner.

"Hey, found you at last! Where were you? I got a bit distracted in this old forest. Met an old hare that lived all his life there in a secluded patch. We shared a lovely meal. Never tasted anything like it. We spoke for ages. Imagine...this fellow lives on his own with only the odd bird dropping in to whistle and sing and steal the leftovers. The Humaniks probably don't even know he exists. Lucky fellow!"

He slumped down beside Tipsy and leaned against the towering tree whose branches swayed and creaked audibly overhead. He yawned and half-closed his eyes. Words slipped lazily from him. "Well, Tipps...anything strange happen when I was away?"

Tipsy looked at him, shook his head, and drifted into a deep sleep.

***

75

Damn. Another mistake. Annemarie deleted several lines of figures from the computer screen and closed the file. The accountant had been a bit frosty with her. She didn't blame him. Since arriving at the office she'd been unable to concentrate on her work.

She could hear the babble of excitement in the village even with the windows tightly shut. And this was a week-and-a-half after the compound raid. *God, had they anything happening in their lives...you'd think a major crime had been committed.* She sipped her coffee from the polystyrene cup. Her hands were shaking again.

Why had she switched on the radio? It was the number one item on the local station: Police had been drafted in from the capital to assist regional officers in the investigation. Forensic teams were combing the area around the hare compound. Sniffer dogs were nosing about, and police calling door-to-door. Hundreds of volunteers were still scouring the countryside close to the "scene of the crime" in an effort to recapture the hares.

She almost laughed when the newsreader referred to the escaped hares as "fugitives". But then, this hadn't happened before, not on Broc Peninsula. In other parts of Ireland activists had released hares, but this was supposed to be a coursing *stronghold.*

Though many people in the region opposed the blood sport, few dared voice disapproval or join a protest. The demos held were organised by animal welfare groups based in far-off districts.

Trying hard to suppress rising anxiety, she reached for the packet of painkillers. She swallowed two with the dregs of the coffee. Her head pounded as though a pneumatic drill was boring through her skull.

She jumped at the sound of her mobile ringing. *Blast.* She thought she'd turned it off. She recognised the number.

Christine Moriarty was a long-time campaigner who lived twenty-seven miles from the Penninsula.

"Annemarie? Can you talk? Listen, I hope all's well for you down there..."

"Yes...why wouldn't it be?"

"God, Annemarie, the Special Branch have just been. They pulled the place apart. Came barging in raving about a terrible incident. Jesus, I though someone had been murdered. It was about hares being freed at Ballycrossways...near you. They searched my garden shed, every room in the house. Tossed the bed mattress down the stairs. Ripped open the pillows, sent feathers flying in all directions. I asked them what they were looking for. *Evidence* they said. In the end they left with nothing but asked me if I had a wire-cutter hidden anywhere and threatened to charge me with terrorist offences if I held anything back!"

"Gosh Christine I'm sorry to hear that. Do they think you were involved in the...the hares escaping?" She felt a rising panic as she mouthed the words.

"They believe the organisation is in some way linked to it, yes. The house is a wreck. Annemarie, I know you're not...you know...well known as an anti-coursing person, I mean publicly. But please, be careful. They'll surely call to you. I got calls just after the search from three other campaigners. They were raided too. The coursing clubs are well in with the police. You know Charlie who does the leaflets every week in the town centre? They arrested him and his arm was broken when he tried to resist. So stupid. He should have gone quietly. Now they think he's hiding something, which I know he's not..."

"Look, thanks for telling me all this Christine but I'm in the office and the boss is in the next room shuffling about. Better not stay too long on the phone."

"Fine, just be careful, and expect a visit!"

Switching off the phone, she forced herself to complete the work that normally would be completed in the first half-hour. Edginess distracted...about a possible police raid on her home, mingled with a deep unease, verging on guilt, about the fact that other people were suffering as a result of her action.

No, she didn't regret what she did, but why did those decent, compassionate campaigners have to experience this harassment from pro hare coursing police because of her? She reviewed her level of involvement in the anti coursing campaign.

Apart from surreptitiously talking pictures at a coursing fixture and signing online petitions she hadn't done anything that marked her out as a prominent activist. But wait...those forensics people. Would they find those bits of material on the barbed-wire?

No, that didn't matter, she reminded herself. The torn jeans were already dropped off at the charity shop, as were the boots. The socks would have obscured the shoeprints and they'd been discarded in any case.

Traces of blood from the scratches: Would those have remained on barbed-wire strands? Possibly...but surely the rain that morning would have washed all that away. And anyway why would anyone think of looking for bloodstains? Other questions popped up to replace the answered ones. But no...There didn't seem to be anything to implicate her in the...she almost called it a *crime*. *Get a grip!*

She felt better after another cup of coffee. Calmly she forced all thoughts of hares, coursing compounds, and frenzied house searches out of her mind and fixed her eyes on those dreary spreadsheets. The rows of numbers seemed to mock her distraction and she found it difficult to focus on the humming computer screen.

***

76

Waxy was finding it increasingly difficult to contain his anger. "I'm telling you, Superintendent, she's no shrinking violet. Okay she's never been on a picket, not around here anyway, and I'd never seen nor heard of her till she turned up with that blasted camera, spying on us, looking for some mud she could throw at us, or pass on to the anti groups. If she'd go to the trouble of taking illegal pictures of the coursing, don't you think she might... just *might* be capable of teaming up with a few of those hooligans and interfering with the compound?"

The Superintendent didn't seem impressed. "She didn't break any law by attempting to film the coursing event. She breached your club's rules. That's another matter. And her lack of any serious public involvement with the anti-coursing campaign indicates she isn't all that pushed about the cruelty to hares thing..."

Waxy interrupted: "Look, are you sure the forensics team covered everything? I found this...it mightn't mean anything. It was near the compound...it was in a field next to it...hanging from a strand of barbed wire."

The Superintendent took the piece of torn blue denim. "Mmm, you're sure it wasn't any of your own lads, or a farmer, who left it?"

"That's for your people to find out...when you pull her in for questioning...and search her house from top to bottom!"

The officer sighed audibly. "Waxy, we're working flat out on this...but, you see, the other suspects we questioned were red-hot activists...known troublemakers. This woman has never been in trouble. Works for a local accountant. Gentle disposition. And she couldn't have done it on her own, surely. And I can't imagine anyone around here helping her."

Waxy's blood was up. He wanted to roar, but somehow managed to speak quietly through gritted teeth. "Can't you see...she could have got help from outside this area, maybe from some of those hooligans you pulled in already...she could have led them to the field..."

The Superintendent leaned forward across his desk. "Waxy, just to put your mind at rest, I'll apply for a warrant to raid her house and have her grilled. I'll use emergency anti-terrorist legislation, put the frighteners on her. If she's innocent, she'll have nothing to fear. But if she had any hand act or part in that crime, I promise you Waxy...we'll break her like a twig."

Waxy's tone changed. He relaxed and blew out a breath of relief. "That's what I wanted to hear."

Rising from the chair in the station dayroom, he clenched a fist and shook it heartily. "Whoever did it I swear we'll make them squeal louder than the hares they took from us. They'll regret the day they ever set foot in that field!"

***

77

Annemarie yawned and combed her hair into shape after brushing her teeth. She imagined she'd aged a few months, though it was probably the result of anxiety and lack of sleep. A fortnight had passed since that dawn raid she'd undertaken at the behest of a wise old hare that appeared to her. If it wasn't just a dream.

Filling the kettle for her morning cuppa, she thought about how distracting this thing had become. Just when she thought her worries were diminishing they returned with renewed force to niggle her and draw her mind into playing back like a DVD the likelihood of DNA evidence being tested and then compared with her own.

She could scarcely think about anything else. The boss had asked her if she was feeling alright the day before, and the other girl at the office had put an arm on her shoulder, saying "you're not yourself Annemarie."

She had to make up something, a story about bereavement in the extended family. An excuse she instantly regretted. The errors in her accountancy reports were minor and thankfully hadn't been noticed by the boss- she'd caught and corrected them in time- but such shabby and below-par work was alien to her. Her mind just wasn't focused the way it should be.

Images of snapping locks, hares running in the darkness, and men in the country's top forensic science laboratory examining microscopic traces of blood from the barbed-wire at Ballycrossways kept intruding, like midges that wouldn't go away in the summer no matter how often you shook your head and tried to repel them.

Closing her eyes, she tried to blot the sabotage from her mind, but the effort only intensified her focus on it.

Though adamant that her action was justified, she was beginning to wonder if it was worth it. The damage to the compound didn't bother her; nor did the anger of the coursing officials. What they were doing was clearly wrong on so many levels. But...imagine what people would say, even anti-coursing campaigners, if she told them a hare had instructed her in a dream to set his friends free at Ballycrossways?

Okay, it was more vivid and real than any dream she'd ever had, but there was no way on earth she'd be taken seriously. And those arrests: She felt again the weight of responsibility for the upheaval in the lives of those campaigners. Two of them had now abandoned the campaign; such was their fear of being targeted by police in response to any future sabotage at coursing venues. Perhaps that was part of the police strategy: To prick the conscience of the real culprit by leaning on innocent campaigners? *Possible.* Thank God, this was her day off. *Must get out in the fresh air. Stop letting this thing dominate my thoughts and my life.*

What's that?

She rose from the table, the cup falling over and spilling its contents unto the floor.

The doorbell. Twice, three times. And someone was rapping on the door too. *Sweet Jesus, is this it?*

A mild electric shock ran through her body. She was shaking from head to foot. The ringing and knocking persisted. "Okay, I'm coming" she shouted, trying to sound unconcerned when she was hoping the floor would open up and shallow her.

She saw the two shapes through the door's frosted glass panel. She unlatched the door and pulled it open. On the pavement stood a tall overweight man in a military style jacket, wearing green wellingtons and with big bushy eyelashes, flushed cheeks and a mouth full of rotten teeth.

One hand was holding his enormous potbelly that quivered like a jelly. He had a hostile look, his eyes flaring with suppressed annoyance or anger. She remembered him...the official who had grabbed her camcorder. He was wheezing as if he'd just completed a lively sprint or a long bout of exercise. To his right a tall uniformed Guard was smiling, his expression neutral and relaxed.

"What can I do for you?" she asked, forcing herself to remain calm and unconcerned.

The wheezing man spoke, gasping for breath as he did so. From a pocket inside his jacket he produced a camcorder. "I'm returning this to you...The footage you obtained has been deleted. You understand that unauthorised photography is prohibited at coursing here, as everywhere else in Ireland." He handed over the device.

"Yes...thank you. I hope it's not damaged. I was only filming. Not doing any harm..."

"It's not damaged", he replied tersely, "but you know the rules. Don't let it happen again!"

Before she could respond the police officer removed his cap, smoothed back his hair and said: "Ah, Miss Cristobel, Just a word about something else. You've heard about that episode up at Ballycrossways?"

"Yes, it was on the news. Everyone's talking about it."

"Yes, it was...but anyway...I think t'would be fair to say that you aren't well disposed to coursing, if your presence on the grounds with that camera is anything to go by. You wouldn't by any chance know any anti-coursing people who might have been involved in that crime? Did anyone phone or email you about it?"

"I don't know of anyone who'd be involved" she answered.

The officer replaced his cap, glanced at the coursing official, and took a step backwards. "Fine, but if you do hear anything, give us a call. There's a reward of five thousand euro for information leading to the arrest and conviction of the criminals responsible. A nice little earner. We'll leave you, thank you Ms. Cristobel...."

He had the trace of a smirk, she thought. Or maybe she imagined it. The coursing official nodded without saying anything; then they both turned and walked over to the white and yellow police car parked across the street opposite her house.

She went inside, closing the door gently so as not to give any hint or show of hostility. She sank into her armchair beside the rayburn stove. *Of course...the camcorder. I was to get it back, but the officer accompanied him to ask a routine question. Or were they sizing me up, testing my reaction?*

She checked the camcorder. *Nothing broken. So they know I'm anti-hare coursing, but then a lot of people are. I'm sure they'll be making inquiries, asking around to see if I've been noticed getting up to any suspicious activity. They might ask the neighbours.*

They'll draw a blank there. There was nobody out and about to see me leaving or returning to the house on the day. Not a soul. No, I'm probably okay...

***

78

Tipsy yawned as his eyes flickered open. Cupid was snoring beside him. Where was the sun? The wooded glade was shrouded in a murky gloom. Night hadn't fallen. The moon was also absent.

Tipsy moaned. It was fog, one of his least favourite weather conditions. You couldn't see very far, and that wasn't good when you were on the lookout for predators, Humanik or otherwise.

He nudged Cupid, who cursed him for disturbing a pleasant dream. Cupid looked around him. He groaned: "Better stay put since we can't see anything."

Tipsy wasn't so sure. They'd been resting in the same spot for quite a while. It was a large clearing. They'd be easy targets if Humaniks with death rods turned up. Cupid grudgingly agreed they'd be safer in thicker woodland, with plenty of foliage to conceal their movements, but how would they know which way to go with that blinding vapour swirling about them?

Tipsy remembered that a short distance to their left was dense shrubbery. They ambled unsighted through the cold blinding mist. "Can't be much further" Cupid mumbled, "and anyway, other creatures won't be able to see us if we can't see them."

Then, as if to confound Cupid's insight, the mist began to abate, growing weaker by the heartbeat but still persisting enough to obscure vision. Tipsy stopped and stood still, hushing Cupid to do likewise. "See that?" He whispered.

Cupid strained to see the oscillating shapes in the fog. Tipsy saw them more clearly now as the vapours thinned and dissipated. *Humaniks!* And yes...that was a dog with them. *Are they searching for us? Could be.*

The dog was on a lead. Not just any dog... a greyhound, like the ones that chased Tipsy and the others in captivity. The two hares froze. Not daring to move a millimetre. They sat silently. Staying perfectly still didn't guarantee safety. It might even spell disaster, but it seemed the best option. Tipsy lisped a prayer to Ostara. *You've got us this far, please...*

Cupid whispered: "They're heading right this way. If they come much closer they'll spot us. We'll have to run for it!"

Tipsy countered: "Steady...we're concealed by these brambles. We can see them through the tiny spaces, but they won't see us..."

Nestled close to Cupid, Tipsy felt his friend shivering with fright. He fought hard to fight back his own fear. As always it throbbed within like another creature occupying his body. *Must stay calm.*

The two Humaniks stopped at a clearing. Tipsy's heart fluttered. Cupid glanced at him; then refocused on the Humaniks. They just stood there, chattering away in hushed tones, the dog held by his leash. The creature looked confused, and was sniffing and darting his eyes about. Had he smelt the presence of hares? Tipsy whispered: "Don't panic...he might suspect we're here but those Humaniks don't seem interested."

The one holding the dog made an adjustment to the leash, allowing the dog to move further from him...closer to where Tipsy sat. *Still mustn't move. Danger...what will I do?*

Cupid was ready to bolt. But they both stayed put. Then it happened...so quickly that neither had a chance to do anything. The second Humanik raised with both his arms a long stick with a shining rectangular shape on its end. He held it high for an instant, and brought it crashing down on the head of the greyhound: A sharp whacking sound, accompanied by a watery splat.

Blood sprayed from the dog. Its eyes rolled around dismally, its tongue lolled. Its whole body quivered. It fell into a pile of fallen leaves that crumpled under its weight. It wasn't dead yet. It made low muffled yelping noises. A second blow to its backbone made Tipsy almost jump out of his skin.

Cupid was staring in terror at the scene. Then, abruptly, the Humaniks turned and went back the way they came.

Tipsy gave a deep sigh and relaxed, but his relief was matched by horror. Motioning to Cupid, he opted to have a closer look at the dog, which he presumed was dead as it wasn't moving. The animal was lying on its side, blood spilling from its head and also from a wound on its back. But one of its eyes was partially open, the lid flickering weakly. Tears streamed down its face, diluting rivulets of blood. Tipsy had mixed feelings. This was the type of dog used to chase, terrorise and kill hares. But this one was a victim of the Humaniks.

"Are you alive?" Tipsy asked nervously.

Cupid was agitated. "Forget him Tipsy", he'd eat us if he could!"

But Tipsy was overcome with a sudden inexplicable compassion. The dog raised his head slightly, coughing blood onto the leaves. There was none of the aggression or bullying fierceness left that those dogs had demonstrated so frighteningly on the coursing field: Only a pitiable, pleading stare.

He struggled to get the words out, each sentence a painful rasp. "I'm dying. Only a matter of seconds...Look, nothing personal you guys. The Humaniks...they care nothing for us. I lost three races in a row. That's why they whacked me I reckon. It's not just you they like to see suffer. I...oh...do you see it? Someone beckoning me! The pain is easing...so cold."

The eyelid closed slowly and feebly...and stayed shut. No more tears to lighten the mats of blood. The dog was dead, but Tipsy felt sure that its spirit was elsewhere. If there was an afterlife for hares, then surely dogs had somewhere to go too.

Cupid circled the dog with curiosity, not displaying any sadness for its demise. He suddenly leaped on top of the carcass and boxed it... punch after punch. "One less dog to chase us!" he guffawed; let's get out of here before we encounter any more crazy Humaniks... or dogs!"

On they journeyed, across fields that seemed to stretch to infinity, under hedges and over walls. They traversed stretches of hard surface unlike any Tipsy had been accustomed to on the island, and dodged more of those Humanik monstrosities that sped past with frightening speed. Day followed night, and now another day was declining. "Let's get some sleep", pleaded Cupid, and they rested in a hollow close to a towering hedge that sagged with the weight of juicy red berries.

As they settled down to rest, Tipsy felt soothed by the tweeting and warbling of little birds from within the hedge.

***

79

Annemarie rubbed her eyes. *Can't be the alarm.* It was set for eight pm. The clock said...*what?* She strained to see it. *No numbers on it.* They normally shone in the dark. *God! Am I still asleep, dreaming? Ah, so this is a trick my mind is playing on me. Dreams can be so silly.*

Then it struck her. She'd read somewhere about people controlling their dreams. Once you knew you were dreaming you could direct its course.

The room was in darkness apart from the clock face with its missing numerals *and hey*, the hands were gone too. *How weird. But no weirder than ...what's that?*

From out of the darkness a tiny golden light had appeared. Somehow a living presence, she felt...piercing a veil of inky blackness. She sat up in bed... or in the dream if it was one. She extended her left hand to switch on the reading lamp on her bedside locker. She moved her arm, but her hand touched nothing. She tried to get out of bed but her legs refused to budge.

The pinpoint of light swelled, expanding soundlessly until it comprised a circle directly in front of her. But instead of illuminating the room it resolved into a vivid rectangular landscape scene, as if a painting by someone like Constable had materialised in her room: a lovely pastoral view... a blue sky peppered with fluffy white clouds, emerald green fields with bustling hedgerows, bluish-grey mountains in the background and in the foreground she saw...

Oh, now I get it...The Golden Hare again!

There he was...sitting and nibbling on a carrot: The only moving feature in this tranquil composition. An aura swirled around the hare as in the previous dream, visitation, or whatever it was.

She rubbed her eyes again and then shut them tight. Was this a hallucination? *Let's see.* What had she eaten or drank before hitting the sack? *Nothing, apart from a mug of cocoa.* That didn't usually affect her sleeping.

Opening her eyelids slowly, she half expected the strange image that hovered in front of her to have vanished. Instead, it had swelled to fill almost the entire room. The Golden Hare was sitting just inches from her...somewhere between the ceiling and floor. He was looking straight at her with those electric blue orbs that exuded an all-knowing vibe. "What...what do you want with me?" she stuttered.

"Be calm, Blessed Human", he replied, his thoughts somehow forming into words in her mind as he communicated.

She couldn't contain herself. "Are you the same...hare... that visited me...previously...and suggested I cut loose all those hares at Ballycrossways coursing field?"

"Yes, I am at the Golden Hare of Gooseberry Island, and I come with further advice..."

Annemarie felt her anger rising. Fearing the dream would end at any moment she moved quickly to get in her piece: "More advice...look...I don't mean any disrespect. I don't know how you do this...appearing to me, or if this is just a crazy dream, and the last visit too...but I've been really worried about that caper you advised me to pull off. Don't get me wrong. I detest coursing, and I'm glad those hares escaped. Yeah, and I'm glad I was the one who intervened to help them...but lots of decent people have suffered because of what I did.

"Their lives have been directly affected by my actions. Hassle from the police, pressure from workmates. The hares escaped, but I can't deal with the consequences...I still don't know if I'll be arrested...there's evidence against me if they find it. For months to come I'll be obsessing about this. I'll be jumping out of my shoes at every ring of the doorbell, thinking every policeman or woman I pass in the street is watching me, suspecting...."

She paused for breath. That's assuming she had spoken at all since this had to be a dream of *some* sort.

The Golden Hare, who had listened patiently without interruption, resumed: "Had you finished speaking? Yes, I understand your plight and that, among other reasons, is why I have returned with the aid of the Higher Hare Spirits, to offer further guidance. What I have to say may disconcert or anger you. But I implore you to consider carefully the advice I will render. It is of the utmost importance and will greatly aid the good work that some high-minded Humaniks are engaged in on the Big Island that you call Ireland.

"You are worried about the possibility of being publicly accused of liberating my brethren from that evil Place of Captivity, and also you feel uneasy about how your fellow compassionate humans are...paying the price... of your own brave deed?"

"Yes, and I don't see a way out of this. What if the police take me in and confront me with evidence that can't be refuted?"

Rays of love and understanding washed over her body...or was it her disembodied spirit? The visitor seemed to grow brighter and his aura shone like a miniature sun. His voice had a peculiar sweetness to it, a soothing reassurance.

"Here is how your destiny can be fulfilled, to the betterment of humans and hares alike: Stop worrying about the police and their activities. You must own up publicly to having released my brethren from enslavement. You must find a way of proclaiming yourself as the liberator of those innocent captives. Don't wait for the police to come to you. You must beat them to it!"

"But...how...I'd have a criminal record. I'd lose my job...."

He shushed her. "The Higher Hare Spirits have consulted with me on this. In the human chamber of justice you can strike a blow for the enslaved and tormented hares of your land. The Great Ones tell me that if you do as advised all will be well for you. They will intervene on your behalf if you take that difficult but immensely courageous and ethical step..."

Annemarie was confused "How can these...hare spirits... help me if I *..confess...?* I don't get it. I'm sorry but this sounds just crazy to me. God...Are you even real? Is this is dream. Am I imagining all this?"

"You are not imagining. When the time is right, we will help you..."...

Annemarie felt sleepy. But how could that be if she were already asleep and dreaming this? Drearily she asked: "How...why...does this seem so real if I'm dreaming? Just before you...appeared...I was sitting up. I saw the chink of moonlight through the curtains, as I often do when I wake early. And the clock... Why are the hands and numerals missing from the dial?"

The Golden Hare was starting to fade, and the rest of the intense landscape imagery with him, but his voice lingered inside her head: "It's not a dream, Blessed Human. When the body sleeps the spirit roams free, for us hares, as for all creatures of flesh and blood. The spirits of some of the wisest hares that ever ran upon the surface of your world have mandated me to establish contact with you, for the greater good of our brethren on the Big Island. I am allowed two visitations, so I will not be returning to you after this contact ends..."

"And the clock, why am I not seeing it as it ought to be?"

"Its appearance is symbolic. The face is blank because this communication between you and me is outside of time. In the world of spirit there are no clocks and no time...Farewell, compassionate human. May you succeed in your mission!"

"Mission?"

The strange wise creature disappeared, dissolving into thin air, and the resplendent backdrop for his visit was gone too. Annemarie felt a sudden jolt, like a mild electric shock, and opened her eyes.

She reached for the reading lamp and flicked on the switch. The room was exactly as it always was. The numerals and the hands were back on the clock, which tick-tocked as normal. But no time had passed since she'd closed her eyes to sleep. What had occurred, dream or otherwise, had unfolded in the space of a few seconds. She switched off the lamp and snuggled down to sleep.

The experience remained with her, visually and audibly, as she drifted into slumber: the powerful image of the Wise Hare and his discomforting advice pursuing her into a succession of mini-dreams that lacked the intensity of the visitation.

***

80

Tipsy froze in his bed of fallen leaves. He and Cupid had been roused from a long slumber that followed their sighting of those cruel Humaniks killing the greyhound.

Tipsy focused his hearing. What was that noise? *Could be a predator. Mustn't draw attention…or has it already seen us?* A high pitched growl somewhere to his left was the culprit. *Not Humanik by the sound of it.*

"Is it a dog?" Cupid rasped. His friend was panicking. "Now we're for it. It might have seen me jump on that dead mutt back there. He'll make us pay for that!"

"Shush!" Tipsy caught an unfamiliar whiff, a pungent aroma he couldn't quite place…possibly because it emanated from a creature unknown to the island. It wasn't repellent, and neither was it pleasant to his nostrils. But he intuited one ingredient immediately: The unmistakable smell of fear. Tinged, he sensed, with a seething rage and desperation.

He strained to see in the enveloping darkness. Those accursed clouds had thickened, blocking out the soft rays of moonlight. Again, there it was…a frantic growling, then a yelp, followed by a low cry. Was the dog in pain? Maybe those Humaniks they'd seen earlier had battered another dog but hadn't quite killed him.

Tipsy's eyes adjusted to the almost complete darkness and…*yes*…he recognised the grayish outline of a creature. It was on the same side of the long high hedge as Cupid and himself. An oddly-shaped dog, but then dogs came in many shapes and sizes. The collie the Humaniks set on him in captivity was starkly different from the sleek greyhounds that ran so much faster.

This must be another type of dog. One used by Humaniks for some arcane or wacky purpose beyond hare comprehension. The creature was confined somehow and wriggling, seemingly to extract itself from that spot, as if part of its body was stuck to the ground.

"He's in trouble!" Cupid exclaimed triumphantly. "He's not going to bother us! Let's get under this hedge and forget about him. If we get too close he might still be able to snap at us."

Tipsy couldn't argue with that advice, but something held him back even as he prepared to continue on his journey. Cupid was already easing himself under the hedge, but Tipsy stopped him with a preventive paw. "Not yet, I want to take a closer look at him. If he's suffering we might be able to help."

"Help? Are you stark raving bonkers, Tipsy? That dog would kill us if he could. It's only because some Humanik or other creature has disabled him that he's not running at us right now! Your concern for non-hares is going to get us killed, or recaptured!"

Tipsy closed his eyes. He knew Cupid spoke sense, but that inner voice urged compassion. "No, I've got to see what's happened to him. Call it curiosity. Humour me, Cupid, come on. I might need you if anything goes wrong."

"Need me? We'll both need the Goddess Ostara to fly down from Hare Heaven to rescue us if that dog recovers. He might decide to have us for dinner!"

"At the first sign of him getting to his feet we run…without hesitation. Out under the hedge and away. Okay?"

Cupid shook his head and gasped. "Fine, I'll go along with you… but hey…no more crazy risks after this!"

Tipsy shuffled along, hugging the hedge to his right. As he advanced, Cupid gingerly hopping nervously behind him, he saw that the creature was struggling to break free from a restraining device of some kind. The moon had partly emerged from the thick concealing cloud and now Tipsy had a clear view of the creature.

A thin shiny string was wrapped around its short thick neck. Its fur was white with black stripes across its eyes and black patches elsewhere on its sturdy covering. A bushy tail swished and thrashed about as it struggled.

Suddenly it looked straight at Tipsy and barked. It was a loud noise. Then it emitted a low sad whine, before barking again. "Sounds like a dog, but doesn't look like one" Cupid muttered, half concealing himself behind Tipsy as he eyed the strange creature.

Tipsy edged closer, halting as the animal strained to run at him on four powerfully-built legs. But it fell back abruptly, seemingly held in place by that device circling its neck. The creature emitted sorrowful whines and yelps, harsh on the ear at first but as tipsy focused his mind he understood its language. "Please, please, release me…please…" followed by plaintive agonising cries.

Catching sight of Tipsy it growled and spat, the restraint around its neck again preventing it from getting closer to the hares.

"Let him be, he'd kill us if he got the chance!" Cupid cautioned, nervously sitting and observing the creature from a safer distance than that separating it from Tipsy.

"Are you ill" Tipsy asked, framing the question telepathically as the creature's speech was difficult to replicate. Suddenly it stopped struggling and sat, panting heavily, its sad eyes glaring at the two hares.

"You understand me…how…?"

"Never mind, what's ailing you? Are you trapped by that thing fastened to your neck?"

Again trying to wrench itself free, it rasped: "Yes, I can't get away, and the more I try to the deeper it cuts into my flesh!"

Tipsy quickly explained the problem to Cupid, who began nosing around the creature, but far enough away to ensure it didn't attack him. Tipsy was about to query the creature's predicament further when Cupid cried out, "Ah, I see what's holding him, look!"

Tipsy followed his gaze to a wooden stake protruding from the earth and partially obscured by undergrowth. The shiny string extended from the creature's neck to the stake and was attached to it. The creature transmitted the plea mentally: "Can you loosen it somehow?"

Tipsy ventured closer to the creature. He fastened his teeth unto the shiny contraption- it was rock hard, slippery and tasteless- and he pulled with all his might. To no avail. His teeth rattled…he felt them creaking and being pulled from the roots. The device was fashioned of some substance impervious to his efforts. His mouth ached from repeated attempts to remove the devilish thing. Pausing, he braced himself for another frantic tug, but the creature groaned: "Stop. You're making it tighter!"

Tipsy withdrew, feeling helpless, his heart full of sorrow for the stricken creature. Cupid was busily engaged behind him. How clever, Tipsy thought. His friend had dislodged the stake. It lay flat on the ground beside the hedge. The creature still had its neck held by the device but was now moving about more freely, the uprooted stake trailing along. "Thanks, hare. I need to get to a safe place where a sympathetic Humanik will get this thing off me. This is the second time I've been caught in one of these damned things!"

Suspecting the cause of the creature's predicament, Tipsy asked "Did Humaniks do this to you?"

It heaved a long sigh and sat facing them, the neckband reflecting a silvery moon beam. "Who else?" it spat; distress giving way to anger. "They've taken my brothers and sisters, and many other badgers I know."

Badger, thought Tipsy… *So it's not a dog.*

"You've got that right," the badger retorted, having picked up Tipsy's transmission, "I've met some dogs though, and not the pleasant kind." He went silent, his head sadly contemplating the ground at his feet. He looked up again, tears forming in those soulful misty eyes. The little rivulets rolled down the black stripes to moisten the white fur beneath his jaw.

He continued, falteringly: "I was put into a trench by Humaniks, and the dogs were dropped in to fight me. I killed both of them. What a scrap that was. My claws and my teeth worked hard for me- a ferocious battle. I fought them with every fibre of my being, all my strength. But they roughed me up bad. Ah, the agony and the terror of it! My whole body was racked with such pain I wanted desperately to escape from it, leave it behind and join my ancestors in the world beyond. But I didn't, as that would mean death, and I wasn't ready for that.

"It wasn't my time, you see. I survived and escaped. Mad roaring Humaniks chased me, swinging big sticks over their heads. I got far away from them, only to be trapped by this neck restrainer. They use these to capture us alive so they can kill us later, or set their dogs on us. They're not all bad, though… the Humaniks. I'm off now to the one I know will help me. Her stony abode is deep in the forest some distance from here."

Tipsy wished him well, thinking of the kind Humanik who had helped him and the other hares escape. The badger, his white face with its long back stripes illuminated by the orb that bore Ostara's image, nodded his thanks to Tipsy and Cupid. The evil device gleamed, sending shudders through Tipsy who imagined it around it his own neck. At least it wasn't causing as much aggravation to the badger as it had earlier.

The creature went on his way, the stake bouncing and twisting as he ran on those squat, muscular legs. Tipsy prayed the badger would find the kindly Humanik he sought, and that hostile members of the same species didn't catch up with him first.

***

81

Annemarie walked up to the office of Liz Franklin, solicitor. A week had passed since that second night-time call, real or imagined, from that captivating Wise Hare. His first advice had led to her breaking the law by freeing the hares. Now he wanted her to confess to the whole thing and was promising this would somehow benefit hares throughout Ireland.

And, as if that didn't sound over the top and truly bizarre a notion to get her head around, he expected her to believe that a hare would turn up to make life easier for her and help her achieve her mission.

Mission!

And all of this advice comes from a hare that appears in a dream, except, according to him it's *not* a dream and he's on the inside track with hares that died long ago and are keeping contact with him from somewhere Up There...

Yeah, that's a great story to tell this legal eagle. Or maybe I can leave that stuff out. Get straight to the point. I'm taking responsibility for something I did that was technically illegal, but morally spot on.

She'd decided, after days of wrestling with the rational side of her being, her intuitive sense, and the niggling feeling that the visitation was somehow real, to confess.

But not directly to the police. She'd do it through a solicitor and only after establishing what the penalties were likely to be. It wasn't exactly a major criminal offence. Turning loose a few hares?

Okay, she'd broken a padlock, and deprived a coursing club of its so-called sport for a day. It would damn her in the estimation of the hare coursing fans. But so what? *I don't want or need their respect.* It wouldn't ostracise her in the village since many locals also disapproved of hare coursing. A criminal record, though, was the one inevitable consequence of confessing and going to court that almost held her back from the drastic course she'd settled upon.

Standing outside the office, she stared at the gold nameplate. She could still change her mind. As she raised her hand to press the doorbell, she hesitated, removed her hand and turned to walk away. *Is it a psychiatrist I should be seeing instead of a solicitor? Maybe I've cracked up. Something inside my head has come loose. But I haven't experienced hallucinations or heard voices, just those two visions that could have been dreams.*

Abruptly she forced herself to press the doorbell, her heart pounding, her mouth drained of moisture. *Let's get this over with...*

***

Liz Franklin rose from behind her desk to shake Annemarie's hand. "And what can I do for you? She asked after the introductions.

Annemarie nervously made eye contact with the bespectacled middle aged woman facing her whose greying hair was tied back into a bun. The solicitor had a broad compassionate smile. She nodded. "Go ahead, and bear in mind that everything you tell me is in strict confidence."

"Thank you."

Annemarie settled herself in the leather-backed chair, suppressing a powerful impulse to jump up and run from the office. *Will she think I'm crazy? No. She's not hearing about THAT.*

She told the solicitor the full story of how she'd freed the hares from captivity, and her reasons: her heartfelt opposition to the proven cruelty of hare coursing.

Ms Franklin, who had been utterly focused and listening intently, let out a long sigh, removed her glasses, wiped them with a pink handkerchief, and put them on again. "So, let me get this straight...You haven't been arrested or questioned about this, and the only contact from the police was that officer calling with the coursing club secretary?"

"Yes, that's right."

"But you wish to confess to...what you did...?"

"Exactly."

"But why? More than three weeks have passed. Why not let it all blow over? You haven't a high profile as an activist so maybe they'll never bother you?"

"They mightn't, or then again they might, but...it's the anxiety, and there's another consideration. Several campaigners have been arrested and put through the mill...for what I did...I'm not comfortable with that..."

"I see".

"Ms. Franklin, can you tell me, if I own up to this, what will the charge be, and the penalty? And will I be able to...you know...make a speech in court letting everyone know I acted on behalf of those unfortunate animals. I want to use the case, if I can, to highlight what coursing clubs are doing to Ireland's hares, the cruelty..."

The solicitor raised her hands: "One thing at a time..." She reached for a thick volume on her desk and flipped through the pages. Stopping at one page, she read silently. Without looking up she said plaintively: "You'd likely be charged with causing malicious damage to the property of the coursing club...and face a fine or possible imprisonment...Yes, you could state your motives and reasons etcetera but the result might be to your own detriment. The judge might be sympathetic to hare coursing, or he might just dislike the notion of somebody using the precious time of the court to advance a particular cause...he might then impose the maximum penalty."

"So you think I should just confess, take my punishment and say nothing?"

Ms. Franklin closed the hefty tome with an empathic plop and folded her arms. "There is another option. It carries risks, but you might wish to consider it. You want to confess to freeing the hares. You could admit to that but plead Not Guilty to the actual charge of causing malicious damage and opt for a jury trial, rather than allowing a single judge to decide the issue in the lower court. Your fate would then be in the hands of twelve citizens, giving you a reasonable chance of acquittal. It would also net you more publicity than a case in the lower court..."

Annemarie saw glimmers of hope, a way out of her difficulties that would leave her untainted by a criminal record and yet vindicated.

"You mentioned risks. What are those?"

"Well, because it's a higher court the penalties are higher too...if the jury were to find you guilty..."

Gloom returned, brushing away brief stirrings of optimism.

"Always a catch", she lisped nervously.

"It's a decision only you can make, Annemarie. Think it over. Also, I'll accompany you to the police station when you go to make a statement. It's important that you don't say the wrong things. Just admit to setting hares free at Ballycrossways coursing venue. Give the date it happened. Nothing more. You're aware of how powerful these coursing people are? If this were an incident involving damage to a cowshed or a car or farm fencing or whatever there wouldn't be a fraction of the police time devoted to it. I had to shield my ears from the racket that police helicopter made...and I saw those elite army rangers being deployed the day after the hares escaped, and top forensics people were on the scene before noon on the day. Completely OTT. But that's what happens when somebody steps on well-connected toes. You certainly picked on some serious folks..."

Rising, she shook Annemarie's hand again and showed her to the exit. "Get back to me as soon as you can. It looks better for you if you come forward on this sooner rather than later. You understand that?"

Annemarie thanked her. When the door closed behind her and she stepped back into the street, she felt as though a weight had lifted from her shoulders. She inhaled the cool autumnal air and her eyes welcomed the rays of weakened sunlight that bathed the street and twinkled on the shopwindows. Life felt a tad less oppressive than before she'd entered the solicitor's office.

But anxiety still nagged. Yes, she'd plead not guilty and opt for a jury trial. *If it all goes wrong? Don't even think about that.* One other thing: What if the police *did* intend to arrest her? Better call to them before they called to her.

***

82

They walked, ran and crept through field after field, nimbly avoiding Humaniks whose menacing forms could appear anywhere. The trick was to see them before they saw you. Tipsy drew solace from the fact that Humaniks were harmless, despite their lethal intent, unless they had those fire rods or dogs with them. The rods spat death or painful injury and the dogs, under instructions from their masters, would do likewise if they could outrun the hare.

Some Humaniks, he noticed, carried rods that didn't shine and those ones, thankfully, didn't seem to spit fire. They peered through a ditch at a Humanik strutting along a lane after those large lumbering creatures that made a dull "moo" sound and had whirling clouds of breath hovering over them. The Humanik was using his rod that resembled a bare tree-branch to tap the sides of their bodies.

Had he captured them... like the hares had been abducted from the island? Tipsy wondered if these slow-moving animals would be chased by dogs also. The voice within quickly dispelled the notion. Those are for eating, it hinted, not chasing.

Cupid had slowed a bit, and looked forlorn. "I need a rest", he moaned.

"Over there", Tipsy pointed, "another wood. We should be safe in there..."

They covered the short distance, Tipsy finding it difficult not to stop and grab a quick snack amid clumps of juicy weeds. They threw themselves down in a readymade bed of fallen leaves at the base of a tree. Cupid asked: "Do we just keep moving, or what? We don't know if we're approaching danger or getting further from it."

"I follow my instinct Cupid and trust in Ostara to guide us. Something impels me in this direction. I'm certain we must pass through this wood and then...at the other side I have a task to perform...I can't say what it is...but I'll get my next round of inspiration when I need it."

Cupid stared at him. "You're the oddest hare I ever met, but I hope that inspiration of yours isn't leading us back into captivity. I'd rather die...I mean it, than to be at the mercy of those Humanik creeps!"

Cupid complained a little more, but his voice grew fainter and the words less distinct. He was snoring. Tipsy closed his eyes and offered a prayer to Ostara. He felt himself falling and drifting gently, or was it his spirit leaving his body?

His sleep was haunted by dreams, some short and sharp, others seemingly endless, though they all played out inside his head in the space of...less than twice as long as the time it took a hare to wash his whiskers. Then, just as he yawned and opened his eyes he found himself still in dreamland.

Or so it seemed. The wood looked the same. Cupid was snoring nearby, a leaf fragment partly covering a nostril and rustling with every breath. Dawn was breaking, though the trees obscured its collage of orange and velvet and drained the sunbeams of their lustre.

But Tipsy had that "awake but still dreaming" sensation, and sure enough, there he was, His Eminence, or rather the great one's spirit, sitting calmly in front of him. Tipsy could see right through him, the translucent form.

You are progressing well, Tipsy. The words came telepathically. No need to speak.

I wouldn't have thought that. I'm here on the Big Island, far from home, in the middle of a wood. I've narrowly avoided having my bones broken by powerful dogs, I've risked my life to save an animal called a fox, who had earlier tried to eat me, I saw just how cruel those Humaniks can be even to the dog creatures that serve them. I helped a badger in distress, I ran the gauntlet of those crazy Humanik death rods...progress?

The Golden Hare smiled. *Fear not, you are on the right track. Learn from all you see and hear and experience. When you exit this wood, you must depart from Cupid. Tell him to turn right and keep walking. Other island hares await him in a nearby meadow. You will cross the road and enter the Humanik settlement. You will approach the rear of one particular Humanik dwelling and await developments that will point the way to the next phase of your mission. This will be the residence of the female who freed you and the others from captivity.*

Tipsy was perplexed. *Which dwelling? How do I know where?*

His Eminence glowed brighter but then began to fade. *You will know. Trust that inner voice...*

The ethereal form grew indistinct and disappeared. Tipsy awoke, his confidence renewed. He nudged Cupid, gritting his teeth as he prepared to tell him they must part company. He had to fight back a feeling of deep sadness and regret. But his mission came first.

***

83

Tipsy felt awful, even guilty, though he'd done nothing wrong. He'd said goodbye to Cupid. He couldn't have him with him where he was going. He must somehow reach the Humanik who liked hares and the Golden Hare had stressed the importance of being unaccompanied when he made contact with her.

Though he didn't doubt the Great One's wisdom, he was perplexed. How on earth was he to find the Humanik settlement where this creature dwelt, let alone the sympathetic Humanik herself? He supposed he'd have to rely on instinct and a possible telepathic clue from His Eminence. Could there be hateful Humaniks waiting for him there?

Still, he had to fulfill his mission. He could ask directions from some unthreatening creature. Yes, why not? Unlike Cupid, they wouldn't insist on tagging along for the final stage of his trek, being complete strangers to him.

He trod more of those smooth Humanik roads, trudged along muddy pathways and through damp fields, the wet grass cold and hostile under his feet, as if determined to slow his progress. Or did he imagine that? Grass didn't think or feel. It didn't have a heart ticking inside its thin blades. It stirred or sighed only because the wind forced it to.

Tipsy slid under a ditch and paused. Facing him was a large grassy mound of earth in the middle of a field. Resembling a small hill, it was studded all over with daisies, dandelions, buttercups, which he recognized, and other flowers and weeds unfamiliar to him. Apart from the mound, the field seemed to be dominated almost completely by high growing plants of a type he'd never seen before. Certainly not on the island. They towered above him like trees. Large, bright green, heart shaped leaves dangled from the long crispy stalks that crackled and trembled in a light breeze. They sounded almost hollow. Sniffing a stalk he caught a delicious pungent aroma.

Was it edible? It could be poisonous. Temptation trumped fear and he sank his teeth into the stalk. It snapped and broke, and fell into the grass, a canopy of green leaves and severed purple shoots falling and brushing softly against his fur. Usually it required a few attempts to shear a stalk like that. He settled himself to have a snack, nibbling on the piece that had broken off. His mouth filled with a juice that tasted divine. He then sampled a leaf, chewing it ravenously. What a nice plant this was.

A sudden swishing of grass made him freeze. Pieces of half-chewed vegetation dropped from his mouth. His heart raced. Had a predator spotted him? Was the creature about to pounce? Should he run...or hope his enemy was hunting by scent and hadn't yet seen him? Horrible choices…*decide…decide.*

"Enjoying the knotweed, I see!"

Tipsy looked behind him. There, partially concealed by plant leaves and grass, sat what he took to be a…*a leveret, or a small hare?* No…it couldn't be. Leverets were grayish, and this creature was brown, and its eyes were black, not reddish-brown like a hare's. And its ears stood up sharply.

"Yes…I've never come across a plant like this. I wasn't sure about it but I just couldn't resist. Nice!" Tipsy blurted.

The creature's ears quivered, its nostrils flared, and its eyes bulged. Tipsy had frightened it. It quickly regained composure, laughed, and spoke hesitantly: "How can you speak our language. Hares don't speak Rabbitese."

"So you're not a hare, then?" The creature puffed out his chest. "I'm a rabbit. We're kind of related, in a far-off distant way. But we're different creatures."

"I'm Tipsy. I can converse with all creatures…except Humaniks. I'm searching for a Humanik settlement somewhere not far from here. I need to find a certain Humanik's home…"

The rabbit hopped closer, its whiskers twitching and its shining black eyes narrowing. "I can show you the settlement. After that it's up to you what you wish to do. Personally I wouldn't go anywhere near those Humaniks or their dwellings."

Tipsy was about to thank him when the rabbit punched him playfully, crooning: "But first have a little meal and a chat with us. I have some friends nearby. Come along!"

Anxious not to offend the helpful creature, Tipsy followed him to the other side of the big grassy mound with its lush floral growth. At the base of the mound sat six more rabbits, all nibbling on the tasty knotweed and other shrubbery. Tipsy introduced himself, causing the usual consternation among creatures who didn't expect to hear someone from another species speak or understand their lingo.

A rabbit three times bigger than the others stepped forward and extended a paw to Tipsy, which he shook heartily: "Benjamin's the name. I run things around here. That's Clarence who brought you here. He's our scout. Knows this countryside like the backs of his front paws… We live in there." The burley creature pointed to several holes in the side of the mound near its base.

"You live inside…?"

"Burrows…unlike you hares. How you get away with living above ground I'll never understand, especially with all those nasty critters out to get you!"

Benjamin enlightened him further on rabbit life and Tipsy was fascinated by the differences between rabbits and hares that belied the outward similarities: leverets were born fully sighted, for example, while rabbits were born blind and took quite a while to see. Like hares, rabbits faced many predators: foxes, large birds, Humanik death rods that killed them…and snares that choked them. Benjamin sighed: "Before the sun goes down we know that rabbits somewhere in the land will fall to Humanik predators."

The Rabbit Boss invited Tipsy to eat with them, pointing to a wide selection of edible plant fragments. He recognized carrots and lettuce among these, recalling the Humaniks who fed him in captivity. The food tasted better this time, among friends. They sat and dined in silence, the only sound being the low hissing of the wind that shook the knotweed. It carried a light drizzle that sprayed all of the rabbits and Tipsy as they munched and swallowed.

But another sound mingled with the soft sough of the wind and the patter of the rain. A strange sobbing or sniveling, Tipsy thought. His attention was drawn to a small clearing in the field he hadn't noticed amid the ubiquitous knotweed. Rabbits were clustered there, motionless apart from a slight, barely perceptible quivering and that eerie lamentation that seemed to come from where they sat or lay prostrate. Tipsy's unspoken question was answered by Benjamin, but in solemn, scarcely audible tones, the cheery note gone from his voice. "They are the doomed ones…they have the sickness that never heals."

"Sickness?"

Benjamin nodded sadly: "Come closer. I'll show you. But not too close."

As they approached the rabbits Tipsy's stomach heaved. Their eyes, noses, mouths and ears were swollen and disfigured, and from each orifice oozed revolting mucus. Amid their weeping, Tipsy could hear them struggle to breathe. He felt a deep revulsion, tinged by helplessness. There was nothing he could do. Unlike the healthy rabbits sitting at the mound, they were covered in sores and now he heard their sobbing grow louder. None of them turned to look at Tipsy or Benjamin, so engrossed were they in their fearful anguish.

Benjamin patted Tipsy on the shoulder: "Let's move back. Let them die. Once a rabbit is debilitated by this sickness there is no hope. This condition is no chance event in our lives. Nor is it an act of vengeance by the Rabbit God, as some rabbits believe. The wiser among us know it was devised by our most devious tormenter to kill us."

"You mean…the Humaniks?"

Benjamin rolled his eye to Heaven. "Who Else?"

Back at the mound, Tipsy chatted further with his gentle hosts, exchanging stories and information and listening to accounts of their peculiar subterranean existence and crafty survival strategies. When Tipsy signaled it was time for him to resume his journey, Benjamin quipped: "Clarence tells me you want to reach a Humanik place of habitation. It's running from them you should be, but best of luck!"

Tipsy thanked him for his hospitality, adding that he had a mission to complete and contact with a Humanik was an essential part of it. Benjamin laughed, clapping Tipsy on the back with a sturdy paw. "That's something we rabbits find odd about you guys. You're bigger than us, you run faster, but every now and then you go completely mad. You do things that make no sense but you do them anyway. Is this one of those bouts of madness, Tipsy?"

Tipsy gazed up at the grey drizzly sky, partly obscured by the leaves of the towering knotweed. He sighed. "I'm not sure what it is. It's just something I've got to do. Though I wish it was over."

***

84

On the hilltop, Tipsy felt lightheaded as he beheld the weird spread of yellow, white, blue, green and purple shapes and protuberances that stretched below to left and right. Clarence and he squatted, observing from amidst a clump of high weeds that would conceal them from any curious or sharp-witted creatures below. Clarence pointed with a front paw at the sprawling panorama of Humanik living space.

Tipsy adjusted his sight- and his mind- to the lines of square structures, each of them exhibiting smaller square shaped openings, and fronting all these dwellings were patches of grass or vegetation, framed by little white walls. Or they seemed small from his vantage point on the hill. Wisps of cloudy bluish-grey vapour, fanned by the wind, rose meanderingly to the sky out of blocks of hollowed stone that protruded from the tops of some dwellings.

Clarence nudged him. "The Humaniks live inside those structures. Sometimes we sit up here, watching them from this safe distance. Those shiny openings in the dwellings…they're not what they seem. They are invisible barriers. You can see right through but if you try to enter you get a bump on the head. You can see your reflection in them like in a pool of water. We're looking now at the rear of the Humanik settlement. Those spaces behind their abodes have grass, or lovely vegetables growing in them…lettuce, carrots, asparagus, scallions; cabbage…our kind of food. We sneak down occasionally to steal some. Dangerous. Rabbits have entered those vegetable patches and never returned…"

"Were they spotted?"

"Yeah…by Humaniks…or cats…or dogs. Or they got caught in snares. Hardly worth the risk, but sometimes a rabbit just can't resist those scrumptious greens!"

Tipsy noticed the creepy silhouettes of Humaniks moving behind the transparent barriers, and saw that some of the barriers were partly draped with coverings, as though to conceal what could otherwise be perceived within. Scanning the line of dwellings he saw tiny lights flickering at the mouths of some Humaniks, which they removed and then returned to their mouths. Others appeared to be talking, or ingesting food behind those see-through barriers.

His heart sank. He'd need to be extremely careful not to attract the attention of hostile Humaniks down there. Problem was: how was he to know which abode contained the sympathetic member of that frightful species?

"Best wait till nightfall". Clarence suggested.

"I wonder", Tipsy lisped. He saw both advantages and drawbacks in that advice. True, he'd more easily avoid detection or capture by Humaniks at night. A hare's vision was better than a Humanik's; he'd been told by some of the Big Island hares while in captivity. He could move about unseen and unheard by his foes down there. But the problem was he'd have more difficulty locating the friendly Humanik in darkness.

And she wasn't likely to be up and about with no sunlight to illuminate her path. Humaniks were averse to navigating the world without light, whereas hares were *more active* by night than by day on the Big Island, more so than on his home island where they ventured out in daylight because they had less enemies to contend with. After much contemplation and weighing up of pros and cons he fixed on a compromise: he'd move into the settlement at twilight and lie low until sunrise, whereupon he'd resume his search.

Then other snags obtruded: Would he recognize the Humanik? He'd caught only a fleeting glimpse of her, a shutter of motion in the half-light of dawn when she'd freed him and the others. And how would *she* react? Would she grasp the significance of his arrival? And what would happen if he approached the *wrong* Humanik, someone who resembled her?

He gritted his teeth, shut his eyes tight and consciously pushed away these nagging doubts and worries. They were, he knew, just irritating expressions of his natural timidity as a hare. He'd gotten this far, against overwhelming odds…outrunning, outthinking and outmaneuvering the greyhounds, escaping from the compound, surviving contact with a wily fox, dodging death rods and Humanik road monsters. All these obstacles in his path had been swept aside.

He felt blessed…and somehow protected. Ostara was watching over him. And he felt the Golden Hare's soothing presence again right now, on top of this hill overlooking the homes of his deadliest foe: Those ferocious predators… all cozy and secure inside their strange abodes, so much more classy and sophisticated than the simple nest in the grass that served as home for the Irish Hare.

"So I'll be leaving you then?"

Tipsy jolted. He'd forgotten the rabbit squatting beside him in the long grass. "Oh yes, and thank you Clarence. I'll never forget you and your honourable friends. Please look after yourselves. Avoid that dreadful disease spread by Humaniks and their other conniving tricks and devices. I'll wait awhile here till the shadows fall…"

Clarence smiled, tapped him on the shoulder with a paw and departed, hopping back to the grassy mound in the field with its comfy burrows. Tipsy opted to sleep. He needed to be strong, in mind and body, for the next phase of his mission.

***

85

Tipsy slept, but only in short intervals, ensconced in his temporary nest on the hilltop. Each time he awoke the sky was a shade darker. More stars had pierced the great velvety expanse, twinkling from their eternal positions as if winking at him.

Down below lights also shone, but these not of divine origin, nor as remote from this haven where he awaited dawn. He assumed Humaniks produced those shafts of light, as they emanated from the openings in their dwellings. And he saw smudgy Humanik shapes in the openings, silhouetted by the light. Last time he wakened, almost all the openings were illuminated. Now, he noticed that less than a third of them had this brightness, and it had grown dimmer in those, possibly diluted by those coverings the Humaniks seemed to pull across the portals, perhaps to prevent light escaping.

Tipsy drifted off, wondering how closer to dawn his next awakening would bring him. His consciousness swayed and dissolved, and after what seemed like just half a dozen heartbeats but was probably longer, his eyes fastened on a sky dominated by a crescent moon and a glittering infinity of stars. He'd been lying on his back. Sitting up he surveyed the scene below. No lights now in the Humanik dwellings, but still some burning in the midst of the settlement, seemingly overlooking those vegetable patches that extended from the bases of the dwellings that the rabbits loved to invade now and again. The rabbits were right about the Humaniks. They were active by day but not in darkness, except inside their dwellings. But they were least active just before dawn, when they slept.

When Tipsy awoke next, the sky had changed again, draining of darkness. The first rays of pink and red dawn were slicing through the celestial canopy. He braced himself. *Time to move.* He began his descent of the hill. It was steep enough and he had to control his movements to avoid sliding down in a mad rush. The grass was slippery with morning dew. About halfway down he came to a stop, stumbling onto a little stone ledge. He arranged himself into a sitting posture.

The Humanik settlement loomed ever closer, and more menacing. He glanced to left and right, and opted to head for the first dwelling on the right. *Have to start somewhere.* If he could find a suitable hiding place he'd hopefully be able to explore each of the homes in turn to see if he might recognise any Humaniks who showed themselves. The trick would be to see them without them seeing him.

A shrill whistle shook him. His eyes turned upwards. Birds, all sitting side by side on a long string. Whistling, chirping, warbling, and trilling. *But...how can this be?* Then, following the length of the string, which swayed under the weight of the feathered ones, he saw it was attached on both sides of the hill to high branchless trees with weird shiny protrusions on top. The trees were so bare. Not a leaf or even the smallest trace of foliage remained.

He wondered if Humaniks had created this anomaly too, though he suspected they hadn't created such a convenience out of love of birds. A thrush saw him looking up and tweeted: "Who are you? Do you fancy my singing voice? I'm the loudest and sweetest singer on the wire this morning, the envy of the whole choir!"

"Wire? Is that what you're sitting on?"

The startled bird, having gotten over his surprise at being addressed in avian, blurted: "Yes...weird creature. This wire serves as an occasional perch of convenience for us. It also enables Humaniks to talk to each over vast distances!"

"You mean, like telepathy?"

"Kind of...though that's a rare gift...even among birds. What are you doing down there?"

"Long story; and I don't have time to tell you...I'm off down to find someone."

"Beware of the cats!" the thrush chirped, before fluttering up into the softening dawn-light, followed by other songbirds that seemed to tire of balancing on the wire. Some of them stared at Tipsy as they ascended; no doubt baffled at his interspecies communication skills. *Cats?* Tipsy had heard of them from hares in captivity. They didn't bother him though, as they only posed a real threat to helpless leverets or injured hares. An adult hare could easily deter them.

The last stretch of the slope was especially slippery. Tipsy lost his grip and slid almost to the bottom of the hill, finally regaining his balance when he struck another rocky protrusion. The impact dazed him. He felt queasy, and his sight blurred for a few heartbeats, but then everything came back into focus. He stood and rubbed his aching head with a front paw. No cuts...just a slight graze under his nose. A backward glance showed the hill extending behind him and upwards.

The wire overhead now hosted different birds...less melodious and not inclined to sing, he noticed. The grumpy, squeaking crows fanned out along its full length, all shouting at him. But he couldn't tell whether it was ridicule or encouragement as they all spoke at once so that no voice could be heard. It sounded like a mixture of contempt and curiosity.

A short distance in front of him, dimly illuminated by the moonlight and weak sunbeams, was the dwelling he had set his sights on. He approached it quietly, looking out for any Humanik presence, or any other creatures who might threaten him. *Nobody about.*

There was an entrance in the wall fronting it. He could see it led into a Humanik vegetable patch. It had a crisscross of obstructing rods and bars, supposedly to avert access by unwanted creatures, or maybe other unwelcome Humaniks. Tipsy managed to squeeze through a space in the entrance barrier and pattered silently along a stony path. On either side grew lines of lettuces. He thought of the rabbits. They'd love this place.

Facing him, high up on the Humanik dwelling was an opening that reflected the dawn-light in little reddish blue twinkles. Seeing no Humanik movement behind it, he resolved to try the next home, but not before grabbing a bite to eat. He nibbled at a piece of lettuce. He was smacking his lips and preparing to leave the patch when a ferocious racket erupted: Noise from inside the dwelling and from somewhere nearby outside it.

He was about to make a quick exit when he saw a small dog with an extra large head and huge snapping jaws emerging from around the corner of the dwelling, attempting to reach him but unable to get beyond a few paces. He noticed the reason for its frustration. It was tethered to the wall of the dwelling. It must have been asleep and roused by the intrusion. "Sorry!" Tipsy whispered.

The dog faltered, momentarily struck dumb. Then, as Tipsy dropped back out of the patch, it was whining and muttering incoherently. Tipsy could just make out the words: "A hare talked to me...I must be mad!"

Tipsy considered his position. He reckoned the only way he'd get to find the Humanik was to investigate every dwelling until, hopefully, he spotted her. She had to make an appearance at some point. That's assuming she wasn't away somewhere else, travelling about as Humaniks did. He sighed. *What on earth are the chances that I'll ever find her?*

He moved to the wall fronting the next patch, squinting at a sudden glint of sunlight mirrored by one of the square openings in the residence. He looked up at the openings, draped with those coverings Humaniks seemed fond of: Probably to prevent any creature from seeing them inside their nests. An abrupt pulling across of the drape on one opening startled him. A Humanik face pressed against the opening, the creature's nose almost flattened and its eyes darting about in searching mode.

It was a male of the species so clearly not the one he sought. Tipsy knew he was in the Humanik's line of sight, but remained as still as a rock, trembling slightly. He hardly dared to breathe, but he had to and feared the little puffs of vapour would give him away. The Humanik then closed the covering, to Tipsy's heartfelt relief.

Then, just as he began to move to have a look at the next home, loud rapping came from the dwelling he had just inspected. A big rectangular orifice appeared at ground level in the home and out ran...the Humanik that he'd seen higher up just a few heartbeats ago. The creature had seen him and was howling, its front paws flailing and its face a shade of purplish red which Tipsy knew denoted anger, thanks to Big Island hares who'd filled him in on Humanik facial expressions.

He ran along the line of dwellings until he reached a wooden entrance to a home that was ajar, swinging and creaking. In he dashed, the raging Humanik's hollering still audible but growing less distinct by the heartbeat.

He found himself in a patch that differed from the others. It had no vegetables: Just a big square of short grass, fringed to his right by flowers. How tall they were…dazzlingly bright yellow discs on sturdy greyish brown stalks. He sniffed and caught the fragrance of fresh dew on the grass. *A pleasant tang.*

He glanced up at the dwelling attached to this patch. It had higher and lower square openings, all draped; so he couldn't see anything inside. Probably another grumpy Humanik, possibly wielding a death rod or some other nasty implement to turn live hares into captives- or carcasses. He was about to leave the patch when something prompted him to stay. He felt, or imagined, the presence of the Golden Hare. Closing his eyes he focused. *Eminence, is it you?* An image of the Great One formed, but indistinctly. *Tipsy...wait. Be patient.*

Had he really heard him? The mental picture dissolved. Tipsy's eyes flashed open. There were a dozen questions he wanted to ask, but the spell was broken. *Well, nothing for it but to sit tight. I must be getting closer...unless I just imagined. I could be cracking up under all this craziness. The fright I got from that hot-headed Humanik back there could have affected my brain. Maybe Benjamin the Rabbit was right and we hares are all a bit mad.*

If he was going to hang around in this patch for a while, as his intuition, or the Golden Hare-enjoined him to do, then he'd better conceal himself. No cover in the short grass. Why did Humaniks cut the grass shorter? *You'd swear they wanted to make life difficult for us.*

The flowers. He positioned himself behind the row of swaying yellow discs. He'd never seen flowers like these on the island. The long thick stalks provided good cover, and he felt a strange sense of relief here, as if these radiant happy plants were bidding him welcome.

Peeping around a stalk, he reckoned someone watching from the dwelling wouldn't see him so easily, but he had a fair enough view of those openings. He wondered how many dwellings he'd have to visit before he'd find the Humanik. He was itching to move to the next dwelling, but that momentary instinct, or possible message from the Great One, held him back.

He opted to wait for whoever lived in there to make an appearance. He'd have to be quick to avoid death or capture if a hostile creature surfaced. And then, if he survived, he'd resume his search.

86

Tipsy was getting restless. Dawn had passed and now the molten sun had completely displaced the fading moon and a solitary star maintained its presence in the firmament. Golden beams streaked across the sward and the sun's orb imprinted itself on the transparent openings of the home he was observing. His eyelids drooped and he had to shake himself to stay awake. Whenever nothing was happening sleep tempted and beguiled.

A robin landed nearby, pecking the earth at the base of a flower, causing its luscious yellow disc to wobble slightly. Spotting Tipsy, the red-breasted little bird opened its beak wide with surprise. "Hello!" Tipsy lisped, not too loud for fear of rousing some irate Humanik. The robin almost fell over.

Tipsy quickly apologised and explained his linguistic gifts. Then he whispered: "Are you familiar with this patch? Can you help...does a female Humanik live in there?"

Recovering its wits after the shock of hearing a hare speak to it, the robin spluttered: "Yes, I think so...she leaves out crumbs for me on the lawn...that's the grassy surface you see...but this morning it seems another bird got here first. Worse luck. She likes birds. But hey...what's a hare doing here...are you lost?"

"Not lost...Searching. I wonder if this Humanik...in there...is the one I seek. I'll just have to wait for her to emerge from the dwelling. If it's not her, I'll keep searching until..."

The robin, listening intently, raised a wing pointedly. Its eyes gleamed and dilated. It bobbed along the line of flowers and stood on its tiny feet facing Tipsy. "Tell you what...I'll fly to her window...that's the watery square hole up there that sunlight bounces off...and I'll see if I can get her attention. She looks out some mornings and I chirp up to her. Humaniks are funny sometimes. Some of them want to kill us...but others like to hear us tweeting..."

"Gee, thanks!"

The robin fluttered upwards and swerved towards the...*window*...Another word to add to his vocabulary. He learned a new one before every sunset, it seemed, whether from hares or other creatures.

The bird alighted on a ledge that protruded from underneath the window. It began striking the see-through barrier with its beak, pausing now and then for a break before resuming its effort that produced a rattling sound. It obviously wasn't loud enough. How was the occupant ever going to hear that? Tipsy's hearing was extra sharp and he scarcely noticed it.

The robin stopped and cast a forlorn glance down at Tipsy, shrugging with its tiny wings. Well, the bird had tried hard and was so obliging. He'd have to thank it for that. *But wait...*what was that movement in the window?

The drape divided, revealing a Humanik head. Tipsy felt a tingling in the back of his neck and a pulsing behind his eyes as the form resolved itself into a distinctive image. The lips and head-growth arrangement denoted a female of the species. *Not just any female.*

Though he'd only seen her once...in that place of captive horrors, he instantly recognised her: The female matched his recollection...his perpetually frozen mental picture of that wonderful creature that had set him and the others free.

She was dreamily surveying the grassy patch. *Move...no time to lose.* He must make himself known to her. He dashed from the hiding place, a cluster of flower discs tickling his ears and forehead as he leapt into the middle of the short grass.

His heart sank...the drape had closed again inside the window. She'd not seen him. *Nothing for it but to wait.* The robin had roused her before her waking time. Later, perhaps, she'd resurface. And at least he knew he'd found the right dwelling.

***

87

The drapes were being pulled open on the window. Tipsy leapt out into the grass. *Too late again.* She didn't even show herself this time. Wary of other Humaniks who might see him, he returned to his hiding place between the flowers and a mossy wall.

The day progressed. Weak sunbeams played with shadows on the lawn. Tipsy yawned, and shuddered: Those gruesome Humanik contraptions passed by continuously from both directions outside the patch. He cringed at the discordance of the noise they made. It rattled inside his head and jolted him every time it assailed his consciousness.

Unlike anything he'd ever heard on the island. Had he not exercised scrupulous care since escaping he'd have been rolled over by one of them. The Humaniks controlling them wouldn't be too concerned about crushing a hare into the ground, he surmised; given the other grizzly things they did to all kinds of animals.

Footfalls on a hard surface resounded inside the dwelling. He waited...but no sign of her. Perhaps she didn't frequent this part of her abode. What if she didn't see him? Then it struck him. She mightn't see...but she might *hear.* Hares had a way of getting inside the heads of Humaniks when they cried out in pain. He wasn't hurting right now but that didn't mean he couldn't make himself heard.

There was a risk, he knew; that other Humaniks would hear him too and come charging at him like that angry creature had earlier. Risk or no risk, though, it was better than waiting for....it could be days. Or she could leave her dwelling by another exit and not reappear for ages.

*Here goes...*he emitted an ear-piercing shriek...followed by the most mournful series of sobs and lamentations he could conjure from the depths of his being. Birds overhead stopped in mid-flight to remonstrate and shriek down at him. Others, perched atop the Humanik dwelling, stopped chirping and stared at him quizzically as though he were stark raving bonkers. A blackbird's wings blocked its ears.

Tipsy began to doubt his own sanity. His whole body shook with the vibrations of the blood-curdling racket he was making. The birds all deserted the dwelling top. Even the shrill crows squatting on a wire over a neighbouring patch, creatures known for their own strident cacophonies; flew skyward in furious haste.

Tipsy gave himself a rest, before resuming his haunting plea to the Humanik.

What was that? He stopped hollering, and peered around a flower stalk. That large blue rectangle was opening in the Humanik home, and yes...she was emerging...heading now right towards him.

This is it. Must be careful not to alarm her...

***

88

Annemarie awoke. No alarm clock this morning. Her day-off. *God!* Would she have many days off when her boss heard she'd been charged with a criminal offence?

She'd try to persuade him to await the outcome the court case that must follow her confessing to releasing those hares. After all, any accused person was innocent until proven guilty. That's the way the legal system worked. If he feared a loss of business, and she knew some of his clients were pro hare coursing and possibly members of that horrible club, then her position would be shaky. She hadn't yet got around to calling to a police station to confess. She kept putting it off. The thought of it made her cringe

She shut her eyes tightly when she drew open the curtains on her bedroom window. The sudden flash of sunlight, weak though it was at this time of year, always threatened to blind her. Yawning, she turned to dress and stopped. Listened.

What on earth is that? A strange crying. *Is it a baby?*

She looked out the window, along both ends of the street. No babies about: Just the postman pushing his bike and a woman with a huge bag of shopping passing him in the other direction. *Must have imagined it.*

She dressed and filled the kettle. As it hummed on the desktop she set about filling a dish with cornflakes. There it was again. For a moment she thought it might be the kettle. Maybe it was making strange sounds due to an electrical fault. But no. She'd heard it in the bedroom and the kettle wasn't switched on.

Listening intently, she felt it was coming from...the backroom. *Couldn't be.* She rushed to the room, fearful of what she'd see. The room was empty of anything except the usual spare bed, chairs, and stacks of old magazines on a bookshelf. Still she heard it...like a baby sobbing, or looking for attention. Then it struck her. It could only be coming from the garden. *Oh My God. Has somebody abandoned a baby?*

She returned to the kitchen and from there to the back entrance. *Here goes.* She opened the door and cast her eyes all around.

Nothing...The lawn spread before her as always. The fringes of tall sunflowers along one side of the patch of green to her right were swaying in a soft breeze. *But...blast.* She'd left the little half rotted wooden door in the garden wall open. How on earth had she forgotten to shut it? Might as well post an invitation to burglars. Anyone could have slipped in. Why had she even opened it in the first place? Must be all the tension and worry about a court case.

She pushed across the deadbolt securing the door. *Nothing on the lawn. Must have imagined that crying.* Relaxing, she edged along the line of sunflowers. Each of them tantalised, with its joyous circle of exuberant yellowish-gold and that dark central disc exuding mystery. They'd be taking their leave in another week or two, but how beautiful a sight in late autumn, that strip of bright celebratory flora defying the seasonal emphasis on decay and approaching winter. A theme she warmed to right now in the depths of anxiety and that nagging fear of the future.

She held one to her nostrils and inhaled its aroma, resisting the urge to pluck it. No point in hastening its demise. *Optimism.* That's what she liked about this flower: All day it tracked the sun's movement, never losing sight of it...always striving to look on the bright side of existence. She must do likewise. Whatever the future held she must remain positive, draw upon her inner strength.

She returned to the house and was about to close the door when she heard a swishing among the sunflowers. She looked around and noticed movement. She stepped back onto the lawn. Something was shuffling about behind the stalks, causing the flowers to quiver and gyrate like little dancers.

Could be a cat. Nothing unusual about that. It wasn't Ginger. He was asleep in the sitting room. But others occasionally dropped in to have a snoop....over the wall or this time, possibly, through the open doorway. She walked pointedly towards the flora, expecting the intruder to either run away or, if it happened to be friendly, come purring to her.

She stopped dead. From between two sunflowers squeezed...*a hare!*

No! Not here...in the village. In my garden!

She backtracked, anxious not to frighten the animal. How had it strayed so far? She went into the house, grabbed a carrot from the fridge and, heart thumping, returned to the lawn, and almost tripped over him. "I'm sorry!" she lisped, fearing she'd frightened the hare and he'd be making a fast exit from the lawn.

Unbelievably, he just stayed there, sitting in the grass...and looking straight up at her. What a lovely noble creature he was, with that reddish brown fur, and the white lobes of his big long ears. She saw herself reflected in his soft watery amber eyes.

She moved towards him, expecting him to flee any second. Was this really happening? She placed her hand on his head and patted the soft fur. No sudden burst of movement. *Still no fear from him. Has he been stunned or something?*

She'd forgotten the carrot in her other hand. She offered it to him and he gently took it in his mouth. Dropping it in the grass, he nibbled on it. Without finishing the carrot, he rose and rubbed against her right ankle, much as a cat would do.

A Cat. She glanced back at the open door. Better make sure Ginger isn't up and about. She tiptoed inside and quietly inched open the sitting room door. Sure enough he was happily asleep and snoring on his favourite couch. She dashed outside. The hare startled her. He was sitting and looking straight at her.

She went to stroke him and again, astonishingly, he showed no fear. *Could he be a pet…maybe he wandered from his owner. Never heard of anyone with a pet wild hare, whatever about a rabbit. Best to let him alone. Maybe he'll return to his owner, if he's a pet, and to the wild if he just happened to stray in here.*

She remembered reading about not interfering in any way with a leveret if you found one. She reckoned the same advice might apply to an adult hare. He wasn't injured, judging by his free and easy behavior. He hadn't limped. *But hey, what's this?*

Dangling from his right ear was a tiny yellow tag or label of some kind. On closer inspection she saw it was plastic and had been attached, clipped on, obviously by a human hand. She leant on the grass and pulled lightly at the tag but it didn't budge, though the hare gave a low moan as if it hurt. She patted him gently.

She stood slowly, a sudden realization dawning. *That dammed coursing club.* She remembered the hares in the compound. It was dark, but she'd caught sight in the moonshine of those yellow ear-tags on the hares as they made their dash for freedom.

She now saw the hare in a different light. If the animal were discovered in her garden she'd be in even worse trouble. Added to a likely charge of wrecking the compound she'd be accused of harbouring a fugitive hare, the property of Ballycrossways Coursing Club.

"What am I to do with you?" She moaned, and as she asked this question the hare rubbed off her ankles and circled her. "What are you doing?"

She decided to wait until evening and then she'd take the hare to the nearby wood outside the village. He could survive as hares did in the countryside. He couldn't remain where he was. He'd be recaptured if anyone reported him to the police or the coursing club and both he and she would then be for the high jump.

With a heavy heart she closed the door, trying not to think of him sitting out there. *Maybe he'll be gone next time I look.*

***

89

Darkness was approaching. *Time to take my furry friend to where he'll be safer.* Annemarie peeked through the curtains at the garden. At first she thought he'd gone. But then, as if he knew she was watching, he reappeared and stood in the middle of the lawn, gazing at the window she was looking through.

She slumped back into the couch and covered her eyes. *What am I to do?* She sighed and lisped a prayer, though she wasn't terribly religious "God…will you please show me the way on this?"

Taking the hare in her car could prove problematic. Would he panic if she tried to pick him up, and how would he behave in a noisy moving vehicle? She didn't have any sort of cage or container to confine him in, and the thought of confining him in any case didn't appeal to her. The tag probably meant he was one of the hares she liberated, and the last thing she wanted was to incarcerate him again and possibly frighten the wits out of him.

Kathleen! She'd phone Kathleen Dempsey, the anti-coursing campaigner who was a wildlife expert. She'd know what to do. She'd forgotten her number. Grabbing the phone book she scanned the listing of Dempseys. *Blast.* Her number wasn't in it. Must have gone ex-directory. *Why is nothing going right for me?*

She was about to throw down the directory in exasperation when an ad caught her eye. "Mrs. Rosalind McCauley, psychic medium specializing in communication with animals."

A wacky idea popped into her head. "I wonder…"

Curiosity took over from her gnawing anxiety about the fugitive hare being spotted in the garden. Probably just spooky hocus pocus… *but what if?* She pushed all reservations from her mind and reached for the mobile. She keyed in the number of the psychic. When she heard the ringing tone on the other end she felt a frantic urge to cancel. *This is crazy…*

She poised a forefinger to abort…but the call was promptly answered. "Yes, can I help you?"

Annemarie hesitated, an urge to hang up battling a stronger compulsion to continue. "Yes…I see an ad here…you can communicate with animals?"

"Yes…it's part of what I do. I can pick up telepathic signals and messages from animals…cats, dogs and horses mainly. Pets. I can't promise I'll succeed. But I'll always try. Money back if I can't tune in or I get nothing…"

"Okay, well…it's not a pet animal I'm concerned with. It's a…a wild hare. Can you read the mind of a hare and tell me what he wants…or why he's…I'd better explain. This hare turned up in my garden and he's quite friendly. But I can't keep him. I mean, he's wild and…"

A soft chuckle from the other end. "That's interesting. I'm afraid I've never had anyone bring me a hare and I've never tried communicating with one. A pet rabbit once and I have to say it was a difficult reading…"

"But, sorry for interrupting, could you give it a try…"

"Yes…yes, of course. My hours for readings are…"

"Sorry, sorry…but I have a problem in getting to you. I'm wondering…could you possibly call to me instead…if you do house calls?"

"Mmm, on rare occasions yes, but it'll add to the cost, you understand?"

"I'll gladly pay the extra, Mrs. McCauley…"

"I happen to be free tomorrow, Sunday…"

"Great…"

Annemarie arranged for the psychic to call at four pm next day. *Am I completely mad* she reproached herself as she put away the mobile. Hands shaking, she poured boiling water into her coffee mug.

A sudden feeling of mild euphoria swept over her. Somehow, she felt, she was doing the right thing, even if it also seemed more than a little weird. Had this something to do with the Golden Hare's dream visit? It looked that way.

Once she confessed she'd have a court case coming up in a few weeks and she'd be using it to promote the anti-coursing cause. *This must be part of some cosmic plan: A hare almost certainly from the Ballycrossways compound drops in to see me, and now I've got an appointment with someone who…well, who claims at any rate, to be able to communicate with animals, a real life Dr Doolittle if she's genuine.*

She paced the floor, her heart thumping. Coffee splashed from the mug onto the carpet. *Darn. Calm down.* Things were falling into place, into a pattern of sorts, she thought, though what exactly the point of it all was she wasn't sure. She felt like something or someone "up there" was playing her like a puppet to fulfill that *special mission* the Golden Hare had spoken about in the vision, dream, or whatever it was.

She sipped the Americano, lips trembling, as she maneuvered her way around Ginger. The cat was purring loudly and pressing against her jeans.

Well. If I'm a puppet, please keep me safe and make sure those strings don't snap. After all, I never signed up to be in a real life Punch and Judy show!

***

90

Mrs McCauley wasn't what Annemarie expected. She had a fixed prejudice about psychics as being small women draped in shawls and maybe hunchbacked.

She felt guilty about this misconception, based on vague notions of quayside fortune tellers... more so when her visitor turned up. The woman was tall and thin, with high cheekbones, lively hazel eyes and blond hair that fell over her shoulders. And she was soft spoken. The phone had somehow made her voice sound sharper.

Annemarie had earlier fetched some carrots and lettuce from the fridge for the hare. He seemed attached to the garden, moving between it and the little DIY shed that she'd opened to let him shelter whenever he felt the urge. She'd checked just minutes before Mrs McCauley's arrival and he was sitting contentedly in the shed, as if patiently awaiting developments.

Annemarie showed the psychic to the long sofa in the sitting room. "Tea, coffee?" She offered.

"Glass of water will be fine".

"Will I fetch the animal?"

"In a minute or two. Firstly, I'd better explain what this involves. If the session proceeds as I'd like it to, the animal will transmit a range of thoughts, mental impressions, images, or emotions…or all of these. He will try to convey as best he can his problems, past experiences, illnesses, or anything that is bothering him right now…" She paused, leaning forward on the sofa and eyeing Annemarie with concern. "Then again, I may draw a complete blank. I could be having an off-day or he may be unwilling- or unable- to connect. This is not an exact science. The results vary from animal to animal, and from session to session. You understand?"

Annemarie nodded, though not fully grasping these unfamiliar concepts. The psychic continued: "Now, when I begin, try not to make any sudden noises, or becoming emotional. The animal will pick that up. They're highly sensitive, more so than many people realize- and it may distract or disrupt the process."

The psychic drank from the glass. "Good, now, if you can place a table between you and me- this will be for the animal to sit on, have it draped with a soft mat if possible. And have paper and pen ready...you might like to write as I speak to record the messages...assuming that communication occurs."

Annemarie pulled a coffee table into position. She covered it with a spare piece of curtain, and went to collect the hare. A sparkle appeared in his eyes when she appeared at the shed door. She didn't need to coax him. He immediately brushed against her legs and followed her into the house.

Mrs. McCauley broke into a board smile as Annemarie took the animal in her arms and placed him on the coffee table. The hare sat obediently, gazing at the psychic. How could a wild animal be so quiet and obliging? Annemarie wondered.

The psychic tentatively patted him on the head and the hare purred. The purring reminded Annemarie that Ginger might enter at any moment and throw a spanner in the works. She excused herself and took the still sleeping cat into the garden.

When she reentered the sitting room, the psychic had her eyes closed and was breathing deeply. Then the woman quivered as if she'd suffered a mild electrical shock.

A long sigh issued from her, followed by a smile. "Ah yes, I'm getting pictures, vivid ones...*birth*, he's showing me his first sight of the world, *his world*. He's shuffling about in long grass, his mother nursing him. Now, he's older...and exploring his immediate environment. Scents of wild thyme, salty air. He's wading about in sand, sneezing, water lapping at his feet. It's a beach or sheltered bay. Now he's circling what looks like...an old monastic ruin.

"He's exploring a deserted village...roofless houses... his feet pressing on laneways of mossy turf. He relishes the taste of juicy mosses and succulent tree bark, but seaweed is his favourite. He's rolling joyously in a carpet of yellow gorse under a molten sun.

"Pastures untouched by humankind. Happy days and nights on the island. *Oh my God*…a sudden stab of fear…a bird of prey hovers overhead…swoops…He sees a friend being seized by the predator…now he's on his hind legs, boxing…competing with other hares in a mating ritual…He's running and tumbling in greenery…passing through a patchwork of fields…he's looking up at, and then running towards… rocky formations…cliffs…

"Fear takes over again…men with nets stalk his territory, but where is it? Ah, he's telling me! It's an island off the Irish coast. *This is astonishing.* Usually it's pictures only and impressions…but this hare is sending me word messages, as if…as if…he can relate to language. *Impossible!*

"He's contradicting me…he's a *special* hare, he tells me. *Oh dear*…I must take a break…this is…*not possible…"*

Her eyes fluttered open and she regarded the hare with a mixture of fascination and nervousness. Annemarie was holding the pen, also incredulous at the hare's seeming superior intelligence.

"I'll resume in a few minutes. Before I do, may I ask you…are you sure you haven't encountered this animal before, that there isn't more to his appearance at your home…something you'd like to tell me. I've never had an animal communicate via coherent word messages in the past, let alone in my own language!"

Annemarie hesitated. She didn't want to tell her story, but felt impelled to speak. She told the psychic about releasing the hares, a likely upcoming court case, the visions or dreams in which the Golden Hare had appeared, and his messages to her about helping the cause of persecuted hares in Ireland.

The psychic switched her focus from Annemarie to the hare sitting on the coffee table. The animal just sat there, barely moving, just staring impassively at her. "There's something special, or most unusual about him…I'm sorry, I don't mean to speak of you as if you weren't here, my fine fellow"

She petted him and he purred. "Yes, that dream visitation is interesting, and possibly significant. Animals have been contacting humans in dreams since time began. Pets mostly, of course. They have an attachment to humans who care for them. Animal spirits, I mean animals who have died, routinely visit in dreams, but the humans who see them assume it's only fantasy. It's not. Dreams can offer symbolic messages and help with solving problems that perplex us during the day, but some dreams have a different purpose, and in fact are not really dreams at all, but experiences on higher levels of reality…"

"You mean that the Golden Hare was real, and I was in some other dimension when I saw him in my room."

"Yes, he was a spirit, but whether of a dead animal or one still here on earth…well, let's ask our friend here shall we?"

Again she composed herself, lying back on the sofa and shutting her eyes. Her breathing changed from casual to an audible whooshing. Annemarie noticed the hare had also altered his posture, but his eyes were wide open and fixed on the psychic.

"…He's telling me his mother was taken by cruel humans who landed on the island. They came in…shapes…ah yes, *boats*… thank you…They fanned out across the island, spreading terror where they showed themselves. His mother was among the hares they captured, using…I see them… wide nets. The hares had seen ones like them before and assumed these were the same…what fishermen used around the island. But these nets were not for fish…

"He's transmitting a deep sadness. Grief and longing. He watched the men take friends and relatives down to the beach in little…boxes…I see them. These men left the island in the boats with all the captive hares on board, including his mother.

"Harrowing scenes. Lamentation and sobbing as hares discover they've lost loved ones. Anger too, but tempered with…he's telling me the hares on the island sought guidance from…the Wise One…I see the inside of a cave…so many hares all bunched together…a radiant creature appears.

"Ah, so it's him…this is the Golden Hare, he tells me. He meets this great entity again on another occasion and…our friend says the Wise One assigned him a mission. Thank you…I understand. Oh God…he says the humans killed his mother. He saw this in a vision…but he'll see her again in the afterlife. He says his task is to help a kind human, the one sitting in this room right now, to end the maltreatment of hares in Ireland. He says he had to make a terrible sacrifice…he allowed himself to be captured when the men…returned to the island with their nets.

"He says his understanding of his role in the human's mission extends to the present moment, but that it is up to her…that's you, Annemarie… to decide how he can help…when and where. He hopes his transmission of information will assist you…and…this is important he says. He *is* one of the hares you released from captivity…the magical one…"

Annemarie gasped, and stopped writing. Though she suspected the hare was from the compound, confirmation jolted and set her heart aflutter. And she suddenly recalled that the Golden Hare had referred in his first visitation to this hare. He was the one who had so skillfully outwitted the dogs. She rose and embraced the hare.

Simultaneously the psychic's eyes flashed open and she shook her head. "Oh dear, this is absolutely draining, I need another break. Our friend doesn't seem to be in the least bit fazed."

The hare seemed to have taken a break too. He was washing his whiskers in a carefree manner, occasionally glancing at either Annemarie or the psychic.

Mrs. McCauley leaned towards Annemarie, conscious maybe of the possibility that the hare was still tuned in to her thoughts. "I think I see what's happening here. At this court case, and there's bound to be one if you confess…you'll have an opportunity to explain why you felt driven to release those hares. Perhaps….I know it may be difficult to arrange, but I wonder if you could persuade the court to allow you to tell this animal's story, how he and other hares were snatched so cruelly from their peaceful island…for this awful coursing event. What I've got already from our friend here is so graphic, so relevant to what this whole coursing controversy is all about. I suggest that I return here in a few days and see if he'll tell me more about what happened when those people took him…."

Annemarie sighed. "I'm not a legal expert. I'd have to ask my solicitor about that, but I can't see a court allowing…well, a hare's testimony. I'll ask her tomorrow."

The psychic looked a little dizzy. She seemed to have drifted into a trance. "Ah, he's telling me he grasps the situation more fully now. He must recount *everything* that has happened to him. The world must know the truth, he says. He will happily stay in the garden shed and on the lawn for as long as he is needed. He has a good feeling about this…"

Annemarie, hearing Ginger scratching at the back door, was prompted to ask: "Just one more thing, Mrs. McCauley, could you inquire if he'd be okay with a cat being around, or frightened of him…I'd forgotten about that?"

The psychic again focused on the hare and seconds later her face erupted in a wide grin. She laughed, nodding at the animal.

"Well?" Annemarie tensed.

"You won't believe this, but it seems he can communicate with animals not of his own species…birds, dogs, anything. He hasn't met a cat yet but he reckons he'd get on okay provided the cat isn't hostile to him."

"Right, I'm going to find out" Annemarie quipped. Opening the back door, she picked up Ginger and tentatively approached the coffee table.

The hare turned to regard the cat. Ginger hissed, and Annemarie felt the hairs standing on his back. "Hush, he won't harm you!" she soothed, rubbing his head.

"But will the cat want to harm our friend?" the psychic asked, "That's a bigger worry!"

"I'm going to leave him down…if he makes a run to attack the hare I'll grab him."

Ginger crept a millimetre at a time towards the coffee table, a picture of suspicion and vigilance, and still hissing. Annemarie leant over him, ready to intercept any attempt to attack the hare, who seemed completely unfazed. Ginger stopped suddenly and was looking straight up at the hare. The hare was gazing into the cat's eyes. Was he communicating?

The psychic smiled. "He's transmitting words of peace and comfort" she whispered.

Then, astonishingly, Ginger leapt up on the table, catching Annemarie by surprise. She panicked, thinking the hare was in imminent danger. Instead, Ginger pushed gently against the hare, rubbing his head against the strange visitor to his house. He purred, and the hare responded by returning the friendly rub.

The psychic clapped her hands in triumph. "Well, that's a little miracle in its own right!" She rose from the sofa. "I'll call back; say three days from now…This has been a most enlightening day."

***

91

Annemarie braced herself for a blast of disbelief or even a polite refusal to represent her from Liz Franklin. Sitting in the solicitor's office, she winced at the reflection of her own furrowed brow from the polished mahogany desk. Her body tensed. Her stomach was in a knot. Her heart sank and she wished, not for the first time in her life, that the floor would just open up and swallow her.

She had just recounted her strange story, right from the beginning. The solicitor had nodded sympathetically but with raised eyebrows as Annemarie began with the night, or early morning rather, when she had a vision, or intensely vivid dream, in which a Golden Hare advised her to free the hares at Ballycrossways, how the same mystical creature appeared again advising her to hand herself in to the police with a view to airing the plight of hares generally in Ireland; how a real live hare had subsequently turned up in her garden and had, through the services of a psychic medium specialising in animal communication, told her the astonishing story of his life on the island, his capture by Ballycrossways Coursing Club, and his escape, along with a few dozen other hares, after Annemarie's one-woman raid on the coursing compound.

Ms. Franklin said nothing. The silence lasted almost a minute. She leaned forward as if about to speak, seemed to change her mind; then clasped her hands on the desk.

Clicking her tongue, she said curtly: "That's quite a story Annemarie…and, of course as you know I'm obliged to act on your instructions. If you wish to give that version of events to the court, and you want me to instruct our barrister accordingly, then I and counsel will respect your wishes…."

Her face broke into a broad nervous grin. She cast her eyes downward, shaking her head despondently. "However…and I've read about people who genuinely believe they've seen, heard, or otherwise experienced psychic phenomena, and have always tried to keep an open mind about these things, I'm afraid it would be extremely difficult, impossible more likely, to get a jury to take all that on board…unless…"

Annemarie was all ears. "Yes, Ms. Franklin?"

The solicitor gritted her teeth. "Unless you'd be prepared to change your plea to guilty…"

"But that would…"

"Hear me out…please…What I suggest is a plea of insanity…yes…I know you believe all this…happened, the hare appearing to you and what the psychic told you about what the other hare had on his mind and all that, but it's just...well, I believe it's more than any twelve men and women out there would accept.

"But I *can* envisage a court accepting a Guilty but Insane plea. I mean…after hearing what you've just told me, and no disrespect, Annemarie…I'm not sure that any other outcome to the trial is possible. The most likely alternative to an insanity plea, in my opinion, would be a plain guilty verdict, because it's also quite possible that the jury might conclude you were perfectly sane… but concocted the whole story to fake insanity. Either way, an outright acquittal would be highly unlikely if you insist on including this…testimony."

Annemarie swallowed hard, tears welling up in her eyes. She forced herself to remain calm and resolute. She took a deep breath. Somehow she found the strength to say: "I expected you'd not be impressed, Ms Franklin, but this is how I want my defence to be conducted. And furthermore, I wish the psychic medium to appear on my behalf. She's agreed to testify…"

"You mean…to translate…or whatever…what the hare, ah…told her…?"

"Yes!"

The solicitor tapped her pen on the desk delicately and then, as if struck by an especially intriguing thought, raised the pen and wagged it for emphasis "Look, I'm trying to take this on board. But let's suppose…just for a minute…that something extraordinary is going on here, and I really am trying to keep an open mind. Is there anything in the way of hard independent evidence…I mean apart from what you…*believe* you've seen and heard etcetera, to back up this idea of the hare's harrowing ordeal…and what you…or this hare as you believe…had to say about the activities of the coursing people?

"For example, do you know of anyone who could confirm that Ballycrossways Coursing Club took hares from the island? That would look bad for them, and help your defence. The jury might take a less sympathetic view of them, and a more lenient view of your actions, if we could show…*prove*…that they snatched those hares from the island…"

Annemarie racked her brains. She shrugged. "Apart from cross-examining Waxy Bumbleton-Crossbar…he's the top honcho in the club. He might admit it…if he had enough cause to believe we knew about it."

"We'll put the question to him. What about that incident on the coursing field…where you videotaped the special hare you mentioned…"

"As I told you, Ms Franklin, the camcorder was confiscated from me. They erased the footage…"

"Are you sure?"

"Certain…when I got it back I checked and it's gone."

The solicitor's eyes sparkled and the traces of a smile began to lighten her grave demeanor. "It might be worth reexamining it…the recording device I mean. The footage may be retrievable. Can you bring it to me?"

Annemarie felt better. If anyone had come to her with such a story a few weeks ago, she'd have either laughed out loud or asked them not to be wasting her time with such thorough cock and bull. But Ms. Franklin, in the circumstances, was being reasonable. How a jury of twelve ordinary fellow citizens would react was another matter.

As Annemarie rose to leave the office, the solicitor held a hand up. "Oh yes…I wouldn't put off much longer that visit to the police station to make your statement of admission. I have a feeling they'll be paying you a visit soon. A tipoff from a friendly officer. Nothing definite, but he told me your name's been bandied about in the last few days."

Annemarie felt deflated again. She knew the solicitor was right. The officer who accompanied Waxy Bumbleton-Crossbar to her house when he returned the camera might have been testing her reaction when he mentioned the hare release. She must quit stalling and call to the police station. "I'll do that Ms Franklin."

"Good, let me know in advance and I'll meet you at the Broc Café beforehand."

***

92

Annemarie settled her hair into place. *No need to overdo it, but I must look respectable when I drop in to that police station to confess.* She found it hard to believe she was dong this. *Let's just get it over with.*

The café where she'd meet the solicitor was around the corner from the station. She'd accompany Annemarie to ensure that nothing other than a formal brief statement admitting to the act was made. No trick questions or admissions to anything other than setting the hares free to save them from cruel injury or death.

Before heading for the front door she had a niggling worry that she'd forgotten something. It wasn't Tipsy. He was sitting in his usual spot, just inside the DIY hut, and she'd left out adequate food for him earlier.

Was it to switch off the lamp on the bedside locker? It was easy to overlook; with the light streaming in through the net curtains you'd scarcely notice it. She ascended the short spiral staircase and swung open the bedroom door. It was still on. No point in wasting electricity. She leaned down to switch it off...and froze.

What was that?

She heard loud voices on the pavement outside, carried to her from the bedroom window that overlooked the street. Above the sound of running engines came sounds… menacing and heart-stopping.

She stepped over to the window and peered through the filmy lace.

Oh Jesus! Two police cars parked; one in front of the other, the doors all thrown open. Almost a dozen uniformed men and gritty-faced plainclothes detectives were gathering in front of her doorstep.

Then that dreaded pressing of the bell. The buzz hit her like a stone in the forehead. She almost fell but kept her balance, her hands clasping her mouth as if to prevent screaming. *Please, anything but this! Why on earth didn't I call to the station a week ago? Putting if off was just plain stupid.*

If they arrested her now she'd lose the advantage of having come forward of her own volition to confess.

And Tipsy. They'd put two and two together quickly when they saw him in the garden, and add another charge…theft of a hare belonging to Ballycrossways Coursing Club.

The back door! The lawn.

She quickly dashed down the stairway on tiptoe, pulled on her coat that lay on the sofa in the sitting room and grabbed her handbag. Carefully, so as to make no noise she unlocked the back door, stepped into the lawn and quietly shut the door behind her.

Tipsy was sleeping. Thank God he hadn't been frightened by the racket on the street.

The doorbell was still ringing incessantly, accompanied by loud rapping. Stepping over the wall that skirted the lawn she walked briskly towards the narrow lane that would take her to the café from another direction, her heart pounding like a jackhammer.

At the end of the lane she looked around the corner. No police about. She crossed the street to the café.

How crazy was this? Dodging the police so she could confess to them?

But on my terms!

She ran the last few yards to the café. Seeing Liz Franklin sitting just inside, alone, she almost threw herself at the solicitor. "Like a coffee, take a seat. I'll...?" Ms Franklin was beginning to ask.

Leaning over Annemarie rasped. "They're at the house...a whole squad of them. A raid..."

The solicitor rose instantly, left some coins to pay for the coffee, and led her client by an arm outside. "Straight to the station. Not a word about them being at the house. We walk in calmly and you act as if you know *nothing* about any raid on your home, understood?"

"Yes...yes."

She forced herself to relax. They stepped around the corner and pushed in the entrance to the police station. Luckily there was nobody else in the waiting room foyer.

Annemarie's heart was trouncing, and she felt beads of sweat breaking out on her forehead. Ms. Franklin tapped her knuckles on the square glass panel for attention. Annemarie noticed a bored looking young police officer sitting inside, a little distance from the panel, working on a crossword.

The station was soundless apart from the scratching of his pen on paper and a clock tick-tocking behind him on the wall inside his compartment.

The officer laid down the pen and rose from his desk to approach the panel. "Can I help you, ladies?" he asked, suppressing a yawn.

The solicitor cleared her throat. "Yes. This woman, my client, wishes to help you with your investigation into the release of hares at Ballycrossways coursing venue..."

The officer seemed to expand in height and width. He left his compartment and stepped into the waiting room. Astonishment distorted his pale features. His eyes bulged, his mouth quivered… but no words escaped. He scratched his head, pulled a chair around to face the two women, signalling them to be seated.

Eyeing Annemarie quizzically, he addressed Ms. Franklin. "I see...and what does she know?"

"She will give you a very brief statement, and then she leaves with me. Understood?"

"Fine. Excuse me a minute." He returned to his compartment and seconds later was back in the waiting section with a large writing pad. He opened the pad and wrote something at the top of a page. "Now...what is it you want to say..."

Annemarie took a deep breath, looked the officer in the eye and said: "I wish to make it known that it was I who, alone and without any help from any other person or group, entered the field containing the hare compound of Ballycrossways Coursing Club. Having gained access to the compound I opened a hatch and released all the captive hares. I did so to ensure that none of those animals would be terrorised or mauled or otherwise made to suffer at the live baiting fixture planned for the following day. End of statement..."

The officer was scribbling furiously to keep pace with her. "Right...and you have nothing to add?"

Annemarie shook her head.

"Okay sign there...and there."

Her hand trembled as she added her signature to that brief factual admission that could have far reaching consequences for her. She handed the pages back to him. He took them and placed them in a folder resting on his left leg.

"Well, that's fine...but you know you'll be hearing from us about this...And that it's likely, just about certain actually, that you'll be charged?"

"I understand".

Ms. Franklin nodded too when he cast a searching glance at her.

"Excuse me" he blurted. His mobile was ringing.

Annemarie and the solicitor were walking towards the exit when he shouted "Just a minute..."

They turned around. His free hand was suspended in midair, pointing at them as if he expected them to perform some unheard of illegal act. They waited, standing looking at him as he continued talking on the phone.

"Yes...Superintendent...she's right here. And...yes...she came in as I said...to confess to the raid on Ballycrossways. Yes, I'm sorry...I had no idea that you'd planned to arrest her. Yes, she's given the statement...signed. Yes. ..."

Suddenly he withdrew the phone from his ear as if it had electrocuted him. "Glory be to God...I had no idea they were down at your house. You may go, Ms. Cristobel, but don't leave the area. There's a lot of interest in you, young lady, at HQ. I have your statement here and they'll have it inside the next ten minutes..."

93

Tipsy sat inside the comfy wooden nest in the corner of the lawn, happily contemplating a cluster of sparrows pecking at crumbs dispersed for them in the opposite corner. The compassionate Humanik was spoiling him too, tending to his every whim. Each morning and evening she laid food at his feet...carrots, lettuce, and new delicacies he'd never tasted before. The nest was a Humanik construction. He smelt the tree from which the wood was extracted.

No hare would or could create such a home. It wasn't the type of abode to which any hare was accustomed. A depression in a swathe of grassy terrain satisfied any hare he'd known. But the wooden nest had its advantages. The entrance was always unblocked, so when the weather wasn't favourable he could slip inside.

And it was definitely more natural than the inside of the Humanik dwelling. His introduction to that visually jarring and disharmonious collage of shapes, colours, and patterns almost knocked him off his hind legs: Soft reds, yellows, and blues...weird lights and oddly coloured walls...hard and soft surfaces with not a trace of grass or clay...blobs of black and brown sitting contrivances, and strange sounds of running water and clanging of unknown or unseen objects.

What a shock to his system...to all his five senses and even to his sixth supernatural sense of heightened awareness. He both feared and relished his entry into the dwelling. His discomfort was quickly dispelled though by the female, knowing she was well disposed towards him. He wondered if those ruins of Humanik abodes back on the island once resembled the one facing him across the lawn.

Rain drizzled diaphanously on the grass, so he opted this morning to avail of the wooden nest the Humanik had kindly provided for him, basking in the sunlight that filtered through the sporadic raindrops. Otherwise he'd prefer to be outside, sniffing those lovely sunflowers, as Ginger told him they were called.

What a pleasant fellow the cat turned out to be. Initial suspicion and hostility evaporated like steam in summer warmth once Ginger heard himself being addressed in his own feline lingo. The Humanik was such a decent sort, and Tipsy appreciated her protection, especially after what he'd seen of other Humaniks.

But with each passing day he ached for his faraway home on the island...the rolling hills, the sandy beach, the lake, the friendly Storm Petrels. And he wondered what exactly lay ahead for him here on the Big Island of Ireland.

His head swam with the memory of that other Humanik, the magical one who could commune with him, mind to mind. He'd told her everything he knew, and she passed it on to his protector. But where was all this leading? He had a mission, and though aware it would, if successful, help other hares, he was still in the dark about how he could achieve such a lofty, seemingly impossible goal.

A low purring distracted him. Ginger was strolling towards him from the Humanik dwelling, his whiskers glistening in the weak sunlight, his gleaming green eyes radiating trust and friendship. The rain had stopped, so Tipsy exited the nest to greet him outside the entrance. The cat sat beside him, yawned lazily and seemed about to fall asleep. His eyes half-shut, he looked at Tipsy: "So you think she has plans for you?"

Tipsy had informed Ginger earlier; with a feeling of pride, that he had a mission and he suspected the Humanik would somehow be instrumental in assisting him achieve success.

"She likes you Tipsy. I know that. But then she likes...*birds*...too." The cat almost spat the words. Tipsy evinced surprise.

"And isn't that a commendable attribute in a Humanik...considering the harm that species does to so many creatures?"

Ginger harrumphed. "I don't especially like hares or rabbits, but I can live with the idea of my owner having a soft spot for them...but those feathered *pests*. They make so much noise, and they fly around laughing at me when I sit out on the lawn. They laugh because they know I can't reach them...up there. But I've got the better of them I can tell you. I've killed dozens of birds. You see, they forget that I don't need wings to get my teeth into their feathery little carcasses. I let them whistle and flutter about...but when they let their guard down, disturbing the earth with their crazy little beaks, I pounce and...Bye-bye bird!" He caught a fit of giggles. "Then it's my turn to laugh" he added.

Tipsy was shocked. Hares didn't kill; whatever their other faults. An idea struck him. He looked the cat straight in the eye. "You say the birds mock you...are you sure of that?"

Ginger stared at him as if he was crazy, but said nothing, just resumed luxuriating in the grass, adjusting his whiskers and purring contentedly. "See that bird up there, on the window ledge...the song thrush...he's looking right at you, and chirping..."

Ginger raised his head languidly. "Yeah, I see the silly twerp, what about him?"

"Any idea what he's saying?"

"I'm not like you, Tipsy. I don't speak their silly language. But I reckon he's feeling all smug and superior...knowing he's beyond my reach...for now!"

Tipsy attuned to the bird's chirping and the words came to him.

Ginger shrugged. "So what's he saying, then?"

Tipsy translated: "He's saying...what a wonderful plumage that creature has, unlike any that a bird could ever hope to emulate...what a gorgeous coat of the loveliest hue...how it reminds me of the leaf of a stately oak in its glorious late autumn lustre. How exquisitely delineated his form and features are: a masterpiece of creation...and oh...how gentle he seems, reclining down there on that soft carpet of green. If only I could speak to him..."

Ginger's eyes opened wide. He stared up at the bird. Scratching his head with a clawed paw, he said, almost in a whisper as though afraid the bird would hear him, "Did he really say that?"

Tipsy nodded. The cat went silent. He wandered over to the dwelling to admire his reflection in the lower window, viewing his image from several angles and posing flamboyantly. Then he returned to Tipsy and mumbled: "I've killed so many of them...but how was I know what goes on in a bird's head, or what he's saying?"

"I see your point...dogs, I believe, have the same problem with you fellows...cats I mean. They don't quite understand what makes you tick..."

"You can sing it...I've been chased by loads of them. Never got caught though."

"Nor did I...The Humaniks set the fastest dogs alive on me. I evaded them, and then I escaped from where the Humaniks were holding me."

"Escaped?"

"Yes, thanks to your owner, as you call her...she set us free. Me and the other hares they captured to run from their dogs..."

Ginger scrutinized him closely. "Humaniks have never harmed me...but I know cats who hate them. I imagine some Humaniks are less fond of cats...and hares... than others."

Tipsy sighed. "Not knowing what a creature is really saying, or what they really think of you, can make you suspicious and fearful. If there were no language barriers and all creatures could communicate freely, then the world, I reckon, would be a very different place for us all. It still wouldn't be perfect, but a lot easier to live in."

Ginger rose, stretched to his full length; and yawned. "Now you're getting a bit too deep for me." Raising his eyes to the bird on the ledge, he snapped: "I wonder if that thrush said those nice things because he knew you'd pass on his words to me. You know something, if I thought he faked it I'd hate him, and all birds, even more..."

Tipsy was about to remonstrate when the voice of the Humanik called out. Ginger scampered over to her, displaying his affectionate side and eliciting copious petting from his owner. *So many creatures only think of themselves...but I'm expected to help a whole species. What have I let myself in for?*

Watching the Humanik fondling the cat, he prayed that other Humaniks might open their hearts to the suffering of hares, and that his mission, however outlandish or thorny it might prove to be, would lighten the hare's burden.

***

94

Bang!

Waxy's fist crashing down on the desk of Superintendent McGrath sent files, an ashtray, and a dozen pens hurtling towards the ceiling of the police station dayroom. Before the high-ranking policeman, the five detectives, and the army officer could respond he jumped to his feet, almost knocking Scabby who'd been sitting quietly beside him listening to the investigation team, from his chair.

"What do you mean she beat you to it? How can she be down at the station giving her own cock-eyed statement about her...*her crime*...while you fellas were right outside her house? I've heard of the keystone cops, but this makes even them look professional..."

The Superintendent, settling the files and pens on his desk, soothed: "now Waxy, that attitude won't get you or anyone here… anywhere. It was nothing more than an unhappy coincidence. Minutes earlier and we'd have caught her at the house...."

The army officer had reddened and looked shocked at Waxy's behaviour. The five detectives were twiddling their thumbs or doodling on the backs of cigarette boxes, pretending not to notice anything.

Waxy felt utter contempt for them all. *Mustn't go too far though.* He needed them, incompetent and disappointing though they were. Calming, he spoke through gritted teeth. "Okay...I understand, but can I be assured that this ...*bitch*... won't get off lightly? I mean. She's confessed, so I assume it's an open and shut case? Has to be a guilty plea, right?"

The Superintendent coughed emphatically, glanced to his left and right at the others, and leaned over towards Waxy with his fingers intertwined. "It would seem so...though of course she may, given her warped view of the world, and her hostility to hare coursing, decide to, you know, make a fight of it by pleading not guilty. She might see it as a chance to get some publicity for the cause. These people will do *anything* for publicity..."

He sat back in his chair. Waxy felt anger rising in him again, but suppressed it. "You mean she'd use the court to flog her crazy anti-coursing propaganda?"

"Wouldn't surprise me...and it wouldn't surprise me if she always intended confessing. That's why I'm going to suggest something. Hear me out; Waxy...I suggest that no charges be brought against her. Think carefully. As matters stand, you've got lots of sympathy after the raid. Other coursing clubs have supplied you with hares from their own stocks. You are seen as victims of an illegal act. But if it goes to court this woman could be portrayed by some media outlets in a positive light. She might..."

Waxy exploded. This time he grasped the desk firmly and upended it, sending all the files, the ashtray, and the pens flying towards the coiling.

The desk struck the Superintendent in the jaw and propelled the detectives from their chairs. Waxy also inadvertently elbowed Scabby in the face, eliciting a shriek of anguish. He had no sooner unleashed this sudden torrent of rage when he regretted it.

The scene appeared to solidify before him like a distorted image on a TV screen that had now given way to clarity. The Superintendent was on the floor pushing the desk off his body with one hand, clinging to his jaw with the other and moaning. The detectives all had blank expressions. Two were on their feet, dusting off their suits and straightening their ties. Disorientated, they swayed and meandered like drunken men. One was consoling the Superintendent and helping him to stand. The army officer was rubbing cigarette ash from his uniform and staring balefully at Waxy.

The detective helping the Superintendent also cast Waxy a ferocious look of reproach. "You should be ashamed of yourself. What were you thinking? We're trying to help you? Are you a complete spacer or what?"

The Superintendent, still holding his jaw, motioned the groaning detectives to be quiet. He gasped: "Ah God but that hurt...I don't think it's broken, thank God. Waxy, take it easy man. I was only making a suggestion. Fine. She'll be charged, and justice will take its course. I was only pointing out...never mind. I think you and Scabby should leave now before we have any further unwarranted outbursts. No disrespect to you of course. We'll take it from here. She'll be charged...immediately!"

***

95

Annemarie closed her eyes and sipped the large glass of orange juice.

Her other hand was stroking the bundle of fur that she'd fed after returning from the courthouse in the police car. He preferred being outside...sitting at the entrance to the DIY shed, but she felt entitled to take him into the house for a cuddle. After all, he was at the heart of her current predicament.

What a day...*what a month...* it had been. The knock on her door this morning wasn't unexpected. Having dodged the special branch raid on her house and confessed before they could pounce on her as if she were a dangerous criminal, she knew charges were likely. Especially with the hysteria that swept the whole Peninsula in the wake of the hare liberation.

She felt a surge of relief at the thought that she'd got to the police before they got to her. But she shuddered at the hostility. When she'd answered the door at seven am today, drowsy, her eyes straining to stay open, the three tall uniformed officers almost roared at her: They spoke at once in a frenzy of impatience and giddiness, each anxious to be heard above the other.

"Hah Ha you'll get what's coming to you, you brazen hussy, oh mark my words!"

"Get properly dressed. You have five minutes!" another spat, his eyes flaming with anger.

The third spoke in lower tones, menacingly: "We're arresting you, young lady, and charging you with malicious damage to one of the finest coursing venues in Ireland. No time wasting now!"

When she reappeared at the door, one of them had produced handcuffs, clapped them on her and pushed her into the back seat of the white and yellow squad car.

The one in the front passenger seat craned his neck, glaring at her: One side of his face was smiling, the other twisted into a glower: "The charges will be brought against you at a special sitting of Clancrash District Court. God Almighty, His Lordship had to be awoken because of you. On his day off! Oh, you'll swing for this..."

On the way to court in the town four miles from the village, they maintained a constant barrage of insulting "advice" and hectoring. She blocked it out by inwardly humming a lullaby. Only when the car stopped outside the court building did she retune to their words.

She was nudged and jostled through the wide stone entrance of the building with the enormous carving of Ireland's harp symbol over it. The building had been empty apart from the judge and a court clerk, both of whom had, she assumed, been transported there for this outside-office-hours Special Sitting.

One of the arresting officers had approached the judge's bench while the other two held on to her as though they feared she'd make a break for it. The charges were read out: Despite knowing what she did and why, the formal process was unnerving. The charge was made to sound dreadful and she felt stripped of all dignity as the judge frowned and wrote something in his notebook.

A date was set for the next hearing at which a trial date would be announced. Then they removed the cuffs and she was released.

Ginger's purring ended her reverie. He appeared alongside the half-sleeping hare, rubbing off its head. The cat seemed to know she needed company and consoling. Animals weren't fools.

On the subject of animals, she wondered what had become of the hares she'd released. Was it all worth it? And was that wise old hare serious about her using the court case to ease the plight of Ireland's persecuted hares?

Must prepare a really good speech, and make sure every newspaper, radio station and social media outlet got a copy of what I have to say.

Whether the verdict was guilty or not guilty, the publicity could help the cause. But something was missing. She had a powerful feeling that there would be more to the upcoming court showdown than just fighting the case and reading out a defiant statement against hare coursing.

Thinking this, she felt the presence of the Golden Hare again, but couldn't see or hear him. He'd said he couldn't visit a third time. Yet she had a strong sense of his presence in the room right now. Was he trying to tell her something? Or remind her of her special mission, as he'd called it?

As if to confirm her intuition, Ginger had jumped from her lap and was frozen to the spot on the carpet, hairs standing on end, glaring at something she couldn't see but that was visible to the cat. And the hare was sitting up, eyes fixed on some invisible spot between herself and the sitting room door.

***

96

The moment the automatic doors swung open in the supermarket Annemarie had a strange feeling of foreboding.

She'd been tense all morning since hearing the news of her upcoming court case announced on the local radio and reading the *Broc Peninsula Gazette's* sensational front-page report. She opted to do her shopping before work, hoping to escape the public scrutiny she expected in response to the media coverage.

People she knew nodded and bid her good morning as usual, but not with the same openhearted friendliness. There was curtness in their voices. Or had she imagined that? *Possibly.* She hadn't encountered anyone yet between her home and the supermarket that she knew to be involved in hare coursing or who sympathized with it, but it was the fact of criminal charges that she knew the average person would frown upon, and that might change their opinion of her.

Until, hopefully, the full story of what she'd done, and why, got out. Inside the supermarket she pushed the small trolley forward and began reaching for the usual items. She dropped the sliced bread in, the cornflakes, the teabags, and was examining the used-by date on a packet of biscuits when she felt a presence behind her.

Not someone passing in the aisle, but standing there. She felt eyes boring into her. Still pretending to be checking the date on the biscuits she felt a tiny spray of fluid on the back of her neck, accompanied by hissing, then a voice: "Tramp…you'll get what's coming to you. You'll do time, bitch!"

Glancing around she faced a man with a leering, mottled face, who immediately bowed his head, coughed lightly and walked on past her with a wire basket swinging jauntily. He cast a quick backward glance, making a throat-cutting gesture with his left hand.

She swallowed hard. *Just ignore*…she had barely formed the words in her mind when she saw Josie from the accountant's office beckoning her at the end of the aisle. Annemarie pushed the trolley, trying to appear casual and unworried, even as her heart beat like a jackhammer.

Josie waited until she was within inches of her to whisper: "Play it cool at the office. The boss is furious. He called me on the mobile. He's looking for a way to get rid of you. He can't fire you, but he wants you out of his hair till this coursing thing blows over…that's assuming you're not found guilty. Says he can't afford to have a criminal in the office. Says it could lose him loads of customers. Ruin the business…"

"Thanks for tipping me off…but what am I to do? Won't he give me a chance; wait for the court case?"

Josie blew out a mouthful of air. "He knows he ought to do that, but you know he's got men from the coursing club on his client list, and some of them are big knobs. Listen…don't go to the office this morning. He'll be phoning you later. He'll let you work from home…you know, on the computer…the usual stuff, but don't be seen at the office until this thing blows over…"

Two teenage boys brushed past, ignoring her but one of them blurted to Josie: "See any hares for sale…I'm itching to kill one, I hate them critters". Both burst into laughter as they swaggered on.

Josie blushed. "I have to go Annemarie. Nothing personal, but if himself heard I was talking to you…sorry."

She walked on with her trolley, leaving Annemarie standing alone. Others passed by in both directions, muttering polite hellos but avoiding eye contact.

Hurt turned to anger within her. She wouldn't be fazed by either this borderline ostracism or the moronic behaviour of bullies. The girl at the checkout smiled as always but there was coldness behind the standard friendly demeanor. When she handed Annemarie her change she took her own hand away so quickly you'd think she feared catching some dreaded killer disease.

97

Waxy fixed himself a stiff drink and tossed it off in one gulp. The whiskey stung momentarily but…ah, that pleasant warmth. He followed it up with another and put the cap back on the bottle.

He slumped into his fireside chair. What on earth was going on? First Dr Callaghan, a rational levelheaded man. The last person you'd expect to be raving about apparitions and spooks, let alone a phantom hare frightening the living daylights out of him.

Now, it was Basher Mylan. Basher wasn't even remotely superstitious…never one to give the slightest credence to ghost stories or any of that things-that-go bump-in-the night nonsense.

In his mind he replayed the frantic account Basher had rattled off the night before when he arrived unannounced at the bungalow. The man was drained of colour, like a living corpse. When Waxy opened the front door that stalwart of Ballycrossways Coursing Club looked as if he'd aged ten years in a few days.

"What's wrong, Basher", Waxy had inquired.

"Can I come in?" the man mumbled.

Waxy ushered him to a chair by the rayburn cooker, into which he had just tossed another log. "Have a drink Basher?"

A wordless nod. Waxy handed him a large brandy. The man sipped, his hands shaking, his eyes bulging and his lips trembling like two strips of jelly. Waxy waited patiently.

Basher, who had celebrated his fortieth birthday just a week before, seemed to be struggling to find words for what troubled him. Eventually he spoke, eyes downward, as if ashamed to face Waxy.

The words gushed out: "It started with a dream. I was out in your training yard. I had just fastened the legs of a hare and was ready to dangle the critter in front of a greyhound for

Cracker O' Toole. You know Cracker? Anyway…I had the hare hanging upside-down, waving him around and the dog was snapping away…Then…everything went red. The dog and Cracker just disappeared in a flash. I was somewhere else.

"Oh Waxy…I heard this wailing and screeching. Steam was belching from the ground, like in those National Geographic films about volcanoes. It was getting hotter by the second. My feet burned. I hopped up and down but there was no escaping it. Everything around me was covered in this red mist or fog. Then, straining to see where the weird wailing was coming from, I made out this pair of ears. Hare's ears.

"Then I saw the rest of him. He was walking towards me through the red mist, and the heat from the ground under my feet was ferocious. My legs were on fire. Then…oh Waxy it was awful…His eyes…they were two gleaming sparks. The closer he got to me the brighter and fierier they became.

"And then he started swelling…growing into a giant…he was yellow, almost golden…like the sun blazing in the summer sky…and he was made of fire, Waxy… flames shot from every part of his body. Then, he opened his mouth and laughed. Standing inches from me he suddenly grabbed me with his flaming paw and hoisted me high into the air. I was so far above ground that I could see, through blood-red clouds and vapour, my house, your house Waxy…then the whole Peninsula. His paw stretched like elastic. *Let me down!* I roared.

"At this I felt myself dropping. I thought he'd let go, and I was falling. But I wasn't. He still held me. I came to a stop, hovering above your training yard, Waxy. But instead of trainers or greyhounds, hares sat around chatting, as if they could talk! One pointed up at me and the others began chanting: *Let it begin!*

"Totally confused, I roared: *What do you want from me?* Suddenly this giant hare tipped me upside-down. I begged for mercy but all I heard was the laughter of those crazy talking hares. Then…oh will I ever forget it…a strange black dog with red eyes appeared…redder than that awful red mist that hung over the world.

"I felt myself being lowered closer to the ground as if I were a puppet, then being swung towards this dog. Its mouth gaped and I saw a set of the most vicious fangs you could possibly imagine, and big globules of saliva were dripping from them. I roared and begged, to no avail. The mouth closed around my head. Complete darkness. Then the pain…the agony. Those razor-sharp teeth bit into my head.

"My screams went unheeded. I cried and begged and…oh thank God I sat up in my bed, in a lather of sweat….Sarah Jane had been trying to wake me for more than ten minutes. She'd heard me howling and I was flapping about. She thought I was suffering some kind of seizure."

Basher raised both hands and pressed his head tightly as if struggling to squeeze all remembrance of the nightmare from it. Waxy rose from his chair and laid a hand on Basher's shoulder. "It's okay buddy…it was only a stupid dream. Did you have something to eat before sleeping…or watch one of those stupid horror movies?"

Basher raised his head from his hands, reached for the glass and knocked back the rest of the brandy. Waxy was about to speak but Basher, his eyes bulging and his face distorted with fear, waved him back to his chair.

"A dream…a nightmare. If only that was all, though that was bad enough. Three days later something happened while I was fully awake. I'd just flicked the switch on the remote to knock off the TV. Sarah Jane had already gone to bed. I flung the remote onto the sofa and turned to go upstairs.

"Oh God Waxy…didn't the damn remote make a funny clicking sound. I looked at it…the buttons were pressing themselves. I swear my heart almost stopped. Then…the TV came back on! The screen lit up but there was nothing only snow white fuzziness and static. The volume went up… louder and louder.

"I grabbed the remote but no matter what I did I couldn't switch it off. I thought maybe the remote was out of action so I went to turn the TV off manually. Waxy…I'll never forget what happened next, if I live to be a hundred. This strange form appeared out of the fuzziness. Long ears first, then a full head and a full body. It was a hare, Waxy, except its eyes were almost human, and this…thing…was looking straight at me! The picture zeroed in on its head and those piercing blue eyes. Then it spoke: It said…"

Basher stopped talking and gave Waxy a look of sheer terror.

"What did it say, Basher?"

"It said…In a life to come *you* will be the bait, and it was pointing a big paw at me. Then it disappeared and… and… I saw myself, myself Waxy…on the TV… being dangled before these vicious alien-type dogs…and they started chopping me to bits. I rushed at the TV. If I couldn't switch it off I'd smash it, so help me God. I heard Sarah Jane running down the stairs. *What's wrong Basher,* she was shouting. Before she got into the room the whole picture on the screen vanished, and on came the weather woman rambling about an anticyclone. Sarah Jane told me I was cracking up and imagined the whole thing. But I didn't Waxy, I swear! You believe me, don't you Waxy…say you do!"

Waxy sighed. He had to be tactful. He didn't want to give offence and possibly lose Basher. He was a valued member of the club and never missed a blooding session in the yard. How Basher hollered and fell around laughing when the lads joked as they prepped their dogs. The man never flinched at a hare's death-rattle or screech.

Waxy leaned forward "The way I see it Basher... I don't doubt for a second that you…*believe*…what you saw on that TV screen. But…we…did Sarah Jane see anything weird…I mean on the TV… when she got downstairs?"

Basher scratched his head. "No…like I told you, it was back to normal when she arrived in the sitting room, and..."

Waxy interrupted: "So she saw nothing…and wasn't that a dream you had…when you thought some old hare-monster fed you to a devil dog?"

"Yeah…but Waxy…it was so real. Not like any dream I ever had. And Waxy…how did the remote switch on the TV by itself? No, Waxy, something's up. It's that island. The curse. I should have listened to that old geezer who said anyone who took hares from the island would be cursed. He knew… but we didn't give him credit!"

Waxy had heard enough. "Look, Basher, no offence, but I've no time for this hogwash. You had a nightmare. People have them all the time. They mean nothing...just chemicals in the brain swishing around. Remotes sometimes act oddly. Maybe you hadn't properly switched off the TV."

Basher stood up abruptly. He was shaking, with anger this time. He wagged a trembling finger at Waxy. "Think what you like…I know what I saw. You won't see me again in the yard. I'm finished blooding greyhounds. Sorry Waxy, I can't do it anymore. Someone up there (he pointed at the ceiling) is warning me. I'm finished with blooding and hare coursing…"

Tears moistened his face and his lips had turned a shade of white to match his cheeks and brow. His hair was tossed and standing on end. The hard-bitten courser/trainer headed straight for the door, waved weakly at Waxy as he opened it, and banged the door behind him so hard Waxy feared it might come off the hinges.

A full day had elapsed and Waxy could still hear the sharp emphatic thud and see Basher's gaunt features.

He ran the whole cock-and-bull story over in his head. Pure delusion, mingled with superstition, he concluded. Basher had listened foolishly to the yarns about the Golden Hare and the curse. Throw in some anti propaganda that got to him and maybe a clash between his tablets and his drinking and…that could explain it.

The doctor? Possibly something similar. The mind plays tricks. Happens every day. What's important is the court case. That young hussy must be named and shamed as the criminal who ruined day three of our coursing fixture. That'll boost morale and deter any further hallucinations or hobgoblin nonsense about hares taking revenge.

God knows, coursing has enough to contend with without fellows losing their nerve and going off the deep end. Yes, a conviction is vital. That case will make us stronger… show up the antis as petty vandals…law breaking ignoramuses.

***

98

Tipsy closed his eyes to sleep. Ginger had just left him to return to the Humanik dwelling after a protracted game of hide and seek among the lofty flowers. He was a playful creature, but Tipsy had other things on his mind apart from frolicking on the lawn with a fun-loving cat. How much longer must he spend in this small if comfortable space before his mission was concluded?

He sat inside the entrance of the wooden hut, paws extended onto the grass outside. The sky was dark and overcast. Rain clouds scudded across the expanse of oppressive greyness. *Mustn't complain I suppose...that cat could have been a hostile creature...and I could have been captured by a less well-intentioned Humanik*. She'd called to him earlier with food, eliciting jealous hissing from Ginger who seemed to resent the affection she lavished on him.

Tipsy yawned and let his mind wander but sleep wouldn't come. Something stirred in the hut. He felt a tingling in the back of his neck. He became aware of brightness behind him in the hut. It wasn't sunlight. The sky was still a dark shade of grey, clouds threatening to disgorge their watery loads at any moment. Tipsy turned to face the brightening corner of the hut. With every heartbeat the sharp pinpoint of light grew in size and intensity against the grainy brown backdrop.

Quickly it resolved into the familiar and reassuring form of the Great One. He was more resplendent than ever, suffused with a gently shimmering luminescence. A regal voice pierced the silence. "Tipsy...celestial and astrophysical conditions are propitious to a manifestation, so here I am. You have done well to make it this far...but now the great day of challenge approaches."

"You mean I'll be leaving here...?"

"Yes, the Humanik who dotes upon you will soon be facing danger in a Humanik Place of Justice. The magical Humanik who translated your thoughts for her has relayed the story of how you arrived here on the Big Island from the

Little Island and explained to her that you have a mission. Tipsy, you must enter the Place of Justice and convey an important message to the Humaniks sitting in judgement over your protector...that hares are NOT mere bundles of fur to be tortured or otherwise mistreated by Humaniks..."

"But Great One..." Tipsy blurted out, "Though I can commune with a multitude of other species, the Humanik mind is closed to me...and their language beyond my understanding..."

The Golden Hare smiled, orbs of blue and orange light flickering about his stately head and dancing around his shoulders. His deep sparkling blue eyes shone brighter...exuding supreme wisdom. "The all knowing ones in the Higher World have decreed, after copious and profound consultation, that you are to be gifted with the ability to penetrate the Humanik mind. This power will remain with you for only fifty heartbeats, so you must waste no time in conveying your message to those arbiters of Humanik justice...this will bring you closer to fulfilling your mission, the next phase of which will then be made known to you..."

"So...what am I to do?"

"You wait...other Humaniks will take you to the Place of Justice. Do not resist or seek to avoid them. They will be associates of your protector. They will take you to where you will, with Ostara's guidance, strike a blow for the hares of the Big Island and your own island home."

Tipsy sighed, feeling the weight of a gargantuan task on his shoulders. "Great One...I will do as you request...but what if...if this assignment proves overwhelming... I am just one hare...in a world of powerful Humaniks, any one of whom could kill me in an instant..."

The Great One's eyes glowed with compassion. "You are not alone Tipsy...the spirits of hares long since departed from this sad earth look down on you, and a team of angelic hares have been sapping the energies of hare-hating Humaniks on the Big Island...see."

To the right of the Golden Hare appeared a bubble showing frightened Humaniks running along winding pathways and through woodland from extra-large hares. They panted and wheezed, terror distorting their pink visages. This image gave way to one of Humaniks trembling like trees in the wind as phantom hare-like creatures loomed over them. *Strange...to see hares striking fear into Humaniks!*

Tipsy was about to query this vision when the Great One began to fade, his voice lowering as he dematerialised... "I am called back to the cave...May Ostara guide and inspire you..."

***

99

Waxy pushed in the door to the conference room of the *Fox and Horn* pub. More than half of the hundred chairs were already filled and the meeting wasn't due to kick off until Three PM. The clock said Two Forty Five.

Usually the members of Ballycrossways Coursing Club waddled in late for meetings, the prevailing notion being that it wasn't cool to be on time.

But not today. The emergency meeting had been called by Waxy himself to address three pressing issues. Though each was important in its own way, the upcoming trial of the anti-coursing activist was the least pressing.

This didn't detract from its importance. Were the outcome anything less than the foregone conclusion it was he'd be worried. But with a signed confession and no possibility of the culprit getting off there was no cause for concern. Apart from the danger of an impassioned "speech from the dock" stunt by that silly woman in an effort to exploit the trial to attack hare coursing.

At any other time that wouldn't bother him too much. Antis could be expected to avail of any situation to malign the ancient sport. But this wasn't just any time: Which brought him to the second of his three concerns: the snap election called by the government for three weeks hence.

The coalition of parties forming the government had fallen out and so the country was heading for the ballot box. His concern related to the five opinion polls published since the announcement. The Ecology Party was expected to win four extra seats in parliament, adding to its existing five. That could spell real trouble for coursing if another Bill proposing its abolition was tabled in parliament. Last time his side had won, but only after some serious inducement and arm-twisting of dithering politicians.

Sure, similar tactics could, and would, be employed if the antis made another move, but those additional Green MPs could still tip the balance against coursing.

The third headache in need of urgent relief was that crazy spate of nightmares and hallucinations that had provoked the resignation of seven club members. He had spoken to several longtime coursing stalwarts about it, urging them to reject such spooky nonsense and pull themselves together. Aside from those who'd directly experienced the supposed visitations, others were freaked out by the tall tales and scary anecdotes they'd heard.

Well, he'd be laying it on the line for them today. With another parliamentary challenge possibly on the horizon, he'd be ramming home the message that there was no room in Ballycrossways Coursing Club for weakness, or for superstitious codswallop about ghostly hares getting inside their heads.

Unzipping his attaché case, he pulled out the sheaves of notes he'd prepared. The seats were filling up fast. Good. And he noticed that his "no drinks rule" was being observed. He wanted everyone clearheaded when he delivered what could possibly be the most decisive spiff of his coursing career.

***

100

Annemarie felt like she'd entered another world, so unfamiliar was the village. It was congested with traffic and media people. She had to rush past dozens of reporters and TV people to get to Ms Franklin's car that was to take her to the Peninsula courthouse four miles away. The road was so jam-packed with vehicles of all shapes and sizes that her solicitor's car was just inching along. She blew the horn frantically. "Damn!" She snapped, "Most of these people have no direct connection with the case, they're just sightseers attracted by all the media hype."

Annemarie understood the level of interest, prompted by articles claiming that a hare was to give evidence in her case through a psychic medium. It was essentially true of course, but the salacious presentation of the fact didn't help…it sensationalized the whole issue. She wondered if this would help or hinder her chances of an acquittal…or her objective in using the case to highlight the anti-coursing cause.

Some of the newspaper articles were completely over the top, with headings like: "Bunny to take the stand in wacky Irish courtroom drama!", and "Animal rights activist calls real life Dr Doolittle to testify in vandalism case…" Others screamed: "Animal Crackers down south as hare faces courtroom grilling!" and "Hare Brained…anti coursing activist calls on super bunny to beat vandalism rap!"

She wondered how Tipsy would fare later on. The thought of what he proposed to do, as conveyed to her by the psychic, made her even more nervous. Mrs. McCauley had translated his brainwave in a series of gasps. The hare wanted to intervene somehow to help her chances of acquittal. Yes, he was happy that the psychic would be telling the court his story, but, if possible, he wished to appear himself to make a statement!

Right now, he was in the care of two activists who Annemarie, following consultation with the psychic, had instructed to take him to the courthouse towards the end of proceedings. If…and only if…an opportunity presented itself, they were to get Tipsy inside the building and, again, if it proved possible, into the chamber where the trial would be almost concluded.

After that, it would be up to Tipsy…*to do what?* She had no idea. Instigate a diversion of some kind? Give her moral support when the verdict was announced? A nice sentiment, but it wouldn't achieve anything.

So much was against this seemingly crazy idea. It could go wrong at any point. What if the hare got killed or badly injured? The activists could be delayed in traffic or release Tipsy too soon… or a half-minute too late. Or the whole plan could backfire and make her situation worse. She tried not to think about it. It was out of her hands anyway. God…was all this just a crazy dream? She bit her lip and pinched herself. *No, it's real. Too bloody real.*

Police in riot gear cleared a path to the courthouse for Annemarie and her solicitor. Red-faced coursing fans screamed abuse at her and shook their fists or cudgels. Eggs and tomatoes were tossed that bounced off the riot shields that formed a protective canopy. It reminded Annemarie of those ancient Romans she's seen depicted in movies warding off waves of arrows.

The foyer of the courthouse was crammed with people. A loud babble of chatter ceased abruptly at the sight of Annemarie. Escorting police again intervened to push back both hostile coursing fans and adoring supporters.

The entrance to the court chamber swung open, three powerfully built officers standing with batons tightly gripped as Annemarie, arm-linked to Ms Franklin, was ushered inside.

The last time Annemarie had seen the courtroom it was almost empty. She'd accompanied a friend who faced a minor parking fine. Barely half a dozen yawning locals and one police officer were present.

Unlike today. She gasped at the spectacle: All the seats were occupied and dozens of men and women stood along the walls to the left and right, squeezing against each other as if they'd just acquired last-minute tickets to a major football game.

Barristers in flowing black gowns and those comical wigs from another century sat in front of a long table, facing unto a raised platform that contained the judge's bench in the centre, underneath the golden harp of Ireland.

The wall behind the judge's bench had three large screens, for video showings presumably. *The footage.* Thank God that technician had managed to retrieve it. The coursing club hadn't properly deleted those scenes of stomach-churning cruelty…and Tipsy's paranormal stunt, from the camcorder. She prayed the footage would have the desired effect.

Her heart missed a beat at the sight of all the uniformed men and women in the back rows. Her eyes passed along the astonishing lineup of high ranking police and military officials. What on earth were *they* doing here? Ms Franklin whispered: "It's just for show…to intimidate you. Don't pay the slightest attention to them. Concentrate on your own testimony."

She forced herself to avert her eyes from the shining brass buttons dotting their uniforms, from swathes of glinting medals and multihued insignia. The leaders of the army, navy, air force, and police, Ms. Franklin quipped.

The solicitor whispered recognition of other dignitaries: A Mother Superior from an esteemed convent sat demurely in the third last row. Next to her, with arms folded and gazing impassively, were representatives from the United Farmers Association, the National Hurling and Football League, the Bird Catchers and Game Shooters Federation, and the South Eastern Eucharistic Ministers Prayer Group.

Annemarie also recognized well-known animal rights campaigners and wildlife conservationists, who smiled reassuringly at her when she made eye contact with them. This revived her spirits a little.

"Up here…come along Miss!" A police officer roused Annemarie from her reverie, directing her to a seat located on the side of the room to the right of the judge's bench.

Directly opposite her, at the far wall of the room, she saw the empty two-row jury box. She felt her stomach heave at the thought of what lay ahead. How would her astonishing tale be received?

Her right hand, shaking, reached for the glass of water placed on the arm of her wooden seat. Her throat was parched and she hadn't said a word yet.

***

101

Waxy downed his large whiskey and stepped out of the pub. He needed that to steady himself for the big day ahead.

He shuffled into the waiting car and was taken, along with three other club officials, to the courthouse. Unusually for this part of the Peninsula, the road was congested. Vehicles with registrations of every county in Ireland drove in front of and behind the car. Far ahead, according to the driver, were a number of army jeeps.

The village itself had been thronged since early morning with TV cameras and reporters thanks to that crazy press release that went out from some anti-coursing group promising that the court case would feature a psychic who could read the minds of animals and that, he smiled to himself, *a hare* would testify on behalf of the misguided woman who had wrecked the coursing event.

As soon as he learned of that gimmick, which was no doubt an attempt to distract the jury from the real issue; the unprovoked attack on Ballycrossways Coursing Club, he had arranged some PR activity of his own; to drive home the gravity of the charge against the young hooligan and the significance of hare coursing in Irish culture. He'd made dozens of calls, invoking numerous favours.

Waxy alighted from the car with his colleagues and quickstepped despite his bulk towards the courthouse. He was delighted to see that the car park adjacent to the courthouse was completely full, with additional cars beeping impatiently, their drivers desperate to find a space. A police cordon had been formed around the building, whether to underline the gravity of the case or for security reasons Waxy wasn't sure.

Maybe the police feared those anti-coursing crackpots would try to pull off some crazy stunt if they didn't get their way. Well, they *wouldn't* be getting their way! The whole country would see them for the spiteful vandals and troublemakers they were when that hussy was taken from the courthouse in cuffs, to share company with drug dealers and every sort of spaced-out criminal spawned by the dark side of Irish society.

Entering the building he brushed away imagined specks of dust from his immaculately pressed dark blue dress suit. His reflection smirked back up at him from his polished shoes. The seats were filled, except for a few spaces that the police had ensured were reserved for coursing club officials. The two back rows looked like long stripes of dark blue and emerald green, studded with silver and gold: The chiefs of the army, navy and air force sat steely-eyed. *Good.* And the next row comprised high-raking policemen, their fierce countenances a reminder that no criminal would leave this building un-cuffed.

Marvelous: This was what he wanted. He tried, indulgently, to get inside the minds of potential jurors. They would have to be impressed by all this show of authority and righteousness. This would take their breaths away, lest they harbour any sympathy for the miscreant on trial. Waxy nodded to the phalanx of dignitaries before taking his seat. His colleagues whistled softly to themselves, one muttering: "Jeepers Waxy, them is pretty important people…we can't lose!"

Waxy nodded agreement, though conscious of the fact that those big knobs were only there for show. The Prosecution would do its job with ease, like rolling down a hill. It was essentially an open and shut case, local police had assured him…so what could go wrong?

He relished the hope that the case would, apart from its legal outcome, discourage neutral people from being duped by the antis…once they'd seen the consequences of swallowing their propaganda.

Yes, today might well spell the death-knell of that assault on our stewardship of Ireland's hares. Anyone who throws mud at us after this will have today's conviction tossed back in their faces.

A glance at the clock told him the case was due to begin in just under three minutes. He rubbed his hands together and gave the officials on either side of him a friendly dig in the ribs, whispering: "This will be as good as watching a first rate dog turning a well-weathered buck, lads!"

"Right you are Waxy", the man on his right retorted: "we hold all the aces on this one; she's as good as banged up. And all the antis have is a frigging fortuneteller who talks to hares!"

The three of them suppressed their laughter, in deference to the air of gravitas that pervaded the courtroom. The woman was led up the aisle and pressed into the seat reserved for the accused.

The door to the judge's chamber opened. Out stepped five grimfaced police officers, three male and two female, followed by His Lordship. Waxy joined the entire assembly in rising to his feet.

***

102

With a flourish, Myles O' Rafferty Smith (Senior Counsel) arose, adjusted his wig and turned to the jury on his left. To his right Annemarie gazed at him from her position in the special seat reserved for the accused in the Circuit Criminal Court.

The tension within her mounted as she beheld the Prosecutor's silky black gown swishing about as he launched into his attack on her. His voice was smooth but scary:

"Ladies and gentlemen of the jury, you are here today to try someone who, you may think, is not accused of a very serious offence. You may think, mistakenly, that this is a trivial issue…a matter of little or no consequence in the broader scheme of things. Oh, you may think to yourselves: who cares about a few hares bolting from a little old cage out in the middle of the countryside. And nobody, you may reflect, has been killed or injured, so…who cares? Let's just let the accused person go free and get on with our lives."

He paused, his head moving slowly, his attention fixing on one jury member after another.

"And well you may think or conclude, but" (he raised his voice an octave) "You would be so gravely wrong in thus assessing the crime…yes CRIME, ladies and gentlemen, that this woman stands accused of. By the end of this case you will, I believe, be satisfied beyond a reasonable doubt that Ms. Cristobel is guilty as charged of causing malicious damage to the property of Ballycrossways Coursing Club.

"The evidence the Prosecution will give will leave no room for even a scintilla of doubt. You will hear the evidence of a police officer who took her statement in which she clearly admitted her crime. You will hear of her previous attempt, in breach of coursing club rules, to videotape parts of this year's annual fixture at Ballycrossways, you will hear of her malicious and unfounded opposition to the wholesome sport of hare coursing that has brought joy and economic wellbeing to rural communities nationwide.

"You will, I am confident, understand and accept, having heard all the evidence, that this was no minor offence, but an attack on the heart and soul of this nation by a person who, if she were allowed to go unpunished, might well progress to committing even graver offences against law-abiding sportspeople and their valuable property!"

Annemarie winced as he called to the stand the police officer who took her statement of admission. She listened with unease and a sinking heart as the police officer confirmed that she had admitted encroaching on the property of the coursing club and using wire-cutters to unlock the entrance to the hare holding compound.

She couldn't help smiling when he read the last sentence of the statement: "I was happy to see all those hares running to their freedom in the half-light of approaching dawn. I did not think of what I did as in any way a criminal deed, but rather an act of compassion aimed at preventing deliberate cruelty to these unfortunate animals."

Annemarie's barrister, Malachi Holt, was on his feet to cross-examine. He removed his wig as if it were a cap or hat, resettled it on his completely bald head, and held up his own copy of the statement like a trophy, waving it about as he faced, first the police officer, then the jury to his left, before leaving it back down on the long document-strewn table in front of him. He smiled as if at a private joke that couldn't be shared with anyone. "Did the accused at any point admit to causing malicious damage?"

The officer looked offended. "Ah, well, she didn't use those words, but she admitted damaging…"

"She didn't admit causing malicious damage?"

"No…she"

"And correct me if I'm wrong but did she not call to the station of her own free will to inform you of her action in freeing the hares?"

"Yes"

"No further question for this witness Your Lordship!"

And down he plunked in his seat.

"The Prosecution calls Waxy Bumbleton-Crossbar."

Annemarie cringed as the grossly overweight coursing club secretary took the stand, wearing a blue dress suit that was obviously tailor made for him. He smoothed his red tie and then clasped the bible tightly. He seemed to wink at somebody to the rear of the chamber.

Listening to him swear to tell the whole truth and nothing but the truth Annemarie wondered if he'd admit snatching hares from the island.

The Prosecuting Counsel regarded him with awe and supreme deference. "Mr. Bumbleton-Crossbar, can you recall for the court that dreadful morning…when you became aware of that crime that shook the Peninsula to its foundations?"

The coursing official frowned, inhaled deeply and gave a delicate cough. "Yes. It is a morning I will never forget. I was roused by repeated banging on my front door. Before I had opened it my mobile and landline were ringing in my ears. The night watchmen at Ballycrossways had discovered the empty compound. The entrance hatch had been interfered with, I was informed, and the padlock broken. Not one hare remained in the compound. The men standing guard had taken a very short break, and I presume the culprit exploited that small window of opportunity…"

The Prosecutor swelled to his full height and his chest expanded by several inches. "And, would it be true to say that the sabotage had far reaching implications…?"

The witness went silent, withdrew a handkerchief from his breast pocket and rubbed his eyes, though Annemarie couldn't detect any tears falling.

"It was…more than a piece of vandalism. Ballycrossways Coursing Club has been the pride of the Peninsula for generations. Some of the finest greyhounds in Ireland have run down that stretch of superbly maintained sward, in pursuit of hares that have always received a sporting chance from the club. Not only that: the hares in our care are better fed and watered than hares anywhere else in Ireland. Our love for coursing is equaled only by our love for those fleet-footed creatures…"

The Prosecutor beamed, and cast a fleeting gaze at the line of jurors. "And Mr. Bumbleton-Crossbar; isn't it true to say that you and other club officials suffered considerable mental trauma and anxiety attacks as a consequence of the crime?"

"Oh yes, I'd been off the drink for three weeks. Once I heard what happened and saw that empty compound, I hit the bottle big time. And I've been affected by bouts of insomnia. Other club officials had to receive counseling and one man is on an intensive course of medication. They can't come to terms with the idea that a brazen fanatic would commit such….such an outrage…against their sport…"

"Indeed, and you were obliged, were you not, to confiscate a camera from a person who attempted to record the action earlier that day at the coursing event, in defiance of a clear prohibition on unauthorised photography?"

"Yes."

"And is that person present in this courtroom?"

"Yes, she is sitting over there."

Annemarie shifted uncomfortably in her chair when he pointed at her.

"And what was her demeanor when you nipped in the bud her unauthorised, reckless and irresponsible interference with the coursing fixture?"

"Oh she had a vicious look…pure hatred…she spat defiance. She was like a cornered rat. She lashed out with her arms and fists and it's a miracle she didn't land punches on some of us. It took five of us to remove her from the grounds before she could do somebody an injury. It was very clear to me that this woman hated coursing, and hated the people who pursue this great field sport."

"And, in spite of her disgraceful behavior and disrespect for coursing, did you not return her camera to her?"

"Yes, we felt that we should do this, even knowing how much she despised us. We are a fair minded group of people and we opted to let her have the device back, though she didn't thank me, just mumbled something under her breath."

"Thank you."

***

103

The frosted grass crunched underfoot as Tipsy sauntered around the lawn. He shivered and cast his eyes skyward. A heaving smutty cloud mass had replaced the soothing blue canopy of daybreak. His protector had left food out for him earlier than most days, and she had fondly embraced him before she returned to her abode. That felt a bit strange. He'd noticed tears on her cheeks too and listened to sounds of lamentation, followed by that cackling that indicated Humanik laughter or an expression of relief.

Then she'd let him alone with his carrots and lettuce and he heard the now familiar impact of wood knocking on wood as she exited her dwelling somewhere out of sight. Upon hearing that definitive thump he instantly realised that this day was special. The time was approaching fast when he'd be called upon to complete his mission. The Golden Hare had mentioned that he'd be leaving this interim sanctuary for a Humanik place of justice, where he would somehow help his protector and strike a blow for the hares of Ireland.

The weak sun cast a pale lustre on the little patch of the world to which he'd been confined now for...how long? He felt guilty about thinking like this. His protector was keeping him safe from harm, unlike the other Humaniks who took him into captivity for their own twisted pleasure. Still, he yearned for the wide open spaces, for the rolling contours of a leafy, verdant and unrestricted landscape. A hare didn't belong in a Humanik's garden, any more than in a place of bondage awaiting a contrived chase that made his captors yowl with merriment. So yes, he was glad the hour of departure was near.

To keep himself warm and occupied, he scampered around the lawn, leaping and tumbling in the slowly melting frost. Startled birds chattered noisily overhead, in the air and on window ledges, probably unaccustomed to such bursts of frantic activity in this normally quiet grassy patch. He darted in and out between flower stalks at the edge of the lawn, noticing how the joyous plants with their sunny dispositions had begun to wilt.

They would soon die, he lamented, pausing to contemplate one flower that had a sadness radiating from its petals that he hadn't seen since his arrival at his protector's dwelling. It knew that inevitable death loomed, he surmised. But later, when the season changed once again rebirth would occur, and these flowers would resume their devotion to the sun as it traversed the heavens, following its progress with their cheery silent heads. Plants never spoke to him, but Tipsy felt they too had life, though of a kind known only to Ostara in her wisdom.

"Exercising, Tipsy?" The plump little robin was gazing wistfully at him as he geared up for another run around the lawn. He relaxed, sat back on his haunches and laughed.

"You could say that. It's safe here...but I need to be free, like you. And I think today is the day I'll be leaving here."

The robin was nibbling furiously on a piece of food, what birds called *bread.* Crumbs of it lay at its tiny feet. After swallowing, its eyes lit up. "Leaving?"

Tipsy nodded. "I'll miss you and...Ginger of course...I know you birds aren't his favourite creatures, but he's been good company."

The robin cast a nervous look around him, and then up at a window in the dwelling where, following the bird's line of sight, Tipsy saw the cat peering down at them. He'd said goodbye to Ginger that morning, acting on his strong hunch that he'd soon be parting company. "Well, wherever you go the best of luck" said the robin, extending a wing that brushed gently against Tipsy's right front paw.

With that, the red-breasted singer fluttered up to the window ledge to taunt Ginger, who scraped at the glass frustratingly and narrowed his green eyes at the bird. Having sufficiently annoyed him, the robin flew into the next garden, leaving Tipsy alone again. But not for long. From the dwelling came sounds of opening and closing, sharp footfalls that echoed within the abode, and lively Humanik chatter.

The rectangle of wood opened to reveal two female Humaniks, both sporting woolly coverings on their heads, their bodies draped with multicoloured clothing. The projection of friendliness and unbridled compassion from both of them left Tipsy in no doubt as to their benign intentions. They were here to help him in his quest. The Humaniks stood staring at each other for a few moments on the lawn, then walked towards him.

One of them leant and gently took hold of Tipsy. He felt himself being raised from the frosty grass into a warm and welcoming embrace. Her clothing felt softer than fur. The second Humanik stroked his head, whispering something that sounded soothing and self-indulgent. He felt himself swaying as he was carried into the dwelling and then back out of it, but not as roughly or frighteningly as when Humaniks manhandled him in captivity.

He beheld a smooth featureless pathway between lines of dwellings. He was being lowered to one of those damnable Humanik contrivances that rolled on silvery discs. He'd lost count of how many of them he'd dodged after the escape. You had to be hyper-alert to avoid being crushed by them, as many hares had been when they failed to hop aside fast enough. And now he was almost touching this vile contraption that wrought such havoc.

He was about to protest when an opening appeared in the monster and two Humanik paws reached out to take him from the one that held him. The interior had less light than outside, though nothing awful happened. But why should it? These were sympathetic Humaniks, so he must stop worrying. They presumably knew what they were doing.

He found himself sitting on a soft shining surface similar to the seating apparatus in his protector's dwelling. Another Humanik was already stroking his head. The seat was comfy enough, but he'd prefer a patch of high growing grass or a warm sandy hollow on the island any day.

A loud roar assailed his ears like a gust in a raging storm and he felt himself moving, though he remained sitting in the same spot. Another Humanik induced anomaly. He closed his eyes and sighed. *Just trust in Ostara and take each moment as it comes. I'm sure there's a purpose in all this!*

***

104

The Prosecutor sat and the Defence barrister rose promptly, his face contorted into exaggerated questioning mode.

"Mr. Bumbleton-Crossbar, you say you were *devastated* by the release of the hares from Ballycrossways coursing grounds?"

"Yes, absolutely and I…"

"Are you a sensitive man…troubled by, for example, the sight of an animal in pain?"

"I am sensitive where appropriate, but a practical man too, not given to sentimentality or deluded by the notion that animals have the same rights as humans!"

"But you did say you care deeply for the hares that serve as bait in coursing?"

"I…yes…we look after them better than…"

"Can you appreciate that there are people, like the accused woman here today, who care about animals too?"

Yes, but not in the way that we do."

The barrister shook his head, glanced at the jury and then back at the witness. "In other words, people like the accused woman do *not* share your concept of animal welfare?"

"They are a million miles removed from us!"

"Mr Bumbleton-Crossbar, can you tell the court how your coursing club captures hares?"

The club secretary beamed, looked around the chamber and his enormous frame seemed to swell even more with pride. He had a wistful faraway look. "Hare catching is a sport in itself. We, that is, the club members, backed up by supporters from all walks of life, set out into the countryside, beating the ground with sturdy sticks and branches, in the time-honoured manner.

"Teenagers, who might otherwise be twiddling their thumbs or hanging about the streets doing mischief, assist us. The hares are netted, carefully boxed, and taken to the club grounds to be fed and dosed and trained to run to an escape hatch…The boys and girls who help us with the catching are given refreshments and free passes to the coursing fixture and some of them may go on to be proud coursers…"

"So it's a day of fun for all the family, in keeping with a sporting tradition that means the world to you?"

"Of course, and each hare is ear-tagged so that it can be released back to where it was found once coursing has concluded…"

"I see. And are there ANY circumstances in which you would deem the release of hares by a member of the public a justifiable act? For example, you say you and your colleagues are devoted to a sporting ethos: If, say, a coursing club was to capture hares from a nature reserve or…say, a patch of our national territory long respected as a no-go area for coursing clubs, would that justify the kind of intervention that resulted in the defendant appearing here today, accused of *malicious damage*?"

The witness's comfortable demeanour evaporated. "What do you mean…no…we don't take hares from such locations. That is against our tradition…our ethos."

The barrister motioned the technician who had retrieved the deleted footage from Annmarie's camcorder and he immediately pointed a remote control at one of the big screens behind the judge.

The barrister addressed the coursing club official again: "Would it surprise you to know, Mr. Bumbleton-Crossbar; that the footage you thought you'd deleted from Ms. Cristobel's Camcorder was recovered?"

The witness's jaw dropped, and his eyebrows rose in disbelief. He opened his mouth to say something but closed it again.

"Please observe and I will resume cross-examination presently."

The coursing club official turned around to watch, as did His Lordship and every eye in the room was fixed on the screen as it came to life, filling with a stretch of green grass, before panning across to the red-coated man unleashing a pair of greyhounds.

The hare darted out of its box and the dogs closed on it quickly. The animal was pinned down by one dog and struck at high speed by the second. It limped away, before being struck again. A man ran onto the field and ushered the dogs away. As he exited the field, the footage showed him stretching the hare's neck, a scene accompanied by loud screeching.

No laughter or catcalls this time, but gasps of horror and low muttering. Annemarie noticed the coursing fans looked embarrassed, which was odd because this happened at all their fixtures.

More footage followed, showing hares being propelled into the air, falling to earth and being pummeled by the dogs. At this point, the film was paused, and the barrister turned to the judge.

"Your Lordship, the next piece I would commend to your special attention, and to that of Mr. Bumbleton-Crossbar…resume please."

The technician pressed a button and another hare could be seen dashing forth from its little box, pursued by two greyhounds.

Annemarie had partly forgotten just how out of the ordinary Tipsy's evasion of the dogs had been. The entire assembly, pro and anti, and the rows of State officials, gasped audibly as Tipsy first led a dog in a long meandering chase that culminated in the unfortunate animal breaking a leg and stumbling, and then, the camera focused on the bizarre sight of the hare teasing the second dog…even casually circling him, as if he were no long visible to the frenzied pursuer.

No catcalls or booing from the coursing fans, either on screen or in the courtroom, as Tipsy sauntered towards the escape and the dogs wandered about aimlessly in search of him. The barrister paused the footage and rewound a few seconds, enlarging a frame and zeroing in on the tag attached to Tipsy's left ear.

"I direct the attention of Your Lordship, and the jury, to the ear-tag. You will observe that it has, alongside a number, the letter "I" in brackets. Some of the other hares also have this "I", while others again do not have it, on their ear-tags."

Still pointing at the video screen, he turned to the coursing official who now looked distinctly uncomfortable. "Mr. Bumbleton-Crossbar, what is the purpose of the ear-tags on those hares we saw in the film, and the others used at your annual coursing fixture?"

The witness spoke haltingly, his brow oozing trickles of sweat. "In line with our sporting ethos, and wildlife regulations, we tag all hares captured so that when we release them after the event, they will be identifiable as coursed hares and left in peace."

"You are aware of alleged incidents in which the ear-tags are removed so that the hares can be coursed repeatedly…especially in parts of Ireland where hares are hard to come by?"

"I abhor such unsporting behavior!"

"Do you indeed?"

The barrister uttered the three words with great emphasis, shaking his head at the jury.

"And, tell me, would you abhor the capture of hares from an offshore island to make up for a shortfall in the numbers of hares required for your fixture?"

The coursing official opened his mouth to speak, but said nothing.

"Look at the screen again…what does the "I" stand for? Perhaps you could tell the court?"

"I…would prefer not to, if that's alright Your Lordship?"

He regarded the judge with a hopeful peek, his eyebrows raised and his lips quivering.

The barrister leaned forward, as if trying to bridge the gap between himself and the coursing official. "Come now, Sir. A woman's reputation is at stake, and I'm sure you are as anxious to get to the truth as anyone else here today. Am I right in presuming that the *I* on the ear-tag denotes *Island*, and that each hare so identified was taken from Gooseberry island by your coursing club?"

The judge interjected: You will answer the question, Mr. Bumbleton-Crossbar."

"Yes…I…yes. Hares have become scarcer, as you mentioned, especially here on the Peninsula. We had no option but to…cast our nets elsewhere. That episode had…had…slipped my memory. Yes. Regrettably, we had to procure additional stocks …from the island."

Annemarie noticed how this statement had some coursing fans holding their heads in embarrassment, or regarding the witness with little or no sympathy. The barrister indicated he had completed his cross-examination. The Prosecutor looked bewildered. He rose and mumbled "Nothing further from this witness, Your Lordship."

The judge nodded. "You may step down."

The coursing official shot a hostile glance at Annemarie as he passed her on the way to his seat.

***

105

Annemarie felt a slight weakness when her name was called. *Hold your nerve…think clearly.*

She moved to take the stand, blocking out the packed chamber…all those eyes that followed her steps to the dreaded seat that had, she knew, enfolded many a tensed and sickly posterior. She almost dropped the bible, eliciting a flurry of whispers and grunts from the assembly, but caught it with her other hand.

Her words sounded muffled and scarcely audible, at least to herself, when she took the oath. Her stomach churned and her head felt light as she settled herself in the seat, leaning closer to the microphone.

Her barrister led her gently through the events of the day. She recounted how she'd attended the second day of the hare coursing fixture.

"And what did you see at this event?"

"I…I went with my camcorder. I'd attended the previous year, and I decided then that next time I'd try to record part of the proceedings. I watched as hares were released from those little boxes and pairs of greyhounds were unleashed in pursuit. They ran and dodged, and some of them suffered horribly.

"The dogs mauled them, or pinned them down, and hares got tossed about…like they were little paper toys blown to and fro in the wind. I found it hard to watch, and also to listen, as these harmless animals cried like babies. I took out my camcorder and started filming. I recorded their pitiful plight.

"Then, to my amazement, something happened that I didn't expect and seemed to baffle the coursing fans also. A hare ran faster than usual, but instead of passing through the escape hatch as he could have done quite easily after outrunning the dogs, he doubled back and seemed to… to taunt them….as you saw in the footage earlier.

"One dog was injured and the other…well, he seemed to lose sight of the hare. The dog had stopped running and he was just wandering around the field…and all the while the hare was hopping about in front of him, or sitting inches from the dog. Eventually this hare ran casually to the escape…"

Jeers from some coursing fans in the room and outbreaks of what sounded to Annemarie like nervous laughter from others.

The Judge intervened. "Enough of that. Silence in my court. I'll have anyone removed who engages in catcalling or rude utterances! Continue Ms Cristobel."

"Yes…what astonished me, and I'd just watched awful scenes of cruelty, was how this hare seemed to be *invisible* to the dog, the only other explanation being that the dog had suffered temporary sight loss. I heard coursing fans to either side of me express bafflement. After I'd finished recording this curious incident, a coursing club official rushed to me and confiscated the camcorder. I was ejected from the grounds and returned home…"

The barrister interjected. "And then, later that night, you had a dream. Perhaps you could tell the court?"

"Yes…it was late. I was sleeping. I wouldn't describe it as a dream. I was roused from sleeping by a *vision*…"

Muffled giggles, suppressed laughter, and stifled jeers. The judge frowned, and silence returned. Annemarie described how the Golden Hare had appeared to her and asked her to free the Ballycrossways hares.

The judge had to intervene more than a dozen times as catcalls erupted. Roars of laughter echoed around the room and bounced off the walls. As she completed her recollection, he called on the police to remove anyone heard or seen misbehaving. This was greeted by further interruptions and police immediately swooped on several rowdy men at the entrance who had failed to find seats and were squatting or leaning against the walls.

Annemarie assumed they were coursing fans, as her own supporters had no reason to be angry, whatever difficulty some of them might have accepting her account of the psychic experience.

"Ms. Cristobel…Though you could have avoided any brush with the law, you opted to turn yourself in. You might tell the court why you did this."

"Yes…I didn't believe that what I did was wrong, but other campaigners were being arrested and harassed as a consequence of my action. That troubled me. I couldn't allow that to happen. Also, I made it clear to the officer who took my statement that the damage caused to property during the release of the captive hares was not *malicious*, as I understand the meaning of the word.

"I just broke the padlock to facilitate opening of the hatch in the compound. That was necessary to achieve my objective, which was simply to prevent deliberate animal cruelty…to save those unfortunate hares from what the coursing club had planned for them. There was nothing malicious in what I did. I saw it as an act of compassion…"

Roars from the back of the chamber muffled the barrister's voice as he begun to ask Annemarie about her decision to engage a psychic. A man with eyes blazing and a shock of tangled white hair protruding like barbed wire came running up the aisle, screeching and shaking a fist, "Hanging would be too good for you!" he roared.

Though a heavy-set man he moved swiftly and undaunted, driven on by a rage that Annemarie thought must be ripping him apart. Her heart missed a beat as he was wrestled to the floor by three police officers less than a metre from where she sat, trembling.

Others were restrained and held back as they too embarked on an ill-fated storming of the chamber that Annemarie feared might result in her sustaining an injury, or worse.

The judge was calling for order, his voice crackling like static on a broken radio set as he fulminated against "outrageous and provocative behavior." He announced a ten-minute recess to allow the court to recover from the unseemly conduct "of people who must think this hallowed house of justice is a place of brawling and unbridled mayhem."

The removal of the more disruptive elements made it easier to continue with her testimony. Still, it elicited a palpable hush, lines of gaping mouths, and a chorus of tongue-clicking. The dignitaries in the back rows had lost their stiff upper lips and were staring at her if she'd just appeared in a puff of smoke.

The judge politely interrupted. "Just a moment, Ms. Cristobel; I want to be sure I understood you. Are you saying you engaged the services of a…*psychic*…to act as an interpreter between you and…this hare that arrived in your garden…and that the hare informed you, as it were, that he was the…the *chap*…that performed so impressively at the coursing event…evading the dogs etcetera?"

"Yes, Your Lordship; I realise how extraordinary all this must sound, but it's the truth, and I'm very conscious of the oath I've taken."

No laughter this time and Annemarie saw the jury was transfixed, whether from sympathy or just plain incredulity she couldn't tell.

Malachi Holt bowed reverentially to the judge and resumed his sympathetic examination. "And isn't it true to say that it was your honestly held conviction that releasing the hares was not only ethically justifiable but an absolute *obligation*…in the circumstances."

"Yes…I did what I did with a clear conscience."

The barrister glanced at the jury and resumed his seat.

Up rose the Prosecutor. With a swagger he removed his spectacles, quickly wiped them, and put them back on. He surveyed the jurors as if to ensure they were paying attention, and fixed Annemarie with a reproachful glower. "Ms. Cristobel, would you agree that you have strong views on hare coursing?"

She nodded assent. "And that you would do *anything* to cause inconvenience to a coursing club…to frustrate their work, as you clearly indicated when you breached the No Unauthorised Photography rule?"

"Not …*anything*…exactly. I wouldn't do anything to hurt them…physically…but I believed that a little damage to a rusty old padlock was a tiny price to pay for saving those hares from…from being battered and terrorized…"

The Prosecutor went silent, his face flushing. Suddenly he roared, causing Annemarie to shake: "A little damage…*a little?* Is that how you describe your deliberate act of vandalism, your premeditated attack on some of the finest sportspeople this country has ever produced?"

She opened her mouth to answer, but he wasn't finished. Raising a quivering forefinger, he hissed, his voice lowering by several octaves, "Ah, but you admit that what you did amounted to damage…"

"Yes, but not *malicious* damage…from my point of view."

"Oh dear…not malicious you say! You dress up like a common thief…a vandal… a vag…you sneak out under cover of darkness with wire cutters to wreck the enjoyment of hundreds of sportspeople…and you expect the court to accept that this was not malicious behaviour? Come now, Ms. Cristobel, I put it to you that you have concocted this outrageous fantasy tale about a hare appearing to you to hoodwink the jury…to feign insanity…and I can tell you here and now…you have failed miserably in that cynical stratagem!"

Annemarie took a deep breath and was about to answer, but the Prosecutor dismissed her with a contemptuous glare. "No further questions to the accused…for now!"

The judge excused her and the Defence called to the witness stand Mrs. Christine McCauley.

***

106

Annemarie crossed her fingers as the psychic medium took the Bible from the court clerk. When she stated her name and occupation the jury lurched forward in openmouthed bewilderment. Guffaws and headshaking again swept the courtroom, with even some of the animal rights people seemingly perplexed.

One woman cast a worried look at Annemarie. There might have been a livelier reaction, Annemarie suspected, had not many of the rowdier fellows already been ejected from the building.

Mrs. McCauley swore the oath and stated her name and profession: "I have practiced for eighteen years as a psychic medium and for fourteen of those I have answered my calling as an animal communicator."

Malachi Holt thanked her, glanced at the jury, presumably to gauge their reaction so far, and then smiled indulgently: "Can you briefly explain the nature of your work Mrs. McCauley, before proceeding to the substantive issue that may have relevance to my client's Not Guilty plea?"

Calmly, with just a hint of nervousness, she explained her gift, how she could receive messages from animals and read their thoughts, under favourable conditions. She then recalled being phoned by Annemarie and agreeing to help her with a "peculiar problem."

"And you might elaborate on how this engagement differed from your customary activity?"

"Yes, normally I deal with cats and dogs, and occasionally horses. Rabbits very rarely and I had never dealt with a hare prior to this occasion."

"Mrs. McCauley, let's skip over the various preparations you went through before ah…tuning in, was it…to the thoughts of this wild creature. You might let the court know what transpired, from the beginning of this…ah… transmission, and forgive my unfamiliarity with the correct terminology applicable to this field of endeavor. You'll appreciate that it is a subject many people, me included, may struggle to grasp."

She bowed her head, raised it again and looked from the barrister to the judge, and then at the jury box. She reached for a notebook and opened it on the first page. "I hope it will be in order for me to consult my notes of the reading…I transcribed the account almost immediately after the conclusion of the hare's story?"

The judge harrumphed and fixed her with an icy stare. "Mrs. McCauley, I must remind you that hearsay will not be admitted in this case. I am granting the Defense very considerable latitude in allowing such testimony as you are about to give. I will, however, be reminding the jury that certain kinds of evidence must be discounted and rejected in total by them…"

The barrister was on his feet. "My Lord, I would emphasize, lest there be some confusion about this matter; that this witness does not propose to indulge in hearsay. She is, according to her deeply held belief, acting as an interpreter or translator, just as the court would allow if a non-English speaking person were to give testimony…"

The judge motioned him to stop talking and sit down. "I have grave misgivings about this since the…witness…whose alleged words or thoughts are to be interpreted and read out is a wild animal (sneers and suppressed laughter from the pews and twelve incredulous faces in the jury box) "but continue, Mrs. McCauley. I will rule later on the admissibility or otherwise of this…extraordinary presentation!"

The microphone amplified the ruffling of pages as the psychic put on her spectacles. Then, after clearing her throat with a little cough, she read from her notes.

Annemarie closed her eyes to listen. She noticed immediately that Mrs. McCauley was endeavouring to present the testimony in a tone similar to that of an interpreter conveying the thoughts and speech patterns of one who needed to be understood. She found the effect mesmerising, at times chilling:

"Life on the island wasn't perfect- survival was a fulltime occupation- and I'm told perfection exists nowhere in the world. My mum was the first hare to tell me. And from that moment I braced myself for a tough life. But even the worst day on the island was better than captivity on the Big Island of the Humans.

"On our island we learned to evade the falcon, we quarrelled over small things, and we might occasionally vie with each other for the same clump of seaweed or tasty sliver of tree bark. I had days of pain when my love betrayed me, and days of sorrow when my second love died.

"Leverets might be swept out to sea if they ventured down to the beach and dozed off or ran too close to the cliff edge. Or they might die of exposure to the ravages of nature. But this we understood as part of life's inevitable challenge. Not so the unnatural practises imposed on us by the invaders.

"Five of my dear friends from the island departed this world on the running field, their lives crushed into the ground by dogs. Dogs unleased by cruel humans. Others survived being used as playthings only to be killed later. I was in the place of captivity when a human entered to skulk amongst us. He battered an injured hare to death and I saw that friend's spirit leave his body.

"The human killed others too in this way, but those were unknown to me, being natives of the Big Island. In captivity I spoke to hares from your Island…they told me of being forced, time after time, to dodge the dogs of death, of running at different locations and how they were moved from one location to another to run; of friends or relatives of theirs that, after repeated chases, died on the Field of Torment.

"I was relieved, and so grateful, when a female human ended our captivity. By the faint light of dawn she rescued us from evil. Many of my colleagues didn't realise what was happening, and had to be encouraged to make their escape, but I was alert, having received telepathic messages from the Golden Hare.

“During my period of freedom, before I met my liberator for the second time, I saw humans indulge their baffling addiction to cruelty. They killed hares with rods that spat fire. The bodies were laid out row upon row. I was lucky to evade the death flames but the memory of the still bleeding bodies I cannot forget.

“I saw too the humans mounted on large animals chasing a creature I encountered for the first time, as he didn’t live on our Island. The fox, I learned, is no friend of the hare. But he doesn’t hate us. He devours our flesh to survive. The humans who pursued him with great pomp and feigned urgency had no such need: Their aim, I learned, is to make the fox suffer for their own pleasure.

“I still can’t understand this. We, on the island, took pleasure in the arrival of new life…the leverets playing in the long spring or summer evenings; sunrise over the mighty ocean, in the simple joys of living; in the splendour of earth, sea and sky as we played or ran or slept or sought love amidst the heath and the heather.

“What joy to see sunbeams dancing on the surface of the lake, or the innocence in the eyes of a newborn leveret! But no joy for us in the arrival of the humans: Just foreboding and a paralysing fear. The day they stepped ashore and pulled their wooden sea-craft along the sand everything changed for us. Something died within all of us even before they laid those giant webs and the snatching began.

“The dogs: I don’t blame them. Yes, they bring pain and death, or the threat of either or both. My heart raced and my head pounded and I feared; even I who was the fastest hare on the island, when the humans unleashed the dogs. For other hares it is so much worse, for they have not the gifts I was born with. But I felt pity when I watched the humans dispose of a greyhound.

“Yes, my heart went out to the dog as the human beat him over the head, repeatedly, with a pole that glinted in the setting sun. I recognised the dog. He was one of the creatures I had outwitted on the Field of Torture. A surge of remorse shot through me. I knew instantly it was because he had failed, and because I had thwarted his pursuit, that the humans now vented their disappointment and rage on him. I realised then that humans have only contempt for the dogs they use to harass and kill us.

"I thank the kind human who intervened to save us, and the other wise female whose thoughts and words I could understand and through whom I relate my story. I ask you all in this assembly of human justice to look favourably on the human known as Annemarie, for she is blessed among the hares of both the Big Island and the Little Island. She was merciful, when others wanted to demean, confine, and torture us.

"Try to understand that we, like you, are capable of suffering. When we hurt we cry out, as you may have heard at those gatherings where the dogs are set on us. The pain that passes through our bodies when attacked by those creatures controlled by humans is beyond your understanding.

"It is unbearable…it encompasses every nerve and fibre of our being, and from the moment it begins a hare craves release…desperately. We prefer death to torture by humans.

"Those of us who survived the human "sport" and escaped urge you to reward, not punish, our human protector. Just as she released us from captivity, from impending terror, distress, and agony, you can now set *her* free. Tipsy the Hare thanks you!"

Stunned silence followed, broken after a few seconds by loud cheering and applause from animal protection lobbyists and conservationists, interrupted by banging of feet and howls of outrage and ridicule from the coursing fans.

Annemarie noticed some of her adversaries looked less scathing than earlier. She spotted three whose demeanour had changed. One regarded her with a puzzled vacant gawk. The National Chief of Police had unfolded his arms and was staring at Mrs. McCauley, scratching his head, a look of complete bafflement distorting his normally expressionless features.

The uniformed men alongside him fiddled uneasily with their medals. One looked troubled, another was scowling, and two more were grinning nervously. The judge called for silence as a bout of frenzied whispering erupted. Chatter filled the room. When the babble subsided, the Prosecutor sprang to his feet, waving loose pages, clutched tightly, at the judge.

His wig dropped unto his desk. Blushing, he whisked it back on, adjusting it quickly before emitting a high pitched shriek: "Outrageous, Your Lordship! Absolutely outrageous! This is not merely hearsay. It cannot be construed as evidence at all. It is a clever stunt to pull at the heartstrings of the jury...I protest. I urge you now to direct the jury to disregard every word uttered by the hare...I mean by this... psychic person. I am flabbergasted by the audacity of the Defence in putting forward such... unadulterated poppycock!"

The judge sighed. "When I address the jury in summing up I will advise as appropriate in relation to how jurors should rate all the relevant evidence. Mrs. McCauley, you are excused."

The psychic resumed her seat near the rear of the courtroom; incredulous eyes riveted to her every step down the aisle.

107

A ten-minute recess was called following Mrs. McCauley's evidence. The judge looked deeply uncomfortable as he exited the courtroom for his break. Tipsy's heartrending narrative, as relayed by the psychic, had the chamber in throes of disbelief and speculation. It buzzed loader than a swarm of angry bees whose hive had been disturbed.

Annemarie sighed. Was it a step too far to allow the hare tell his story? If she'd heard it a few months earlier she'd have either laughed or rejected it outright as pure fantasy or charlatanism. Now, she prayed that others wouldn't be so dismissive.

It's a miracle I need.

She detected ridicule on some faces, embarrassment on others; and pitying glances were directed at her. She felt a small weight lift from her. At least the presentation of the evidence for and against her had concluded but she couldn't relax, because now came the scary part, when Defence and Prosecution got to make their final pitches to the jury.

The ten minutes stretched to a mini-eternity. The hands on the wall clock seemed to crawl slower than two lazy snails. Then, the buzzer crackled and the judge swept back in to resume his seat under the golden harp of Ireland. He gave the go-ahead for the final summaries.

Malachi Holt went back over the testimony, laying great emphasis on the fact that, although she had admitted releasing the hares and causing minor damage in the process, Annemarie's action was motivated not by malice but by a sincere desire to save animals from the kind of ill-treatment clearly shown in the footage.

Yes, she believed, he said cringingly, that a ghostly hare had advised her to so act, but she was entitled to that belief. Psychic phenomena was controversial, he conceded, and there were many schools of thought as to what exactly was happening when people saw or heard, or believed they did, such extraordinary things. Entire religions were founded on human interpretation of such phenomena.

Whatever the jury thought of apparitions, or of psychics like Mrs. McCauley who believed they could communicate with animals, they should, he insisted, be in no doubt about the unsporting and downright nasty practice of encroaching upon the tranquility and scenic loveliness of a little island where hares lived free from human interference.

For it was incontestable, he said, following the admission under cross-examination of Mr. Bumbleton-Crossbar, that among the hares released by the accused woman were creatures taken secretly from the island.

He concluded with a flourish: "I ask you, ladies and gentlemen, to take this damnable deed into account when you deliberate on the guilt or innocence of the accused. I urge you to reject the Prosecution's case and acquit her!"

The Prosecutor rose to his feet, adjusted his wig, and strode with great deliberation to the jury box. Hands clasped behind his back he began his final speech. Head bowed as he paced slowly along the front row of jurors, he began almost in a whisper:

"Ladies and gentlemen, I do not envy you your task today. In all my years as a prosecuting counsel I have never heard such absolute balderdash presented in a courtroom. Yes. I accept that there are mixed views on hare coursing, but nothing put forward by the Defence has altered the proven facts of this case; Annemarie Cristobel admitted in her statement to police that she entered the grounds of Ballycrossways Coursing Club, snipped the padlock and released the entire stock of captive hares.

"She wants you to believe that although she caused damage to the property of the club, this damage was somehow not malicious. In the course of her testimony… that was as conniving and manipulative as it was outrageous and phantasmagorical… she spun a tale that might have come straight out of the Arabian Nights or a fanciful bedtime storybook.

"She would have you believe that she sabotaged the coursing event on the instructions (sniggering) of *a hare* that appeared to her. To bolster this contemptible and conspicuously asinine malarkey the Defence called a woman who claims, like the fictional Dr Doolittle, to be capable of communicating with animals. Mrs. McCauley purportedly transmitted, for the benefit of the court, the alleged testimony of…and forgive me for having to repeat such poppycock in this hallowed chamber of justice…*a hare!*"

He paused, fixing his gaze in turn on each juror. Annemarie thought some of them looked ill at ease as he eyeballed them.

"A hare, ladies and gentlemen…you were asked to take into account the… ah…*evidence* elicited from a dumb creature by a mumbo-jumbo merchant!"

Malachi Holt rose. "Objection, Your Lordship…Mrs. McCauley is a distinguished psychic medium. Her reputation is being impugned by the Prosecution!"

The judge nodded: "You will not refer to the witness disrespectfully, carry on!"

"Yes, My Lord."

The Prosecutor refocused his piercing eyes on the jury. "Even if you were persuaded by these fantasy stories, from both Ms. Cristobel and Mrs. McCauley, the fact remains that the accused by her own admission released the hares. That action on her part is in no way ameliorated by the fact that some of the hares had been captured on Gooseberry Island, whatever one might think of encroaching on our offshore islands in that manner. Her action was an unlawful act regardless of how she might view it; and regardless of who or what person, or figment of her imagination, may have prompted her action. Even if you believe in fairy stories and idiotic fortunetellers you must, on the basis of the compelling evidence presented to you, find the accused guilty as charged!"

When the Prosecutor resumed his seat the judge commenced his direction to the jury, summarising the Defence and Prosecution cases.

Annemarie's heart sank when he instructed the twelve jurors to disregard all of Mrs. McCauley's evidence and to banish from their minds the alleged testimony of the hare as translated by the psychic.

"It may have been entertaining for some people in this chamber; or deemed a diverting little series of phantasmagorical tidbits to fill up the columns of tabloid newspapers…but in my court such flights of wild hearsay and tendentious twaddle will not be tolerated. I allowed the psychic's evidence only with the gravest misgivings and to accord the widest possible latitude to the Defence, but you must now erase it from your consideration of the case. You never heard it. Understood?"

Mumbles of assent from three jurors, reluctant nods from the rest of them.

He continued: "On the issue of malicious damage and the accused person's denial that her action…" He halted midsentence. He was frowning and straining to see something.

Annemarie followed his gaze, as did the entire jury and dozens of people in the rows of seats. Some were standing and pointing excitedly. Eyes were riveted on the entrance, the door to which was slightly ajar. Annemarie caught the glint of a silver *Save the Hare* badge on the jacket of the activist, her friend, who was holding the door open at the same moment that she spotted…*Tipsy! God, it can't be…* But it was.

So he'd got here…and in time. But in time for what? He must have something pretty important to say, but the judge wouldn't allow any further translations by Mrs. McCauley…and even if he did he wouldn't let the jury pay the slightest heed to the hare's message.

There he was…sitting calmly inside the entrance…as if deciding what to do next. Then a shriek: "Catch him! Get that damned creature out of my court!"

The judge's demand was amplified through his microphone, interspersed with whistling and static. He was standing and gesticulating. "This is an outrage…remove that…*thing!*" A quivering bony forefinger was aimed directly at the uninvited one.

Police who'd been standing to either side of the entrance immediately rushed at Tipsy. He hopped forward up the aisle between the rows of long benches. Police jostled with each other to catch him, colliding and bumping into colleagues or falling sideways onto the seats, eliciting shouts and protests as legs and elbows struck members of the public and coursing fans.

Tipsy veered sideways, hopped onto the lap of the nearest person, skidded across dozens of laps and then, seemingly changing his mind, doubled back and resumed his dash up the aisle, as if to cause maximum annoyance and disruption. Or was he possibly just finding his way?

The naval, army and air force commanders shuffled out of their seats in the back row and joined the chase, but couldn't get past the police who blocked their passage.

Annemarie watched in disbelief as a four-star general jostled past the other military personnel, elbowed the police out of the way and leaped rugby-tackle style in a bid to either restrain if not flatten the hare. He reminded Annemarie of a soldier in a war movie…sacrificing his own life to take the full blast of a grenade.

He missed Tipsy, collapsing and banging his head off the floorboards. A policeman pulled him to his feet, the general's arms clasped around his head. His medals jangled and his lips had formed into an "O" as pain distorted his commanding countenance.

Tipsy proceeded further up the aisle; then stopped abruptly. The pursuing police stopped too, the officer in front holding back the others. "What's he at?" the leading officer rasped.

Then, before they could make their next move, Tipsy bounded through the air and landed right inside the jury box.

The six men and six women reacted differently. Two of the women were on their feet, screaming. One was leaning over with the apparent intention of patting him on the head, though she wasn't quite sure of herself. The men were scratching their heads, or pointing, or laughing. One man was shaking with fear and his right hand covered his mouth.

It seemed to Annemarie, though she couldn't see Tipsy; that he must be inching from left to right at their feet as they appeared to be following his movement, their eyes aimed at the floor of the jury box.

Then, no more than ten seconds after invading the personal space of the twelve "good citizens and true", as the judge had called them, Tipsy hopped out of the jury box, eliciting renewed gasps and shouts from the assembly.

The police came charging after him up the central aisle, now with batons drawn and swinging pointedly, reinforced by dozens of coursing fans who were pouring down the side aisles and hollering like demented ancient warriors or men hyped up on stimulants.

Undaunted, Tipsy remained static. Then, with the first baton about to make contact with his head, or at least one of his long ears, he leapt into the air. Annemarie's heart fluttered. Was he really headed *that* way?

The entire assembly followed his ascent, astonishment and alarm bursting through their composed features as they saw where Tipsy seemed intent on landing. The chamber erupted with a raucous spasm of gasps and excited exclamations as a creature they might have dubbed dumb dived down through the dusty atmosphere of the courtroom and alighted with a resounding plop on the judge's desk.

His Lordship emitted a low squeal. He looked petrified. He put up his hands to protect himself. "No…don't do it…when I called you a thing and a damned creature I wasn't being personal. I do not tolerate unauthorised intrusions or interruptions in my court…what am I saying is… well, you're a hare!"

Readjusting his wig, which had started to fall off, and straightening his tie, he grasped the microphone tightly: "I said…remove this intruder…how often must I…"

Before he could finish the sentence and as police rushed to stage an assault on the judge's bench, Tipsy sprang right into His Lordship's lap. An earsplitting roar echoed around the chamber. The windows rattled and policemen's eyes bulged with horror.

Silence again.

Annemarie couldn't believe it. The judge was holding Tipsy in his arms and patting him on the head as if he were a cat. Tipsy was staring up at him, his low purring audible via the microphone.

The police, availing of the hare's apparent distraction, quickly surrounded His Lordship. One, standing to his full height, raised his baton and was carefully aiming it at Tipsy.

"No need for that" the judge rasped, a benevolent smile softening his normally impassive expression. "He seems to be harmless enough…"

The officer put away his baton and signaled to the others to do likewise. The Prosecutor, possibly feeling a bit left out of the drama, rose to his feet and hollered: "Your Lordship, I would remind you that justice will not be served by allowing this display of theatrics that may well, for all we know, be a ploy orchestrated by someone who wishes to influence the outcome of this trial…."

Tipsy instantly hopped down from the judge's lap and retraced his steps back to the entrance. A frenzied chase recommenced, with Tipsy dodging swinging batons and inaccurate kicks. Others applauded or urged him on, while some doubled over with laughter.

The activist, standing at the entrance, drew open the door and Tipsy made good his escape. *Not for the first time,* Annemarie marveled.

Everything was a blur of sound and movement from the moment Tipsy disappeared from sight. The Prosecutor, looking deflated, grumpily plopped back down into his seat, indicating with a dismissive hand gesture that he'd nothing more to say. The judge then completed his summing up, emphasising in sombre tones that jurors must not allow themselves to be swayed by the hare's unwarranted and quite unprecedented intervention.

He cautioned them to erase it from their minds and also to completely expunge from their memories his own distracted and regrettable stroking of the animal after it had approached the bench "willy-nilly" in a flagrant violation of courtroom rules and etiquette and hallowed legal tradition stretching back more than eight centuries.

The jury appeared to be only half listening, their eyes continually straying to the entrance as if expecting Tipsy to stage another "unwarranted entry."

The Jury retired to consider its verdict. The fifteen minutes it took the twelve arbiters to decide her fate seemed more like hours to Annemarie.

When the buzzer sounded and they trooped back in through a little doorway to the left of the judge she bit her lip. Then she closed her eyes and crossed her fingers.

Please…please, God, I know I don't talk to you often, but please...

"Will the accused be upstanding" the judge ordered.

She forced herself to stand, wobbling at the knees. She was shaking. Every bone in her body trembled. Her lips went cold and quivered. She inhaled deeply. Felt a sick revolting emptiness in the pit of her stomach.

"Have you reached a verdict?" the judge asked the jury, his bewigged head leaning towards them in a woebegone emasculated glower.

The foreman stood and nodded, holding a copy of the charge sheet. His dried lips parted. "We have, your Lordship. We find the accused, Ms. Annemarie Cristobel, not guilty on the charge of causing malicious damage to the property of Ballycrossways Coursing Club."

Thank you God, she lisped. She almost collapsed with relief, clasping her face with both hands, tears already forming.

Not Guilty. The sweetest two words she'd heard in a long time. Sweeter even than the three words *I Love You* her last boyfriend had uttered, a few weeks before he betrayed her.

One side of the room erupted with applause, while from the other howls of derision, strings of obscene curses, and mawkish outrage assailed her ears. The judge was banging his gavel and calling for order, and police were jostling both rowdy coursing fans and chanting anti-blood sports activists out of the courtroom.

Annemarie stepped down from her seat, to be embraced by her solicitor and barrister. Activists pushed flowers at her, which fell to the floor in the chaotic outpouring of conflicting emotions. "We'll get you, you bitch" a chubby twenty-something lad howled, just inches from her, before being dragged away by a policewoman. "Good on you, Annemarie" another voice soothed.

She was escorted by police through a back entrance, to avoid, one officer warned, "potential serious injury or loss of life."

***

108

Waxy heaved and sweated. On the summit of the hill he sat on the rocky chair and surveyed the Peninsula. It was a steep enough climb as always, but Waxy didn't mind that today. It wasn't exercise that brought him up here this time; though losing a few pounds was always desirable. He tackled the hill to get his mind off multiple predicaments. His attempt to stamp out the ludicrous spate of hallucinations and nightmares revolving around ghostly hares and other phantasms afflicting club members had backfired… badly.

His plan had been to knock some sense into them at the meeting; to mount such a withering no holds barred attack on their delusions that they'd pull themselves together. It didn't work.

Instead, before he could begin to address the problem, hands started rising, and faces with haggard, woebegone looks vied for his attention. Several more members announced that they, too, had been visited by creepy hare spooks or had awoken in lathers of sweat after dreaming of hares exacting vengeance on them.

He'd called for silence, and launched into a sturdy refutation of all the gobbledygook. Without success. If anything the infection seemed to be spreading. Expelling the affected members wasn't an option, as some of them were long standing and valued officials and one was a national award winning hare catcher who'd been presented with his trophy by a government minister two years before amid a fanfare of merriment and backslapping.

To see him now, running from shadows and afraid to answer his front door, sickened Waxy to the core.

With time, maybe, they'd recover…snap out of this crazy, debilitating condition. Waxy believed in God, but not in phantom hares bothering decent coursing men. That just didn't happen in the real world.

On top of those silly imaginings had come the shock result from the court case. Every coursing fan in Ireland had written it off as an open and shut affair, but then it went the wrong way. He refused to contemplate that the psychic had been telling the truth. It was just a fabrication concocted between the accursed Cristobel woman and that…damned witch! It had to be.

First there were coursing fans seeing furry ghosts…then a jury seemingly believed a wild fairy tale about a hare giving his life story through a wacky interpreter.

Waxy rose from the rocky seat and stretched himself. As always on a perfectly clear day he could just about make out the distant shape of the island: A benign protrusion on the horizon. Chalk white with a stripe of green across the top.

Again the question bothered him: How did that blasted hare get to do exactly what was likely to benefit the saboteur in court, to influence the outcome of the trial? And now that animal's antics were being exploited by the antis: Another Bill attacking hare coursing was due for debate…thanks to that blasted hare.

He wiped his sweaty forehead with his equally moist arm. *Better be getting home. Calls to make.* No time to be lost with another assault on his beloved sport in the pipeline.

Why did he ever set foot on that God forsaken island? It seemed like a great idea…It solved the hare shortage problem for two years running. But damn it…that dissenting chap was right. The trip had brought him nothing but bad luck. Not that he'd ever give credence to the notion that hares could have any power over humans. It was unlucky in the same way that men bet on the wrong greyhounds…nothing to do with hobgoblins.

Strange…a breeze fanned the back of his neck. He looked around; again glimpsing the far off island and the mighty ocean separating it from the Peninsula. There was no wind. *And not many flies about in this weather.*

He started his descent of the hill, so refreshing after the long climb to the summit. He'd walked about a hundred yards when he stopped abruptly.

What on earth?

The familiar terrain seemed to have changed. A bush that ought to be on his right was now on the left side of the dirt road. But, more startlingly, there hadn't been an apple tree on the right side. He stepped over to it, baffled also by the shaking of its branches and leaves. There was definitely no breeze, let alone a wind strong enough…He held up both arms. *Not a hint.*

He went to touch the tree. His hand went straight through it. He withdrew it in shock, almost falling to the ground. Regaining his balance, he looked around him to make sure he hadn't strayed unto a different pathway.

Then…the tree wasn't there anymore. *Oh God, not me too*…could it be all that tension and worry…the hares escaping…then the court case…and another anti coursing Bill on the way? *That must be it.*

He'd show those antis that coursing would NEVER succumb to their furry bunny campaign. They could huff and puff all they liked and brag to the world about their "wonder hare", but when it came to a vote those slimy politicians would see which side their bread was buttered on. Their eyes would open wide, as they did last time, when all that dosh came tumbling out of the brown envelopes and shopping bags.

Oh yes, that regrettable but efficacious tactic need only be applied to a few… enough to tip the balance against the Bill. The numbers would be tight, even with the election of additional Green MPs.

Reaching his bungalow, he inserted his key in the lock but, *blast*…he couldn't turn the key. His hand had gone cold and numb. Worse…it was stuck to the key and the key was stuck in the lock.

Alarmed, he sought frantically to wrench it free.

What's that?

Against the light grey façade of the handball alley wall opposite his home a misty form had materialized. Waxy blinked, shook his head and then shut his eyes tight. Opening them again the ethereal shape had resolved itself into... *a hare.*

Though not a typical reddish brown one. The semitransparent...thing... was...almost golden. Little flames danced and flickered around it as it hopped menacingly towards Waxy.

Again he tried to free his hand from the key but he couldn't. His fingers wouldn't loosen. He stood facing the apparition, his back pressed to the door and his hand attached as if by a powerful magnet to the key that was stuck in the lock. The hare's eyes glowed a fiery blue, its ears towered above its luminous head, and then its mouth opened slightly as if the thing was about to speak.

No sound emitted but Waxy thought he heard, somewhere inside his head, the words *Your Race is Run,* as the phantom shuffled and shimmered ever closer, its luminosity increasing.

It was just a few feet from him. He could see his reflection in its eyes, the look of sheer terror on his face... like a man pleading for his life.

No! He pleaded, first in a low whimper, then louder and louder until he was screaming. He roared until his voice had risen to the highest pitch he was capable of. Then he stopped and broke into crying. He felt helpless, resigned to his fate...his will broken.

Suddenly, the numbness left his fingers and the hand gripping the key recovered. He turned it in the lock without a backward glance. He slammed the door shut, squinting to avoid seeing the apparition. He ran to the front window and peeked out through the drawn curtains.

It was gone. Not a trace of it. But two passers-by were standing and staring at the house. He pulled across the curtains and waved at them, saying under his breath: "Get away you nosy fools!"

He already hated himself for allowing a trick of the mind to unsettle him. A small inner voice nagged at him that hare coursing might be against God's wishes. He quickly ejected that thought, anger mounting at its intrusion. *My hand went numb because I let fear have its way, and that stupid hallucination. Tricks of the mind may frighten some... but not me. Never!*

He stormed to the drinks cabinet and grabbed the whiskey bottle, pouring himself a generous measure that he downed in two gulps. The first of many.

Slumping into his chair beside the rayburn he studied, through a groggy haze of alcohol, the oil painting on the wall opposite. His father had acquired it at an auction decades before. It showed a gathering of 18th century gentlemen at a hare coursing event.

The archaic costumes oozed nostalgia and the surroundings were idyllic, with lovely mountains, glens and leafy glades. The hare had just been caught by one of the two pursuing greyhounds, which had sunk its teeth into its neck, with the second dog about to fasten on to a struggling hind leg.

Waxy sighed and, putting aside the empty glass, swigged from the bottle. *There was no one opposed to it then. God, I wish I'd been born in that time. No hippies with tattered placards. No need to suck up to greasy politicians.* His head swam and the painting seemed to sway in empathy. *Just the drink,* he assured himself.

What's that? He stood and approached the wall, unsteadily, to take a closer look. Just to be sure.

For a moment he'd imagined that the hare on the canvass had blinked and that its eyes had grown brighter. But now he saw it was another silly trick of the mind, like that episode outside the house, and seeing a tree that wasn't there.

He went to his chair, reaching for the bottle as he did. Then his whole body shook. His heart pounded. An ear-splitting crash reduced him to a bundle of fear. He lisped a quick prayer.

Waxy Bumbleton-Crossbar turned slowly to see the hare coursing scene on the floor, twisted out of shape in the varnished mahogany frame and lying in shards of broken glass.

Fallen? He whimpered, *how has it fallen?*

109

Have I really done all that? Tipsy asked himself.

He was resting now, savouring the taste of food lovingly given to him by his protector. She was so grateful to him, he knew, for his part in helping her avoid the wrath and censure of her fellow beings.

It all happened so quickly, in a blur of turbulence and speed. He'd blanked out his normal timid disposition, his natural timidity as a hare, and shut his eyes tight. Then he'd focused hard to avoid thinking of Humaniks as those treacherous creatures who could hurt hares in so many unspeakable ways.

He hadn't forgotten how the Humanik in the place of captivity had finished off the injured hare, those muffled thuds and the rapidly diminishing cries as the hare expired… and the strength of the Humanik…his powerful limbs gripping the hare's back legs. *Yes, they have that advantage over us.*

But Tipsy judged that his speed gave him an edge over Humanik brawn and superior intelligence. He tensed all over again thinking about it.

When the large square hunk of shiny wood squeaked open, revealing the packed Humanik assembly, he wondered if the Golden Hare had underestimated the scale and terrifying nature of the challenge.

His Eminence had appeared in his usual style, when Tipsy was on the cusp of waking and sleeping. Radiant as ever he'd asked Tipsy to undertake one final act. It would be risky, he said, which prompted a "what's new?" reaction from Tipsy, but would, the great one emphasised, help the cause of hares in a special and unprecedented way whilst also boosting his protector Annemarie's chances of avoiding Humanik punishment.

I will guide your movements once you cross the threshold, he assured. *Remember how you dodged the falcon…and the dogs the*

Humaniks set upon you? You can do this Tipsy. You can show those creatures in there that drape their bodies with wrappings to conceal their pale skin…that we too matter, however simple or silly our ways appear to them...

Tipsy had to suppress his rising and ever escalating doubts. But then…once the trembling paw of his right front leg stepped inside that oppressive building, his body took on a sudden surge of power and energy.

Dozens of Humanik heads swiveled to gaze upon him. He felt the Golden Hare's presence and heard his voice within: To the left at the top of the big space crammed with Humaniks he saw the twelve creatures seated behind a wooden barrier. He knew what to do. The inner voice urged him on.

They needed to see him; he knew, and to be reminded of his importance in the broad scheme of things. And so he had introduced himself briefly to those twelve Humaniks who, he noticed, were looking straight across at his rescuer, who was sitting alone and looking mightily worried.

One by one, he had pleaded telepathically with them not to let the kind Humanik be punished by the hare-haters.

And they seemed to get the message, as they all reacted with shock when his inner voice reverberated inside their heads.

He had then transmitted his concern to a frazzled old Humanik sitting alone who seeming to be in overall command of the proceedings. This creature reminded him of how the Golden Hare held forth in the cave, except this was no hare, and his head was partly covered by what Tipsy took to be a clump of dried seaweed.

Getting into this assembly was one thing. He had taken them by surprise, but getting out was hectic, though he had nimbly evaded the grasping paws and stamping covered feet of the Humaniks who fell about in despair in their vain efforts to apprehend him.

Dashing out through the opening, he felt the same relief as when he outran the dogs, even as the roars and curses of the baying Humanik throng ripped at his skull.

Nibbling on a carrot outside Annemarie's wooden dwelling looking unto the patch of grass, he felt both relieved to be safe and yet curiously deflated. How on earth was all that commotion and prancing about in that weird place going to make life easier for hares?

As he pondered and sipped the water his rescuer had left for him in a container on the grass, he felt a tiredness coming over him, which gave way to an abrupt intensity of perception.

A familiar form materialised. *You have done well Tipsy*, the Golden Hare soothed. *Your work on the Big Island is now complete. The hares of the Little Island will soon welcome you home. You will assist me in catering for the spiritual and ecological wellbeing of the population.*

His Eminence faded and a dizzying vision replaced him…of the island in full summery bloom. Vast swathes of shimmering vegetation, flowers of myriad colours dancing in a light warm breeze. He saw them and also caught their sweet fragrance.

The lake, fringed by multi hued flora, reflected a bright blue sky across which chirping birds zigzagged crazily or flew in neat formations. Frogs croaked their greetings to him at the lakeside.

He saw the storm petrels in their colony, a chorus of raucous chatter complimenting the sound of the ocean. Butterflies traced patterns in air or fluttered on tree boughs or along the wild hedges.

Then he saw the leverets, care-free in the morning sunshine, chasing each other and leaping jauntily over rocks or clumps of heather. He saw the little sun-kissed beach, the waves gently caressing the sandy shore and just below the surface of the ocean fish darted to and fro, heedless of the gulls that hovered and swooped overhead. Older hares dozed in the shade afforded by trees and abandoned Humanik dwellings.

The vision dissipated and His Eminence re-appeared. *You will meet them shortly. I have good news for you Tipsy. Your achievement has set in motion a process that will free them from the threat of the Humaniks and their giant webs. Never again will the Island hares have to run or hide from them, or feel the pain and terror of captivity or be forced to run from Humaniks or their dogs with the weird face masks.*

Tipsy had a dozen questions to ask, but the Golden Hare faded again. How he looked forward to the return, to seeing all his old friends again: The ones who hadn't been snatched or killed for the amusement of Humaniks. He lisped a prayer for those who had parted this world of challenge, but couldn't contain his joy even as he contemplated their absence.

He felt as though a dark stifling cloud that had blotted out the sun was now dissolving, to let the light shine again on the hares of the Big Island and the Little Island.

***

Epilogue

Annemarie basked in the lively sea breeze, her hair blowing and fluttering.

It irked her at first but then she let nature have its way as she caught her first sight of the island. She sang along with a tune that carried from the radio playing in the skipper's control room, the music mingling semi-harmoniously with the hum of the motorboat engine.

The chalky cliff face resembled a white ghostly wall emerging out of the sea, with a jagged green stripe running along its top.

Tipsy was below deck in the company of three volunteers who had begged to accompany Annemarie. She let them on board, but on the strict condition that the boat trip, or rather its purpose, be kept a closely guarded secret.

After the dramatic events in court, Tipsy had become mega- popular. Social media went crazy when images and footage of him in the courtroom went online. It got millions of YouTube hits within an hour of this *hare with a mission* gamboling unto the world stage.

Thousands of chat boards obsessed about the furry messenger from Ireland. Millions of text messages crisscrossed the globe eulogizing him. He'd become too popular for his own safety, Annemarie feared. Tipsy mania had blazed a trail across cyberspace and she'd been inundated with emails, tweets, Facebook messages and requests from mainstream media for interviews and photo ops.

Most were well-meaning but with all that publicity there were bound to be some wackos anxious to make a name for themselves by harming the second most famous hare in the world, next only to the fictional Bugs Bunny, and maybe even poised to overtake the TV cartoon icon in the celebrity stakes.

She'd done interviews, but with only one aim in mind: to exploit Tipsy's X Factor cachet to highlight the plight of Ireland's hares and the obscenity of hare coursing. She marveled at the extraordinary rapid fire succession of developments that had led to this ocean-crossing, this secretive mission to return Tipsy to his home off the Irish coast.

Smart phones and I pads recorded his courtroom gymnastics, culminating in his "appeal" to the judge. Cameras weren't allowed in court, but it's not every day that a hare enters a courtroom and performs feats of acrobatics that make even the greatest Olympian sporting achievements look amateurish.

Tipsy had helped to secure her acquittal. Even her barrister, who had cringed at the idea of allowing the psychic to give evidence on Tipsy's behalf, grudgingly admitted that "the hare may have tipped the balance."

Then the anti-hare coursing lobby, still despondent after its parliamentary setback two years earlier, quickly grasped the potential of Tipsy's superstar status. Politicians were lobbied, their attention drawn to the fact that a hare, representative of a persecuted species, had broken through barriers of human ignorance and cruelty to touch the hearts of millions.

The *Save the Hare* Bill was re-launched in parliament. A snap General Election had shifted the balance slightly in favour of the anti-hare coursing side, but nobody could predict which way a vote would go owing to a small number of MPs who might either abstain or "flip-flop" at the last minute and switch support from one side to the other.

Campaigners hoped the *Tipsy Factor* might take the Bill over the line, just as he'd swayed the jury to acquit Annemarie.

Then, just when the anti coursing lobby was confident of success, three politicians who had pledged to vote for the Bill did an about-face, the same three who had switched sides two years before. One was Joey the Fixer Lannigan, who represented the *Peninsula and the Islands* constituency.

Luckily for the campaign, however, the Fixer hadn't noticed a hidden recording device that an undercover reporter had installed in his clinic. It recorded an exchange between him and a delegation from Ballycrossways Coursing Club and the footage clearly showed Lannigan scooping bundles of cash into a desk drawer, as the coursing officials laughed and congratulated him on his "change of heart".

The resulting TV news report sparked outrage and his immediate resignation from parliament. When the six pm news carried the report the anti-hare coursing Bill was due to be voted on fifteen minutes later.

The nine pm news reported that the Bill was passed by a majority of two, this result down to the two politicians who had switched to the pro-coursing side suddenly opting to switch back and support the Bill. Both of them vigorously denied that they'd received any generous donations or inducements of the kind the Fixer had been filmed accepting.

The news scene changed amid excitable voice-over commentary to images of a handcuffed Lannigan being shuffled into a police van, turning to scream defiance at a cameraman before the twin doors slammed shut behind him.

Scenes of jubilation flashed across TV screens later that night and next morning. Fifty years of campaigning had finally achieved protection for the Irish Hare.

Tipsy had helped to consign one of the worst forms of organized animal cruelty to the scrap heap.

Annemarie glanced in through the cabin window to see all three activists petting the Wonder Hare. The boat had begun to divert to the right towards a small beach. "Another few minutes and we're there", the skipper hollered.

Annemarie wondered how Tipsy felt about the journey. It would certainly have been less stressful than his transportation in captivity to the Peninsula.

Inhaling the salt sea air, she heaved a sigh of relief that a new chapter had opened in the long history of the Irish Hare.

Thousands of years ago, this gentle creature had, against all the odds, survived an Ice Age. Now a small nation nestled in the middle of the Atlantic had halted the persecution of hares. No more would *Lepus Timidus Hibernicus* serve as live bait for dogs, animals that, like the hares, were killed when it suited humans to be rid of them.

The boat approached the horseshoe beach. The three activists came up on deck to join Annemarie, their furred fellow-traveler in the arms of a woman whose t-shirt proclaimed: "I knew Tipsy-the Psychic Irish Hare!"

The End

Afterword and Acknowledgements

Sincere thanks to those who encouraged, inspired, or in any way helped me while researching this book, especially Aideen Yourell, Campaign Director of the Irish Council Against Blood Sports, widely known for her tireless advocacy on behalf of the Irish Hare and against all forms of animal cruelty; Philip Kiernan of ICABS who designed the book cover that serves as the all-important initial introduction to the novel; immensely gifted wildlife photographer Lindsay Hodges, whose picture of an Irish Hare in his natural habitat features so prominently in the cover design; Bernadette Barrett of BadgerWatch Ireland, for her advice and information on that intriguing (and wrongfully maligned) creature, the badger; Mona Ward, Bernadette Wright, Jim Murray, Fiona O' Connell, and Nicky Fitzgerald (my brother) for their helpful tips; and kudos to the following publications and organisations that shed further light for me on the fascinating story of the Irish Hare:

The Hare Book, published by the Hare Preservation Trust in the UK

Wild Hares by Henry Tegner (1969) John Baker Publishers Ltd

Talking Wild by Eanna Ni Lamhna (2002) Town House and Country House Ltd

Ban Blood Sports, official website of the Irish Council Against Blood Sports

The Irish Wildlife Trust

The Irish Society for the Prevention of Cruelty to Animals

A final word...

They all lived happily after: Except they didn't...not beyond the confines of this novel set in the Republic of Ireland where, unfortunately, hare coursing is still legal.

The Waxy Bumbleton-Crossbars of this world continue to capture hares for coursing. And, while hares can perform seemingly miraculous athletic feats in their flight from hyped-up dogs on the coursing field, none of them has the remarkable extrasensory prowess of our Tipsy or can run, or think, as fast as he can.

There really is a Golden Hare. Well, two actually. They live peacefully on Rathlin Island off the coast of County Antrim. They have lovely blue eyes and almost golden fur. They are albinos - rare genetic mutations - and treasured as such by the islanders.

When hare coursers attempted to capture hares on Rathlin a few years ago, a large group of locals successfully blocked the netting gang. Apart from wishing to safeguard the hare population, the islanders were especially protective of their precious Golden Hares.

As mentioned in the story, a big majority of the Irish people DO want hare coursing banned, but, as also emerges in the novel; "nod and wink" politicians connive in the shadowy backrooms of the *real Ireland* to prevent its abolition.

Since 1966, animal protection groups have been campaigning for an end to the hare's sad plight. Since 1993, greyhounds used in coursing have been muzzled. The change was initiated by wily politicians who believed this would weaken opposition to the blood sport.

But, as again depicted in the story, greyhound muzzles do *not* protect the hares: They are mauled, battered, pinned down, have their bones crushed, and are tossed about like broken dolls. The ones that physically survive the ordeal may die afterwards, having succumbed to stress-related ailments.

Anyone who hasn't personally witnessed this so-called "sport" can go on YouTube anytime to see what's being done to our wonderful Irish Hare. This great survivor of the Ice Age has to run the gauntlet of sadistic man-made games, its torment exacerbated by loss of habitat due to urbanisation and modern agriculture.

But, while the scandal of coursing continues in Ireland, so does the campaign to abolish it. There are many people in the real Ireland similar to the fictional Annemarie Cristobel. They work tirelessly on the hare's behalf...lobbying, protesting outside coursing venues, spreading awareness...bringing closer the day when coursing ends and the gentle hare can run free in our countryside.

You can find out more about them, and what they do, on www.banbloodsports.com

***

About the Author

John Fitzgerald is a freelance journalist and writer living in Callan, County Kilkenny, Ireland. *Escape from Grievous Faults* is his first novel. He has had hundreds of articles (news reports, opinion pieces, and human interest stories) published in local newspapers in Ireland and in the *Irish Examiner's* former County Kilkenny supplement.

He is also the author of seven books dealing with local history and heritage: *Kilkenny-People Places Faces* (2002), *Callan in the Rare Old Times* (2013), *Callan through the Mists of Time* (2004), *Kilkenny-A Blast from the Past* (2005), *Are We Invaded Yet?* (2008), *The Nore View Folk Museum-a chronicle of real people's lives* (ebook-2015), *Kilkenny Pubs and Bars* (paperback and ebook-2015) *Bad Hare Days* (paperback and ebook-2009), a stranger than fiction autobiographical account of his involvement in the campaign against live hare coursing in Ireland, and, *Escape from Grievous Faults* (2016), a novel set in Ireland's grim industrial school era.

***

14456606R00247

Printed in Great Britain
by Amazon